REBEL HEIR

ELIZABETH MICHELS

sourcebooks
casablanca

Published by Sourcebooks Casablanca, an imprint of Sourcebooks,
Inc.
P.O. Box 4410, Naperville, Illinois 60567-4410
(630) 961-3900
Fax: (630) 961-2168
www.sourcebooks.com

Printed and bound in Canada.
MBP 10 9 8 7 6 5 4 3 2 1

For Webb—you're perfect exactly as you are. I love you.

One

Berkshire, England, 1817

"ANY CHANCE YOU CAN PAINT A BIT FASTER THERE, Stapleton?" Ash leaned out the carriage window to ask. If the young man hunched outside with the small paintbrush didn't increase his pace, the two of them would be in chains by sundown.

It had to be midmorning by now, judging by the stables' shadow cast on the ground outside Ash's window. Stapleton had spotted the cover of the inn from the driver's perch and pulled the carriage off the road from Bath not twenty minutes prior. Paying a groom for his silence, they'd slipped behind the building to make an adjustment to the carriage.

The men giving chase would be gaining ground every minute Ash and Stapleton stayed here, but a change of identity would be more helpful than gaining distance from their enemies.

"Depends," Stapleton muttered a moment later without looking up from his work. His cap was pulled low over his short blond hair and angular features, but

Ash could hear a hint of annoyance in his voice. "Do you mind if the lions you asked for have the general look of large dogs?"

Ash leaned back against the velvet-covered cushions and propped his boots on the opposite seat, crossing his legs at the ankles. It was true that they were in something of a rush, considering the angry mob chasing them. But a lord's seal and emblem said a great deal about his personal attributes. "Lions do give the impression of strength," he mused, staring up at the tufted fabric on the ceiling. "Lord Crosby should be a strong fellow."

"Crosby now, is it?"

Ash mouthed the name again: *Lord Crosby*. It was a fine name, a name that would command respect. It was certainly better than his given name of Ashley Claughbane. Of course, that didn't take much effort to achieve. "Rather rolls off the tongue, don't you agree?"

"As long as you're paying, I'm agreeing."

Ash ignored the pointed comment on their friendship—having spent every day with the man since they'd left home seven years ago, he knew better. Stapleton wasn't interested in coin beyond what he needed to live, nor was he prone to keeping his opinions to himself. No, Stapleton was in this for the grand adventure of it all and always had been—unlike Ash. His own reasons were a bit more complicated.

He shot a glance at the inn, visible out the opposite side of the carriage. The scent of eggs and sausage on the fire wafted from the open windows of the inn. Ash might as well have gone inside for a plate of food, considering how long Stapleton was taking with the blasted paint. He hadn't had a bite since some dry cake yesterday at that tea in Bath, the event where everything had begun to fall to pieces.

It wasn't the first time he'd had to abandon his plans in favor of keeping his head. In his line of work, one learned to keep moving regardless of the circumstances. But he'd been careless in Bath; he knew that. He'd grown brazen in his actions. Every job in the last month had left him more irritated than satisfied. Was ennui possible for someone like him?

"On to the next village," Ash muttered as he reached into his pocket and pulled out the calling card that he'd kept for the past year. He read it over again.

Fallon St. James
The Spare Heirs Society

Perhaps it was time for a change.

As the fourth son in a newly titled family, he certainly met the qualifications. Membership to the secretive London club hadn't appealed to him in the least when he'd met St. James last year, yet Ash hadn't tossed the man's card out. Some part of him had known he would travel this path one day.

Had the time now come?

He rubbed his thumb over the embossed swirls of ink that formed the word *society*. He would be part of something, like a family. He cringed at the thought of signing up for another family after so long on his own. But if the London job was to be a success—and it must be—he would need more assistance than Stapleton could provide. He narrowed his eyes at the calling card as though it held the answers to his questions.

Ash had been working toward his goal since his father's death seven years ago. Unceasing travel from village to village, selling schemes and potions, honing his skills of persuasion in preparation for this moment—the moment when he would take back what his father had lost. He'd scouted the potential for his scheme last year, but he only had one chance to put it to action, only one chance to finally set things right for his family. Was it finally time? What a decision to rush through behind an old inn.

"Where am I taking the much-esteemed Lord Crosby?" Stapleton asked, interrupting Ash's thoughts.

Where to next? Ash stuffed the card back in his pocket and looked out the window. There was no turning back toward Cornwall or Devon now; the men trailing them from Bath would see to that much.

When Ash didn't answer right away, Stapleton continued, "It's north from here to Oxford. South goes to Hampshire. Hampshire would be nice this time of year. Wouldn't mind finding a house there and staying through the spring. We could see the sights, slow down a bit…"

Ash turned in surprise, but Stapleton was focused on the brush in his hand. Slow down? Why would Stapleton want such a thing? "You know we only have two rules, mate: no staying, and no becoming attached. That would be breaking one of them."

"Aye, I do." Stapleton paused in his work, looking up at Ash. "But a bit of a stay would be a welcome change of pace, don't you agree?"

"I hate to dash your hopes, but there's an angry mob chasing us. We can't *stay* anywhere."

"I can evade pursuit faster than anyone in the business," Stapleton said with a grin.

"And you think a sedate spring in Hampshire would suit the likes of us? What will we do for entertainment? Take strolls along the shore?" Ash laughed at the thought of the two of them on holiday together like a pair of matronly aunts.

"Wouldn't be so bad. Might remind us of home," Stapleton mused as he rested his arm on the side of the carriage.

"You long for home?" Ash made a face. "There's nothing back there for us. You can't want to return to a servant's life for my brother after all this time."

"There was this maid there," Stapleton said, a faraway, dreamy gleam filling his eyes.

"There are many maids—a country full of them, in fact—and none of them require travel back to the blasted Isle of Man for a visit."

"Aye, but this one…"

Ash shook his head, putting an end to the other man's dreams of a seaside holiday. No amount of time spent by the water would make him amenable to the idea of returning home. "Hampshire is filled with widows, remember? The old and bitter kind, not the amusing kind."

"I'd forgotten," Stapleton said with a chuckle, his momentary bout of nostalgia disappearing in an instant. "Oxford, then, is it?"

"Or it could finally be time," he said, testing the waters of possibility. St. James's card was a stone weighing down his pocket—and his thoughts.

"Time," Stapleton repeated, staring at Ash for a

second as he considered the meaning of his words. "You can't be serious, Claughbane. London?"

"You want amusement for the spring. I want—" Ash broke off at a sound in the front yard of the inn. Craning around to see through the sliver of space between the buildings, he watched Lord Braxton dismounting from his horse and surveying the inn. The men from Bath had arrived. That was the problem with losing someone on an empty span of road—they didn't stay lost for long.

"Forget the lions. I find I'm quite fond of dogs." He was also rather fond of his own head. The men hadn't spotted them yet, but they would soon. If he and Stapleton slipped away now, they might escape for good.

Stapleton nodded and stood, dusting his hands on his breeches. "You're lucky I'm as skilled with a brush as I am with the carriage reins."

"Indeed. You might want to take up those reins soon if we're to leave here free men."

Stapleton paused, looking up at Ash through the carriage window. "London, then. You're certain."

The gravity of the moment reflected in his friend's eyes. They both know what this meant.

"London."

⌇

Thank goodness the quadrille offered one room to breathe, because a waltz with this particular gentleman might have led to her untimely death.

Evangeline circled Lord Winfield with practiced steps and offered him her hand, ignoring the overpowering scent of his cologne. Truly, had he taken a swim in the vile concoction before arriving at the ball tonight? She took the smallest breath she dared, focusing on her steps.

The arch of her wrist was in exacting accordance with the dancing instruction her mother had insisted upon. She stepped forward, pointing the toe of her beaded slipper until it just peeked out from beneath her ball gown.

Her mother had this season organized down to the second, and at this second Evangeline was executing the perfect quadrille in spite of a distinct lack of breathable air around her dance partner. She tilted her chin to a pleasing angle and tossed a smile at his lordship. Moving back toward him, she placed her hand on his arm with a featherlight touch. Two more smiles and this dance would be over.

Most ladies allowed the music to dictate dance length, but Evangeline thought of dances as a matter of many practiced steps, two elegant curtsies, no more than one allotted lingering hand on a gentleman's arm, and five smiles.

If she accomplished every step as rehearsed, she would find a match her family would approve of. The gentleman's identity didn't matter—even his lordship of the cologne. If Evangeline Green had any skill, it was that of dressing for a part and then playing it flawlessly. The role of wife would be no different from the others she had played in her life: daughter, sister, cousin, and friend. She would wear the proper gowns, offer the perfect responses to those who would call upon her, and always have a warm smile for her lord.

What more could a man want? For that matter, what more could she want?

There had been a time last season when she'd thought she desired a different path, but she'd been wrong. Her mother had been correct after all—Evangeline could not be trusted to choose her own future.

"I do so enjoy the quadrille, Lord Winfield."

"The pleasure is mine, Lady Evangeline. Your ability to conduct yourself properly at a ball is certainly as Lady Rightworth promised. You were the finest lady on the floor tonight. I must admit, though, I find the glass ceiling of the Dillsworths' ballroom to be a bit concerning." He glanced up as he spoke, sneering at the elegant transparent roof, which danced with merry dots of light. "All those candles suspended from such a small amount of roof seems dangerous."

Her mother's list of rules for conversation circled through Evangeline's mind. *Never offer an opposing view* and *Always honor your hosts* collided into a gray area with his last comment. She took a breath, considering the appropriate response. "I suppose some might say it adds a bit of excitement to the average dance. I'm pleased we survived."

"Excitement isn't an ideal I hold in much regard. Predictability gives one comfort for years to come," he intoned as he led her from the floor.

"I too enjoy knowing what is to come." She supposed that was a true statement, in a sense. She did enjoy knowing that in a moment she would be away from Lord Winfield's excessive scent. And she enjoyed knowing her next dance was free and she would have a few minutes to chat with her cousins. Of course, the twins were anything but predictable.

She forced her attention back to the conversation at hand. She was ever so close to ending this encounter without a single misstep. With the correct phrases and the execution of a perfect dance, she would be wed in but a few months' time if she could simply maintain her performance. "What if summer couldn't be trusted to be warm, or winter cold? It would be quite a mess to cope with."

"Winter warm as though it were summer. Such fanciful thoughts, my lady." He chuckled and shook his blond head, studying her for a moment.

Evangeline maintained a serene look on her face, hoping he didn't now think her overly whimsical. She'd stepped over the line with her comment, and after trying so to be the lady Lord Winfield would want for his wife. Perhaps she did require more practice...

"I believe I prefer the seasons as they are," he finally continued.

"As do I, my lord," she offered as relief flooded through her body. "As you said, some things should be able to be relied upon."

"You make quite agreeable company, my lady. May I rely on the promise of a dance with you at the next ball?" He leaned in a fraction too close to ask, the stench of his cologne filling the air around her.

She resisted the urge to pull away to breathe. He was pleased with her company. Everything was as it should be. She smiled the final smile of the encounter. Then she allowed her hand to trail over his arm in the one allotted lingering touch to make him remember her before letting it fall back to her side. "One in which we will remain quite safe from falling ceilings, I hope."

"Lady Evangeline," he offered in farewell as he bowed and took his leave.

Evangeline was still taking breaths to keep from coughing when her cousins joined her, pulling her back toward the wall of the ballroom where they couldn't be overheard. It was a precaution deemed necessary near the end of last season after the unfortunate incident with Lady Smeltings. The woman had heard Victoria's rather loud opinion that her ladyship's new style of hair made her look like an angry bee about to move in for the sting. It had taken far too many smiles over tea to settle that score, and the three of them had agreed to be more careful of their talk in the future.

Her mother appeared none too thrilled by their move away from the action of the room, but she was thankfully locked in conversation with two other ladies and wouldn't be able to berate Evangeline until later. But that didn't stop her narrow-eyed glare. Busy ignoring the scowl that burned into the back of her head over the abandonment of her previously prominent location at the side of the ballroom, Evangeline took a glass of lemonade from a passing footman.

She would no doubt pay a high price for her behavior on the carriage ride home, but her two cousins were worth the browbeating. The three of them had become quite close over the three years since Victoria and Isabelle's father had unexpectedly inherited his title and estate. Evangeline mourned the lost years when she and her older sister hadn't been allowed to visit *such common gentry*. Even if they were family. But at least she'd had Sue for a sister…until last season.

The only correspondence she'd received from her sister in the past year had been small sketches of sights Sue must have seen while on her wedding trip with Lord Steelings, and even those had been few in number. There were no messages or locations— nothing but the drawings. Evangeline understood Sue's reasons for such distance, but it made her heart ache all the same. She drowned the maudlin thoughts in a large swallow of lemonade. She had her cousins for company now, as well as her new friend Roselyn, and she would not make a mess of things as she had with her sister last season.

"Who's next?" Victoria asked, grabbing the card from Evangeline's wrist and squinting at the names written there. She winced. "You'll want to watch your toes for the remainder of the evening. Not a single good dancer—or interesting conversationalist, for that matter—in that lot."

"Victoria," Evangeline admonished through teeth clenched in a polite smile. "Even with us standing here, someone could hear you."

"I'd be doing them and all the other ladies here a kindness. Someone should tell these gentlemen that they dance an awful waltz, and that their conversational skills are no better than their abilities on the dance floor. Have you heard Lord Herring drone on about his crop rotations? I almost drifted off to sleep on the floor mid-twirl."

"Victoria does have a fair point, Evie," Isabelle

mused, investigating her cousin's dance card for herself, a frown on her pouty lips. "You seem to have selected your dance partners based on their ability to make a girl nod off."

Evangeline pulled her wrist away from her cousins' inspection. The gentlemen in question had been selected based on rank, wealth, and good standing in society. Her mother would consider no other factors. "Really, Isabelle. I expected you to understand. Exceptions must be made." She hid a grimace behind her glass of lemonade. "Such things matter little in the game of marriage."

"In the game of marriage, even I place no bets," Victoria said with a shake of her blond head.

Evangeline eyed her cousin. "We're expected to play a hand or two at least. Show some effort, Victoria."

"I don't care for the odds." If Victoria was anything, it was sure of her own opinions on everything around her. Evangeline admired her strength. There was no place for such talk in her own life, of course, but her cousin's words always made her smile.

"I, on the other hand, want to play this game forever. Isn't it wonderfully romantic here tonight? The candlelight, the roses, all the gowns and dashing gentlemen…" Isabelle sighed and looked out across the ballroom as if soaking in a particularly beautiful sunset.

"You would find romance in being paraded about town like a cow at the local harvest festival. I'm sure you'll get the winning ribbon this year, Isabelle, worry not."

Isabelle huffed and turned her back on her sister, her perfect blond ringlets bouncing as she moved.

"A cow at the local harvest festival? Really, Victoria." Evangeline shook her head. Although they bickered, her cousins truly did adore each other. Evangeline thought the comfort of their relationship gave them the ability to say such things. They could say what they wished, but she'd seen them laugh and cry together over the last three years. She knew their true nature.

Victoria chuckled, as unrepentant as always, enjoying the situation even more when Isabelle shot a murderous look over her shoulder.

Evangeline watched the gentleman she was to dance with next move past them, treading on a lady's toes when she came too close. Leaning toward Victoria, she whispered, "Perhaps you were right about my next dance partner."

"Of course I was. What you need to survive the remainder of this evening is champagne. What you were thinking with that lemonade, I have no idea."

"I was thinking that I had a thirst," Evangeline replied as she set her lemonade glass on the tray of a passing footman.

Isabelle spun back around, apparently having followed their conversation while acting put out. "Are we going in search of champagne? I believe there's a parlor with refreshments nearby."

Evangeline looked around to answer her cousin, but at that moment the crowd parted, and there he was. She blinked, not trusting her own eyes.

It couldn't be. Perhaps she'd imagined him.

She craned her neck to see through the crush of people to the ballroom's main entrance. *He* looked into the room, his eyes sweeping across the dancers, before he turned and moved away into the hall. He was here. He'd left her with empty promises a year ago, and now he was back. She was already moving in his direction.

"Will you excuse me? My gown is in need of repair," she murmured without taking her eyes from the door.

"Your gown is fine, Evie. You always fuss so. Let us go and find some champagne so you'll be fortified before your next dance."

"I really must repair my gown." Evangeline was crossing the room before Victoria could reply.

Perhaps her eyes were bewitched. She'd thought she would never see him again. And yet at the same time, she had never stopped looking for him. She'd found herself searching crowds for his face countless times over the past year. Her mother had accused her of madness when she'd abandoned their shopping last month to follow someone down Bond Street. That gentleman had turned out to be Lord Wellsly, to her everlasting embarrassment. Evangeline gave a mental shudder at the memory. This time was different. This time it wasn't simply another tall gentleman with the same lean build or coal-colored hair. This time she'd seen his face.

She slipped from the Dillsworths' ballroom without her family taking notice, which was a wonder in itself. Now, if she could only discover which direction the dratted gentleman had gone. Dillsworth House was a large home on the outskirts of the city. Its opulence made it the perfect location for such a large ball. But its size also made it a challenge to find a single gentleman in the crush of guests wandering the vast halls.

Evangeline turned at the end of the hall, delving deeper into the less-populated areas of the home. Perhaps she'd lost his trail. Who would wander a dim hall during a ball? But even as she thought it, she knew Lord Barnish would do exactly that. She'd first met him in just such a location at a ball last year.

Her eyes narrowed on the flicker of light coming from the crack under the door just in front of her. She lifted her hand to the edge of the door, her palm sweating beneath her snug glove. What would she find inside? What if the gentleman she'd seen wasn't even Lord Barnish? Or worse, what if he was? Taking a breath to regain her usual calm facade, she opened the door.

Across what appeared to be a small library, she saw him again. He had his back to her as he flipped quickly through papers on a desk. The room was lit by a few candles placed in ornate sconces on the walls, but they shed only enough light to dissuade one from tripping over furniture—hardly enough to read by. A lantern burned bright on the desk though, throwing dancing light across his hands. He lifted one piece of paper and studied it in the light. His head tilted and she could see the edge of a triumphant smile—the same smile she'd searched for since last season.

"My Lord…it *is* you," she muttered, trying to gather her wits about her. For all the rehearsing of what she would say if she were ever to see him again, now, in this moment, all she could manage were benign niceties? "I didn't expect to see you here this evening," she continued, inwardly rolling her eyes at her own words.

"Nor I you," he replied as he turned toward her, lowering the paper in his hand, but not replacing it on the stack on the desk. "It is, however, a pleasure to see you now." He was as handsome as ever. The nonchalance that seemed threaded through every fiber of his body had him leaning a hip on the desk. His eyes raked over her body before landing on her face. His quick blink was the only sign that she'd surprised him. The rest of him remained suspended in a show of languid enjoyment.

After quickly checking the hall behind her, she stepped into the quiet of the library. Licking her lips, she searched for the words she wanted to say to get the answers she needed to hear. Closure, that was what she wanted of him. That was *all* she wanted of him, and then she would leave without looking back. After all, the gentlemen on her dance card were approved matches, and he was not. "When I last saw you…"

"I was unavoidably detained, my lady." His voice was as smooth as his appearance—smooth like glass. And just like glass, anyone in reach was likely to be sliced to pieces at a moment's notice.

Evangeline winced at the slight. He acted as if he'd only stepped outside for some air and not disappeared completely both from society and from her life for a year. Did he have her confused with a dance partner from earlier in the evening? Perhaps, unlike her, he didn't remember their time together at all.

She shouldn't have come here. She shouldn't have ever looked for him on the crowded London streets. And she certainly shouldn't have kissed him that night after knowing him only a short time.

"Allow me to make amends," he added. The corner of his mouth quirked up, the promise of a smile hidden beneath the surface.

"Unavoidably detained," she repeated as she balled her hands into fists at her sides. "For a year."

"A year. That does sound rather damning, doesn't it?" He made a face of dismay. "My lady, has anyone ever told you how candlelight reflects in your eyes like the stars on a cloudless night?"

"Yes. As a matter of fact, you told me just that— last year."

A muscle twitched in his jaw. Was that to be his only acknowledgment of his obvious misstep? "Still, it's no less true today."

It would seem he wasn't the sort to offer an apology. And she'd spent a year pining for this man! She shook her head as her mind rushed to make sense of what was happening. "Lord Barnish, I can see I've made a horrible error in my judgment of you. It seems time has also served to make me wiser in my dealings with rakish gentlemen."

He pushed from the desk at the mention of his name, something akin to concern filling his eyes. "Well, now I know the issue. This Lord Barnish seems a rather unreliable and foolish fellow since I take it he abandoned you. His loss, the daft prick." He smiled in that way that haunted her memories, his clear blue eyes twinkling with humor. "I'm Lord Crosby."

She blinked. He was going so far as to give a new name? No. This was not the manner in which their reunion would take place.

She took a step forward, looking up into the face

she would know anywhere. "Crosby, are you? It's odd that you would possess the same tall, athletic build as Barnish, the same tan coloring from too much time spent outdoors. Why, even the lift of your brow as you study me, the quirk of your lips as if amused by your own thoughts, your coal-black hair tousled in the same careless manner. Tell me, did you just emerge from a lover's bed, or do you simply enjoy making proper ladies envision such…" Evangeline stopped herself, realizing too late that she was rambling on about his appearance and causing the heat of a blush to rush to her cheeks.

"My lady…"

Clenching her fist so as not to cover her mouth at her carelessly spoken, horribly inappropriate words, she watched him. "You don't remember my name, do you?" She couldn't believe how wrong she'd been about him. "I've spent the past year chasing a wisp of smoke that vanished into the air."

He took a step toward her. "Smoke from embers that burn still, judging by your anger now."

"Smoke from a foul fire I now wish I'd never encountered."

"Lady Emily," he offered with a hint of an apologetic smile, clearly attempting to get back in her good graces. He took another step toward her, wincing when she narrowed her eyes. "Lady Ethel?"

"Good day, my lord," she ground out.

"It's actually night at the moment—not that we'll quibble over such nuances at a time like this."

She shoved him hard in the chest, annoyed when he didn't budge, but only looked down at her gloved hands.

He looked back up at her, his eyes twinkling in the candlelight. "*Good evening* would be appropriate though...Lady Elizabeth."

"You"—she hit him again, putting the force of her body behind the blow, but he still didn't flinch—"do *not* have leave to use my given name, therefore it scarcely matters if it is Irene or Penelope!" She realized after the fact that she was yelling. *A lady never yells.* The words played in her mind in her mother's voice.

Giving her gown a tug, not so much to straighten her skirts as to calm herself, she said, "You may call me the lady who left you standing alone in the library."

And with one final fluid motion—one that would have made her dance instructor quite pleased—she plucked the paper from his hand and glided out the door. For all the upset he had caused her, she would not allow him to steal from Lord Dillsworth on her watch. She was Lady Evangeline Green, daughter of Lord Rightworth, and that was simply not how things were done in good society.

Two

ASHLEY CLAUGHBANE HAD DONE MANY THINGS IN his life, but chasing impulsively after an ill-tempered lady wasn't one of them. Still, he muttered a curse and took off after her.

He'd known London would be a troublesome bear of a job, and this was why. All right, perhaps this wasn't why. How could he have anticipated this turn of events? But the task was proving troublesome nonetheless. What were the odds that the chit would remember him from last year, let alone that she would be in attendance tonight? Truly. A hundred to one? A thousand, perhaps? He'd only been in town one week last year. Yet here she was, fleeing with the document he needed for his plan to move forward.

He reached the hall and spotted the flick of her skirt as she moved out of sight. What the devil was her name? When he thought back, he could remember the soft caress of her lips against his, that her dark hair felt and smelled like rose petals, that she'd worn yellow. But her name was a mystery. He shook his head and rounded the corner after her. She was walking toward the crowded ballroom. He had to stop her. She could destroy everything. He would have to leave town, and there was no way he would be able to return. "I've waited too long for this to walk away now," he growled to the empty hall.

Diving through a door that looked like it led to an unlit service hall, he ran to the opposite end. If he could cut her off before she reached the ballroom, all would be well. He simply had to get to her in time.

He found the door at the end of the hall and flung it open, the passage leading directly back to the ballroom. He blinked into the candlelit room, his eyes adjusting from the dimness of the service corridor. There she was. She was smoothing her skirts and looking the part of an angry ice queen, the paper he needed still clutched in her hand. She was searching the room, and he would venture a guess it wasn't to find him again.

There was no time for thought. There was no time to consider his options. Leaning out from the doorway, he grabbed a fistful of her gown and pulled her backward. She staggered on her heels, recoiling into the dark hall with him. He gave her gown a final tug and shut the door on the ballroom, throwing them into relative darkness.

She gasped. Would she scream? One never knew if a woman was a screamer or not, at least until the opportunity presented itself. This sort of event was his least favorite means of having that question answered.

"What do you think you're doing?"

Not a screamer, it seemed. "Saving you from making a horrible mistake," he replied.

"Saving me? I don't require saving. And certainly not by you."

"Ah, but if I'm not wrong—and I'm rarely wrong—you were about to hand this paper over to our gracious hosts." He ran a finger down her arm to the gloved hand where she held the document.

There was a telling pause before she pulled her arm out of his reach. "You're wrong. Everything about this situation is wrong."

"It is, isn't it?" He lowered his voice to a suggestive rumble, grinning as he spoke.

She huffed but made no move to put more distance between them. "You're despicable."

"True."

"And I'm guessing not on the guest list this evening."

"Also true."

She studied him, her soft blue eyes reflecting the sparkle of a lone candle on the wall. "Then why are you here?"

"The more interesting question is why you haven't yet left. For someone who finds my company so unpleasant, you've now followed me into two darkened spaces."

"I did *not* follow you here," she stated, her eyes flashing with ire.

"Details," he countered.

"A rather important detail, if you ask me."

"Is it? At the end of the story, we're here either way."

"So we are. Lord Barnish…I mean, Crosby…or whatever you call yourself these days, I am sorry to leave you alone once again, but I really must return to the ball."

"To turn me in for appearing here uninvited," he finished for her.

"Among other things." Her gaze fell to his mouth, and she blinked her focus back to his eyes. It was a small glance, but he noticed nonetheless.

"Oh, we shouldn't forget the other things," he said, closing the gap between them by a fraction.

"No, we shouldn't."

"You're right, of course." He reached up and traced the line of her jaw with his fingers. "It would be wrong."

"Quite wrong," she whispered.

"Yet irresistible," he murmured as he slid his hand over her cheek.

She took a quick breath. He could feel the tension in the delicate line of her jaw. He hadn't read her interest incorrectly. When it came to charm, Ash knew no equal.

When he touched his lips to hers, her eyes drifted closed and she pressed forward into him. Suddenly, what he'd planned as a stolen kiss, meant to distract, didn't seem stolen at all. This kiss was freely given. And if something was offered, he was a smart enough fellow to take it.

Her mouth was lush and willing beneath his. He deepened their kiss, tracing the seam of her lips with his tongue. A hint of lemon lingered there. Her kisses were sweet yet tart, matching the lady in question. Damn. He still didn't remember her name.

He slid one hand into the dark hair that hung in shining ringlets at the back of her neck, pulling her closer with the other. She rose to her toes, pressing a hand to his chest. Where had this minx come from, and how had he possibly forgotten about her?

He slipped his hand down her arm to the hand where she still held the document. He twined his fingers with hers as he plundered her mouth. He now had what he'd come for in his grasp, but he didn't want to leave—not now.

This had not been part of his plan. What had begun as *his* winning move in this game of theirs had somehow become *hers*. He needed to leave. He couldn't stay here with her—too much was at stake. He broke their kiss. The next minute passed on a tide of blinks, questioning looks, and ragged breaths.

Finally, he gave her a small nod and took a step away. "I appreciate the kiss...even more than the document you returned to me."

"What?"

He leaned in and kissed her once more for good measure. She didn't fight the touch, but a second later when his actions clearly registered, she made a different type of contact—her palm against his cheek.

A loud slap filled the hall, or perhaps it only echoed in his own ears. Either way, it stung like the devil.

"At least tell me your true name," she demanded. "You owe me that much."

He waved the piece of paper in the air in farewell. "You may call me the gentleman who left you standing alone in a servants' hall."

He opened the door to leave her there as promised. All had worked out quite well this evening—unexpected, but well.

A grin was still on his face when she ducked her head beneath his arm and tried to stop him from fleeing. Was the lady mad? She was a fine-boned woman, though the smallest woman he'd ever seen, but she could hardly stop someone his size. His hand was on the door behind her. She was pushing and still sliding backward on the polished hardwood floor as he moved forward.

"You will not get away with this. Not again, not this season."

Again. The word caught him off guard. He paused to look down at her, seeing some emotion shining behind her eyes—emotion that had nothing to do with a stolen document.

He wasn't certain of her meaning, but he knew he couldn't linger to find out. He grabbed the hand splayed on his chest and lifted it, spinning it in the air and sending her twirling into the crowded ballroom. Her hair was a bit mussed at the back of her neck where he'd delved his hands into it. He hadn't noticed in the darkness of the hall. Perhaps his hadn't been a well-thought-out plan, but a few hairs out of order were surely a forgivable offense. He stuffed the paper into his pocket and shook his coat into place.

"Evangeline!" an older lady said, stopping her movement into the crowd. "Your hair looks a sight. I knew that new maid didn't pin it properly."

That was her name. Ash recognized his cue to run as clearly as though it had been waved on a great red flag. "Lady Evangeline," he said with a grin and a bow just before he tore toward the front door of the Dillsworth home and fled into the night.

⁓

The correct thing to do was to forget that the entire evening had occurred, of course. Nothing had happened last night. She hadn't seen the gentleman she'd been searching for since last season. She hadn't followed him into the library to confront him. Kissing him in the servants' passage *certainly* hadn't happened. And Evangeline's mother had not spent the following three hours ripping her to shreds for her disappearance from the ballroom and her less-than-perfect hair.

She straightened her spine against further thought on the matter and tried to focus on the shop windows as they passed. After slipping from her home this morning while her mother had met with their housekeeper, Evangeline had gone in search of Isabelle and Victoria. Her mother would have a fit once she discovered Evangeline had left home, having left only a note that she was shopping for new gloves for the next ball. Her excuse would gain her a few hours away from her life anyway, and she found that she required some extra time this morning. Evangeline glanced over her shoulder as they moved down the street to make certain they were alone. Mother's fit would be even worse if she heard news that the three of them were *walking*, of all things, to visit their new friend Roselyn Grey. But Isabelle had declared today too fine for closed carriages, and Evangeline had agreed.

Evangeline had met Roselyn when she'd first arrived in town. It was her friend's first season and the poor dear wasn't off to the best start, considering the recent passing of her fiancé. The circumstances around both his death and their brief period of engagement were all hush-hush, of course, but Evangeline knew the unfortunate truth about the Duke of Thornwood's sister. Like many other ladies, she was sure, Roselyn had been served a foul dish to swallow in her come-out season. With one season beyond her, Evangeline wasn't in much better condition.

Passing a small shop filled with gloves, fans, and ribbons of every color under the sun, she paused, her gaze falling on a display of ornate hairpins. They appeared the sturdy sort in spite of their pearl, jet, and glittering paste ends. Perhaps those pins would have held her hair in place last night. Then her mother would not have seen it slip from its confines.

Having known the true reason her hair had fallen, and that it had nothing to do with the poor maid who'd arranged it, made the news of the maid's dismissal at first light this morning even more painful for Evangeline to hear. But Evangeline couldn't risk speaking up on the matter, a situation she was unfortunately accustomed to bearing the burden of. All Evangeline could do now to help matters was to send a glowing reference for the maid without her mother's knowledge, and she would do so. If only he hadn't touched her hair when they'd kissed, but he had. And shamefully, she'd enjoyed it.

Evangeline bit at her bottom lip, the memory of his lordship's touch lingering there like a burn from scalding tea on one's tongue the next day. Burn, indeed. The heat of that kiss had singed her to the core. His hands in her hair, on her skin, were what her dreams had been made of since she'd first met him. Closing her eyes, she wished she could relive the past day, though with a few differences—the gentleman in question would remember her, for one.

Following him had been a terrible idea. What had

she been thinking? The entire series of events that had transpired was so unlike her. She was the proper one, the perfectly behaved one, the one everyone could count upon to be sensible... She had to be. But there was no rewriting the past now. The very sight of that man had caused her to act impulsively and go where she ought not to have been, where she would never go again. She hadn't been the ideal lady last night and now, just like during that terrible childhood summer, she would pay the price for her poor behavior.

I hope that kiss was well worth your current regret, Evangeline.

Heaven help her, it had been. She would never admit it aloud, but Lord Crosby—or whatever he was calling himself now—was a wicked gentleman in all the ways that mattered. Which was precisely why she needed to stay far away from him. Assuming he hadn't already disappeared once more.

"Are you wearing the rouge we found in that shop last year?" Isabelle asked as she peered at Evangeline's reflection in the glass of the shop window.

"Of course not. I'm not joining a theatrical troupe, Isabelle."

"You're delightfully rosy today for no good reason, then."

"Am I?" Evangeline lifted her chin and continued down the street, hoping to have a moment for the color in her cheeks to calm.

Isabelle, however, added a small skip to her already pert steps and caught up with her. "You're not so pink-cheeked that a life in the theater is in your future, but the morning air agrees with you. Wouldn't the theatrical life be grand, though? Traveling to cities far and wide…"

"Staying in questionable establishments and singing for food?" Evangeline added. "I fail to see the appeal."

"Oh, Evie, must you see the dreadful reality of every situation?"

"Apologies, Isabelle. I find I'm out of sorts this morning. Please, continue your romanticizing of an otherwise seedy form of employment. I find it refreshing." It was certainly a better place for her mind to dwell than where it had been since last night. Even after the tongue-lashing she'd received from her mother over her disappearance and the state of her hair, not to mention her guilt over the dismissal of yet another maid, her thoughts kept returning to his lordship and his sinful mouth.

"Is she going on again about the demimonde?" Victoria asked as she caught up to them, and the ladies crossed a small street. "How many times must I tell you, Isabelle, that there's more to the life than scandalous clothing and masks at parties?"

"This time it's the theater," Evangeline corrected with a small smile for her cousin.

"Oh." Victoria shook her head in acceptance. "Very well. Glad to see your dreams have taken a step toward respectability."

"I'm not planning to become an actress or a kept lady, I'll have you know," Isabelle replied, her usual dreamy look vanishing long enough for her to glare at her twin sister. "I simply find the idea intriguing."

Victoria rolled her eyes.

The twins continued their discussion as they walked

down the street. Isabelle was a beauty down to her bones. She always managed to find the grace, excitement, and romance in any situation, no matter how difficult. Some—namely Victoria—thought she lived in a dream of her own making. But more truly, she chose to see the world around her in a lovely light, and Evangeline rather enjoyed sharing her cousin's view.

Victoria, on the other hand, was more likely to stomp on a romantic notion and do a bit of a dance on its head than admit she agreed with her sister. She was the very definition of the word *hoyden*, and Evangeline loved her for it. She was quite fortunate to have such wonderful ladies in her life. Their presence might just make this season bearable—her second and hopefully last season...

Her mother would busy herself with making Evangeline a shining example of a lady. Her father would scowl from the depths of his library every time she passed his door. She would dance with more gentlemen of title and means, like the overly cologned Lord Winfield. And if she pointed her toes just so when they danced and smiled as she ought to do, he, or someone like him, would offer for her. She would be someone's wife. And she would finally have a fresh start.

Escape from her current circumstances was the only thing she wanted, and marriage was the vehicle that would take her far away. But was escaping her mother's wrath her only desire in life?

A different sort of desire had her leaning in for more just last night in the service hall. In that moment, she'd done what she pleased instead of what she must do.

There in the dark hall, she'd ignored everything but her own desire for a man she knew to be a rake.

In a lifetime of pleasing others, shouldn't she be allowed one brief encounter that was her own? What would happen if she took another moment for herself?

Just then her toe caught a bit of uneven ground, tossing her forward. Righting herself before she fell on her face, she took a steadying breath and continued along beside Isabelle.

"Are you all right?" Isabelle asked with her hand on Evangeline's elbow.

"Quite." In truth, the thought of indulging in anything she desired without concern for the consequences had caught her more off guard than the uneven ground. Where had the rebellious thought come from?

She banished the last few minutes from her mind, more ashamed of her wayward musings than the misstep she'd taken on the walk. Evangeline, of all ladies, couldn't afford such liberties. She must do as she was told, without complaint.

She knew, however, exactly who inspired such thoughts in her once again, just as he had last year. His eyes still lurked in her memory, a clear, piercing blue and laughing at the list of rules he'd broken in one evening. This was yet another reason to stay well away from him. Not that she had much of a choice in the matter. He would already be on the road out of London by now. One thing she knew for certain— *Lord Crosby* never stayed in one place for long.

They ascended the stairs to Thornwood House and were shown into the parlor. Roselyn was already there, thankfully not wearing black on this visit. Her new friend had a flair for the dramatic, but Evangeline imagined that growing up on a ducal estate where the duke in question was said to be mad would have that effect on anyone.

"There you are. You certainly made a fast retreat last night," Victoria said in greeting.

"The only redeeming quality of the Dillsworths' ball was getting to wear my new gown," Roselyn replied as she sank into one of the chairs.

"Was it as bad as all that?" Evangeline asked, eyeing Roselyn. Her wild, dark curls were trapped in a braid today, twisted and pinned at the base of her neck. She was as lovely as ever, even if dark smudges could be seen beneath her eyes, indicating a troubled night's sleep.

"Isn't your first ball supposed to be the makings of fond memories for years to come?"

"Who told you that?" Victoria asked, drawing back in shock. "It's complete bollocks."

"Victoria!" Evangeline exclaimed.

"It is," she returned with a shrug.

"Then it lived up to its illustrious reputation. After my brother scared away most of the gentlemen in attendance, there was really no saving the evening."

Evangeline could see how having the Mad Duke of Thornwood looming over one's shoulder would put a pall on events. She offered Roselyn a sympathetic smile and took a seat by the window.

Something tightened in Roselyn's jaw as she continued. "After a truly wretched time of it, I went to find the carriage and return home." She shook her head, and a wry smile crossed her face. "The only *friendly* gentleman I managed to meet over the entire evening was on the front steps—one Mr. Brice."

Isabelle's eyes lit with excitement. "You must tell us every word he said, Roselyn," she rushed to say as she practically fell into the chair beside Roselyn's.

From there the conversation turned to Mr. Kelton Brice, of course, as he was the long-time gem of Isabelle's eye. Tea must have been served at some point, because a cup was growing cold in Evangeline's hand, but her mind couldn't be further away.

"Evie, what do you think? You're always proper," Victoria said, cutting into her thoughts. "Should he be in town this season?"

Who? She was ashamed to admit she had no idea about whom they were speaking. She blinked, forcing her mind from the man she would most likely never see again.

"Evie?" Victoria asked again.

"Yes?"

"Is something wrong?" Isabelle asked.

Yes, something was terribly wrong. She'd fallen into the clutches of the man who'd haunted her dreams since they'd last met. She'd dared to have a single notion about what she might truly desire this season. She shouldn't have even considered the idea, but for a small shining moment she had. And unfortunately for her, what she wanted was a liar, a seducer, and a thief.

She couldn't allow it.

Her cup rattled against the saucer with the vehemence of her convictions.

Hadn't she proven herself to be stronger than her

temptations? She'd seized control over her situation when she was still a child, had learned to follow her mother's command. Since that dreadful day when she was twelve, she'd devoted herself to the pursuit of a proper life, just as she should do. She hadn't indulged in more than three bites of any sweet in the past seven years. She had never uttered a contrary word to a gentleman who was under consideration for marriage, either while dancing or over tea. She even wore dresses she privately found unappealing.

The worst example in her mind, though, had to be her actions toward her sister, Sue. Evangeline had destroyed their relationship last season in order to remain in good standing with her family, and that was a hurt she could never repair. She took a sip of tepid tea to keep any emotion from showing on her face. Her past misdeeds were terrible enough without exposing her sins to those around her.

Evangeline had withstood quite a bit in her life thus far, and she would withstand whatever hold that dratted man had on her. After all, he was gone once again and she had an appropriate husband to find.

"No. Of course not," she finally answered. Nothing was wrong. Nothing at all.

Three

ALL HAD GONE RIGHT WITH ASH'S PLANS THUS FAR—
Dillsworth's financial document, his perfect scheme,
his new affiliation with the Spare Heirs, and last but
not least, that kiss with Lady Evangeline. He hooked
his hand around the oak banister cap, swinging
around the corner to the main stairs with a spring in
his step.

Ash had arrived at headquarters for the Spare Heirs
Society yesterday and had been immediately welcomed
and offered one of the available rooms upstairs for his
stay in town. The grand home was quite accommodat-
ing, with a number of guest rooms, comfortable beds,
and ample storage. Personally, he didn't require the
shelf space since he never unpacked anything from his
trunks, but the other gentlemen who resided under St.
James's roof seemed quite settled, with living quarters
for valets as well as space for horses in the mews at the
rear of the building.

Stapleton had been shown to his room, and space
was made to store the carriage. "Ah, London life," Ash
muttered to himself with a grin. Moving from inn to

inn, he wasn't used to living in such style. He'd best not get too comfortable, though.

Hearing footsteps along the hall at his back, Ash turned and saw the very man he needed to meet with this morning—Fallon St. James. As much as Ash would rather carry on with his business in town alone, a job this size required discussion and planning.

"Interesting place you have here, St. James," he called out while waiting for the gentleman to catch up with him on the stairs.

Ash's gaze lingered on the set of cherubs painted on the ceiling far above his head as he leaned back against the stair rail. The headquarters for the Spare Heirs Society was a strange place—pleasant, but strange nonetheless—much like the group itself. Ash had seen a great many buildings across England and Wales, and he could honestly say this was the first time he'd encountered such a concentration of gentlemen huddled within a building decorated in such a feminine style. But it wasn't just the fact that the home was at odds with its occupants. These gentlemen in particular were all of a similar ilk—secretive, risk-taking individuals willing to use whatever skills they possessed to better their situations. It was a bit disconcerting to think there were so many other gentlemen with similar minds for business, when he'd spent so much time on his path alone.

He had to admit that it was an interesting idea, this notion of banding together when society gave no assistance to those gentlemen born after the first in a family. An interesting idea, but not one he wanted to dive headlong into for the foreseeable future.

Ash's gaze fell across the large paintings in ornate frames depicting various ladies in front of landscapes and gentlemen seated in libraries, none of whom bore a resemblance to the mysterious head of the secret society. How had St. James obtained such a property? Ash glanced up at the man as he neared. "I'm certain there's a story behind the acquisition of a home such as this. I've relieved a fair number of women of their—we'll call them unnecessary—possessions, but a house? That's impressive."

St. James didn't answer as he descended the steps. From what Ash knew of him thus far, Fallon St. James was a man of few words, even though Ash suspected the man's thoughts were unceasingly spinning. His dark eyes flashed even when he said nothing. That, of course, only made Ash's curiosity about the leader of this group of misfit gentlemen increase. St. James joined Ash at the bottom step and studied him in silence, just as he had done when Ash had arrived yesterday. Was staring the man's only form of communication?

Ash raised a brow, a smirk drawing the corner of his mouth up. "You don't have to get squeamish on my account. I understand." He pushed off the stair rail and took the final step down into the main hall. "It was won in a fair card game, was it not? Signed over in a deathbed promise, was it? Listen, I'm sure it was obtained in complete honesty. Have I told you the story of how I got my carriage?"

"This has been the headquarters for the Spare Heirs for a number of years now. It suits our needs. Your accommodations are to your liking, I presume?" St. James waved a hand toward the double doors near the base of the stairs, indicating for Ash to follow him.

Ash threw his hands up in surrender and grinned. "Secrets are what lives like ours are built upon. You may keep yours, for now. Whoever she was, the lady had a fine home. My rooms are more than adequate for my stay here. As I mentioned before, I'll be gone in no more than one month."

"If you're certain you can accomplish your task in that time," St. James said over his shoulder as he moved across the hall.

"If you knew of my quick work in the Welsh towns, you wouldn't be concerned."

"I *do* know of your reputation in Wales," St. James said with enough confidence to make Ash wonder exactly how much of his past this man knew. "I think, however, you'll find the *ton* to be a more difficult group to persuade away from their purses."

"I'm aware of the difficulties involved." The thought of what lay ahead washed over him again, just as it had on the road to London. His jaw tightened in the face of the challenge before him. Ash had to succeed. He'd waited long enough, practiced long enough. It was Lord Rightworth's turn to pay for what he'd done to Ash's family. This time he would be the one left in ruin as Ash rode away in *his* carriage.

He'd tracked Lord Rightworth ever since the day he'd taken everything from Ash's father. After all, one must know his target well. Ash knew the man's information from his home in the country, and the one in town, to the fact that he was married with two school-age daughters, to his interest in politics and his propensity to cheat at cards, …at least he knew the man on paper. And it would soon be time to know him personally.

He patted the document he'd acquired at the ball last night, still in his pocket. Obtaining Lord Dillsworth's financial statements had been the first step in the process. The men of the *ton* followed that gentleman's lead in all monetary matters. Ash had seen that during his visit to town last year. Convincing Dillsworth to invest in Ash's false company was the first and most important step in bringing his long game to fruition. Then it would finally be time to set things to rights.

A steam engine small enough for everyone to own one—ha! He would make people believe it was the next move in society. Once Rightworth had placed all his funds in Ash's care—far more than that of any other gentleman involved—Ash would vanish just like…well, just like steam! It was brilliant. His father's fortune would finally be back where it belonged: with his family. And it all started with the document held safely in Ash's pocket.

He followed St. James into the main gathering space of the Spare Heirs Society. It appeared to have been a drawing room in a previous lifetime, an open space that ran the length of the large home. Now billiard tables sat in the center of the room, while representations of every style of leather chair were scattered across the floor. Was this one drawing room or five mashed together into furniture stew? The mismatched seating seemed to swim within the large, pale-pink walls, while golden swirls of paint made bows on the ceiling. Ash shook his head and followed St. James until they reached a table in the corner of the room, situated to overlook the street below.

After signaling for drinks, Ash settled into one of the chairs and regarded St. James. The man was secretive, but Ash supposed that made him the perfect leader of a secret society of second, third, and in his case, fourth sons. It was an odd line of work. Ash had been on his own so long with only Stapleton for company that remaining in one place, never mind being surrounded by a brotherhood of sorts, was like treading on foreign soil. He'd spent the first eighteen years of his life trying to escape the brothers he'd been born with, the next seven dodging their notice while on the road, only to come here and join more?

He shifted in his seat. One job. He would see this one plan through to the end, and then he would leave.

"You didn't need to go to such lengths last night, you know," St. James began. "Kelton Brice is Dillsworth's youngest son and a member here. Had you informed me of your plans, I could have made arrangements."

Ash bristled. "How did you hear of it? There was a bit of a chase when I departed, but I've escaped worse."

"I assume you retrieved the investment and financial information you needed."

"How did you…"

"Dillsworth's knowledge of investments is hardly a secret. And his current holdings point to how you might gain his support. However, if you need anything further, Brice can retrieve it without breaking into the man's home."

"It was no trouble," Ash replied with a grin.

Evangeline, he repeated to himself. At least he'd learned—and vowed to remember—her name. No matter the blunders, it had been worth the venture into the servants' hall. That kiss had distracted him for the remainder of the evening.

Who was he bluffing? It was morning and he was still thinking of it.

"To be clear, Dillsworth is only to be involved to a minimal degree in your business here, only as much as absolutely necessary." St. James nodded to a footman and a tea service was placed before him, while Ash accepted his glass of liquor. "There have already been enough brawls within these walls without you swindling a member's father."

"You think me a swindler? St. James, you wound me." Ash took a sip of his drink, allowing the burn of it to simmer through his limbs. If he had been honest about his plans while in town—which he hadn't been—St. James would have known that Ash only skimmed the surface of any individual's wealth. He could never take everything away from a family as Rightworth had done. Of course the exception to that rule would be Rightworth himself. Ash planned to take everything from that man—down to the last crown. He settled back in his chair with a grin, stretching his legs under the table. "I am but a peddler of the future, a purveyor of hope and destiny."

St. James shot him a glance as he poured his tea. "How long have you been working on that last bit?"

"The carriage ride to London."

"You should have ridden a bit longer."

"Hmmm…too much? I'll work on it. I'll need

everything in place in the next day, if I'm to begin tomorrow night."

"With no documentation, no prototype? Your words will only take you so far."

"It's 1817, St. James. The future! These men can either fear change or benefit from it." He leaned forward, waving his hand through the vapor that rose from the man's tea. "Steam—it's all around us. And the future will be dominated by it. Soon every home will be transformed by it. An investment in steam is an investment in tomorrow."

"That's going to convince gentlemen to give you investment funds?"

Ash lifted the teapot from the table and encouraged more steam to escape the top of the pot. "It will if they fear for the security of their estates and livelihoods."

"You require more than a bit of vapor if this is to work," St. James replied. "And kindly put my teapot back on the table. I happen to be fond of it."

Ash placed the piece of pink floral china back on the table with a roll of his eyes. He hadn't answered to anyone in the last seven years, and he hadn't been known for listening well before then. Was joining the ranks of the Spare Heirs a mistake? He swallowed the retort that lingered on his tongue along with his whiskey.

"You knew what I was after when you invited me here," Ash said after a long minute's silence.

"It's my duty to ensure all endeavors of the Spares find success—success beyond the destruction of one lord in town. If Lord Rightworth's demise is the only thing of interest to you, then by all means, show him a hot cup of tea and talk about hope for the future. I'm certain he'll come around."

"Look, St. James, you can either be involved or I will continue on without you and the Spare Heirs."

"Am I interrupting?" A somewhat familiar-looking giant of a man in a bright-blue coat sank into an open chair at their table, not waiting for an answer to his question. "I had a hell of a night trying to catch up with some gent causing a row at my family's ball." He leaned his blond head back and closed his eyes, raising one hand to signal for a drink without looking to see if it had been noted.

"Chased the man through the streets until I lost his trail, and wasn't even told what he'd done. I don't mind doing a bit of running for the Spares, but when the order comes from my father, you know how that can irritate. And at the end of it I lost the bastard. Of course, that was when I ran into Harriett. You remember Harriett, St. James. It was dawn before I could remove her talons from my—"

"Brice," St. James said, trying to gain the man's attention. "*Brice.*"

Brice opened his eyes and looked around the table for the first time. "Who the devil are you?" he asked Ash.

"Lord Crosby, purveyor of the future, and the future is steam," Ash offered, lifting his glass in salute.

"Still needs work," St. James muttered.

Brice looked from Ash to St. James and back again. "Bloody hell. *You* were the man I was chasing last night. St. James, you could have mentioned a Spares operation happening at my family's ball. Not to mention why the devil there was anything occurring at *my* family's ball last night. I thought we'd established this wasn't to happen after that incident a few years back with the—"

"Calm yourself, Brice. Crosby here didn't know of your affiliation, or he would have involved you. Isn't that correct, Crosby?"

"Of course, mate," Ash said, knowing it would be easier to get the man's father on his side if Ash had his assistance. Not to mention that Brice's involvement would save him some effort. As for last night, Ash regretted nothing. If he hadn't gone to the Dillsworths' ball, he wouldn't have seen Evangeline again. Ha! He still remembered her name. "I don't want to upset the balance of things, having just arrived and all."

"Crosby, is it?" Brice asked.

"It is," Ash said with a grin. "You know, I have a healing tonic upstairs that would make last night all but disappear from your memory." He gave a wave of his hand as he said it—an affectation he'd picked up from a fortune-teller last year. People seemed to like the drama it added to his words.

"Do you?" Brice asked as he took a drink from his glass.

"No, but the tonic will get you foxed to the point that you don't mind the memory so much."

"I like him, St. James." Brice released a hearty laugh that shook the windowpanes. "We could use someone with a sense of humor around here, after enduring your secretive glares."

"Good to know I'm not the only recipient of that look," Ash said.

Brice leaned closer even though he made no attempt at lowering his voice. "You didn't ask him about the house, did you? He doesn't like to talk about that at all. Clams up tighter than ol' Harriett's nether regions, if you know what I mean."

"Brice," St. James interrupted. "Before you arrived, we were discussing a bit of business."

"Never mind me, then. Continue. I'll stay silent as the grave."

"That *would* be a feat," St. James replied as he raised his hand and signaled for a footman to come forward. The man laid a large piece of paper in the center of the table, then backed away with a nod. *Crosby Steam Works* was printed in large, official-looking letters above a drawing of some sort.

"I believe this will lend some credence to your words, beyond waving your hands about to suggest vapors."

Ash looked down at a sketched diagram with intricate wheels, lines connecting them, and notes scribbled in pencil around the borders. It did seem technical, but what was it? He looked up at St. James. "This…whatever this is…will produce steam?"

"At the moment it produces squeals and the scent of burning hair." St. James took a drink of his tea. "Of course, the *ton* doesn't need to know the details."

"It does give the impression of actual scientific advancement," Ash offered as he studied the paper, spinning the drawing to look at it from all angles. If he was to use this document, he would have to memorize it and give the marks meaning in his own mind. "How did you come across such a diagram? And the name at the top…Crosby Steam Works." It did sound as if it would be a legitimate organization. He ran a hand over it in admiration.

"I know a scientist of sorts." St. James shot a look

at Brice that Ash didn't quite understand. "I paid him a visit after I last met with you. The Crosby name was added after your arrival at headquarters of course, but the remainder of the diagram was completed a month ago."

Brice leaned forward to study the paper with them. "This was what that visit was about, then? Steam? And I thought we were only there to wish Dean well with his upcoming leg shackle."

St. James shrugged and looked across the table at Ash.

"How did you know I would come to London?" Ash asked. *He* hadn't even been sure, and yet this man had taken a trip to have scientific-looking sketches drawn.

But St. James only twitched the corner of his mouth up in a hint of a grin, revealing nothing.

Ash glanced to Brice, but the large man only shrugged and said, "Welcome to the Spare Heirs."

As for Ash, he still wasn't sure about the entire thing. If the group could assist him with his plans, then he was glad for that, at least. But one month of belonging to any sort of group would be long enough. The last thing Ash needed was something tying him to London society. One month and he would be gone, no matter how great the temptation to stay.

❦

Her mother had insisted that she stand just so in order to tempt every gentleman present into a dance. Evangeline pursed her lips and moved her fan to her waist where she'd been instructed to keep it to accentuate her shape beneath her gown. She paused, waiting for someone to notice. Her arm was growing numb, but she didn't dare move from her statuesque position.

Her mother had left her side to chat with a well-connected lady she'd spotted in an adjoining parlor. This was Evangeline's first small piece of freedom from the woman's watchful eye since the last ball, and she was not going to fail.

"Evie, don't you agree?" Isabelle pleaded at her side. "Tell Victoria she's being ridiculous about the rules of the card rooms."

"Don't bother her, Isabelle," Victoria responded. "Can't you see she's too busy posing for an invisible portrait? She can't possibly answer questions at a time like this."

Isabelle shifted beside her. "You simply know that she will agree with me. Ladies do not belong in the card room with the gentlemen."

Evangeline kept her gaze on the swirl of movement on the ballroom floor, wishing Roselyn had been able to attend this evening. In Sue's absence, Roselyn seemed to be the only voice of reason beyond her own. And Isabelle and Victoria required constant reasoning. She blinked as she'd been taught to do, allowing her lashes to fall with grace to her cheeks before opening her eyes wide again.

Victoria gave a snort of derision in a most unlady-like fashion. "If you were truly *hunting* for a husband, you would go where the prey is plentiful. Gentlemen congregate together over a hand of cards. It's logical to walk up the stairs and join them."

"Where Mother would surely catch you gambling again? Victoria…" Isabelle's voice trailed off in concern.

"I'm not gambling. See?" Victoria stepped forward into Evangeline's field of vision with extended arms. "I am here, bored out of my wits at the side of a ballroom where sweet young ladies such as myself belong."

Evangeline sighed, abandoning her pose and turning toward her cousins. "No one is going to be caught gambling, because no one is planning to gamble this evening. Isn't that true, Victoria?"

"Of course it's true." Victoria rolled her eyes. "Everyone knows the stakes at this sort of event are dismal anyway."

Evangeline narrowed her eyes at Victoria, then stretched out her fingers. They'd gone cold from clutching her fan with the utmost intensity. "Comments like that are not helping to keep Isabelle from fretting."

Victoria's full lips twisted in irritation. "I only suggested we stroll up the stairs to try to find her some fresh meat for the husband hunt."

"I'm fairly certain referring to gentlemen as slices of flesh isn't advisable," Evangeline whispered, glancing around to see if anyone had heard.

"If society can force me onto the marriage mart like a pig being led to the slaughter, then I can damn well refer to gentlemen in the same terms," Victoria retorted.

"Shh. For heaven's sake, Victoria. Someone could hear such talk and then you'll never find a husband."

Isabelle stepped between them with a hand laid on her cousin's arm in a gesture of kindness. "Don't mind her, Evie. She has no desire to find a husband. I believe she longs to be my children's unwed, elderly aunt." Isabelle turned to look at her sister, a rare fond smile passing between them.

"And I shall teach them all the things they need to know," Victoria added.

"Like how to out-curse a sailor?" Evangeline asked.

"Precisely. I look forward to it."

"My poor children," Isabelle muttered, but she was beaming at her sister with obvious affection.

Evangeline sighed and slid her gaze beyond her cousins. And that's when she saw him. Hair dark as sin, and arrogance that could be seen from across a room. Crosby hadn't left London. He wasn't on the road to some other place far away from her... He was *here*.

Her breath caught as she watched him ascend the open stairs to the balcony above the ballroom floor. He was talking to the gentleman at his side, whom she didn't know—imparting some secret, she was sure. Secrets seemed the only language he knew; even his name was false. But why? And who was he truly?

He was moving in the direction of the card room Victoria had been so interested in visiting. Soon he would be inside the walls of a room where no lady was permitted, and she would have lost her chance to learn the truth.

Evangeline gave Victoria's arm a tug to spin her in the proper direction. "On second thought, perhaps the card room is just the place for us this evening."

"You can't be serious, Evie," Isabelle said, attempting to follow her gaze, currently fixed on a point moving up the stairs. "We mustn't go inside there with the gentlemen."

"I'm not suggesting we do," Evangeline replied. There was no need to do something that brazen. She only needed to get close enough to learn why Crosby was still here. "But I think we would be remiss not to take a trip up the stairs. Only for a moment, of course."

"See, Isabelle?" Victoria said with an air of triumph. "Evangeline understands the rules of the hunt, and I'm only too happy to assist her."

"Wait for me," Isabelle cried. "If you're to go in search of gentlemen, I'm coming with you. Perhaps Mr. Brice is in the card room."

Evangeline gave the parlor door a fleeting glance. Her mother's attention was focused on smiling at the appropriate times in the conversation that surrounded her. Things such as smiles and laughter didn't come naturally to the stern woman, and never had. She wouldn't notice if Evangeline moved for only a few minutes. And as usual her father had wandered away the moment they'd arrived, no doubt to discuss politics with their host. He'd been quite clear in the carriage about his reasons for attending this evening.

Leaving the ballroom for even a minute, two balls in succession? She would have to be more vigilant with her conduct for the remainder of the season. But tonight… If she could slip away, then return in a timely manner to her position at the edge of the ballroom floor and stand appropriately as if nothing had occurred, no one would be the wiser. Quickening her pace, Evangeline moved through the crowd, gliding around the groups of people gathered at the edges of the room.

The Tottings' home boasted a lovely ballroom that was open to a gallery above. It was only a few steps to the base of the stairs. For once her mother hadn't been able to manage a position for them farther from the entrance, and Evangeline couldn't be more thankful.

The staircase to the gallery hung in the corner as if suspended from the ceiling. She led the way, leaving her cousins to scurry up the stairs behind her if they were to keep pace. He'd come this way, and if she hurried, she could catch him before he disappeared into the realm of gentlemen.

She paused at the top of the stairs, glancing to each end of the open gallery. Seeing two dark heads turn the corner at the far end of the room, she followed. Serene-looking Tottings ancestral portraits lined the walls, giving the appearance that they were watching the ladies twirl about to the music below. It was a charming effect, if one didn't consider that they were doomed to spend eternity living every ball as a wallflower with both an unfortunate visage and an inadequate dowry might be forced to do. Evangeline gave the portraits of the ladies a sympathetic nod as she passed.

"Evangeline, what is your hurry?" Isabelle complained at her back. "I can't walk any faster in these slippers. They match my gown to perfection, but I cannot say the same for their fit on my feet."

"Then why did you tell Mother they were divine?" Victoria asked. "I believe that was the exact word you used—*divine*."

"Did you not see them? They are divine," Isabelle replied, her usual dreamy tone back in her voice.

"As long as your plan is to admire them from afar," Victoria countered. "You can hardly walk, Isabelle."

"Yes, but look when I point my toe…" Isabelle's words trailed away as she paused to show off her shoes to her sister.

Evangeline didn't even slow her stride, much less

turn to look at Isabelle's shoes. She could admire them after she'd found Crosby and learned why he was here tonight.

"Damn if that isn't divine," Victoria exclaimed.

"See? I told you."

Evangeline shook her head, making sure to stay well away from the railing overlooking the ballroom where she could be seen. Her cousins could hobble in her direction when they were finished discussing the finer points of Isabelle's dancing slippers. She only slowed when she reached the end of the gallery. The portrait of a sour-looking gentleman seemed to be giving her a set-down about the direction she was taking. "Hush," she whispered to him as she turned the corner toward the card room.

Bracketed sconces provided scallops of light that swooped down the long hall like the trim on a lady's dress. If Evangeline and her cousins kept to the shadows, they could reach the far end without drawing notice. She glanced around to see if Victoria and Isabelle were coming, only to have them collide with her as they rounded the corner.

"Oof," Evangeline muttered, taking a step back to find her balance. She lowered her voice to a whisper. "If we're careful, we can reach the door to the card room without notice."

"Without notice?" Isabelle asked, appearing deflated by Evangeline's plan.

"I agree with Isabelle. If we're going to lure a gentleman for either of you, it won't be done in the shadows."

"What do you plan to do, walk right down the hall where we know we shouldn't be?" Evangeline asked.

"Yes." Victoria smiled. "And with style. This is for your sakes, after all, not mine."

Evangeline opened her mouth to argue, but Victoria had already linked arms with her and was pulling her down the hall. She was the one who'd started on this path of wrongdoing so she could hardly complain now.

Her nerves jangled like a bell in the hands of an eager child as they slid from light to shadow and back to light again. The gentlemen seemed to be gathered at the opposite end of the hall, still a distance away. A door had been left open, and gentlemen spilled out in a mass of dark coats and rumbling voices. The smell of liquor burned Evangeline's nose even at this distance.

"Do you think they could spare a measure for me?" Victoria mused. "The only drink offered in the ballroom was lemonade. Dreadfully dull gathering this evening."

"That is not why we are here, Victoria," Evangeline whispered.

"Why do I get the feeling that you are not here for the same reasons as Isabelle and me?"

"I'm sure I have no idea what you mean." Evangeline lifted her chin higher at the accusation in her cousin's voice.

"Don't you?" Victoria asked, cutting her eyes in Evangeline's direction.

Evangeline didn't answer and Victoria said nothing further. Thankful for Victoria's rare silence, Evangeline focused her gaze and her thoughts on the group of gentlemen ahead.

She could see Crosby standing alongside the

gentleman he'd taken the stairs with. It seemed he had a fondness for dimly lit halls during a ball. The ballroom was most likely too bright for his tastes. No dancing and chatting for him, no—he couldn't deceive anyone under the bright light of the ballroom.

"Evie," Isabelle whispered at her other side. "Is something wrong? You look as if you might start bashing gentlemen on the head at any moment. I don't think that will help us to find husbands."

"I'm quite well, thank you. I'm simply not accustomed to such environs."

"We could go back," Isabelle offered.

"No, we've come this far." After risking the worst her mother had to offer for leaving her post in the ballroom, she at least wanted answers for her effort.

They stepped from light to dark once more as the gentlemen chuckled at some jest Crosby made. If only she could hear, she might learn why he was in attendance tonight. But from the looks on the men's faces, the conversation was not as serious as that.

She watched as Crosby stirred a lightness in the crowd, making them seem less inhibited than they had been moments ago. It was the same as he had done with her last year. Was it simply his way to tug people out of their day-to-day lives and submerge them in a dream? Back then, she had foolishly followed along.

His words from last year rattled around in her memory: *It seems I require assistance. Do you mind lending a hand?* But he hadn't needed her assistance at all. Had he ever truly needed someone's help? He seemed the sort who had backup plans for his backup plans.

"Always consider the doors," she whispered, remembering her mother's rule about where to stand at a ball.

"What was that?" Victoria asked as she sauntered down the hall at her side.

"Nothing," Evangeline replied.

Last year, Lord Crosby had been considering the door he'd walk through while she was still in his arms outside that parlor, and again the other night in the service hall. She should have known on both occasions, should have seen it in his eyes, but he'd revealed nothing.

"Evangeline, you're scowling at the gentlemen we're here to hunt," Victoria said, cutting into her memories. "Or perhaps your prey is someone specific this evening?"

"Apologies." Evangeline pasted a pleasant look on her face so that no one would guess the directions of her wayward thoughts—no one except for Victoria, apparently.

As they crept nearer, she could hear bits of the conversation of which Lord Crosby was the center.

"…I told her all the pies she wanted were hers if she would only be so kind as to remove her goat from my carriage. Of course, her goat had already eaten his way through the pies I was delivering. That was the last time I visited the tenants on my estate, and the last time I trusted my driver to close my carriage door after I stepped out of it."

There was a round of laughter before one gentleman asked the same question she was wondering herself. "Where is your estate, Lord Crosby?"

Evangeline stilled, listening.

"Northwest of here, where the goats grow to the

size of horses by feasting on stolen pies," he answered with a grin.

Another round of laughter filled the hall, but Crosby was no longer paying attention to the gentlemen he was entertaining. His gaze met hers through the crowd and didn't let go. She watched as a smile lit behind his intense shade of blue eyes. He was pleased to see her. He shouldn't be. He should have left town while he had the chance, with his secrets intact.

"Ladies," Crosby offered with a bow, drawing the group's gaze to where she stood with her cousins.

"My lord," Evangeline offered in return, forcing a confidence she did not feel into her voice. "Do continue with your tale. I find I'm now quite curious what happened to the woman you encountered after you made your undeniably heroic escape."

"Evangeline?" A familiar voice spoke from the fringes of the group—too familiar. "Is your mother unwell?"

"Father," she managed to say, every part of her body tensing in an instant. Isabelle shifted at her side, but Victoria didn't flinch. Evangeline's eyes had been locked on Crosby with such force that she'd missed key pieces of information, just as she had last year. Curious gazes had turned in her direction, including her father's. What was her father doing outside the card room listening to Crosby's story about a pie-eating goat? He was supposed to be discussing some terribly boring parliamentary matter with Lord Tottings downstairs in the man's library.

Her eyes flitted over the group who were now watching her and her cousins. Crosby seemed to enjoy the attention, but it only served to make her jittery.

She needed to say something in response to all the gentlemen's stares. She certainly had enough practice in proper conversation. Yet her mind was blank.

She'd stood here far too long already. She'd acknowledged her father's presence and proceeded to turn into one of the statues her mother was always forcing her to impersonate.

Finally, her brain broke free and began to function. "Mother wishes to leave the event early this evening." She would pay for the lie later, but it would get her out of this dratted hall.

Her father nodded and moved to leave the group. "Will you excuse me, gentlemen? Crosby, pleasure meeting you."

"Likewise," Crosby replied, but his tone was icy and the look he gave her father once his back was turned sent a chill down her spine.

As she watched, Crosby's expression cleared and was replaced by the mischievous gleam she associated with him. What was his game?

She may not know his true name, or where he'd gone a year ago, but she sensed he had some greater intention tonight than gaining a laugh from these men.

With one last glance over her shoulder as her father led Evangeline and her cousins down the long hall, she vowed to find out.

Four

FATHER? LORD RIGHTWORTH WAS LADY Evangeline's...father?

But Lord Rightworth's daughters were school-aged, braids in their hair and hidden away in some nursery. Young ladies. Evangeline was none of those things. She was a beautiful lady of perhaps twenty years of age. She couldn't be Rightworth's daughter...and yet she was. Damn Stapleton and his poor reconnaissance skills!

Ash stared at Lord Rightworth's retreating form, moving away alongside that of his daughter. While Evangeline glided down the hall on a wave of long limbs and graceful beauty, her father plodded along at her side in what could only be described as utilitarian necessity. Or perhaps he was stuffed so tightly into his evening wear that a sturdy gait was the best possible outcome.

Excusing himself from the gathered group of gentlemen, Ash followed them at a distance. He stepped down the long hall leading back to the gallery, looking past the twin ladies who had arrived with Evangeline. There wasn't even a similarity between father and daughter in their hair colors. Ash wasn't sure why any of this bothered him so, other than that he'd been caught off guard by their relationship.

He had a past with Evangeline. He could use her to his advantage in this scheme. He should be pleased. Using associations like the one with Evangeline to help his cause was his normal course of action. It's how he survived. She was no different. Did she challenge him unlike any other lady he'd ever met? Certainly. Was he drawn to her refined beauty and shy smiles more than that of any other lady he'd ever met? Clearly, that was true. But her appeal had no bearing on the matter at hand. It couldn't.

He followed the pair to the corner of the gallery, watching as they led the way for the other two. "Of all the blasted ladies in London…" he murmured to himself. He was an idiot.

"You didn't know." Fallon St. James joined him at the end of the hall.

"An oversight on my part," Ash ground out, silently cursing Stapleton again as Evangeline descended the stairs with her father. "One that I'll avoid making in the future."

"You'll avoid the lady? That seems unlikely."

Ash turned to the gentleman at his side. St. James blended into the shadows in his usual dark attire as, Ash assumed, he intended. But his sharp eyes cut through the darkness, making Ash shift on his feet. "I hardly know her, St. James."

"Obviously." His friend's voice was smooth, as if coated in oil. "You do, however, know her better than you'd care to admit."

"Damn," Ash muttered. He'd always thought of himself as quick-thinking, but St. James was somehow able to best his abilities. "How do you do it? How do you know every bit of information this city has to offer?"

"It's my business to be aware of everything," St. James replied, cryptic as always.

Ash retraced his steps mentally, trying to think where he'd misspoken or left evidence where there should be none. "Only Lady Evangeline and I know of our past."

"The two of you and anyone else who notices the way you look at her."

"I didn't—" Ash began, but stopped with a scowl for the ballroom below.

"A blind man could see the way you look at her."

"I'm going to call on her father tomorrow," Ash ground out.

"Make sure you meet with him about steam and not to negotiate the terms of a dowry."

"Steam is the only thing on my mind."

"That's hardly true." St. James gave a small shake of his head. "Watch yourself, *Crosby*."

Ash turned back to St. James when Evangeline had disappeared from sight, only to see an empty hall. Even the gentlemen who had gathered there had returned to the card room. He could follow their lead and scout out more potential investors over a game, but that didn't seem wise—not now.

Tonight, not only had his ability to research his target been disproved, but also his ability to hide his thoughts from those around him. At this rate, he would be a terrible partner in a simple game of whist, never mind the impact those inabilities had on his work.

He'd come to the city prepared to face down the most daunting opponent of all in the largest city in the country. He'd readied himself for this task for years. Years!

Perhaps he'd acted too quickly. If he'd honed his skills a bit longer, he might have seen Evangeline for who she was. At the very least, he should have remembered that he could trust no one but himself.

Stapleton had been right about one thing—Hampshire was nice this time of year. But it was too late to retreat now. All Ash could do was deal with this setback and adjust his angle of attack.

He stewed over his failures as he made his way from the ball.

By the time he'd returned to headquarters a bit later, he knew the truth. It wasn't a lack of concentration that had led to this evening's shock; it was Evangeline's ability to bring his concentration crashing to the ground. He'd nearly lost the document at the Dillsworths' ball because of her. His first instinct had been correct—avoiding her was the answer. The question was how to accomplish that when she was the daughter of the one gentleman he was determined to have invest in Crosby Steam Works?

The man had taken from Ash's family without any thought of the consequences, and now Ash must do the same. He had planned it all. He would accept only small investments from the other gentlemen in town, but then strip Rightworth of everything he possessed. It's what the man deserved. But Evangeline's involvement complicated matters to a degree that made Ash's head pound.

He muttered a curse as he fell into a chair at the table in the corner of headquarters, where everyone seemed to congregate. There was something soothing about sitting in the dim lighting of a room set aside for the use of gentlemen. There would be no surprises here, no unforeseen family relationships that threatened to destroy all that he'd worked for.

"Am I disturbing you?" a large, dark-haired man asked, moving toward Ash across the open gathering space.

"Not at all." Ash indicated the chair beside his with a wave of his hand. "Have you come to welcome me to the Spares as well? Every day there seems to be more gentlemen to meet. I think they double themselves in their sleep."

"With the Spares, anything is likely. I'm Ethan Moore, Lord Ayton. I'm new about the place, though I was a member here years ago."

"I believe Brice mentioned you last time we spoke. Your title is new, is it not?"

"It is. Fortunately the Spares still let me reside here and support the group."

Ash leaned back in his seat in what he thought to be a lordly posture. "I'm Crosby."

Ayton nodded and signaled for drinks.

Ash relaxed a fraction, relieved to have something else to think about for a moment. "What is it that you do to support this group?"

"I'm a fighter."

"I believe it," Ash said, eyeing the size of the man's arms and his nose that had been broken at some point.

"The Spares trained me in the sport years ago." Ayton paused, glancing down at the table between them. "Now I've returned."

"You gained a title and yet you still fight?" Ash asked as two glasses filled with dark liquid were placed before them.

"It's what I do, who I am. I don't know what else…" His voice trailed off and he was silent for a moment before he looked up from his glass. A crooked smile that seemed to match his nose transformed his face into something rather pleasant. "When I see in my opponent's eyes that he's going to go left and I move in for the strike…"

"You're skilled at your craft," Ash surmised, taking a drink.

"It's the only skill I've ever had."

Ash understood. Reading people in order to sell them whatever wares he had on hand was the only skill he possessed.

"Have you ever been caught off guard by an opponent?" he asked a bit too quickly.

Ayton chuckled and drained half of his glass in one swallow. "Noses don't break themselves."

"I would think returning the next day to fight again was no easy task."

"The next day? It was the next round of pummeling I took that was difficult. I was still sore a week later." He signaled for another round.

Ash studied the man before he took a long drink from his glass. "But you returned to it."

"I did."

The drinks arrived and a companionable silence fell between them. It was true that Ash had been hit with an unexpected punch this evening, but that was no reason to doubt his skills. Just like Ayton had done, he needed to return to his sport. He was here to sell Rightworth and a few other gentlemen on an investment in Crosby Steam Works. Unlike in Bath, he now had diagrams. He knew the terminology. He wouldn't be selling mysterious tonics and potions as he had in the past, but he was ready for this job.

His family's honor was at stake. He'd made a deathbed promise to his mother that he would fix things for his family, and he wasn't about to go back on that. He couldn't allow a pretty face to get in the way of what he'd worked toward for so long, not even if that pretty face belonged to Evangeline Green, the one woman who knew he wasn't who he claimed to be.

"It's a woman, isn't it? Got you in a right tangle."

"What was that?" Ash asked. Had he said something aloud? If so, his problems were worse than he'd imagined. He couldn't go about mumbling to himself and still sell…anything at all.

"It's a lady that has you tossing back that whiskey and doubting your thoughts on life," Ayton clarified.

Ash tensed. "What do you know of it?"

"Not a thing. Simply recognized the look of desperation in your eyes."

"You too, then, mate?"

Ayton let out a harsh laugh. "My situation is rather complicated."

"We should start a society."

Ayton raised his glass and looked around at the relatively empty headquarters. "I believe we're already in it."

Ash didn't know if it was the effect of the whiskey or the knowledge that he'd been selected to join this club for the very abilities he was doubting, but either way his plans suddenly seemed more attainable than they had earlier in the evening.

He would go to meet with Rightworth tomorrow. He would have a backup plan prepared if the man's daughter was at home, but he would not allow her to harm his mission. He'd sold young ladies love potions, old men tonics for youth, and tomorrow he would promise Lord Rightworth financial gain beyond his wildest dreams.

Seeing Evangeline mattered little. The important bit was his meeting with her father...even if his mind kept lingering on her.

"To the Spare Heir Society," he said, tossing back the remainder of his drink.

❧

Evangeline straightened her spine and dipped her chin to the proper angle for but a second. "Lord Winfield, how pleasant it is to see you today. Are you enjoying this fine weather?"

She worked to ensure her gaze was engaging without being too direct, as it had been on every other attempt thus far. Holding her breath, she waited. Was that enough without being too much? Her palms began to sweat inside her gloves as she clutched her fan at her waist.

"Not perfect, but I suppose it will have to be sufficient," her mother finally said. "Once he answers, you reply..."

"I do so enjoy the outdoors. When the trees gain their leaves for the summer, it always reminds me of—"

"What are you doing?" Her mother's voice went shrill, threatening to shatter the glass in the parlor windows. "That is not what you're to say next. It was supposed to be: 'The trees provide nice shade in the park.' Repeat after me, 'nice shade in the park.'"

"I thought—"

"Nice shade in the park!" her mother commanded, sweeping around Evangeline, her hawk-like eyes taking in every detail of her daughter's performance.

What flaws her mother had not already buffed to a high shine were on display, awaiting reprimand. Evangeline worked to remain still, because fidgeting under such scrutiny wasn't tolerated. Some lessons one never forgot. Instead she focused her gaze on the corner of the window. She could see a child across the street, sitting on a garden bench and swinging her feet with vigor, while a governess read from a book. Such a simple joy it must be to swing one's feet and listen to a story.

"The trees provide nice shade in the park," Evangeline enunciated every word before adding in a small voice, "I only thought that if I added a bit of myself to what we practiced, it might sound less…rehearsed."

"Of course it's rehearsed, darling." Her mother stepped forward to smooth down a lock of Evangeline's hair that had escaped its confines, the look of displeasure on her face wrinkling her lips into a small, pursed blotch of color. "Such an important thing as conversation cannot be left to chance." She uttered a humph of disappointment and abandoned Evangeline's hair.

Evangeline took the smallest breath she dared, keeping her gaze on the scene outside the window as her mother continued to circle. "Mother, are you ever concerned that my future husband won't know me at all if I only recite practiced lines?"

"Know you?" Her mother laughed, a rattling hiss of breath from behind Evangeline that sent chills down her spine. "That scarcely matters. We can't allow your future to rest upon a gentleman's interest in your mind." She'd reached a point in front of Evangeline and stopped her slow, circling pace. Grasping Evangeline's chin between her fingers, her mother examined her face, pulling it this way and that with a painful grip. "You are the favored lady of the season. You have your appearance. That is all that matters." She released her pinching grasp and continued to move in her slow circle.

Evangeline pulled herself straight. Her marriage would be built upon which gown she wore and a few comments on the weather. She had known that truth for some time. But she still found it as bothersome as a wrinkle in the foot of one's stocking that couldn't be remedied without removing a shoe in public. Only this wrinkle would last a lifetime stuffed into the sole of an ill-fitting boot. There was nothing to be done for it. She'd once acted against her mother's wishes and almost destroyed her family in the process. Years later, she was still paying the price for her rebellion.

"We can't have you opining on the specifics of trees. Gentlemen might think you too wrapped up in troublesome thoughts. It's best to keep to the words I wrote for you. Now begin again."

"Lord Winfield, it's pleasant to see you today…" Evangeline paused and looked at her mother. "I could continue this practice alone. I wouldn't want to disrupt your morning."

But when her mother inhaled a great breath, puffing up like a bird that was about to go on the attack, Evangeline knew she'd gone too far.

"After your disregard for the rules at last night's ball? Retrieving your father when you knew very well you were to dance the waltz with Lord Winfield later in the evening. The last waltz! He's a marquess! I need to sit. Ring for tea." She waved Evangeline away. "Of all the foolish decisions you've made, this may well be the worst. You are more like your sister than I realized. Not to worry, though. We can be rid of those similarities with just the *smallest* bit of effort on your part." Her mother heaved a weary sigh and sat on the edge of the nearest chair.

"I thought you'd signaled you were ready to leave," Evangeline said, attempting to justify her actions before the situation became worse. "It was out of concern for you that I gathered Father." She took her time in ringing for tea to hide the truth on her face.

"Leeeeave?" Her mother drew the word out in her outrage. "Why would I wish to leave?"

This discussion was careening in an unpleasant direction. Why had she thought she could slip upstairs after Lord Crosby without notice? That one reckless decision could cost her the season. This year was her chance to find a husband and start anew. She couldn't lose it for the likes of Crosby. "Perhaps you grew weary or had a headache."

"Any such state is occurring now because of you. I thought your training had prepared you for this season. Clearly I was mistaken. There will be extra lessons every morning. We cannot have a repeat of your summer of madness."

"Yes, Mother." Evangeline's throat tightened around the words. She'd known this reminder was coming, but it always hurt nonetheless. She had spent all her days like this since that summer, the summer of her twelfth year, gaining favor with her mother to survive the afternoon only to lose that favor by the evening. The memory of that summer had even led Evangeline to betray her own sister last year.

She couldn't survive her mother's wrath again. She would simply have to be perfect. Reaching such an ideal meant staying well away from Lord Crosby and acting just as her mother instructed her to act. If being unblemished in every detail of life kept her safe, then that was what she would do.

"This family barely recovered from that ordeal," her mother continued.

"I know, Mother." Evangeline dipped her chin in apology. "I won't disappoint you again."

"I should hope not!" Her mother's brows threatened to touch her hairline. "You almost destroyed us all. Imagine living without funding for society events."

Evangeline remained silent. She'd learned long ago to not interrupt when her mother wished to relive that terrible summer. It had been an awful idea she'd had that day, one that she'd regretted ever since… Not that her remorse mattered. She'd only thought of being rid of Great-Aunt Mildred for the remainder of the summer. The woman had been awful to everyone around, but mostly Sue and her… Not that her justifications mattered either. The only thing that mattered was her great-aunt's withdrawal of her support for quite some time before her father had sorted things out. Evangeline had been a silly girl then and had acted without thought, something she couldn't afford to do today.

Her mother made it clear on every available occasion that Evangeline would never be forgiven for that infraction' against the family, and if she set one toe out of line again, she would no longer be welcome in their home. Evangeline lived within that harsh reality, but this year she would find a husband. Perhaps she wouldn't be able to put a toe out of line with him either, but at least she could maintain a clean record with him. It would be a fresh beginning.

Last night had been a mistake. In truth, every encounter with Lord Crosby had been a mistake. She would steer clear of that man from now on. She must. Unlike last year, he could take his false name, thieving ways, and questionable intentions and leave town without a backward glance. She would be here not giving him a further thought.

Some other gentleman—like her mother's choice, Lord Winfield—was where her focus would remain. Other gentlemen weren't cloaked in mystery. Mystery was for the horrid novels Isabelle liked to read, not for Evangeline. She liked fact—straightforward, proper fact. And Lord Crosby was anything but straightforward. Which was why she wouldn't be thinking of him ever again—beginning now.

"The blue gown for tonight, I believe," her mother mused as the parlor door opened.

The third new maid in the last week brought in the tea. She wouldn't last long, based on the cheerful look on her face. Clearly she hadn't been warned about the lady of the house. Life in this home wasn't for the faint of heart.

"Tea, my ladies." She practically sang her words.

Evangeline tensed at the storm she sensed brewing even as she fought to contain a smile. It was a welcome breath of air to see a smile within these walls.

"What is your name?" her mother asked as she eyed the now-blushing young maid.

"Jane. Today is my first day, and I greatly look forward to working in such a prestigious home."

"That much is true," her mother stated.

Flattery. Perhaps this maid would survive the week.

"I included some biscuits and cakes with your tea. The kitchen is filled with their delicious scent. Your cook has truly outdone herself. I thought you might enjoy them."

Or perhaps this maid wouldn't survive the hour. Cakes and biscuits? Her mother couldn't abide large amounts of food, let alone sweets.

Evangeline turned her most gracious smile on her mother, drawing her attention away from Jane's blunder and allowing the maid time to slip unnoticed from the room. "The blue gown sounds lovely. What jewelry do you suggest?"

The maid would learn. The key to life in their home was to keep the lady of the house in an even temper. As for Evangeline, she would wear the ensemble her mother wished. She would find a husband, and by the end of the season, she would be gone from this place like so many maids over the years.

❧

Ash leaned against the wall just inside the front door of Lord Rightworth's London home, taking in the details of the house while he waited to be seen by the man. The house boasted a few luxurious items, like the tapestry that hung on the wall above the stairs, and the ornate chandelier, but nothing to the point of excess. It struck Ash as odd. He'd expected excess.

His own home had once been pushed past the point of excess. He could remember the statuary in the garden he used to hide behind when his brothers came looking for him, and the walls filled with art until only slivers of wall between golden frames remained.

All of that had been sold with the rest of his family's possessions because of this man. His father had ended his own life. And his mother had passed away soon after. That was when Ash had left home, and he hadn't been back to the hollow shell of his former life since then.

Pushing from the wall, he examined a vase filled with flowers that adorned the table beside him, but he was no expert on such things. If the vase had been made from stacks of coins, he could guess its value. As it was, all he knew was that unlike the pieces in his former home, the vases in Lord Rightworth's home hadn't been placed in crates and hauled out the door. He could get everything back. There was hope for his scheme yet.

"What are you doing here?" A light, feminine voice sounded behind him, sending a tingle of awareness down his spine.

He turned, knowing who had spoken before he saw her. "Lady Evangeline, what a surprise."

She glanced over her shoulder before she spoke, looking to the empty hall behind her before turning back to face him. "It's not surprising at all if one takes into account that I live here." She moved toward him. The light from the open door behind her spilled over her warm mahogany hair and washed down her arms, giving her the look of an ethereal goddess gliding down a lowly hall. "Why are you here?"

Before he could answer, the door at the base of the stairs opened and Lord Rightworth joined them. "Lord Crosby, good of you to come."

Ash tensed just as he had last night at the door to the card room, but then schooled his expression. He needed this man to trust him, and for that to happen, Ash couldn't go around scowling, no matter what his thoughts about his present company.

"Father," Evangeline said in a quiet voice. She looked away from Ash to greet the man.

"Crosby, have you met my daughter, Lady Evangeline?" Rightworth asked. "She's been enjoying the London season thus far. Haven't you, dear?"

"I have…for the most part." Her eyes flicked back to Ash in challenge.

It was a dangerous game he played, but then, when had it ever been simple? This beauty could end his plans in town with one wrong word to her father, and yet he couldn't seem to help himself. He also couldn't rip his gaze from her upturned face. This encounter was ill-advised at best—but he'd never backed down from a challenge, and he wasn't going to begin now. Certainly not with her. Perhaps he could use their interactions to his advantage. If he kept her off-balance, she wouldn't focus as much on his intentions toward her father. A diversion—that's what this scheme needed.

"Lady Evangeline and I met at the Dillsworths' ball," he explained, finally pulling his eyes from her long enough to glance at her father. "She was kind enough to take a quick turn on my arm on the dance floor."

"That was a dance? My experience with *quick turns* must be more limited than yours, my lord." Evangeline moved to wrap her arms across her chest before dropping them suddenly back to her sides with a grimace.

Ash grinned, thinking of the way he'd spun her into the ballroom after they shared that kiss. "A quick spin about the floor seems to define it quite well, actually. Do you disagree?"

A hint of color infused her cheeks, making her skin a delicious shade of pink, but that was the only sign of her discomfort.

"I believe your daughter finds fault in the dance we shared," he said to Rightworth, although Ash's gaze remained on Evangeline. "Perhaps if I had another opportunity to prove my skill on the dance floor?"

"I have no complaint. I didn't intend… I'm sure you didn't come here to discuss the events of a recent ball," she said with a nervous glance at her father.

"That's true." There was nothing wise about Ash's

current course of action. One misstep here in front of her father, and he would be riding out of town with Stapleton by sundown. And yet, he was toying with her. That was the trouble with diversions—sometimes they even distracted the person onstage. He hadn't come here to see Evangeline. He would be lying, however, if he said he hadn't hoped to catch a glimpse of her. That glimpse was unfortunately over—if only someone would deliver the news to his unruly eyes.

Lord Rightworth cleared his throat a moment later, making Ash realize he'd been staring at the man's daughter for the better part of a minute. "Evangeline, why don't you show Lord Crosby into the library while I see that this makes it into the post?" He held up a note of some sort as he moved down the hall past the stairs.

Evangeline watched her father leave before moving to the library door and waving Ash inside. "If you are here to steal documents from my father…"

"I'm not here to steal anything." He held out his hands as he'd once seen a performer in a fair do to prove he held nothing in his sleeves.

"Then why are you here?" She was still eyeing his hands with concern.

He stepped farther into the library, scanning the room for any clues he could use in his dealings with Rightworth. Unfortunately, the room was of the standard sort. Leather-bound volumes the same as in every other lord's library in every other home in the country. Every home except for his family's, of course. He turned back to her. "Can't a gentleman call upon another gentleman without raising alarm?"

"Not when one of those gentlemen is you."

"You wound me, my lady. I comment on your dancing abilities, and you insult me only a few minutes later?" He shook his head.

"You were commenting on your own escape"—she glanced toward the door before continuing in a hushed voice—"with a stolen document in hand, I should add. We have yet to dance."

"A mistake I plan to remedy immediately." Time to unbalance this lady and be rid of her curiosity, at least for a few minutes. His hand slipped around her waist, and he pulled her into his arms impulsively. He couldn't seem to help himself. At the moment, he was the one who was unbalanced.

A surprised "oh" escaped her lips as he lifted her hand to his and took the first step of a waltz.

He led her around the chairs that sat in front of the fireplace before circling her father's desk. Her eyes were bright as she looked up at him, a shy smile creeping across her face. The moment was almost innocent—almost. Aside from the fact that they were alone together, and that he was holding her closer than society allowed, he was rather impressed with his momentary lack of roguishness. Her thin frame fit easily in his arms as she moved with him across the floor. The warmth of her body soaked through the fabric of her simple day dress and heated his blood.

"Are you always this way?" she asked, shattering his thoughts. "Attending balls where you have no invite, waltzing to no music in the library?"

"Any other way would be quite dull, don't you agree?" He guided her to a halt before the fire. Slowly, he lowered her hand and slid the other from her lower back, grazing her waist with his fingertips as he moved. He didn't want to let her go. But he'd tested his limits, and any moment now her father would return.

Right on cue, footsteps sounded in the hall outside the door and she jumped away from him.

Only a second ago she'd held her hand to his upper arm, but now she moved it to her hair as if adjusting something there. There was nothing to adjust. He'd never seen a lady so put together while at home mid-morning. The only evidence of their dance around the library was the rapid rise and fall of her breasts and the quick blink of her eyes. She was outwardly perfection, but beneath the shine of her perfectly placed hair and the well-pressed folds of her dress, this was a lady who was affected by him. He took a step away from her.

"Lord Rightworth," Ash said in a businesslike tone as the man entered. "I was just discussing the many benefits of risk-taking with your daughter."

"Calculated risks can produce reward." Rightworth moved to his desk in front of the windows. "I do find it curious that my daughter has such a keen interest in financial investment all of a sudden." The man's gaze slid to Evangeline to study her in search of answers to some riddle.

Evangeline didn't flinch under such scrutiny, only turned toward him with a pleasant smile that didn't quite reach her eyes. "What type of risk are you pro-posing today, Lord Crosby…if I might ask?"

"A profitable one," Ash offered, tamping down his thoughts of who would profit from this particular man's risk today. It was time to begin. He had fished a great deal as a child, and he likened this stage of his play to that first cast of the line. The fish in the water only needed to become curious and swim closer to the shiny metal of the lure. Today wasn't for reeling anything in—that would take time. Today was simply about establishing curiosity.

"Evangeline, I believe your mother was looking for you in the hall," Rightworth said. "You may converse with Lord Crosby later. Right now, we have business to discuss."

Ash was somewhat disappointed that she was being asked to leave. True, Evangeline clearly enjoyed picking him apart, which added a layer of difficulty to the situation, but he didn't mind her questions. Of course, since that line of thinking would make his situation even more complicated, he ignored the desire to insist she stay. He was supposed to distract her, not the other way around.

Evangeline's eye twitched ever so slightly with her clear desire to argue about her summary dismissal. When she opened her mouth, however, all she said was, "I'll leave you to it, then."

She was gone in a swish of skirts, and Ash was left with the true purpose of his appointment here today—to sell mist to the man who had destroyed his family.

"Lord Rightworth, have you ever considered the possibilities of steam?"

Five

EVANGELINE GAVE HERSELF ONE FINAL NOD IN THE mirror and turned to leave her bedchamber. The noise of an argument could be heard even at this distance. She sighed, preparing herself to face the battle at the bottom of the stairs.

Her father hadn't attended any of the events in town last season, and her mother had pronounced that Evangeline's unwed status was on his shoulders. Of course, she placed the same blame on Evangeline's shoulders, but her father seemed unaware of their mutual fault. And so it was that tonight he could be found in the hall below, stuffed into his formal attire and waiting to leave for the Rutledge family's evening of poetry. This fact also accounted for his grunts of complaint at being pried from his library, as well as his irritation with everyone of the female persuasion in his near vicinity.

"And it would do nicely if you could befriend Lord Winfield and bring up the subject of your daughter," her mother commanded.

"We're going to this event to sit and listen to Joseph

Rutledge's daughters recite poetry. What would do nicely is if I were able to keep from sleeping."

"Important members of the peerage will be there."

"The ones daft enough to accept an invitation to an evening of poetry?" he clarified.

"Nevertheless…"

"I'm attending. That is what is required of me to see Evangeline wed and out from under our roof, and that is what I intend to do."

Evangeline stopped listening, still poised at the top of the stairs. Tonight, she would sit and listen to poetry. She would smile at every available gentleman at least once, and by the end of the season, she would be smiling at only one gentleman. Glancing down one last time at the gown that had been selected for the occasion, she patted the folds of fabric. Everything was in place. Even her father, it seemed. This evening would begin and end with no issue. She kept reciting similar words to herself as she descended the stairs. *You will smile. Some gentleman will offer for you. All will be fine.*

"Evangeline! Stop muttering to yourself and come downstairs at once."

"I'm coming. I only had to find the hat you wanted me to wear with this gown."

"Hmmm, much improved. I don't know where you found that pale-green one you were going to wear. It needs to be thrown out with the rubbish."

"I liked it," Evangeline muttered. The green hat had been Sue's, but she didn't dare mention her older sister's name. Not in front of her mother.

"Your hair is displayed to your advantage now."

Her mother studied her. Evangeline knew that unsettled look in her mother's eye, as well as the meaning of her guarded compliment. She was going to make another change. Evangeline was presentable, but not yet up to her mother's standard of beauty.

"Might we leave today at some point?" her father asked, bringing the examination of Evangeline's looks to a close. "I would like this evening to end, and that doesn't seem likely as long as we stand around here."

"Just a moment." Her mother held up one elegant finger. Her focus was still on Evangeline, from her pinned-up hair to her beaded slippers. "I'm not entirely sure of Evangeline's gloves."

"I thought they matched the ensemble well," Evangeline said just above a whisper.

"I suppose." Her mother touched the gloves with a single finger, her face contorted in disgust as she considered them.

Her mother was disgusted by most things in life and offended by the remainder. But as long as Evangeline made no move to disagree, her mother would weary of her critique and move on to something else. Evangeline held her breath. Standing in the manner her mother preferred, she waited. Soon. Soon she would only have a new husband to please. Surely that would be an easier task than dealing with her mother.

When the woman finally turned without making additional changes, Evangeline released the smallest sigh she dared and moved past her to the door, grabbing her pelisse as she left. The night air was cool against her skin, pushing away thoughts of hats and proper gloves. Truth be told, she cared little for such fripperies. It was a fact that would surprise most who knew her. She was known for her appearance, and fashion played a large role in how she was presented in society, but she wouldn't call it an interest.

She knew of several appropriate pursuits for a lady her age, but none seemed to hold her attention. She'd always envied her sister's love of art, even if Mother hadn't approved of her paintings. Sue had something to hold dear. She had a passion. Evangeline had a list of hobbies she could live without. And yet she was as perfectly dressed as any fashion-conscious lady would be; she practiced embroidery at first light every morning; and now she was on her way to listen to poetry. The lackluster thought of tonight's entertainment churned within her, but she tamped it down as she descended the steps to the garden. She would simply dedicate herself to the pursuit of a husband this evening. That was the purpose of this outing—not the Rutledge ladies' recitations, even if they were cousins by marriage now.

"Evangeline, ladies do not go striding out into the dark of night," her mother commanded from the door.

"Yes, Mother." She was stopped at the garden gate, prepared to wait there for her family, when it swung open from under her hand. "Oh!"

Jumping back a step, she heard a familiar voice.

"Good evening, Lady Evangeline."

She blinked into the night. Lord Crosby? What was he about, scaring her out of her wits in such a manner? "You know my name. What a surprise," she bit out to cover the racing of her heart.

"How could I forget?" he asked. Even in the dark she could see the hint of a grin playing about his mouth.

"It can be accomplished quite easily, it seems." She took a breath, trying to regain order in her mind.

"Allow me to make amends. I was passing by and thought to call…"

"After nightfall?"

"Your father asked me to call this afternoon, but I was detained elsewhere."

"As you can see, we're on our way out for the evening."

"If you would rather I leave…" he started but then fell silent, watching her from the opposite side of the gate.

The word *no* flew to her lips, but she kept silent. She didn't know what interested her in life; she didn't know what she liked or disliked. What she did know, however, was for whatever mad reason, she didn't want Lord Crosby to leave again.

"Crosby," her father offered as he reached them.

"Lord Rightworth," Crosby stated, his jaw grinding out the name without the teasing note he used when he addressed Evangeline. "I was just discussing my poor timing with your daughter. I should have called hours ago."

"Evangeline, darling, I hope you didn't insult his lordship."

"No, Mother. Lord Crosby enjoys a good jest. Why, he even pretended to forget my name at a ball last week," she said in the smooth voice her mother preferred. "His jest was ever so amusing."

This time she could see the entirety of Crosby's wide grin, shining in the dark. Did he think this was a game? And if it was, had she just made the first move against him?

Her mother took a step forward, scowling at the man who had invaded their evening. "I don't recall witnessing your introduction to my daughter, Lord Crosby."

"You were busy with Lady Smeltings in the parlor when we were first introduced," Evangeline stated, grasping the first excuse that came to mind.

"At the Tottings' event?"

"You said yesterday you danced together at the Dillsworths' ball," her father interjected.

"Aren't we in danger of being late, Mother?" Evangeline asked, cutting off her father's perceptive comments.

"Indeed," her mother replied, clearly sensing that details were being omitted.

"Apologies for rushing off, Crosby. We're on our way to the Rutledge event at Torrent House," her father said as he swung open the garden gate that separated them.

"The Rutledge event at Torrent House," Lord Crosby repeated. "Of course, I was about to go there myself."

"Then why did you come here?" Evangeline asked before she could think better of it.

Her mother pinched her arm under the guise of adjusting the sleeve of her gown, making Evangeline suppress a wince of pain. She should have known better. Asking a lord any question with an air of impertinence was against Mother's rules. Something about this gentleman made her forget them all.

"Only thought to call for a moment along the way," Crosby explained in a matter-of-fact tone, but his eyes danced as he looked at her as if she'd just been allowed in on some secret only he knew.

"Come with us," her father offered. "We can talk in the carriage."

"Surely Lord Crosby will want his own conveyance available to him at the Rutledge residence," her mother attempted. It was clear she didn't want to arrive with such a gentleman, most likely because she thought he was of a lower rank than Father.

"I'll have my man follow along after us." Ash turned and gave a nod to the driver of his carriage.

"Then there is no reason for you not to ride with us," her mother said through clenched teeth that were meant to resemble a smile. "Come along, Evangeline."

Once inside the carriage, she had no choice but to stare at Lord Crosby because he was seated opposite her and beside her father. His eyes glittered with mischief as he returned her stare in kind. This was going to be a long journey, despite being only a few blocks.

"Lord Crosby, what brings you to London?" her mother asked in blatant inspection of the man.

"Business brought me to town, but I've found myself quite distracted since my arrival."

"The entertainments of town do that to the best of gentlemen. I still remember my first time in London." Her father smiled over some memory of his youth. It was hard for Evangeline to think of her father as anyone other than the man she saw today, but even he must have had a past before her mother.

"This is your first visit to London, Lord Crosby?" Evangeline asked, knowing it was not, and also knowing he wouldn't tell the truth.

His eyes crinkled at the corners in challenge. "Actually, I was here on a brief visit this time last year. Perhaps you recall attending the Geddings' ball last season?"

"Only vaguely, my lord," Evangeline choked out, knowing that was when they'd first met.

"It was quite the crush, as they say. Lady Evangeline was a vision in yellow. Her hair was swept up with some sort of pins."

"Pearl-tipped," her mother supplied.

Evangeline couldn't move beyond the fact that Lord Crosby remembered the color of the gown she'd worn last year. She couldn't recall what color gown she'd worn last week. He was an equation whose parts refused to add up to the proper amount. Her gaze met his in the dark carriage as they bumped down the street. He remembered her hair and gown, but not her name. And if he had taken such notice of her, why leave town? Even more puzzling, why return a year later using a different name and repeatedly seek out the one lady who knew that everything about him was a lie?

"Darling, you remember that yellow gown, don't you? It was the one I was pleased with from the third shop we visited. The second one was a disaster. Dove-gray silk…"

"Certainly." She did recall there had been one gown out of perhaps twelve that her mother hadn't despised. It must have been yellow.

"Lord Crosby, I admire your taste in fashion," her mother complimented, making Evangeline tense. Her mother never said a pleasant word unless it was followed by something awful. As if on cue, her mother continued, "I can't recall hearing of your familial background. Where is your estate?"

"My family has always been quite private in nature. They don't frequent London, preferring life back at Crosing...tonitch to the city life." His eyes darted out the dark window before landing on her mother with a hint of a smirk.

"Crosingtonitch? I've never heard of it. It must be small." Evangeline didn't have to turn to the side to know the look of disgust that was written on her mother's face as she made the proclamation.

"Or it's a well-kept secret. Perhaps they don't care for visitors," Evangeline offered, drawing Crosby's attention once more. She didn't know why she was assisting this man in what was clearly a ploy, but doing so there in the dark carriage, where no one could see to any degree, made her smile.

From the other corner of the carriage her father cleared his throat to gain her mother's attention. "I'm sure it suits their needs quite well, my lady."

"Hmmm, quite," her mother muttered, but it was clear she'd lost her momentary interest in his lordship. Neither a smallish estate nor a secretive large one helped her climb to the next level of the *ton*, and that was her only concern.

"Lord Crosby, you'll have to come see me to discuss our business. It's clear the only conversation to be had in the presence of ladies revolves around fashion and travel destinations."

"There are only so many suitable topics for a lady to discuss. Evangeline is saving her most interesting conversation for Lord Winfield. Aren't you, darling?"

"What do you plan to discuss with Lord Winfield?" Crosby drew back in mock dismay that would have been quite believable if not for the twinkle in his eyes. "I admit I feel cheated by the slight."

"I have quite the discussion about the weather planned," Evangeline said. There was nothing wrong with the words she'd said, but she blushed all the same. She had plenty more interesting topics to offer, but none she was permitted to discuss.

"The weather." Crosby nodded. "Lord Winfield is fortunate, then. I don't know if I could manage such a topic."

"There is no shame in being out of one's depth, Lord Crosby," her mother said as the carriage slowed in front of the Rutledges' home and the light of candle-lit windows flooded their carriage.

"Clearly I have been bested this evening. I'll have to simply dream of a lively discussion of rain clouds." He smiled at Evangeline, and in that smile, she sensed he understood—which was impossible. No one understood.

The carriage stopped, and Lord Crosby shook his coat into place on his shoulders. "I appreciate your company on the trip here."

"Likewise," her father said as the carriage door opened. "It will no doubt be the highlight of my evening."

"Surely not," Lord Crosby returned as he climbed down to the ground.

"An evening of ladies reading poetry?" her father asked. "There isn't much competition for the honor, Crosby."

"Poetry…of course. Tonight's entertainment is a reading of poetry." He glanced up at the home looming above their heads with a hint of dread.

"It is, but then of course you knew that." Evangeline smiled and went inside.

When they were shown into the drawing room, she almost drew back at the sight of the gathered throng of people. Only her training kept her from reacting in surprise at seeing such a crowd. There must be no other ball this evening. The Rutledge family were relatives of Sue's new husband, Lord Steelings, and at least they must be pleased at such a crush. She cast a glance over the chairs set in rows in front of the podium.

"Mother, we may want to claim seats while we are able."

"And miss the time to socialize before the recitations begin? Absolutely not. We are not here to listen to verse." Her mother didn't look at Evangeline. Instead, she had her eye on their hostess across the room. The poor woman was clearly busy directing footmen in the task of bringing in another row of chairs for the rear of the room, but that was of no concern to someone like Evangeline's mother. A second later, her mother was gone from her side.

"May I escort you to a seat, my lady?" Lord Crosby asked as he joined her.

"Thank you, but I must remain standing."

"Oh, I see." He surveyed the room for a moment. "May I ask why?"

"We are here to socialize," she recited.

"I can see where being seated would destroy that possibility. I, for one, find it impossible to speak once I find a chair to sit upon."

"Then we shall have you as a dinner guest. What an entertaining evening that would be."

"I don't think your mother would approve of a silent dinner guest."

Her mother didn't approve of anything at all. She was now on the opposite side of the room and had gained seats for Father and herself with a powerful family in town. It appeared Evangeline was to fend for herself. "Perhaps we *should* find seats, or I fear we'll be left standing for the performance."

"I see just the place," Lord Crosby said, extending his arm to her.

After following him along the wall to the back of the room, Evangeline took the last open seat in the room—the one tucked into the corner beside Lord Crosby. It was the one place where not a single gentleman could see her. Her plan to attract a husband wasn't quite working to her advantage this evening. Of course, it had begun to spin steadily out of her control before she'd even left her garden gate.

She set her reticule and fan down at her feet. Looking through the spaces between dark-clad shoulders and hair swept up into elaborate twisting locks, she searched for an alternate seat, but there was none. She'd known before she looked. She didn't seem to have any choice in the matter, so the husband hunt would have to wait for another day. Locating the podium while the chatter of the crowd still rumbled through the room, she waited.

It wasn't until after Lord Crosby sat and made a show of adjusting his coat on his shoulders that she became aware of how small and dainty the wooden chairs truly were, and just how close she was sitting to him. She simply wouldn't glance in his direction.

Hands folded in her lap, she took a steadying breath. She would survive this evening by refusing to think about the man at her side, or the fact that he remembered what she had worn when they met last year. What, if anything, did that mean? He'd still left her and he would again.

Poetry, she was here for poetry. She ignored the gentle scratch of Lord Crosby's wool coat against her upper arm, as well as the faint, spicy scent of his shaving soap. She focused her gaze on the empty podium at the front of the room. *Do not think of him. Do not think…*

"Rather close in here, isn't it?" His rough voice whispered in her ear, sending a shiver down her spine that she fought to suppress.

Yes, it was dreadfully close. He was dreadfully close, and the blame for this entire situation could be placed on his shoulders—his broad shoulders that brushed against hers every time he moved. He hadn't even been invited to this event. It was his fault there was a shortage of seating. She was supposed to search for a husband tonight and now she was trapped, sitting far too close to an unmarried man who couldn't help her in that respect at all. At least he would have to suffer through an hour or more of poetry recitation. It was a small ray of sunshine on an otherwise stormy night.

"An evening of poetry," she said just loud enough that he would hear her above the chatter of the crowd. "I'm sure you looked forward to this event all day."

"I did," he replied close to her ear, setting her nerves on end once again. "I clutched the invitation to my heart and sighed. Rather wistfully, I might add."

"The invitation you never received," she clarified, pulling her gaze from the podium to look at him.

"Yes, that invitation." He chuckled, his clear blue eyes sparkling with humor.

"Sometimes there is a high price to be paid for your risk-taking."

"And poetry is that price tonight." The corner of his mouth quirked up as he looked at her. "I jest. In truth, I happen to be fond of a good verse."

"Really?" she asked in surprise. "It makes most gentlemen—"

"Want to *curse*? It could be much *worse*."

She sighed. "You're impossible."

"That sounds *plaus-ible*." He drew out the last two syllables and flashed a wide grin.

She shouldn't encourage him; really she shouldn't. But then she did. "Are you certain the poetry won't make you *cry*? Then I'd be forced to cheer you with *pie*."

"I'm simply pleased to be seated, pressed against your *thigh*," he whispered so that only she could hear before nodding to the front of the room with bright eyes. "Look, it appears to be starting." He sat back in his seat with a smug grin. Under the guise of stretching to get comfortable, he pressed his powerful thigh against hers.

Heat seared down the outside of her leg and spread to all her limbs. She should scoot away, but there was no place to scoot. And shameful as it was, she didn't truly want to move away from him. She didn't want to move at all.

Where they were sitting, no one could see them. All backs were turned, and they were shoved into a cramped corner together. Perhaps just for the next few minutes, she didn't need to move. After all, who would know of it if she remained here, pressed against a roguish gentleman's side? No one.

Chancing a glance to the side, she saw that Lord Crosby's gaze was focused ahead as if he had not a care for how he was affecting her. The thin weight of the silk gown her mother had selected for her to wear did little to separate his skin from hers. She shouldn't think about such things. It was improper to notice the muscular build of the scoundrel at one's side. She blinked, turning back to the front of the room as well.

Lord Torrent was saying something in welcome and presenting his eldest daughter, April. Meanwhile, Evangeline darted her eyes back in Lord Crosby's direction. This time her movement drew his attention.

"What?" He mouthed the word.

She only scowled in return. There was nothing a polite lady could say in such a situation, and she wasn't quite sure how an impolite lady would react either.

Nodding toward the podium, he mouthed, "Poetry." Then he added another overeager nod as he grinned at her, clearly knowing how irritating he was and relishing every second of her discomfort.

She was the very image of a polite lady, but images could be misleading. And only he would know of her actions tonight. She pulled her arm up and shoved her elbow into his ribs. That would show him! Only she was the one to flinch as her elbow connected in just the wrong fashion with one of the metal buttons on his waistcoat.

A sharp stab of pain shot up her arm. She squeezed her eyes shut and curled her arm in close to her body. In the next second, warm male hands were wrapped around her arm. She opened her eyes but only saw swimming shapes for a moment while her eyes watered a bit from the impact. She didn't need to see, however, to know that Lord Crosby was pulling her arm back toward him, holding her elbow gently in his hands.

Her gaze cleared in an instant as she searched around them for watchful eyes. But there was no interest from the row in front of them because the lady at the podium held the attention of the room. With the wall at their backs, they were all but alone and Lord Crosby knew it. He most likely had known it when he seated her there. But she didn't pull away on principle.

He silently tugged her glove down to investigate the damage to her elbow, while the lady at the front of the room spoke of flowers or pirates or something. Evangeline wasn't listening. He searched her skin until he found the center of the radiating pain where she'd collided with his button. Without a word between them, he began rubbing away the hurt. Slowly, she turned to look at Crosby.

For the first time, she wasn't able to find a trace of humor about his eyes. "Are you all right?" he whispered, concern drawing his brows together until there was a small line between them.

She nodded but was unsure if that was true since she couldn't pull her gaze from his. What was she doing? This was not how the evening was to transpire—hip to hip with a mysterious and not marriage-minded gentleman as he touched her. And yet she didn't want it to end.

He continued to rub gentle circles around her elbow, relaxing the muscles that had tensed there. The tenderness of his movements opposed everything she thought she knew of this man. He would leave her. Everything about him fairly screamed, *Guard your heart!* She knew better than to allow him to touch her. She knew better than to let the touching continue after the pain in her elbow receded. She certainly knew better than to allow him to pull her glove farther down her arm and draw shapes over the sensitive bare skin on the inside of her forearm. But she didn't pull away. With a thrill of rebellion, she allowed him to touch her, even silently begged him not to stop.

If she so much as flinched, the moment would be gone. He would release her arm, and she would never experience this again. The thought of facing the remainder of the evening without the warmth of his leg against hers, without the tickle of his fingers moving against her skin, or blast it all, the constant attention of this man she knew was wrong in every way possible, was the worst fate of all.

Time only moved in the front of the room where words were said and different ladies stood at the podium. In the back of the room, there were only the two of them and her awareness of the gentle, yet life-roughened hands that drew swirling lines down her arm toward her wrist.

He pushed her glove down farther until it bunched over the palm of her hand. Wrapping her hand within his, he pulled her arm toward him and rested it on his leg. Her breathing quickened. If anyone saw them…but she knew no one could see. They sat in the last two seats tucked away in the back corner of the room. Her eyes darted to his, watching him, waiting for his next move.

He lifted her hand from his leg and placed a kiss on the inside of her wrist. His lips were warm where they lingered on her skin. He'd kissed her twice before in private, and yet, here in the corner of a drawing room while society's eyes were diverted, this was the most intimate moment she'd ever experienced with a man. Placing her hand back on his leg, he slid her glove back into place. He ran the backs of his fingers over the exposed skin above her glove for but a moment, and then the recital was over. He stood and her hand fell back to her lap as if nothing had happened.

Evangeline fought off the immediate sense of loss that flooded her body and blinked. Was it over? It couldn't be—not yet. She hadn't heard a word that was said. Her regret wasn't over the poetry she'd missed, however, but the end of something delicate and magical that would likely never happen again.

She gathered her belongings with shaking hands and stood, avoiding all eye contact with Lord Crosby. They'd had enough real contact over the last hour that something untoward would certainly show on her face if she looked at him. The moment they'd shared was crashing in around her in the bustle of the rising crowd. The truth of her wild thoughts would surely be revealed, even in a glance, and she couldn't allow that to happen.

But then she tipped her head up in his direction anyway. It was as though every day of her life hadn't been spent in preparation for social situations. Perhaps her mother was correct—she did require more training to make proper choices while in London. Even knowing this, Evangeline couldn't look away. She was trapped by something beyond his clear blue gaze, some truth that hid behind his lies.

"Rousing poetry this evening," Ash said, focused on a point beyond where she stood, all of a sudden looking as if his warm gaze had been thrown into icy waters. "Don't you agree, Lord Rightworth?"

Evangeline turned to see her father standing in the next row of seats, and her mother moving through the room in her direction.

"Mmm, yes. Quite," her father replied.

"I believe Lady Evangeline was partial to the last one, *The Vanity of Human Wishes*. She seemed to truly be *touched* by the words." He turned his attention to her. "Do you agree with Mr. Johnson's views on wealth?"

He'd been listening to the poetry? All she could think of was his touch and how her hand had rested on his leg. And all the while, he'd been unaffected and listening to the words being spoken?

How did he do that? He was the one here uninvited, having insinuated himself into her family's plans. He was the one who'd distracted her during the readings and provoked her at every turn, yet she was the one with flaming-hot cheeks. Flustered beyond reason, she stared at him for a second before attempting to speak.

"I found the language used to be quite pleasant, my lord," she finally replied, having no idea what she was speaking of.

"All that talk of treachery and other lands… We're English. We have enough to deal with inside the borders of our own country," her father grumbled.

"I found it to be a bit dreary," Crosby stated with his eyes on her father. "We require no guide as we make our own paths—paths that can lead us to great wealth if we seize opportunity. However I'm a forward-thinking gentleman, not a poet."

Was he referring to some business dealings with her father now and not poetry? Evangeline looked back and forth between the two men, her mind teetering to keep its balance after the events of the evening.

"You sat in the corner of the room?" her mother hissed as she reached them. "Why even attend?"

Evangeline opened her mouth to explain, but her mother was already picking apart her other flaws. She deserved the dressing-down, although her mother couldn't possibly know her true crime tonight.

"Lord Winfield wouldn't have even seen you back here—hidden away in the corner of the room like the lesser gentry." She darted her eyes to Lord Crosby as she spoke. "This will not do. It will not do at all. And what have you done to stretch your glove so terribly?" she asked, her gaze turning back to Evangeline.

"Eyes do become misty during such moving poetry," Lord Crosby chimed in.

There was no need for him to intervene on her behalf. In fact, he should leave. He was experienced in doing just that. Why wasn't he leaving? Having him at her side only made Evangeline's mind turn to soup. She blinked at her mother, unsure what to say while Lord Crosby's gaze was upon her.

"And you used your glove to dry your eyes?" her mother asked her, outrage making her voice go up two octaves. "Haven't you a handkerchief?"

"I did not become misty-eyed over the reading," Evangeline began in a quiet voice, knowing her mother's opinions on tears shed over any subject.

"She's correct. It was me. William Blake always makes me weep," Crosby explained to her family. "Lord Rightworth, thank you for allowing me to join your party this evening. It was most enjoyable. Lady Evangeline, I would like to call on you tomorrow."

"I believe we're otherwise engaged—" her mother said.

"Nonsense," her father cut in. "Never too busy for a fellow like Crosby. I'm pleased to see my daughter finally showing an interest in a gentleman."

"Father..." Evangeline warned in a low murmur, but she said nothing further.

"Very well. Tomorrow then," Lord Crosby promised, but his eyes were not on her, but her father. "And, Lord Rightworth, when I come to call this time, perhaps I'll remember those diagrams I mentioned." Lord Crosby nodded and took his leave.

Evangeline was still staring after him when she heard her father say, "I look forward to it."

Her father guided her mother toward the door as the woman predictably nodded an elegant farewell to everyone she passed. Lord Crosby was gone. And Evangeline was left unbalanced and wondering about him once more. Diagrams? What did he mean by diagrams?

She certainly wouldn't be getting any answers tonight. Tomorrow, however, was another day entirely. She trailed after her father, her mind still fuzzy.

"We'll have her married within the month," her father murmured with clear glee.

"To whom? Please, do not look so pleased with yourself. Our daughter can do a far sight better than the likes of Crosby."

"He's coming to call on her tomorrow," her father said as if that explained everything.

It explained nothing to Evangeline. Gentlemen who were keen on leaving town, had stolen on two occasions, and regularly used a false name didn't call on ladies, did they? And if he had meant his request to call on her—why?

It must be part of his scheme, whatever that might be. Evangeline couldn't restrain the smile that tugged at her lips. If he wished to court her for some gain on his part, she would make him pay for it. Perhaps he had turned tonight back upon her head with his scorching caress, but with a tea service between them, she would be quite safe.

He wanted to call on her? Ha! Let him. He was about to become quite well versed in what it meant to court a lady.

He would surely flee London within the day after such a dull affair, and then she could return to finding the proper husband she required without Lord Crosby about. She rubbed her thumb over the spot where he'd pressed his lips to her bare skin. She couldn't rub away the memory of his kiss, but she could eliminate the temptation for more. Evangeline needed a husband and Lord Crosby—or whatever his true name may be—was not the gentleman for the job.

Six

IAN CULPEPPER, LORD BRAXTON, WAS AN EASYGOING man. He regularly looked the other way when his sisters ran around Bath like the hoydens that they were. He always ignored the fact that his butler borrowed from the house's supply of whiskey without thought of returning a single drop. He even occasionally slipped his younger cousins sweets when his aunt wasn't looking. But he had not been able to stand by and allow his grandmother to be swindled by some charlatan passing through town.

He'd seen the trouble the moment he came upon the man with his grandmother. That false twinkle in the swindler's eye had drawn Ian's attention like a piece of broken bottle left behind in the grass and catching the light. He'd watched the man spin a tale with concerning ease. It was his grandmother's girlish laugh, however, that had urged Ian into action.

He'd done what any gentleman would do: He'd tossed the charlatan from his home in the middle of tea. Perhaps most gentlemen of good breeding would have waited for their tea to be finished, but Ian wasn't one to sit about and wait—ever. He hadn't even stopped at removing the man from his home. He'd chased him halfway to London before losing the trail, and then he had gone in search of more information.

Now, he ran a hand over his weary eyes. Somehow he would find a way to keep his long-ago vow to his father. Ian would care for this family, and that included his rather fanciful grandmother and—in this instance—her investments.

"False name. False estate. False business. Is there anything true about this man?" Ian pressed his fist into the desktop as he stared down at the map that sat atop a pile of clippings from the local posts of surrounding towns.

Rockwale, his perpetually inebriated butler, moved to straighten the pieces of paper strewn across Ian's desk, stacking the scraps of newsprint until the charlatan's face looked up at Ian from a small likeness sketched in black ink on top of the pile. "The truth is in the pudding, as my mother always said."

"Rockwale...I believe that's the *proof*," Ian corrected as he straightened from his desk, muttering to himself. "The *proof* is in the pudding."

The man stepped away with a nod of agreement. "She wasn't much with words, my lord, but she did enjoy a good pudding."

"Perhaps your mother was correct," Ian mused as he turned to look out the window onto the street below. It was a quiet afternoon, but then, most were in Bath.

"I fail to see how a pudding will solve the situation, but I'll ring for the cook."

"No." Ian spun on his heel and began pacing the floor in front of the windows as he often did when he was on the edge of a decision about his family. Over the two years since he'd inherited responsibility for his family's welfare, he'd worn the finish on the hardwood floor dull in the space behind his desk. "We require truth and proof." He turned and set off in the opposite direction. "I don't simply want to have Grandmother's funds returned—I want to see that this man doesn't harm another man's grandmother. Portable steam." Ian shook his head at his grandmother's naiveté. "He must be held accountable for his actions. I will see to it that he's punished for his thievery."

Rockwale cleared his throat, shifting to the side to gain Ian's attention. "Pardon my opinions on the matter, my lord, but don't you have enough to deal with here in Bath? Your sisters—"

"Will be fine for a bit under my grandmother's supervision," Ian cut in, already making preparations for a trip in his mind. Rockwale could argue all he liked, but Ian's mind was settled on the subject. He would return to the point where he'd lost the swindler's trail and track him from there. From Berkshire it would be north to Oxford, south to Hampshire… or straight ahead to London. If he'd continued straight… Ian turned and paced the other direction. The damage the man could do to the good members of society in London was staggering. Ian had to leave. He had to try.

"Your grandmother can't keep pace with your sisters. You can barely manage them, and you have youth on your side."

"You flatter me, Rockwale." He flashed a smile at his butler as he moved across the room toward the door. "I've failed in every effort to manage my sisters."

"You'll need assistance," his butler persuaded. "At least gather a few other local gentlemen. Your family wasn't the only one who encountered that man. Surely others were taken in by his schemes."

Ian stopped with his hand on the doorknob. "You're correct. His foolishness was the talk of the town during his stay. I'll have to move quickly to gather assistance before he gets too far away."

"I've never known you to sit idle, my lord. Indeed, it was surprising you didn't catch the rascal on the road out of town last week."

"He shan't be so lucky this time," Ian said, opening the door. "Have my horse readied."

Ian Culpepper, Lord Braxton, was guilty of plenty of lesser crimes in this world, but he would not be guilty of standing by while his grandmother was swindled. He would travel as far as he must to find the man responsible for stealing from his family. And at the end of his journey, he would ensnare the scoundrel in his own web of lies.

Seven

"LIE ABOUT MY INTENTION TO CALL? WOULD I LIE TO you?" Ash lowered his voice to ask, aware of the maid sitting in the corner with a lap full of embroidery while she pretended not to listen to their conversation.

He'd found Evangeline in a small parlor off the main hall when he arrived this afternoon. A tiny room intended to receive guests was an odd place to spend the day, almost as if she were hiding in her own home.

When Ash first set foot inside the parlor, Evangeline had exchanged a meaningful glance with the young maid who remained in the corner. After an encouraging nod from the maid, Evangeline had turned back to him with eyes as bright as those of a child being allowed unexpected sweets. Ash had taken that to mean the maid was the loyal sort. He certainly hoped that was true, since they were now discussing whether he'd lied about his intentions.

"Yes, I'm quite certain you would lie to me," Evangeline stated. "In fact I'm quite certain you already have and continue to do so. Tea?" Her eyes were lit by some inner merriment as she indicated a serving tray that sat on the table in front of her.

She was a vision in green today. Everything about her was in place, down to the last hair on her head, and he had the overwhelming desire to ruffle her well-preened feathers. Who lounged about their home with such an exacting appearance? Or had she dressed with him in mind today? He'd changed waistcoats twice and retied his cravat at least five times before leaving headquarters. He'd told himself it was to appear appropriate when he saw her father, but as Evangeline suggested, he was a liar.

He glanced back at the door to the hall. Business could wait. Instead he leaned an elbow on the back of the chair opposite where Evangeline sat beneath a row of windows overlooking the garden. The maid in the corner now had her nose so close to her embroidery that she was in danger of poking the end of it with a needle. She only broke her trance for quick looks at the door. All seemed private then.

"Tea," he repeated, leveling a glare in Evangeline's direction. "You wish to have tea with someone who lies to you?"

"Everything is more civilized over tea." She blinked, clearly believing her own words.

"And you believe some water and leaves will make me more civilized as well," he supplied, watching her.

He hated burdening her with unwelcome news, but he'd been quite uncivilized on occasion. In fact, his thoughts about the way she looked this afternoon and what he longed to do to her overly tidy hair and perfectly pressed dress were downright barbaric.

"One can only hope for a bit of civility. Do sit, Lord Crosby. You led my father to believe we have a mutual interest, though I'm certain your intent was to discuss some piece of business with him today and not to join me for tea. Curious, don't you agree?"

She was damn distracting. The only thing he found curious was that he was supposed to be distracting her, not the other way around. "Very well," he muttered as he circled the grouping of chairs and dropped into the one beside Evangeline's.

She smiled as she poured a cup of tea and handed it to him. Perching on the edge of her seat with cup and saucer in hand, she looked at him with the intent stare of a cat about to trap a helpless mouse. "Lord Crosby, I hope you're enjoying this fine weather we are having."

"The weather?" He shifted to note the sunlight pouring in the windows around them.

"Yes, my lord. It is a quite nice day, don't you agree?" She lifted her cup to her lips, pausing before taking a sip.

"I haven't given it much thought." He couldn't stop staring at her mouth. Was she doing that thing with the teacup on purpose?

"That's…" She sighed. "Lord Crosby, this is what we are to discuss over tea, so I suggest you have an opinion one way or another about the brightness of the sun."

"Is this the bit you had planned for Lord Winfield? I'm sure I should feel honored." Instead he was only annoyed. He didn't want a conversation intended for another gentleman—he wanted… Well, best not to dwell on what he wanted if they were to keep things civilized. Instead he asked, "Why are you so interested in the weather?"

"My lord, you jest." She laughed. Why was she laughing in such a false manner? He looked around to see if someone was jesting *him* this afternoon. But he only saw the maid's small, mournful shake of her head as if something tragic was occurring.

He narrowed his eyes on Evangeline. What was this about? Lowering his teacup to the small table, he said, "Listen, I don't know what we're doing here, but—"

"We're having tea and polite conversation, my lord." She stated this as if it should be plain to anyone, and yet something about the situation was off.

"Is that what this is?" he asked, leaning forward to study her.

"Yes. When a gentleman comes to call, I'm to serve him tea and talk of the weather." She took a sip of her tea, her lips curling up into a smile as she looked at him over the rim of the cup. "This is what you wanted. Do play along, Lord Crosby."

"And the only available topic of conversation is…"

"The weather."

"Clearly." He'd turned the tables on plenty of people over a cup of tea, and this must be what it was like to be on the other end of that conversation. He had no idea where this was going, but if she intended to sell the weather, he would take as much as he could carry away. "May I ask a question of you? Do you want to discuss the weather? Because if I'm offending your long-standing devotion to fog or something of that nature…"

Her lips twitched as if she was fighting not to smile,

but losing the battle. This first genuine smile of the afternoon lit her eyes and spread warmth into her cheeks. "I have no ties to fog of any kind."

"And rain? Do you possess a kinship with rain? I wouldn't want to offend."

Her smile broadened. "No, although I must admit a partiality to wind."

"The sort that rips through towns, scattering leaves and turning everyone's hair on end?" he asked with a raised brow.

"Is there any other kind?" she teased.

"Not where I come from. My home was always littered with debris from the winds that blew in from the sea."

"It *was*," she said, her eyes narrowing on him. "You no longer live at home, then?"

"I haven't been there in some time." He worked to keep the emotion from his voice, but failed. "My home is wherever I happen to be."

"And you never stay long."

"No. No, I don't."

"Much like the wind," she mused.

"Ah, and we're back to the weather." He leaned back in his chair with a grin.

A door opened nearby, and footsteps sounded in the hall outside the parlor. Evangeline shot a panicked look at the maid, but the girl nodded for them to continue as she moved to the door and peered out into the hall. Nevertheless, they paused their conversation until the steps faded away.

"That would be Father. He's the one you're truly here to call upon, no matter what you claim." Her gaze was unswerving, as if she was attempting to read his every thought. And God help him, he would let her. Her voice was small and almost frail as she added, "It's all right to leave, my lord."

"And abandon this rousing discussion?" He grinned. He didn't know what he was doing, other than destroying his own plans, but he knew that the *my lords* and *Lord Crosbys* were driving him mad. For the first time in years, the falseness of his life grated on his nerves. He had the absurd desire to be honest with her, if only about his name. *Mr. Claughbane* or even his blasted given name of *Ashley* would be better than hearing Evangeline call him something wrong for one more second. "And it's Ash Clau—" he blurted out before stopping himself. "Ash," he repeated.

"Is that your name?"

He knew what she was asking. He'd used two false names with her already, and she knew it. "I believe honesty is required during 'civilized conversation over tea.'"

She shot a look to the maid before turning her attention back to him, keen awareness in her eyes. Perhaps his desire to hear his real name from her mouth was a bit rushed. He'd pushed the boundary of their tentative friendship. He should have known better, but it seemed with Evangeline he never did.

"Ash," she finally said in a quiet voice just above a whisper, her full, pink lips pursed around the sound, drawing his attention to her mouth. After a moment of thought or perhaps indecision, she added, "You may call me Evangeline, or Evie if you prefer, not that you'll recall it when next we meet."

Or perhaps he hadn't overstepped his bounds. His heart raced at the ease with which he'd procured the liberty of her first name. He'd wager Lord Winfield hadn't reached such heights with his discussion of the weather. "Which name do you prefer?"

"My sister always called me Evie," she said, her eyes lighting with a smile as she spoke.

"I won't forget your name again. You have my word." He paused, watching her. "Evie."

Her breath grew shallow in the quiet of the room, and he watched as a blush crept up her neck. "In the name of honesty over tea, you shouldn't make that claim."

"In the name of honesty over tea, I very much should." There was no way he would forget her name again.

"Where did you go last year?" She looked down at her teacup with a shake of her head. "Apologies. You don't have to answer that. It's none of my concern. I should keep my mind upon…"

"Raindrops and breezes?" he asked. "I was only in town for a few days' time. Business matters, you know," he added, hoping she wouldn't inquire further. It was the one bit of information he couldn't voice, and for some reason he had a devil of a time keeping secrets from Evie.

"And this season?" she asked. "When do you leave?"

"You seem rather anxious to be rid of me." He held his breath, hoping she wouldn't see through his diversion. Leaving was a subject he didn't want to discuss. "What excitement do you have planned once I'm gone?"

"I…" She pressed her lips together and shot a

glance toward the open door, then to the maid in the corner. "I shouldn't answer that. It's unseemly for a lady to discuss such intentions."

"Now I must know." He lowered his voice and leaned in to ask, "Are you to run off with a lover? You know, now that I've called on you, we're practically courting. Have a care. I'm sitting right here." He was teasing her, and yet some small part of him was taking a bit too much pleasure in it. He should stop, but when did he ever follow the smart course of action? "Surely the upstanding gentleman you're courting should be told of such an arrangement."

"No!" She breathed the word with enough force to drive back an army. "I have no *lover*. Why would you think such a thing?" She clasped her hands together in her lap. "This must be why I am to only discuss the weather."

But instead of backing down with an apology, he leaned closer to whisper, "You have followed me into darkened halls three times, kissed me twice, and allowed me to touch you during a poetry reading. And we have only just begun a courtship." He shrugged and leaned back in his chair with a grin, knowing he was irritating her, but enjoying the way she became outraged with him.

"Stop it." She looked around to see if her maid had heard him. "I did not kiss you. You kissed me. There is a difference." She practically mouthed the words, not even daring a whisper.

"Is there?" he asked, as if they were still discussing the weather, before adding in a lower voice, "Because it seemed as if you wanted that kiss." He narrowed his eyes on her. "Did you not want me to kiss you?"

"I... The sun is shining outside," she blustered. "It's a lovely day, don't you agree?"

He ignored her attempt to change the subject, scooting his chair a fraction closer to hers to continue their hushed discussion instead. "Say that you did not want me to kiss you, and I will never kiss you again."

"Hardly a cloud in the sky, which is unusual for London."

"Do you want me to never kiss you again?"

"I'm sure the parks are busy."

"What do you want, Evie?" His question was a quiet one, but it drew her attention.

"That hardly matters," she whispered with a sadness he didn't quite understand lingering about her eyes.

"I would think what you want matters more than any sunny day."

"What I want is to please those around me with my words, appearance, and actions," she replied as if it was a line over-rehearsed for a play.

"What of you?" He shook his head, trying to make sense of what she was saying. "That wasn't what you were doing with me, was it? When you kissed me? Last night when I touched you? Evie, you can't set out to please any gentleman you see in a hall. Do you not know where that can lead?" He shouldn't be dissuading her from this line of thought—it played right into his own desires—but she was wrong. She should be the one who was pleased.

"How tawdry you think me," she hissed. "Of course I wasn't attempting to please you the other night when you...when we...or last night, for that matter."

"Then you did want to kiss me," he said, relief flooding through him.

She didn't answer, which was answer enough.

"That's at least a start," he muttered.

"Might we speak of something more appropriate for the remainder of our tea?"

"Like clouds? They hang in the sky and dump rain upon our heads. They don't require further discussion." He would, however, like to know why she was so determined to only talk of the weather. "Evie," he said, waiting for her to look up and meet his gaze.

Her clear blue eyes were bright with worry, but why? Granted, he wasn't one to have tea with young ladies often because he could further his plans more by spending his time with those who had excessive funds to dole out. But conversation over tea didn't seem the sort of thing even a *young* lady would be upset over.

"What would you like to discuss?" he asked.

Her eyes darted to the door, bypassing her maid's watchful looks in the same direction, before Evie leaned in to whisper, "I'm not to discuss anything of import."

"Why not?" he whispered back.

She considered her answer, some secret hiding in the depths of her eyes. "I'm a lady," she finally stated.

"I can see that." He grinned at her, enjoying the blush that seeped into her cheeks. Whatever concern had filled her, he wanted to banish it forever. And if that meant discussing the weather, he would do so. He watched her for a moment and could see the worry still in her eyes as she busied herself with straightening the already-straight tea tray. "In the name of civilized conversation over tea, however, we could simply talk."

She relaxed a fraction. "I suppose if it is an official rule, I shouldn't break it. I never break the rules."

"I find rules to be rather malleable things. I bend them and they always snap back, good as new, when I'm done with them."

"How many rules have you broken?"

"Bent," he corrected. "And I don't keep a tally. Have you ever bent the rules? Surely on occasion…"

"When you aren't present?" she asked.

"Am I so terrible an influence?"

"Yes."

He gave an unrepentant shrug of his shoulders. "At least I excel at the task."

"What *other* tasks are you excelling at while in London?" Her gaze dropped to the tea service and she refilled her cup, although he suspected that had nothing to do with thirst.

"Honesty has its bounds, Evie," he warned.

She returned the tea to its tray and looked up, meeting his gaze. "You're going to leave again, aren't you?"

"When my business is concluded."

"Your business with my father." Her brow furrowed as she studied him. "Why court me, even if we both know it isn't in earnest?"

"For the tea and civilized conversation, of course." Would his answer settle the matter for now? He found himself waiting, his body tense with anticipation.

She picked up her teacup and nodded in his direction. "Clearly."

That was the problem with honesty. In his line of work, it was always short-lived. He didn't know why he'd allowed himself to become entangled with

Evangeline Green. It was an unnecessary complication. He could have stopped the direction of her
father's thoughts on the matter. He could have met
with the man without barging in on his time out
with his family, without proclaiming a desire to call
on Evie. But he'd allowed it to happen. He'd wanted
it to happen, convinced he could distract Evie long
enough to reach his goal. But he was the one caught
off balance every time she looked at him.

Perhaps there was still a benefit to calling on Evie in
an effort to meet with Rightworth more often. He could
use Evie as a means to get close to the family and the pursuit of his goals. But for that justification of his actions to
be plausible, he would have to actually call on the man.

As things stood, he was here, sipping tea and
chatting about the weather with a lady, instead of
sitting across the hall, hard at work convincing her
father to tender all of his ill-gotten gains to Ash for a
steam machine that would never exist. And the most
troubling part of the whole business was that the only
thing he wanted to do was refill his cup and stay the
afternoon with her.

❧

Evangeline slipped through the door and into her
mother's private parlor, checking over her shoulder to
ensure she was still alone upstairs. All was quiet. She
took a steadying breath. Being in her mother's private
space was risky at best, but she must do this.

Picking up her skirts, she scurried to the bookshelf
that stood in the far corner. She moved a vase out
of the way and grabbed her mother's most prized

possessions, volumes one and two of *Debrett's Peerage*. Evangeline held the large books to her chest. The answers were here; she knew it. Tweaking the vase back into place, she turned and ran from the room.

Her mother was shopping and would be home within the hour. But for now, the upstairs hall was empty as long as Evangeline hurried. She didn't wish to explain her curiosity to anyone, much less the lady of the house. Fleeing around the corner and into her own bedchamber, Evangeline leaned back against the closed door with a sigh. She hadn't slept last night, thinking of what she knew she must do, and now she would see that it was done.

The man was up to no good—that much was certain. Despite his claim of honesty over tea yesterday afternoon, plenty of unanswered questions remained. He'd practically danced around what he was doing in London. *Business*. There was more to it than that, and she was going to find out what, since boring him to the point of fleeing certainly hadn't worked.

He was only playing at courting her before he left town again. Why? She had the right to know the truth about him. Didn't she? And if he was being false in his dealings with her father, she had the responsibility to stop him.

If her mother had taught her one thing, it was that gentlemen should be researched. She'd been made to memorize titles, families, estates, level of wealth, and connections in society of every gentleman in town this season and last. She should at least know the true family name of the man she'd already kissed—twice! His given name was Ash.

"Ash," she whispered to herself with a smile as she sank onto her bed.

She'd seen the truth of his name in his eyes when he said it yesterday. It wasn't much to begin with, but it was better than what she'd had last year. It was surely short for something…Ashford…Ashton…

Dropping the volumes onto the bed at her side, she ran her fingers over the leather cover of the top volume before flipping the book open. Inside was a terribly long listing of families, which seemed appropriate. Good society was called the *ton*. Perhaps not ironically, the name matched the weight of the books.

Evangeline shifted on the bed and leaned farther over the index. This was quite a large number of families when she was trying to find one gentleman. Which was interesting, since her experience with finding one gentleman to marry was quite the opposite—there should be more to choose from. Settling in, she studied the names. She knew many of the family names from her sessions with her mother. Of course, there were plenty she didn't know. Those without fortune, or with no entailed estate, had been beneath her mother's notice.

Page after page was filled with tables and explanations of the peerage. Her head ached with the amount of information before her. She simply wanted to know who Ash was. If only there was a way of narrowing her search… She thumbed through the large book without truly seeing it, jumping as she was struck by a thought.

The wind would blow in from the sea at his home. Ash's home was on the coast. It didn't exactly point to his true identity, but it did eliminate a sizable portion.

Her door was flung open with an unceremonious bang as three ladies peered inside. "Evie, there you are. We looked everywhere for you." Isabelle's smile lit the room as she stepped inside, even her footsteps were cheerful as she crossed the floor.

"Your butler tried to shoo us from the house, saying you *weren't available to callers*." Roselyn mocked the last bit in a dramatic interpretation of her family's butler, making Evangeline stifle a laugh.

"Victoria told him we were far from your average callers, and we wouldn't be long." Isabelle leaned against the window frame without removing her bonnet or gloves. They must have plans for the after-noon, Evangeline thought.

Victoria shrugged one shoulder as she moved to the mirror for a quick check of her hair. "I also mentioned Roselyn being a duke's sister. That really opens doors in town. You should use it to your advantage, Roselyn."

"Yes, it does indeed open doors," Roselyn agreed, pulling a face of resigned disappointment as she adjusted her glove at the wrist. "Unfortunately, those open doors always accompany looks of puzzlement over my sanity, thanks to my family."

"Your brother's title worked today," Victoria said, consoling her while turning back to the room and propping a hip on the corner of the dressing table. "I for one enjoyed the look on Evie's poor butler's face."

Of course dropping a duke's name had worked in this home. The butler had been trained almost as well as she had on the subject of titles.

"It seems we arrived at the perfect time. What are you reading? That looks dreadfully dull," Roselyn said as she investigated the cover of the book lying open on the bed.

"Whatever it is, abandon it. We're on our way to Bond Street," Victoria commanded as if leading a charge. "Isabelle requires a new fan."

"Because you broke mine," Isabelle retorted.

"Because you hit me with it."

"Oh, Isabelle," Evangeline muttered, but she was ignored.

"I did no such thing. I merely tapped you on the arm, just as we were taught to do."

Victoria drew back in horror. "Don't do it that way, or you will have injured all the gentlemen in town by season's end."

"I did advise her that she should practice, Victoria," Evangeline offered, cutting into the twins' argument.

"Perhaps Isabelle doesn't need another fan," Roselyn added. "I often find them overused in fashion anyway."

"What is this, Evie?" Isabelle asked, ignoring the discussion of her skills with a fan and coming to perch beside her on the edge of the bed.

"Mother's copy of the latest *Debrett's Peerage*."

"Why would you want to read that in your free time?" Victoria asked. "Is she forcing more stringent studies upon you now that you're here in London? You poor dear."

"No," Evangeline stated, drawing herself up straight to brace for the impact of her next words. "I'm searching for a gentleman."

"Ooh, who is he? Tell us everything!" Roselyn said. She leaned against the post at the foot of the bed.

"That's the problem." Evangeline ran her fingers

over the edge of the book, flipping through the pages with a sigh. "I don't know anything."

"Did he deceive you?" Roselyn asked. "Because if he's the sort of gentleman who goes about town making up stories, that is someone you'd best avoid."

Evangeline placed a hand on Roselyn's arm. She was only trying to protect Evangeline from her own problems with gentlemen. Roselyn had her own troubles, what with the death of her fiancé and all. "Roselyn, you know avoiding a gentleman isn't as simple as it would seem."

Roselyn smiled and squeezed the hand on her arm. "I do."

"Surely you can research your gentleman later, Evie," Isabelle said hopefully. "Victoria will select some garish fan if you aren't there to help with the decision."

"Not garish," Victoria corrected. "Simply smaller, much smaller."

Isabelle leaned forward, pleading, "See, Evie? I need you."

"I really should stay here," Evangeline stated.

"I can help you find the perfect fan," Roselyn offered. "Perhaps something with flowers on it?"

Victoria pushed off the dressing table and moved across the room. "Come along, dears. I believe our stop here was in vain. Clearly Evie is too busy investigating Lord Crosby's background to shop with us today. We should leave her to it. If we don't find a new fan for Isabelle, I'll never hear the end of it."

"Ooh, it's that new gentleman in town?" Isabelle asked with wide eyes.

"I never said—"

"You didn't need to say his name," Victoria cut in.

"I swear the lot of you are rotten at keeping secrets from showing on your faces. This is why I don't bring you along when I play cards."

"Victoria!" Isabelle exclaimed.

"I was speaking in the theoretical sense, Isabelle. I only entertain myself with drink anymore, which is a struggle since London life is wretchedly dull."

Isabelle might believe her sister, but Victoria wasn't as skilled at hiding truth from her cousin's eyes as she would like to believe. Victoria's gambling would land her in hot water eventually. Evangeline only hoped it was many years from now, and well after she had a husband to look after her interests.

As the three ladies left her bedchamber, she smiled after them. They were the best part of being in the city. If she had to return with her parents at the end of the season—or worse yet, be sent away to live with Great-Aunt Mildred in Scotland—she wouldn't survive. She needed those ladies about.

To keep them in her life, to keep any semblance of life at all, she needed to find a husband. She looked down at the pages upon pages of fine print in front of her. Somewhere in these lines of text lay a family she would join. "And what are you doing? Looking up a man who is sure to be gone within the week," she mumbled to herself. If she was to investigate him, she'd best be done with it before her mother returned home.

Where to begin? Living near the sea was hardly rare in England. If only there had been anything else, some detail she'd missed. She pushed a falling lock of her hair from her face, tucking it behind her ear as she considered everything he'd told her.

"It's Ash Cla…" he'd said. Had he almost said his family name? If he had, it was quite the slip for such a secretive man.

She began thumbing through the pages. An hour later, she was still sifting through mottoes and family crests. Her eyes were weary and her neck sore, but finally she turned the page and two names caught her searching gaze. Two families in the listings met the specification she was looking for: the Clancartys and the Claughbanes.

Her heart sped as she began to fit pieces of the puzzle together. The Clancartys remained quite landlocked in Derby. That eliminated them quickly enough. What if neither family lived near the sea? She swallowed her concern. She would have to search by some other means. Abandoning her quest for answers about Ash wasn't something she looked forward to, especially not after having to give up on the same search last year.

She sighed, quickly flipping through pages to find the other name. Claughbane family…

Following the line of printing with her finger, her eyes darted across the page until she found the words she was searching for. Brennen Claughbane, born seven March seventeen eighty-one, has three brothers… Isle of Man. She tapped her finger on the word *isle*. "Isles are certainly by the sea." She grinned as she spoke. She returned her attention to the page, her eyes flitting across the lines of text in search of more information, but the subject had changed to the Duke of Clermont.

Straightening from the book, she stared unseeing across her bedchamber. "Mr. Ash Claughbane from the Isle of Man, it's a pleasure to make your acquaintance."

Jumping from her bed to dash across the room, she

dropped into the seat at her small writing desk. Her hands shook with anticipation as she lowered her quill to the piece of paper before her.

> *Dear Mr. Claughbane,*
>
> *I'm quite certain you will find this letter unusual because I am a lady and I write to you regarding a gentleman in town for the London season. Please, I beg you, do not form the wrong opinion in reference to my interest in this gentleman as we have only had tea together on one occasion.*

She paused, ink pooling on the tip of her quill. There was no need to tell a stranger that she had kissed the man—twice—simply for the sake of honesty. That small detail could remain unspoken. One shared pot of tea was an innocent enough means of meeting a gentleman without any assumption about her character.

> *I believe this gentleman to be a relative of yours. I would like to inquire after…*

Oh dear. She hadn't considered this portion of her plan. A lady couldn't very well ask after the familial background of a gentleman with no purpose to her query, yet she needed to confirm that Ash was who she suspected he might be. Ignoring the question of why this was so terribly important to her, she drummed her fingers on the small writing desk and stared out of the window. If only there was some manner of asking after Ash without actually committing a social crime in doing so.

*I would like to inquire after the given names of your
family members, as the poor gentleman in question
is quite heartsick over his long absence.*

She glanced to the abandoned embroidery she had
left on the settee. She'd tossed it aside yesterday when
she was too ill of looking at it to make another stitch
and hadn't yet put it away. Embroidery—that was
the answer. She smiled. Finally, a ladylike interest she
detested was coming to good use.

*With your kind assistance, I would like to make a
work of embroidery to remind him of home and ease
his time in the city.*

Lady E.

The letter broke a thousand rules a proper lady ought
not to break. She winced and signed *Lady E.* at the
bottom of the note. At least the return letter would
bring her answers. If this was truly his family, they
would list his name among their relations. He could be
a cousin or nephew of the gentleman she'd written to.
Of course, he could be unrelated and she'd just signed
her name on correspondence to a strange man. "At
least this Mr. Brennen Claughbane lives on an island,"
she muttered, and sealed the note with wax.

Soon she would know who Ash truly was, and
then… She straightened in her seat. And then, what?

Evangeline hadn't a clue what her next step would
be, but she knew she wanted to take that step knowing
all she could about Mr. Ash Claughbane.

Eight

EVANGELINE LEANED AWAY FROM HER COUSIN TO avoid being hit in the face with Isabelle's new fan. Either Isabelle had yet to get used to the new accessory or Victoria had been correct—she was going to wound someone—or both. Evangeline tried to straighten to the proper posture for standing on the side of a ballroom, but almost had her nose removed for the second time.

"As you can see, it is indeed a fan," Isabelle said with a flourish of her wrist that almost sent the contraption sailing across the ballroom into Lady Smeltings's hair. "And I suppose a dreadfully boring fan is better than the broken one I had in my possession before."

That was debatable, but Evangeline wasn't going to voice her opinion to Isabelle. That was normally Victoria's job, but she was currently dancing the quadrille with a gentleman. With Roselyn not in attendance this evening, Evangeline was left to survive her cousin's new fan alone, at least for the moment. "It isn't so terrible," Evangeline attempted. "It boasts a fine handle, quite sturdy looking."

Isabelle stared down at the fan in her hand. "Sturdy isn't really what one looks for in a fan, Evangeline."

"When one's sister is Victoria, perhaps one should," Evangeline said with a small smile, turning her attention back to the dancers on the floor.

"Perhaps you're right," Isabelle said, dropping the fan to her side and thereby allowing everyone nearby to take a breath of relief. "On a happier note, Lord Winfield has a pleasant-looking body."

"Isabelle!" Evangeline warned as she pulled her cousin away from a group of ladies who seemed to be only half concerned with their own conversation. The other half would be devoted to listening intently to everyone else's discussions.

"What?" Isabelle asked as if they'd been discussing something as meaningless as colors of ribbon. "He's next on your dance card. I'm certain that beneath those layers of evening wear, he has a fit bum. Not as fine as Mr. Brice's bum, mind you, but not terrible."

"How would you know what attributes a gentleman possesses beneath his clothing, let alone in his private regions?" Evangeline hissed, refusing to even glance at Lord Winfield's body to see if she might agree with her cousin.

"Mother tells me I have a vivid imagination." Isabelle beamed as she twisted a ringlet of blond hair around her finger.

"*My* mother says you have delusions of grandeur, but what does she know of it?" Evangeline replied.

"Perhaps I do. However, I like it that way. It's quite a cheerful place, the inside of my head."

Evangeline often wondered if Isabelle's thoughts

were coated in candies like the display in the bake-shop window she'd seen with her sister years ago. A great cake had been swirled with candies up to the top, like a mountain of sweets with chocolates pouring from the center. Sue hadn't wanted to leave, but Evangeline had pulled her away.

She gave Isabelle an affectionate bump with her elbow, thinking of the sister she'd betrayed. "I wouldn't have it any other way, even if it does lead to scandalous talk while in the middle of a ballroom." Evangeline couldn't help but notice the gentlemen's forms as they passed on the dance floor, now that the subject had been brought to mind.

Did it matter what features a man possessed? He could have no teeth and an unfortunate disposition, and he would still provide her with an escape from her current situation. She wasn't in a place to be particular, as long as someone would offer for her by season's end.

Just then, a gentleman who offered no escape from her current situation walked in the door of the ballroom. Ash was the sort of man ladies were warned about, and tonight he looked every bit the part of the devil-may-care rake. His dark evening wear matched the jet of his hair.

He scanned the room. Was he looking for her? Her heart sped.

It shouldn't matter, Evangeline, she told herself. He was only playing at courting her—none of it was real. He would soon be gone. Would he return to the Isle of Man? And why pretend to court her while in town? Did his interest have to do with her father? Or perhaps he was only amusing himself out of ennui. She should look away from him, but she didn't.

"Gentlemen look us over, so why shouldn't we do the same?" Isabelle, she realized, was still speaking to her.

"It does pass the time between dances, I suppose," Evangeline muttered, entranced by the cut of Ash's coat as it fell from his muscular shoulders.

Isabelle followed her gaze. "Lord Crosby has a quality bum. You can tell by the fit of his breeches. Though I'm sure you've noticed it already."

"I didn't notice anything," Evangeline rushed to say. The heat of a blush spread up her neck and burned her cheeks, but she couldn't tear her gaze from Ash. The memory of his body close to hers, his hands on her skin… "I would never think such…vulgar…"

"Evangeline," Isabelle said in the flat tone one would use to complain about what was being served at dinner. "He came to your home for tea. You said you sat with him and listened to poetry." She stopped with a dramatic shake of her head. "Poetry," she repeated as if the one word proved her point.

"It wasn't as romantic as you imagine it, Isabelle," she countered. It was true it hadn't been romantic. It had been something far more intriguing that Evangeline couldn't define and was quite sure she shouldn't be reflecting on in the first place.

"You're staring at him this very minute. Admitting a gentleman has a nice bum is the same as complimenting a lady's fine parlor décor or the cakes at tea."

"That is far from the same thing, Isabelle."

"I'm not suggesting you inform him of your opinion—can you imagine the scandal?" She giggled.

"I can see it now. 'Lady E. informed a certain lord of his fine bum at a ball Thursday last.'"

Evangeline had pulled Isabelle away from listening ears, but if anyone heard the direction of their conversation, she would be shipped away to live with Great-Aunt Mildred for certain. Yet in spite of the serious threat that posed to her future, she had to work to keep the amused smile from her face.

"You're clearly interested in him," Isabelle finally stated once her laughter had subsided.

"Am I?" Evangeline breathed.

"Aren't you?"

What did interest matter in her situation? Somewhere in this room, Lord Winfield or some other gentleman was dancing, drinking, or discussing politics, and he would soon be her husband. Ash was only about because… She didn't know his intentions, but she knew enough to know they weren't honorable. "Mother is pushing for a courtship with Lord Winfield," she finally replied.

"So I've heard."

"Father practically threw Lord Crosby in my path." She was still working to understand her father's actions in that regard. She took a breath, knowing that in the end, none of it was her concern. "Mother and Father will resolve the matter between themselves and inform me of the outcome. It's as simple as that."

"Are you claiming not to have feelings on the matter of your future husband?" Isabelle asked.

"Of course I have feelings—" Evangeline stopped herself before she admitted too much. She found Ash in the crowd once again, and her eyes followed him as he moved down the opposite wall of the room. Everything about him was wrong. She knew it. Yet, the small rebellious act of watching him from across the room made her skin tingle with warmth. "In my case, feelings can hardly be trusted as a guide."

Isabelle sighed. "Evangeline, I admire your prudence."

"However…" Evangeline led in, pulling her gaze from Ash's fit body wrapped in pristine evening wear for what might be the fifth time tonight. She turned to look at her cousin. "Mother always contradicts her initial statement. I've learned to sense a *but* waiting to emerge in the next statement."

"But what do you want for your future?" Isabelle asked, making Evangeline blink for a moment.

"I-I don't know."

"When I'm unsure of something, I follow my heart," Isabelle offered with a warm smile.

If only her words were of any assistance in Evangeline's tangled web of a life. "How do I know what my heart wants?"

"Your eyes always follow instructions from your heart. What do you see?"

Clear blue eyes met hers across the dance floor, and a mischievous grin tugged at Ash's lips. He *had* been searching for her. Her stomach clenched at the thought.

"What if my heart can't be trusted to give proper directions?" Evangeline asked.

"It can always be trusted, Evie. And I notice you have yet to spare a glance for Lord Winfield." Isabelle leaned closer to whisper, "I don't blame your heart. Lord Crosby's bum is of five-rose-petal quality and poor Winfield only has three and one half petals."

She turned to look at her cousin. "You have a system of ranking gentlemen's...rears?"

"Of course." Isabelle nodded, her round eyes wide. "How else are we to decide whom to wed? I keep a chart in my journal—or I did before I misplaced it recently. I got the idea from a chart of horses Victoria kept hidden under her bed. If that much thought is put into which horse to wager upon, we should put at least that much effort into our husbands, shouldn't we?"

"You're very wise. You know that, don't you?" Evangeline asked, knowing Isabelle was often considered the whimsical and even naive one in her family.

"Shhh, you'll destroy my carefree image," Isabelle said with a grin. "Now, if you'll excuse me, this amount of thought has me in need of sustenance. I think I saw cakes in the next room...and Mr. Brice was walking in that direction only a minute ago."

"Enjoy the cakes." Evangeline lowered her voice to add, "And the view of Mr. Brice."

"Enjoy *your* view in my absence," Isabelle called back as she walked away.

If Evangeline wasn't already blushing, she certainly would be doing so now with everyone nearby attempting to understand Isabelle's meaning.

"The moldings in this room are quite lovely," she said to an older lady who was studying her.

"I suppose," the woman returned, her wrinkles growing deeper as her brows drew together in confusion. "After your discussion of the gentlemen, I hardly noticed."

"Excuse me," Evangeline said as she fled the spot.

She wasn't certain what her mother would have

her do after being caught discussing gentlemen's physical attributes at a ball, but Isabelle had told her to follow her heart. And right now, her heart was telling her to run.

She moved toward the door with lightning speed. Ash was moving in that direction as well. She shouldn't have noticed him. *Your eyes always follow instructions from your heart. What do you see?* It mattered little what she saw. It was, however, quite disturbing that she could find Ash in a crowd so easily. He would leave again. But her untrustworthy heart would only follow after.

The crush of guests was tighter by the door that led to the hall, and she darted this way and that to escape her actions of the past half hour. Discussing gentlemen's private parts—what had she been thinking? But as she pushed through the throng of people, she knew that wasn't all she was running from.

She found Ash again, trapped in a passing conversation with a gentleman not ten paces away, yet still watching her.

Pushing forward toward the hall, she bounced off a gentleman who had stepped into her path. She really needed to pay better attention to where she was walking.

"Apologies, Lady Evangeline." Lord Winfield extended his arm to her. "I was coming to fetch you for our dance."

With one last glance at Ash, she laid her hand on Winfield's arm and allowed him to lead her onto the floor. "I was hoping to see you."

Ash gave Stapleton a questioning glance and turned the unopened letter he'd been given over in his hands several times. Only one person he knew wrote such scrunched yet precise letters, as if a great weight was pressing down on every line of text. He'd seen that writing many times as a boy, but he had no desire to see it now.

Ash had been in London for several weeks now. Things *were* taking longer than expected with Rightworth, but had he stayed so long in one place as to allow this to happen? He flipped the letter around in his hand again and stared at the writing once more. "Clearly I've stayed here too long already," he muttered.

"We could leave," Stapleton offered.

"No."

Questions of how his brother had found his location so quickly swam in Ash's head. And there was no way to discover the answers unless he read the blasted letter. Ripping the letter open, he held it up to the light of a nearby candle.

Dear Ashley,

I hope this letter finds you. I received an interesting note from a lady in London today. I'm told one of my relations is heartsick for news of home. She asked for a listing of all known family relations so that she might sew some sort of reminder of the land longed for and give it as a gift. You can imagine my surprise to learn this, since I only have one family member who remains unaccounted for, and he has never shown an interest in his home, marriage-minded ladies, or needlework.

*I know why you're in London, Brother. You
needn't do this. It is true that Lord Rightworth took
all Father possessed in repayment of that debt, but it
was his right to do so. No one killed our father, Ashley. Father ended his own life. Nothing you do while
there in London will make things right for our family.
Isle of Man has changed, especially since I gained our
cousin's title two years past. We have no need for you
to take funds from a powerful man in London for our
survival. Please, reconsider your actions…*

Ash didn't finish reading the words scrawled in
ink before him. He balled up the letter in his hand
instead, his knuckles turning white around the paper.
Ashley—only three people had the nerve to call him
that, and he didn't want to see any of them just now.
He exhaled a harsh breath. Brennen knew his whereabouts. The sharp corners of crushed paper pressed
into his palm as he squeezed it even tighter. How had
he been so foolish as to look into Evie's eyes and tell
her his given name?

He threw the ball of paper across the room. It hit
the wall with a disappointing tap and rolled under
the bed as he turned, walking to the fireplace at the
opposite end of the room. He'd never before lost his
sense of commitment to his work, his sense of when
to speak and when to listen.

It was Evie. Or rather, the effect she had on him.
He lost all sense when she was around. And now, with
her assistance and clearly that of Stapleton as well, his
brother knew where he slept at night. Damn. By now,
the lot of his brothers would know his whereabouts.

The walls of his bedchamber seemed to be closing in around him. They would try to stop him. The number of days he had remaining in London had, in an instant, been cut in half.

"That look right there is why I didn't want to give it to you," Stapleton said, still lingering near the door as if unsure whether to stay or leave.

"How did his man find you, Stapleton?" Ash asked through clenched teeth. He knew how his brother had learned he was in London—that blame was clearly on Evie's shoulders. That didn't explain how he'd had the note delivered to Stapleton in the mews behind headquarters. Ash had told no one about this place, because that was nearly the Spares' only rule.

Stapleton didn't answer, but only winced as he ran a hand over the back of his neck. It was a look Ash knew too well after years of living with the man.

"Lady Evangeline is to blame for telling him I'm in town." Ash moved back across the room and kicked the door closed so they wouldn't be heard in the hall. "But Stapleton, he had this letter delivered to you— here at headquarters. How exactly did my brother know where to find me?"

Stapleton hesitated for only a second before he admitted the truth. "You know that maid I mentioned from the kitchens back home?"

"You told one of the maids?" Had he learned nothing from his years with Ash?

Stapleton shifted on his feet and stared at the floor. "I only mentioned that we might be back on the isle soon, once we're finished with things here. She's always been sweet on me, and I thought…"

Ash exhaled a harsh breath and turned away from the man before he did something he would regret. "You let my brothers know where I am so that you could have a woman waiting for you when you return?"

"Of course it sounds bad when you say it like that," Stapleton muttered. "You already said that lady of yours told him you were in London. Surely after that, my actions—"

"I will deal with that bit of misfortune later," Ash cut in as he turned back to face Stapleton. "She only said I was in town. You led my brother's footman to our doorstep." Ash ran a hand through his hair in exasperation. "Do you know what trouble that could have caused if someone like St. James had heard of it?"

"I meant no harm."

"I know you didn't, but…" Ash let out a stream of curses that in no way relieved his distress.

"We can leave, return here some other time," Stapleton offered. "There are plenty of towns in Scotland we haven't visited."

"No," Ash said a bit too quickly. "We stay."

"Truly? I think this job is getting to you. Or maybe it's that lady you've been spending time with."

"She has nothing to do with this." But Ash knew Evie had complicated his thoughts on almost every subject since he'd seen her that night in the Dillsworth library.

"Listen, Mr. Claughbane, I've known you nearly all my life. My father was your father's valet. I've served you since you left the Isle."

"Then you should know why I can't leave," Ash returned.

"Aye. I do. But taking from Lord Rightworth

won't bring back your father," Stapleton said, echoing Ash's brother's words.

"It will return to my family what is rightfully theirs. You've always known my intentions for all of this." Ash raised his arms to encompass the entirety of their lives before letting them fall back to his sides. "We've had an adventure and it's lined both our pockets quite well, but this job, Rightworth, has always been my focus. You know that. You've always known that. Don't tell me now that we're here, you're siding with my brothers."

Over the years Ash had forgotten that Stapleton had once been a footman in his family's home. Before he'd left with Ash that night, he'd had a young lifetime of loyalty to the Claughbane family. It was a fact Ash would have done well to remember.

"I made a promise seven years ago to keep you from harm," Stapleton said without apology, for once looking the part of footman and not the swindler's assistant he'd become.

Ash moved to the bedpost and leaned a hip against it, crossing his arms over his chest. "I made a promise to my mother as she withered away into dust and heartbreak that I would aid this family. That is all I have ever tried to do."

"Your wealth in this game almost exceeds what your father lost. Do you need Rightworth's coin as well? We could walk away. Your brother says so in his letter—you don't need to go through with this scheme. Things on the isle have changed…"

"I should have known you broke the seal and read the letter for yourself. You always did have your ear to the door when you were a footman."

Stapleton grinned. "A quality you've always admired."

"Only when you use it to my gain," Ash corrected. "You read that drivel from my brother and let him get to you."

"He was convincing."

"That's enough to change your mind?" Ash pointed to the spot where the letter had landed, shadowed by the edge of the bed. "You shouldn't have written to the damn maid, Stapleton."

"You would understand if you'd seen her in recent years. You weren't with me when I paid that visit last fall." The man shook the wistful look from his eyes and had the grace to appear apologetic for what he'd done.

"If you wish to return home, then go." Ash had the Spares to assist him, he supposed, although he constantly struggled with involving them. He worked alone with Stapleton at his side, and always had. But he wouldn't force anyone to stay where they had no wish to be.

"I don't wish it. I was only…" He trailed off with a sigh. "Haven't you given a thought to what we'll do with ourselves after this job is over?"

It was true that he'd always dreamed of the next village, the next scheme. But the road he'd traveled had been leading him here. Beyond this job, beyond Rightworth, was further than he'd ever considered before. It was due to the high expectation of his work here in London—that was all. To dwell on anything beyond this scheme would be a complication, not to mention break his two rules: he couldn't stay, and he couldn't become attached to anyone.

Ash put that last rule out of his mind and looked back at Stapleton. "We'll do the same as we always do."

"Move to the next town over and attempt it all again?"

"No, make the decision after we leave." This was the perfect plan. This way Ash didn't have to consider his life beyond London. He tossed out a casual grin. "Only this time, we're going inside when an inn smells of sausages. I've been dreaming of breakfast meats ever since we left that place in Berkshire."

"You'll walk away from this Lady Evangeline?" Stapleton asked, eyeing him in a way that made Ash aware of just how much time they'd spent together over the years.

"I have to, don't I?" he said, his voice sounding flat and lifeless even to his own ears. "She's Rightworth's daughter."

"Suppose so," his man replied, but the sentiment didn't seem to reach his eyes.

"I've only called on her to get close to Rightworth," Ash said with confidence even as the lie caused him to flinch inwardly.

"As you've done before," Stapleton agreed.

"Precisely. Just like every time before. And I'll leave just like every time before." But thinking of it made him slightly ill. The truth was, Evie wasn't like every other lady in every other town. She was special. Perhaps he did need to keep her distracted to protect his identity from her father. And perhaps courting her was a good excuse to see Rightworth and keep the man interested in investing in Crosby Steam Works. But his plan allowed him to see a great deal of Evie at the same time. And that desire was *not* just like every time before—not in the least.

"Apologies for opening the door for your brothers to intrude on things here. I need to go see to the horses...and see if I can get back into the card game that I left to come find you." He flashed a smile, but the look slipped into thoughtful concern as he regarded Ash. "Just so you know, this is the first time I've ever heard you talk about leaving as if it's a chore and not a pleasure. You might want to think on that." He walked out before Ash could reply—a damn trick Ash had taught him.

Ash rolled his eyes and went to the bed to pick up the letter he'd thrown across the room. Dropping into the chair in the corner, he unfolded the paper from the wad he'd formed and ironed it flat on the top of his thigh.

He read it three times through before rising to his feet. He should be concerned about his oldest brother and self-appointed patriarch of the family. Would Brennen make waves for Ash here in town? It was possible, but his family was so far removed from city life that it wasn't likely. As long as Brennen stayed on the island, all would be fine. Evie, on the other hand, had the potential for making more waves than he could navigate.

She wanted to make a piece of needlepoint about his family, did she? She should make a tapestry that covered an entire wall—his family history was quite the sordid tale. He tossed the letter into the fire, watching it shrink into black as it burned, taking the truth with it.

How long could he keep Evie from going to her father with what she knew of him? Another week?

Two if he was careful. Now that she knew his full name, it was just a matter of time. Or perhaps if she only knew a portion of the truth, he could gain her trust and keep her in his life a bit longer.

"You're breaking your own rules, Ash Claughbane," he murmured into the flames as a reluctant smile spread across his face. Rules were meant to be bent until they lay warped on the ground behind him. And he knew exactly who he wanted to coax into bending a few rules with him.

Nine

"I HEAR YOU WRITE A LOVELY LETTER. QUITE THE penmanship," Ash accused in lieu of a greeting as he strode across the empty parlor toward Evie early the next morning.

He'd been up half the night considering why he didn't want another secret added to the pile between them, and he still didn't know what to make of it. Until recently his life had been devoted to the prospect of revenge...and it was still, wasn't it? It needed to be. He'd made a promise to his dying mother, and that wasn't something that should be easily forgotten.

Certainly he'd had an enjoyable time on the road—the freedom, the thrill of the sale, and the fresh start of a new town where no one knew him. But revenge on Rightworth had always been his driving force. Now, after years of work, he was closer than he'd ever been before to his goal.

But then there was Evie, the lady he should be using to have his revenge on her father.

Instead, every day he looked forward to Evie's company, even glimpses of her at a ball. Any thrill he gained from his life as a con man paled in comparison to how his heart raced when he was near her. And for the first time, he wasn't looking forward to a fresh start where no one knew him.

Instead, he wanted Evie to know him further. He wanted to spread the ugly truth of his life out on the table for her to examine, and then perhaps she would do the same for him. He had to pull himself together. A small serving of the truth—that was all he could offer her now. He must remember that. But when he saw her look up from her embroidery and meet his gaze here in the parlor, all of his complicated thoughts of last night faded away.

"The letter! I found your family, then?" Evie exclaimed as she stood from her usual seat in the front parlor in front of the windows, not looking ashamed by her correspondence in the least.

"Shhh! Do you mind?" He spun on his heel to see if anyone was about, but thankfully found the hall behind him empty other than the young maid who was slipping back to her usual corner of the room. She already knew far too many of their secrets, but Evie seemed to trust the girl. He prowled closer, reaching Evie in only a few strides.

"Claughbane… That's your true name? Ash Claughbane?" she asked in just above a whisper.

"I'm Crosby to everyone in London, and I would like to keep it as such," he murmured in a low voice with a finger to his lips.

"Apologies." Without warning, she hit him hard on the arm with her small fist.

"Ouch!" He drew back from her reach. "What the devil was that for?"

"I'm sure I have no idea, Lord Barnish. I mean, Lord Crosby." She shot him a narrow-eyed glare that might have melted flesh if her rosy cheeks and pouty lips hadn't made the look more adorable than frightening.

He'd longed to be honest with her. He could tell her all—it's what he wanted. But she wouldn't easily dismiss what he was doing to her father, her family. Telling her everything would seal his own fate. However, sometimes schemes had to change and adapt. He would simply have to find a balance between complete honesty and what he was accustomed to—a life of lies.

"Very well, I suppose I deserve your beatings," he finally said with a grin, his gaze still on her lips. She was perhaps more beautiful today than she'd been in his thoughts last night, if that was possible. "If you must hit me, I'm at least grateful that this time you avoided my face," he added, intending to tease her over her continuing abuse. Even as he spoke, his smile slipped away and the air around them grew warm. The memory of their kiss in the servants' hall surrounded them as if he'd described every second of it in great detail.

Clearly, she was thinking the same, because a silence fell between them and her gaze dropped to his mouth. If he kissed her again, would she hit him? Would the young maid finally sound the alarm? Kissing Evie again would be worth the risk. It might be too soon to not get slapped again, but he was never one to shy from a challenge. He shifted forward a fraction, closing the gap between them.

"My lord," a footman muttered from the open

door, making Evie jump beyond his reach and the maid leap to her feet.

"Pardon my interruption," the man said, with eyebrows creeping toward his receding hairline. "Your phaeton seems to be blocking the street."

The blasted phaeton. And Brice had said it would be a good idea to bring the contraption. "Ladies like being seen in the park," he'd suggested. Idiot. He'd cost Ash that moment with Evie and what it could have promised. Ash nodded his thanks to the footman nonetheless as the man turned to leave the parlor.

"You drove a phaeton here?" Evie asked, looking around him and out the front window. "A phaeton that makes red apples look dull?"

"Yes, it's quite red. I borrowed it from my friend, Mr. Brice," he muttered, as he tried to force the bitter thoughts from his head. He could still have time with Evie today. "I thought you might like to enjoy the weather. I know you're a supporter of such things."

"I talk of the weather. Experiencing it is another matter altogether." There was a sadness about her expression as she spoke in the soft voice she always seemed to use when others were about. "I might freckle in Mr. Brice's conveyance."

Ash paused, watching her and trying to understand her hesitation. "This means you're not willing to take a ride in the park with me? Due to the threat of sunshine."

"I'm told it's perilous," she replied, but the strain around her eyes seemed to diminish a fraction.

"There's only one way to know for certain." He extended his arm to her and waited. Would she come with him? A thrill of uncertainty sent a chill down his spine.

Evie turned and looked at the young maid in the corner. "Jane?"

"Go. I'll say you're in your bedchamber with a headache if need be," the maid replied with an encouraging smile. "You have no social engagement until this afternoon."

"If you're certain," Evie said before turning back to him. "But we must hurry before anyone notices I've gone. If rides in open carriages at a fashionable hour are frowned upon, I certainly don't want to have to explain this." She took his arm and let him lead her back to the hall. Her eyes darted about in search of some threat he couldn't see.

What was she afraid of? He'd only wanted to speak with her for a few minutes without interruption, and this seemed the best tactic. At least if his friends in the Spare Heirs could be believed. "Am I causing you trouble?"

"Always." She looked up at him with a tentative smile. "I've heard Mr. Brice's phaeton is quite the conveyance."

"You know of it?"

"I know of the man who owns it," she corrected.

"How do you know Brice?" Ash asked with an unexpected pang of jealousy.

"I know someone who speaks of little else," she said, taking a shawl from her faithful maid who'd followed them into the hall. "He drives a bright-red phaeton, wears only the best waistcoats, and apparently is quite the dancer."

"Ah, I should warn the poor man," Ash replied,

watching a wordless exchange between Evie and her maid that ended with the woman giving her a nod of encouragement.

"He should be so fortunate." Evie stuffed a hat onto her head and turned toward him. "I didn't realize you were friends with him."

"We're members of the same club," Ash said, distracted by the strain on Evie's face as she shot one last look at her maid.

The maid mouthed "I won't tell," and gave Evie another nod.

"Oh? Which one is that?" Evie asked.

Which what? He blinked, realizing she was asking about the Spares—one of the many topics he couldn't discuss with her. Ash was spared having to find an answer by the butler's murmured "My lord," as he opened the door for them to leave.

They were almost to the garden gate when he noticed she was watching him. "Is something wrong?"

She shook her head. "My lord... You aren't a lord of anything, Ash."

"That is true," he admitted, holding the gate open for her.

"You don't seem troubled by the distinction."

"I'm attempting honesty. It's a rare occurrence for me. One would think you might appreciate it a bit more." He stepped close to her, closing his hands around her small waist. He lifted her from the ground and into the high perch of the phaeton. It hardly seemed like a private place for a conversation, but Brice had insisted it was. Ash shrugged and moved to the opposite side, taking the reins from Stapleton with a nod.

Stapleton gave him a knowing grin when Ash told him to take a walk until they returned. Ash knew he would hear about it later, but for now he would be alone with Evie. Climbing onto the seat beside her, Ash waited until they were well out of view from her home before he shifted closer to her and relaxed a bit for the drive.

"You have family on the Isle of Man," she said, peering over at him as if he were a riddle in great need of solving. "A brother?"

"Several, actually," he corrected. He shouldn't provide her with information that could lead to his downfall if she turned him over to her father, but that bridge had been crossed some time ago, hadn't it? Or was it merely the faint, flowered scent of her as she sat beside him that forced him to speak? Whatever the reason, his normally guarded words tumbled from his mouth with her, reeking of truth. He sighed.

"Several. Truly?"

"I'm the youngest of four."

She studied him, nodding as if he indeed looked like the young, reckless little brother his family claimed he was. He suppressed an irritated growl and guided the horses around a corner into the park. Then he glanced back to her, almost amused that she was still watching him in an attempt to assemble the pieces of his life.

"And they live on the Isle of Man—which you claim as home," she mused.

Was that home? He had no home any longer. It had been emptied of all memories and sold years ago. A shell of a building didn't equate to a home. "I haven't been back there in quite some time."

"Why are you in London? It's not to enjoy the season like so many other gentlemen, is it? Is it even business, as you claimed?" she finally asked, dancing terribly close to the central truth that stood like a wall between them.

"What, no lengthy commentary on the state of the weather today?" he asked, glancing up into the sunlight that slipped through the leaves of the trees overhead.

"You use a false name. You spend your spare time ingratiating yourself with the gentlemen in town. You stole a document from poor Lord Dillsworth, and then there was the way you slipped away last year."

"Ash Claughbane truly is my name," he said, sounding rather lame in the face of those damning facts.

"Yes," she agreed. "Crosby, however, is not."

Damn. This was normally the point at which he would either redirect the conversation to safer territory or escape town, regroup, and try again in the next town down the road. Yet, here when it mattered most, he was considering other options, even though he knew how horribly this conversation could end. What would happen if he told her? He could hardly tell her everything, but perhaps a bit of it.

What was wrong with him? It was rule two of only two. Could he not even follow his own regulations? But then, he couldn't stop himself. Like powerful waves pulling him into uncharted waters, he couldn't fight against the current with her.

"If you would rather discuss the clouds in the sky…"

"God, no." He chuckled and sank back a fraction on the seat. "I am originally from the Isle of Man. As I said, I'm the youngest of four brothers, though

I haven't returned home in years. I've made my own path since my school days."

"You would have to, as the youngest boy in the family."

"Hmmm," he said, neither agreeing nor disagreeing. He needn't mention his oldest brother's recent acquisition of a title, did he? It didn't affect Ash's life, although from the sound of that letter he'd received, it had made a difference on the island.

"What does one do as the youngest of four?"

"I am in the business of sales. At the moment I'm gathering investments in personal steam machines." He guided them onto a more secluded path. There was no way of knowing where it led, much like their time together. That seemed fitting. All he knew was that Evie sat tucked close beside him and no one was able to interrupt their conversation.

"And before this moment?"

"It depends on the town and the people—what they need, what I have, what they desire." He glanced at her, the word *desire* filling the air between them.

She pulled her gaze away from his with a jerk of her head and stared ahead. "And you change what you sell, just like that. From town to town, always moving."

"I do." He wanted to look at her. Having this discussion would be difficult enough with…anyone at all, but especially Evie, without having to steer horses at the same time. He needed to look at her, to see the effect his words were having. Just ahead there was clear ground where the path curved around a grouping of trees. Pulling the horses to a stop, he shifted until he had one arm resting on the back of the seat. His forearm grazed the back of her shoulder, and his legs were stretched closer to hers as he searched her face.

She almost moved away to keep a proper distance between them. He watched as she glanced down at the crossed ankles of his boots that brushed against the bottom of her dress. He'd been so focused on weaving the vehicle down the path that only now did he notice how she sat impossibly straight and maintained a tight grip on the seat on either side of her legs. Was she frightened of their height, being alone in the park with him, or the turn of topics between them? He didn't know, but he scooped up the hand that clenched the seat between them in an attempt to push the troubled thoughts from her mind.

She stifled a small gasp and looked down at their joined hands. Would she pull away? For a second he held his breath, as if in the presence of a wild animal that might run from him. But when she tangled her fingers with his and looked up at him, she appeared more thoughtful than afraid. Part of him was glad his attempt at reassurance had succeeded, while the other part wondered what the blazes he was about with this lady.

"Gypsies who lived in much the same way as you do once stopped at the border of our estate. They told fortunes and gave out tonics said to heal any disease— for a price. Is that what you do?"

And there it was standing before him—truth. Lost in the depths of her eyes, he stammered, "It's a bit more complicated than that. I…"

"Ash, I speak of only the weather and fashion to everyone I know. Your secrets are safe here."

"That is what you say now," he said, knowing everything would change between them soon. For the first time ever, he dreaded the day that he would collect his reward and take his leave. "What about when it comes time for me to leave?"

"I'll point out how positively leafy I find a tree while you walk away."

"Why?" She shouldn't promise to protect him. She wouldn't if she knew the full story.

"Because I want to know the truth." She twisted slightly in her seat and brought her other hand to his, capturing his palm between hers.

"No." He shook his head, trying to regain his good sense. That was pointless while he was in her company, but he attempted it nonetheless. "Why would you assist me when I leave?"

"Because leaving is what you want," she said with resignation negated by the fact that she clung to his hand as if he were the last ship in the harbor.

"Do *you* wish me to leave?"

The moment slowed between them like cold honey clinging to a spoon. Neither of them was quick to speak, neither quick to look away. She clearly lacked the preparation required to answer.

He gave her a warm smile, letting her know there was no need for words. He wouldn't push her. Not yet, anyway. The more he knew of her, the more he understood that there was more truth in what she left unspoken than in what she said. She spoke through the look in her eye, the clinging of her hand. It was nuance, and he examined every piece of it. What had frightened her to make her so fearful of expressing her thoughts? He would peel away her layers until she was laid bare before him, but today that meant revealing more of himself than he cared to admit. It was a risk—but one he couldn't walk away from.

"How did you begin in this particular field of study?"

"Field of study?" He laughed, breaking the tension between them. "It began in school, I suppose. When I left home, I was able to become someone else. For the first time, I wasn't irresponsible Ash, youngest of four. I was whoever I chose to be—the benefit of calling an island home, I suppose. Off the island, no one knew me or my family. I could begin anew, be anyone. That was when I discovered that people—people other than you—believe what they're told."

"What do you tell people other than me?"

"You already know, Evie." His gaze dropped to where the end of one ribbon from her hat caught in the breeze that had picked up in the past few minutes. The length of shining blue satin tickled the exposed skin along the top of her shoulder. Lifting the ribbon between his fingers as he spoke, he moved it away from her neck. Then, because he wasn't one to resist temptation, he traced the path that the ribbon had taken, the backs of his fingers brushing across her pale skin. "I haven't been honest with you either, yet somehow you guessed the truth."

"That is true," she said, not shying from his touch. "I believe you may need to hone your skills."

"This has been my life for seven years, and you think *now* my skills need work?" he asked, his fingers continuing to follow the line of the back of her neck down to the ridge of her shoulder. She didn't flinch under his question or his touch. In fact, the only sign that he was having any effect on her was the hold she now had on his other hand. He was sure she didn't realize that she was caressing his fingers and gazing into his eyes as she did so.

"You should consider improvements. I wasn't taken in by you for a moment, *Lord Crosby*."

"Not even for a moment?" He grinned. "What about last year? What of the servants' hall? I thought I was quite compelling on that occasion."

"Those are different skills entirely." She seemed to become aware of how she was holding on to him because she made to pull away—at least until he tightened his grip and held her still. How could she tease him about kisses while maintaining such a prim facade?

"A shame. I think I would prefer honing *those* skills with your assistance." Right now in broad daylight with every chance of being seen. He wanted her. He couldn't sit here, allowed to touch her shoulder, her neck, even that tendril of hair that escaped her hat, and not want to feel her lips against his. He wanted to touch every part of her, to taste her, and discover every secret she held beneath that veil of perfect ladyship.

"I-I don't think… That won't be necessary," she stammered, yet she didn't move away.

"Later, then," he promised, more to himself than to her.

She looked down, focusing on some benign point on his shirt as she spoke. "I'm sure you practice such things in every darkened hall across England. I was simply the lady present that night."

Did she think that was true? All right, perhaps there was a hint of truth in it. Very well, a great deal of truth. But that had been before he knew her, before… He couldn't put a finger on what had changed, but it had. She was different. "You were *not* simply the lady present." He moved to lift her chin with a knuckle until she was looking at him again. "You're Evangeline… Evie," he added.

"I suppose the fact that you remember my name now is something to be pleased over," she murmured, still looking troubled.

He'd pushed too far. With others he could always judge that line and where he stood in relation to it, but not with her. And now she was pulling away from him. He dropped his hand to the seat behind them. "I did forget your name, Evie. I admit that much, and I am sorry for it. I did not, however, forget you." He remembered everything about her. Everything, it seemed, but the one detail that mattered.

She cleared her throat and glanced away, allowing the subject to drop with a curt nod of her head. When she turned back, all emotion had been stripped from her face. Whether she'd forgiven him or didn't wish to discuss it further wasn't clear, but everything about her stated that they were to move on. "Even with the pleasant change from your home, why choose to be a…"

He blinked at the sudden change of subject for a second before finishing her question for her. "Salesman? …Swindler?"

"I was searching for kinder terminology, but yes. Surely there were other professions that appealed to you."

No other profession would gain back what his family had lost, not to mention that no other would fit his temperament so well. It had been a natural decision. But did it still fit his temperament? He'd never stopped to ask the questions Evie was now posing. He shot a glance at the horses, which were growing restless beneath their harnesses. The reins still lay wrapped around the edge of the phaeton as the horses shifted and pawed the ground. He should retrieve the reins and continue on, but he remained still, not wanting to leave just yet.

Looking back at her, he said, "It suits my needs… and it simply came about. Have you ever had something come to you so easily that you didn't think about the decisions that led you there?"

"Yes, once. Or I suppose twice, now." Her gaze dropped to his lips for a second before she blushed and looked away.

He kept quiet, sensing that he was about to cross the line again. He didn't want her to pull away just now.

"Younger siblings do have options beyond a life of crime, you know," she said after a moment.

"Ha!" he let out, thinking of the large headquarters across town filled with other gentlemen just like him, younger siblings who had come together for survival in society.

"You could have joined the ranks of the military," she suggested. "Their uniforms are quite smart. A life lived to the beat of the drum and all."

"Do you know how early they must rise in the morning?" he asked, drawing back in shock.

"You live a life of crime so that you needn't rise early?"

"Of course. Isn't that how everyone makes life decisions? Don't enjoy rising early? Life in the military or life as a baker, for that matter, are off the table." He shrugged and gave her an unrepentant grin. He had other reasons for choosing his path—his promise to his mother, for one—but he'd never considered the military as an option. His choices certainly ran deeper than when he would be forced to rise in the morning, but regrettably not by a large margin, he was beginning to realize.

"And the pay in the military is not vast," he added in an attempt to sound more reasonable. "I don't earn a king's ransom, but I do well enough to enjoy a certain style of life. I was brought up with an appreciation for certain niceties. Niceties not often found on the field of battle."

"Very well. Not the military, then. What of the vicarage? Dedicate your life to serving others and doing the Lord's work?"

He started laughing. He hadn't an answer. Ash—a vicar. Another round of laughter shook his body and brought tears to the corners of his eyes.

"I didn't find the notion nearly that amusing," she grumbled, but a hint of a smile threatened to show on her face.

He continued to laugh for moment before wiping at his eyes with the back of his hand. "A vicar," he muttered.

"I suppose a swindler is the only option for you, then." She shook her head in clear exasperation.

"I don't take advantage of people, if that's what you're imagining. I find people with excess means, people who have wealth and are doing no good with it...those who don't deserve it. And even so, I don't leave town with all they have. I couldn't live with myself if I did that to an unsuspecting gentleman," he said in all honesty. That's what her father had done, and Ash would not rob from another family in the same fashion.

Another family other than her own. But he wasn't willing to think about that now. Not with Evie here.

"Only those who have earned the loss of their funds through their misdeeds? There are quite a few of *those* people in society, aren't there?"

"I'm good at it, Evie. It's simply who I am," he tried to explain.

"I disagree." Her words were quiet as she spoke in the small, frail voice she used when others were about. "You are capable of much more."

He looked into her eyes, hanging on to the belief in him that resided there. It was odd that such strength could come from such softly spoken words. Was he capable of more? For now, he only wanted to be capable of the task before him. He would think about *more* in a few weeks, once he was on the road out of town. "Perhaps," he finally muttered. This was to be his largest scheme. He needed to be capable of more than he had been in the past, even if he knew that wasn't what she'd meant.

"You're courting me as cover for your plots, aren't you?"

Her question was sharper than the slap to his face had been that night at the ball. He didn't know what the devil he was doing with her, but it certainly wasn't helping his plots—or his plight, for that matter. "It's never been my intention to use you, Evie."

"If you are in such a line of work, what dealings do you have with my father?"

There it was—the question he'd been dreading. "That's business of another sort."

"Do you have another sort?" she asked, concern filling her eyes.

"Evie, I've been disgustingly honest with you. The thought of it makes me a bit ill."

"And honesty isn't a requirement for rides in the park. This isn't conversation over tea, after all," she said, but not with the same light tone she would have used only a few minutes ago. She directed her gaze forward down the path. "It was wrong of me to ask. Of course you aren't taking advantage of my father. You wouldn't be here with me if that were true. It was a silly question. I shouldn't suggest such things."

He wrapped her hand within his and squeezed it. If he stayed he would eventually have to tell her the truth. He inhaled a sharp breath at the ease with which staying had crept into his thoughts. He didn't stay— ever. He couldn't, could he?

"Ash, are you courting me in truth?"

"I have no idea what I'm doing." Courting Evie was by far the worst idea he'd ever had, and yet he couldn't walk away. Not yet.

"Do gentlemen like you often accidentally court ladies without a purpose in mind?"

"It would seem so," he grated out.

"Not even a purpose that involves business with my father?" she clarified. The intent look on her face almost bordered on haunted.

He'd been honest with her, more so than he had

been with anyone perhaps ever. Therefore, it pained him to do what he must. He gathered the reins, turned to her with a kind smile, and lied. "Of course not."

∽

St. James,

Although my last report was positive in nature, I have encountered a delay. The gearing necessary for the machine we discussed is of a nonstandard size and must be fabricated. I found a blacksmith in Leeds…

Ash looked up from the paper in his hand, but as usual, St. James's face revealed no information. "Gearing for what machine? What is this about? Oliver Dean—is that who drew the diagrams?" he asked, handing the letter back to the man and shifting the large rolled-up diagrams in his arms.

St. James had stopped Ash in the main hall of headquarters. His meeting with Lord Rightworth was in less than an hour, and it wouldn't be wise to make the man wait, let alone for a letter Ash didn't fully understand. But it must be of some importance for the leader of the Spare Heirs to share it with him because St. James wasn't prone to sharing anything at all.

"He's referring to your steam machine, Crosby."

"My… Do I need to further explain to you what I do, St. James? There isn't a real steam machine. I collect investors; we split up the profits—"

"I know how the business works," St. James grumbled as he pulled Ash to the side to allow a group of gentlemen to pass. "Wouldn't it appear a more legitimate operation for gentlemen to invest their money in if you had a prototype? I asked Dean for the diagrams, but then he mentioned a model, turning gears and all."

"Do we need turning gears?"

"It's a far sight better than you waving your hand over a cup of steaming tea for the effect of it."

"I thought it rather clever," Ash said.

"It wasn't."

"Very well. At any rate, I have the diagrams now."

"Nevertheless, I'm going to have Dean continue his work."

"Until then, this will do," Ash said, holding up the roll of paper in his hand.

"You memorized the terminology?" St. James asked, nodding toward the diagrams.

"Along with Dillsworth's financial investments in the past year. I've spent every night since I arrived in town poring over the document I retrieved from his library."

"Anything of use?"

"He sold his interest in corn in the last year and invested in two different factories."

"His investment in the factories was in the *London Chronicle*," St. James pointed out. "I hope you have more information than that for your trouble."

"Did the *Chronicle* mention how heavily invested he is in iron and tramways over on the continent? It's nearly his entire fortune." Ash whispered the last bit out of respect to Brice, who was about somewhere in headquarters. They were discussing the man's family finances after all.

"No, it didn't," St. James said.

"I plan to use that to point to steam and industry being the future. If Dillsworth is out of farming, others will want to be as well. It's 1817, mate. If we can cart goods about the continent on iron rails, we can have steam for every home."

"Is that the new line?"

"Did you like it?"

St. James shrugged. "It's improving…"

"Glad to hear it. I'm off to meet with Rightworth."

"Not to call on his daughter?" St. James asked with one brow raised in question.

"No." *Not today*, Ash finished to himself.

"Be careful there, Crosby," St. James warned as he turned.

"This job is why I'm here. You have no need to worry on my account." Ash watched the head of the secretive club walk away before he moved toward the door. St. James had every reason to worry on Ash's account. Ash was worried on his own account. He'd spent the better part of last night and this morning thinking about his ride with Evie in the park. But now was not the time to dwell on the man's daughter.

He took a breath, focusing on the plans in his hands and the words he'd rehearsed. Tomorrow he would seek out Evie. Today…today was spoken for.

❧

"Evangeline?" She heard her mother call from somewhere in the house beyond the door to the small receiving parlor.

Evangeline hated the way her mother said her

name. From the woman's lips, her name sounded like a weapon, all sharp edges and piercing points. Evangeline didn't wish to spend the remainder of the afternoon reviewing proper conduct and the many ways she fell short of perfection, but she also couldn't hide in this parlor forever. Or could she? She pressed herself against the window frame in an attempt to blend into the draperies, allowing the sun to warm her skin for one more stolen moment before stepping back with a sigh. It was pointless. No one could hide from that woman, especially not Evangeline.

"Evaaaaan-geliiiiine!" Her mother's voice grew shriller the longer she was left alone in her search of the house.

With a sigh, she moved away from the sunny window where she'd spent a precious few minutes enjoying the view of the day on the other side of the glass. She should know better. There was no place for the sun in her life; she could only speak eloquently of it. Her mother's footsteps grew louder, and Evangeline scurried across the room to grab her abandoned embroidery from the one chair that sat in a shadowed corner far from the touch of sunlight. Falling into the chair, she arranged a pleasant look on her face just as the door was flung open.

"Good afternoon, Mother."

"Did you not hear me?" Lady Rightworth asked with accusation in her voice as she stepped into the room.

"Apologies. I must have been absorbed in my needlework. Did you call for me?"

"Never mind that." Her mother marched into the room. Blinking into the bright sunlight for only a second, she went straight to the closest window and slung the heavy brocade fabric over the opening. The room dimmed in an instant and her mother turned to stalk across it. "The moment you finished with your dance instructor, you were to come and see me, Evangeline. We have much to prepare for this afternoon. I daresay you aren't giving this season your full effort. Now, on your feet."

"I am trying, Mother," Evangeline stated as she laid her embroidery aside and stood.

"Yet your attempt is disappointing to me." Her mother stepped closer, examining her. "You don't wish to disappoint me, do you?"

"Of course not."

Lady Rightworth pursed her lips and looked closer at Evangeline's day dress. "A smaller waist."

"Pardon?"

"We must increase your appeal to the gentlemen this season," her mother explained. "I had a nice chat with Lady Smeltings yesterday at that awful garden party. She advised that I purchase stays that lace tighter and have your gowns taken in. Your gowns will still be fashionable, mind you. But tighter nonetheless. She's quite wise, and *her* daughter was betrothed within the first two weeks of her first season."

"That's quite fortunate for her daughter," Evangeline said, wishing the same had been true for her so that she wouldn't be standing here at this moment. Even tighter stays? She was already bound into every gown she wore, none of which were gowns she liked. She never complained about it, but her mother discussing her underthings with a neighboring lady was too much. "You discussed my stays with Lady Smeltings?"

"She only wants to help, darling. You do wish to find a husband, don't you?" her mother asked, squeezing her fingers around Evangeline's ribs.

"Certainly. I only…" *Want to breath while doing so*, she finished to herself.

Her mother's fingers bit harder into Evangeline's sides. "Are you complaining? I already allow you too much liberty as it is."

"No, ma'am. I…"

"Don't stammer, Evangeline. It's so unbecoming." Her mother's hands fell away from Evangeline. "I thought you were fashionable. If a much-admired lady like Lady Smeltings believes that you require more tightly laced stays, then tighter stays you shall have. Anything for you, my special daughter. Maid!" she called with a snap of her long fingers.

"Her name is Jane," Evangeline whispered as she watched the young maid step into the small receiving parlor.

"My daughter requires a tightening of her stays. Take her to her bedchamber and do what you can to cinch in this sack of a day dress. Tomorrow we will buy tighter ones."

Jane nodded in acceptance of her orders, but then her gaze shifted to Evangeline's. The maid's brows drew together as she seemed to read the discomfort Evangeline was feeling despite her efforts to keep it from showing on her face. The young maid took a breath and straightened her spine, a new light turning her eyes bright. Then she shifted her gaze back to the lady of the house. "Am I to do that before she's to go to the park with Lord Winfield in ten minutes' time?"

"Lord Winfield…in ten minutes' time?" Lady Rightworth fairly screamed. "Why was I not informed of this?" She spun back toward Evangeline. "Did you know of this event?"

"I…" Evangeline began, not knowing how to answer. Truthfully, this was the first she'd heard of such, but she could hardly admit that to her mother. Someone must take the blame for the oversight—and it was either Evangeline or Jane. She froze, her gaze going to Jane who still stood just inside the parlor door.

"He left word with Lord Rightworth this morning, my lady," Jane offered with a kind smile, saving her from her mother's wrath—for the moment, anyway.

"Oh. I see." Her mother took a step away as her temper waned. "Well, my husband is a busy man. It must have slipped his lordship's mind. Go on then, Evangeline. Your tighter stays will have to wait until your return." She pierced Evangeline with a glare when she didn't immediately move. "Why you're still standing here with me, I have no idea. Go!"

"Yes, Mother." Evangeline moved toward Jane, not understanding what had just happened. Lord Winfield hadn't seen Father today. Father had been in the library with Ash all morning. Then she saw the maid's mouth twitch with satisfaction in the same fashion that Victoria's did when her cousin was planning some scheme. That was when Evangeline understood. There was no plan to go to the park with Lord Winfield. Jane had lied to save her from her mother for the afternoon. If her mother found out…

"Do wear the new gloves I got for you, and the hat that matches that dress," her mother commanded.

"Mother, those gloves…" *Don't fit at all*, she finished to herself. She should stop this charade. She'd get a brief reprieve from her mother's company, but she would pay the price later. And the price with Mother was always too high.

"Maid, tidy up her hair before she leaves the house." Her mother tugged on Evangeline's dress until it hung in a manner that caused the look of disgust on the woman's face to diminish slightly. "Lord Winfield won't appreciate her arriving in such a state."

"Yes, my lady," Jane said, already pulling pins from her pocket and sticking them in Evangeline's hair.

"Evangeline, you do recall what you're to discuss with Lord Winfield?" her mother asked with narrowed eyes.

"How could I forget proper conversation?"

"Quite easily, it would seem, or you wouldn't require practice every morning. Remember this, no man wants your company for your opinions." Her mother stuffed Evangeline's fingers into the too-small gloves and yanked them up over her palms. "You are to look smart on Lord Winfield's arm and keep quiet. That is all. And you *will* do as I say."

Of course she would do as her mother asked— she always did. This woman whose tight grasp left Evangeline tender and somewhat bruised must be kept happy. But that was the problem. Lady Rightworth would never be happy. She would never be satisfied with Evangeline. Evangeline looked down at her hands, crushed into the gloves her mother had chosen

for her. Her life was comprised of fashionable appearances made to raise her mother's standing in society.
This wasn't for Evangeline's sake. This was about
her mother. Evangeline cared nothing for fashionable
appearances; she only wanted a moment's peace and
the freedom to feel the sun on her face.

Her mother placed a hat on Evangeline's head,
blocking any sun from reaching her skin and causing
her to freckle. "It's all wrong, of course, but I suppose
it will have to do."

"Jane, didn't you say we're to go to the park for this
outing?" Evangeline asked.

"Yes, my lady," Jane said with a sly smile. "And we
don't want to keep his lordship waiting."

"I do so enjoy the outdoors," Evangeline replied.
"The trees provide nice shade in the park. Good day,
Mother." Evangeline walked to the front door and
stepped out into the bright spring afternoon with
Jane at her side. If she was to talk of the weather for
the remainder of her life, the least she could do was
experience it just once.

❧

Evangeline stepped away from her maid on a wave of
whispered encouragements, leaving Jane to sit alone
beneath the shade of the large tree.

Her mother would be furious if she knew Evangeline
hadn't come to the park with Lord Winfield, but
instead had come to enjoy the day beyond the confines of their home. And Evangeline was quite certain
that she would bring the roof down upon her head by
leaving the shade of a tree to walk the sunny paths of

Hyde Park when she spotted Ash from a distance. But Mother and her rules weren't present today.

Her maid's quick thinking had provided Evangeline with a much-needed break from such things even if for an hour or two, and for that she was grateful. Jane, of course, would be gone within the week—kindness never seemed able to survive under the same roof as her mother—but Evangeline accepted the woman's gesture today anyway.

Her heart pounded in her chest. The grass dampened her stockings at her ankles, and the sun beat down on her head with delicious freckle-causing heat, but she only moved faster toward Ash. It had only been a day since she'd seen him last, but it seemed a lifetime. Their carriage ride yesterday had changed everything, and not in the way she'd imagined.

Although logic told her to avoid him now that she knew who Ash Claughbane really was and why he was in town, she was walking faster in his direction. Granted, Evangeline had been told repeatedly that she made terrible decisions, and perhaps this could be counted in their number. But when he'd explained his decision to lead such an unusual life, when outrage should have filled her, she'd found she only felt a sense of rightness, justice even.

Evangeline had seen the evil that lurked beneath the surface of society's most respected members. She'd experienced it firsthand in the case of her own parents, having been ignored by her father and managed by her mother her entire life. Did the two of them not deserve to have her mother's pin money taken to afford Ash a nice meal? Let him take it. Evangeline would never steal from her family, but if Ash chose to do so, she wouldn't stop him. After all of her mother's schemes, it would be rather fitting to see the woman on the receiving end of someone else's plot for a change. As for her father, he would no doubt gain from Evangeline's marriage. What was a bit of money? Even if Ash was swindling her father, she trusted Ash.

She may not have Ash in her life forever, but she certainly wouldn't turn him in for his crimes and cut her time with him short. She was finding that she wanted this too much to force him away. Perhaps she couldn't be trusted to make decisions for her life. But she didn't care about that just now. She neared where he stood in the path and picked up her pace.

He'd dismounted from his horse and was waiting for her on the path. With the reins hanging from his loose grip, the stylish cut of his riding coat, and his hair catching the light breeze, he looked as if he might be posing for a portrait and not simply waiting for her to join him. She suppressed a dreamy sigh that would have made Isabelle proud.

Ash smiled at her as she approached, extending his free arm to her. "I was under the impression that you didn't participate in the weather."

"I took a ride with you just yesterday," she countered as she joined him on the path.

"A ride I had to convince you to indulge in. And now I discover you secretly lounging on a park bench, weather all about you." He nodded toward the spot where her maid still sat, watching her with a smile.

"Was I secretly lounging?"

"Positively dipped in weather," he replied, his

eyes raking over her for a second before returning to her face.

"Can one be dipped in sunshine?" she asked, focusing on the path ahead to cool her thoughts. "I'm sure Mother wouldn't approve, if that's true."

"You look dipped in sunshine."

She glanced down at the yellow of her day dress. "Oh, I suppose I do look a bit…"

"Radiant," he supplied.

Her breath caught. She'd been complimented on her looks before, but somehow his one word carried more sincerity than any other she'd ever heard. Making the mistake of glancing in his direction, she almost stumbled when she saw the corresponding look in his eye. She scrambled mentally to find words to continue their conversation so that they wouldn't spend the remainder of the afternoon staring at each other in giddy silence—thrilling though that may be.

"I slipped away with the new maid, who will most likely lose her post over arranging for me to have a moment outside the walls of my home," she explained.

"You make it sound as if a jailer locks you in at night."

She often felt as if she were locked away. Could she be truthful with him? He'd told her about his family. She never spoke out of turn against her family, but Ash would protect the information she gave him. He might be a swindler, but she trusted him. It seemed odd to hold such confidence in a man who'd given her two false names already, but not when that man was Ash Claughbane.

"There is more than one type of prison," she finally said with her mind on the overnight stays she'd be wearing by morning. "Mine has ribbons and beads instead of bars, but I feel the cold metal wrapped around me just the same."

"Surely it's not all bad. You make it sound as if you're being tortured," he said with a cursory glance over her.

He didn't understand. How could she explain it? "Do you know who selected this dress for me? And what of this hat? These gloves?" She looked down at her hands encased in what felt like vises. "I despise these gloves," she said with a whisper.

"Do you?" He stopped walking and lifted her hand from his arm to inspect it. Then lifting the other hand, he began tugging on the fingertips. "Blasted tight, aren't they?"

"They are," she agreed, watching his face instead of his work on her gloves.

He finally pulled the gloves off and held them with the reins of his horse that was following slowly behind them. "And yet you willingly put them on your hands."

Or didn't fight when they were put on her hands—there wasn't much difference from her position. "I do what I must," she replied, stretching her fingers to allow blood to flow there once more.

"For fashion?" he asked, inspecting her gloves in the light.

She reached for them, but he pulled them away, out of her reach. He still didn't understand. "For survival," she corrected.

"This is what holds you captive? You're told every detail of what you must wear?"

"And what I must say, how I must stand, and who is allowed smiles," she added.

"Do I rank high enough to earn a smile?"

"Your smiles are stolen," she said truthfully.

He shrugged and grinned. "Coaxing things I want from people is what I do."

"You want my smiles?"

"Always." It was quite possibly the most romantic comment she'd ever heard, but then he destroyed the effect by adding with a wicked glint in his eye, "Smiles, kisses in service halls, perhaps more when you follow me next at a ball..."

"Might I have my gloves back now?"

"This is no way to live, Evie," he said, shaking the gloves in his hand.

"They're only gloves. It's not the end of life in England."

"This is about more than a pair of too-tight gloves," he countered, concern filling his eyes as he looked at her.

"Most of my life is binding."

"Why would you wear such a painful fashion?"

"Because my fingers are unladylike!" she exclaimed before sucking in a breath as if she could pull the words back into her mouth along with a great gulp of air.

"What?" He grabbed her fingers and lifted them to inspect them. "Who put it into your mind that your fingers are anything less than perfect?"

"Please return my gloves," she muttered.

"So that you might stuff them back onto your hands and crush your otherwise lovely appendages?" He ran his fingers gently over the red pressure lines her gloves had left on her hands.

"Ash, I must wear them," she tried to explain, but he didn't release her bare hands.

"You're miserable with them," he said without looking up at her as he continued to smooth the lines pressed into her hands.

"Someone might see."

"Does it matter if someone sees?" he asked, finally releasing her hands. "It's hardly criminal. They're only gloves." He waved them in the air once before dropping them to his side. "What is the worst that could happen?"

What *was* the worst that could happen? Surely she wouldn't be sent away from London for the crime of removing ill-fitting gloves for a moment while in the park. "I'm not sure what could come of this."

"Want to find out?" The mischievous grin that covered his face made her want to do more than walk gloveless in the park.

She watched him, unable to speak the words. The temptation he presented was too great in every way imaginable. The last time she'd dared to do as she wished, it had cost her every small freedom that should have been hers. Would it happen again? Surely the lack of gloves on a warm afternoon in the park wouldn't lead to her family's downfall like before.

With a knowing look in his eye, he tossed her gloves into the air. His horse huffed at his back, but no matron of the *ton* shot out from the shrubbery to reprimand her.

She watched as the gloves fluttered to the ground

like a pair of wounded birds. "Quite dramatic, but I think I'll put them in my reticule for safekeeping. I wouldn't want to be caught without them upon my return home."

He studied her for a moment before asking, "Why are you frightened so?"

She froze with the gloves in her grasp, taking a moment before standing upright again.

"Don't say you aren't frightened. I see what you do to keep those around you happy, the way your voice changes when we're alone. You're afraid to speak above a whisper when anyone is about. Why?"

She wanted to run. This must be the benefit of Ash's lifestyle. Anytime someone became close enough to rub the grime from the windows and peer inside, he was able to walk away and start anew. Yet, she stood rooted to the ground in the middle of the path, facing down everything she'd worked to hide for years. "You're fortunate, you know. You can be anyone you wish to be. You can dress how you see fit, walk outside with the sun on your face…"

"I suppose that is true," he hedged.

"I must follow the wishes of my family," she said, willing him to understand.

"Isn't that true of all unwed ladies?"

"Some more so than others." Couldn't he see? She had to do everything asked of her without question. Even this conversation was a violation. She was in the park, gloveless, with the wrong gentleman on a sunny afternoon. She would pay for this misdeed. She would—

"Evie," he said, claiming her attention. "They may be your family but they don't own your heart. We're here in the park on this fine day, and you're free to wiggle your fingers for the first time in what I can only assume is years. They don't own this moment. This is yours and yours alone."

A smile flooded her face as she looked at him. He was right—this was her moment in the sun. Her mother wasn't here. Today, on this afternoon with Ash, the sunshine belonged to Evie.

"I sincerely hope that smile wasn't stolen, because I would like to keep the memory of it."

"I stole it on your behalf," she said, her heart racing faster the longer she stood here with him.

"Then I shall take it." His eyes twinkled with mischief. "Come. Those free fingers need to experience a bit of the park while we still have time to enjoy it."

She stuffed her gloves into her bag and wrapped her bare hand around his arm. The scratch of warm wool covered the thickly corded muscle beneath her fingers. It wasn't ladylike to notice such a thing. Of course it was also unladylike to remove one's gloves in public. Perhaps she wasn't the lady who had been honed into perfection for years. "Perhaps I could become a lady who walks in the park gloveless," she muttered to herself.

"Evie, you already are that lady."

She blinked up at Ash. Did she dare to discover more of who she truly was and who she wished to be? It was a dangerous proposition—one that could cause terrible damage if acted upon. She wiggled her fingers, aware of the flinch of strong male muscle beneath her grasp. This danger also brought a smile to her lips. She could be more than the shell of perfection everyone else of her acquaintance believed her to be. And wasn't it wise to examine who she was now before she found a husband?

With Ash at her side, she could brave the danger. As long as he didn't leave her. But as much as she trusted him, staying at her side was the one thing she knew he couldn't promise.

‸

STEAMING THROUGH TOWN

"An investment in steam is an investment in tomorrow," says Lord Crosby of Crosby Steam Works. A scientifically minded gentleman with his eye on the future, Lord Crosby plans to produce the first steam engine for personal use. This advancement in science is poised to be a means of power for every home in the country. He suggests it could change the way lands are farmed and shorten travel times from village to village, perhaps even eliminating the need for horses altogether. While all of London waits for this most anticipated invention to be revealed, the industrious lord has been gaining popularity and investors in town at a rapid pace. This writer found Lord Crosby after the recent evening of poetry hosted by Lord Torrent. Ladies and gentlemen had gathered together in celebration of the written word, an event Lord Crosby tells us he quite enjoyed.

Ian leaned back in the rickety chair near the main door to the inn with a loud creak, pulling the copy of the *Times* with him as he moved. The article went on to describe the evening's entertainment and even the style of Crosby's coat and the quick flash of his smile. But Ian's gaze drifted over to the small sketch of his lordship that accompanied the printed words. He knew that scheming face. That man's smile might have charmed the writer of this article, but it only made Ian scowl.

"Lord Crosby, we meet at last," Ian muttered, clutching the paper tighter in his hands.

Finally Ian had a name and direction. The gentlemen he traveled with would have to listen to reason now. Ian had insisted days ago that the thief had gone to London, and he'd been right. They'd wasted too much time already, making inquiries on the road leading to Oxford. His eyes darted to the date printed at the top of the page. Two days ago. Surely Crosby, as he was now known, was still in London.

"There's still time," Ian muttered, abandoning his cup of coffee on the table and taking the paper with him.

"On yer way out for the day, m'lord?" the innkeeper asked as he paused in his sweeping to allow Ian to pass.

"With any luck, my group will be off to London today."

"Must be good news from town," the man said, nodding toward the paper in Ian's hand.

"Very," Ian said with a smile. Of course *Lord Crosby* may not think it such good news when he had to face down seven angry gentlemen from Bath. That was the danger of news—it traveled fast, even across the English countryside to small inns where adversaries awaited. Crosby would do well to remember that.

Ten

ASH CLIMBED INTO HIS CARRIAGE, THE SMALL PACKAGE now in hand. It was still early for tonight's ball. The unexpected errand to Bond Street this late in the day had left him only enough time to return to headquarters for a few minutes before he would depart again. When he did leave for the evening, at least he would do so in a cravat that wasn't stained red. He tossed the package onto the seat at his side and looked out the window.

Bond Street was quite a different place when the sun sank low in the sky and the ladies and gentlemen who kept the street bustling with activity during the day returned to their families. A single lamp flickered farther down the street, leaving the section where he sat waiting for his driver to return quite dark by comparison. The merchants were either gone for the day or closing their doors and sorting their wares for tomorrow, giving the street a peaceful quiet tinged with an eerie lack of life. He was pleased he'd caught the tailor before he left for the day, or he wouldn't be attending any events tonight. "Blasted bottle of tonic," Ash muttered to himself.

Earlier he'd spilled an entire bottle of the colored water he'd sold as a tonic last year. The shirts in his trunk had escaped damage, but his cravats hadn't been so fortunate. He could have unpacked his belongings weeks ago into his rooms at the Spares headquarters, but he'd never unpacked. It wasn't a rule—he simply didn't. *Maybe it's time you did.* He ignored the voice that had grown steadily louder within him for the past week. His effort was aided by the fact that the voice in his head sounded terribly like that of his eldest brother.

"Been waiting long, your lordship?" Stapleton asked with an overly formal bow, clearly enjoying Ash's present identity over that of the doctor or landed gentry he'd played in the past.

"Long enough that I'm surprised you can stand. How many pints did you have while I finished my shopping?"

"Enough," Stapleton replied with a smile. "Envious?"

"Thoroughly. I must ask, however, if you're fit to drive? I would draw looks if I were seen driving my foxed servant about town, since I'm such a *powerful lord*, but I will do so to save both our skins."

Stapleton waved away his offer. "I'm not totally foxed. I know well enough to slow my consumption when—"

"Is that…?" Ash interrupted, squinting in the direction of a shop on the opposite side of the street. "Is that Brice in the jewelry shop?"

Stapleton turned in the direction Ash was looking, peering across the road and into the store window. "I can't claim to know him well, but when I saw to his horse last week, he didn't mention a word of being a clerk in a store."

"Precisely." Furthermore, Ash was certain the jeweler's had been dark only a few minutes ago. "Perhaps you should take your seat in case we need to leave quickly."

Stapleton nodded and slipped around the corner of the carriage, leaving Ash to silently study the scene before him.

Kelton Brice moved about the inside of the shop by the light of a single lantern. He was searching for something. Clearly the Spare Heirs had some interest in the jewelry trade in London. Were shopkeepers selling paste for the price of true jewels, or possibly selling stolen goods? Ash had witnessed many such plots over the years. Yet Brice seemed to be searching through documents, not jewels.

Ash could leave his carriage with Stapleton and go inside. He was a member of the same society, and he worked on the same dingy side of the law. Yet he didn't move.

Through the large glass window, he saw Brice move to a desk in the far corner and begin sifting through papers there.

Ash had always been the one on the outside looking in—alone. When he'd signed on with the Spares, he hadn't realized the extent to which he'd been trading one set of brothers for another, but even now there was a wall between them. There had always been walls. His three brothers were always together, always deep in some endeavor, while Ash watched from a distance. And now he sat in a carriage and watched a brother of a different sort steal about a jewelry store after close of business. Some things never changed.

Nevertheless, he was pleased with his life. He didn't need anyone.

He crossed his arms over his chest and leaned back in his seat, propping his feet on the opposite cushion. He didn't need brothers of any sort. Relations became complicated and cumbersome. Eventually he would leave the Spares. He would even have to end his time with Evie. Though the thought of watching the gentle swish of her skirts as she walked away was...difficult.

He tensed for a moment before he became aware that the swish of skirts was real. A lady was now opening the door to the jewelry store. Wasn't that a friend of Evie's? He was certain he'd seen them together at balls and such. She was one of the twins. What the devil was she doing with Kelton Brice after dark, and while he was on a mission?

He couldn't hear their words, but he was somewhat thankful for that small bit of fortune when the lady placed her hands on her hips in the standard stance of any fishwife. Brice could barely open his mouth to respond. That itself was rather impressive, since he was known for his ability to chatter incessantly in a voice that could be heard on the other end of town. Evie's friend was moving toward Brice now as he held his hands out to the sides as if to show he held no weapons.

Ash leaned forward for a better view, only to see her disappear through a door in the rear of the shop. It appeared to lead into a shared storeroom for the milliner's next door, for in the next moment, Brice had followed her into the dim light of the neighboring shop. What the devil was happening? Brice was talking now, and for the first time since he'd met the man, Ash found himself wishing his friend would speak up. His normally loud voice was muted by the wall of windows between them. Ash's eyes widened as the lady flung a hat at Brice's head, catching him on the ear.

"Did you see that?" Stapleton said from atop the driver's seat, his voice echoing through the empty street.

But before Ash could call out a response, the lady started to pull hats down from the shelves of the shop and hurl them at Brice's body. He wasn't putting up much of a fight for such a large man, merely using the back of his arm to block the hats from hitting his eyes while the lantern swung in his hand. Ash winced. That lantern needed to be put on a table or…

It flew from Brice's hand and landed amid a large basket of ribbons in the shop window.

Flames lapped up the walls in an instant, but neither Brice nor the twin lady seemed to notice, too deep in their argument. Ash had his hand on the carriage door, ready to jump to the street and call out a warning, when something crashed inside the building and his carriage jerked forward. Stapleton was getting them safely away before the authorities could arrive, as he always did. But Ash couldn't run this time. He had to help…didn't he? He couldn't very well leave them to die in the smoke.

"Stop! Wait! Stapleton!"

When the carriage came to a sudden halt, Ash shoved open the door. But before he could spring into action, he saw a chair fly through the front window with a great crash. As empty as the streets had been a moment ago, now people gathered, merchants streaming out of shops.

"Claughbane, we leave now," Stapleton called down to him. "No good can come of getting involved."

Ash hesitated a moment, then settled back into the carriage without a word.

He stared into the dark velvet cushion opposite his seat as the carriage rattled down the street. Leave—that's what he always did when things began to heat up. In this case that heat was literal. Brice and the lady would escape the flames. The window had already been shattered, and enough people were nearby to offer them assistance.

Yet, he hadn't seen them on the walk outside. He couldn't be *certain* they made it out unscathed. The thought gnawed at him. He raised his hand to pound on the roof, prepared to demand that Stapleton turn around and return to Bond Street. His fist was in the air. His fingers curled in until the skin on his knuckles grew tight, but he didn't knock on the roof. *Don't become involved. Don't stay.* His own rules held him like a vise.

And yet as the carriage pulled him forward, he knew. When it came to Brice and the Spare Heirs— and, damn it all, Evie—his only steadfast rules needed to be bent to the point of breaking.

Could he become involved and stay for a bit longer than usual? Or would the rules he bent so readily to suit his needs finally snap back to hit him with a force strong enough to end him?

≈

Evangeline slipped through the crowd that had gathered close to the entrance of the ballroom, anxious to find Roselyn—if the poor dear was even here tonight. When she heard her mother pause to greet someone behind her, Evangeline only increased her pace. That small move would gain her at least ten minutes of peace, along with twenty minutes of verbal lashing later this evening, but it was well worth the price.

Glancing back only once to ensure her escape, she saw that her mother was now enveloped in the group of ladies she'd paused to greet. Fans fluttered as tomorrow's on-dit was decided upon. Roselyn had mentioned that her brother referred to them as vultures, and Evangeline quite agreed.

It was unfortunate that her friend had become a topic of gossip based on their vicious assumptions about her past. Roselyn wasn't to blame for the way things had ended for her fiancé before the season began, even if Evangeline did have misgivings about the details of Roselyn's story. But a mysterious story was hardly enough reason to destroy a young lady's first season. That was, however, the fickle nature of London.

Evangeline turned back, her gaze sweeping the room. She told herself she was looking for Roselyn, but she knew that wasn't the only person she sought out.

The afternoon she'd spent with Ash in the park had been the happiest of her life. The warmth of sunshine on her face, the ability to wiggle her fingers without binding gloves—everything about yesterday had been freeing, but there had been more to her enjoyment of the day than just an elusive taste of the freedom most ladies took for granted. Her fingers twitched at the thought of her bare hand on Ash's arm. The warm look in his eyes as he shot her that troublesome grin of his… She pulled herself together as she moved around a group of gentlemen.

She had yet to see Ash tonight. She did, however, spy Roselyn standing near the terrace doors at the rear of the room. Mother would require smelling salts if she saw her associating with Roselyn when her friend was the current source of the chatter on the opposite side of the room. Evangeline quickened her pace to join Roselyn before her mother could stop her.

Roselyn released a grateful sigh when she saw her. "I thought you'd abandoned me."

"Never," Evangeline promised. She hoped her smile was reassuring, even if it did hold an edge of concern she couldn't conceal. "Victoria and Isabelle haven't arrived yet?"

"They did say they were attending this event—I believe so anyway. I was set to meet Victoria on Bond Street this afternoon, but then I became distracted by the shattering of my hopes and dreams."

"Surely it isn't as bad as that," Evangeline offered, knowing it was most definitely as bad as that. Her mother had regaled her with all the talk on their carriage ride here. She'd seemed very pleased to announce her daughter's friend's social downfall. All Evangeline could do was listen.

"I'm using the news as an excuse to wear my favorite gown," Roselyn said, giving her skirts a bit of a flounce as she spoke. "I may not be fit to marry, but I will not enter my decline in poor fashion."

Evangeline couldn't imagine Roselyn Grey doing anything in poor fashion. She didn't take the interest in fashion that Roselyn did, but she knew enough about it to know her friend was the best dressed lady this season. Even tonight, she was the picture of elegance in bold color, with a simple necklace at her throat and her elaborate braids piled high on her head to tame her dark, wild curls.

"The talk of your presence at Lord Ayton's passing won't last forever, Roselyn," Evangeline assured her. "Soon, the vultures will swoop down upon some other unsuspecting soul and you will be free to dance with any gentleman you choose."

"You know your mother is among those you call vultures, don't you?"

"A fact that only proves the truth of my statement," Evangeline said quietly, making Roselyn chuckle.

"Speaking of vultures, she's flying in this direction."

Evangeline stiffened her spine against the coming storm that whisked ever closer in a dark-emerald gown. "I'll spare you the uncomfortable greeting and leave you."

"Much appreciated," Roselyn said with a thin smile. "I shall be here, alone yet looking fabulous in my new gown."

Evangeline gave her friend one last smile before turning away. She moved between the clusters of conversation and avoided a lady who seemed to have taken her skills with a fan from Isabelle's example.

Now that Evangeline was moving away from Roselyn, her mother had clearly decided to wait for her on the opposite end of the room. The woman only walked when necessary, as if even that small act showed too much humanity and, as such, was beneath her. The scowl hidden behind her watchful eyes promised more than twenty minutes of threats and reprimands during the carriage ride home.

Ah, well. Roselyn was worth the sacrifice.

As Evangeline moved around a group of gentlemen, the heat of a gaze sent a shiver down her spine. Someone was watching her. But instead of snapping to attention and parading past with the falseness her mother encouraged, she smiled. Ash. She wasn't sure how she knew it was him, but she did.

Already blushing, she turned and found Ash at the center of the group. He'd clearly been in the middle of some sort of discussion, because he held the attention of every man within earshot. She understood their fascination. Of course, now that same attention had been transferred to her as she paused in front of the gathering.

"Lady Evangeline." Ash's deep male voice wrapped around her, sending her heart into a stampede of wild beats.

"Lord Crosby," she returned with a small curtsy.

"Will you excuse me, gentlemen?" Ash asked, not taking his eyes from her. "I'm quite certain I've missed a dance with Lady Evangeline."

"You shouldn't let the lovely ones wait too long, Crosby," an older gentleman teased Ash as he passed by.

"My thoughts exactly." He pulled his gaze from her and turned to the gentleman with a grin. "I knew you were among the most intelligent here, Lord Randmore. When I return, we'll set a plan for how to spend all the money I'm going to help you earn."

"A visionary, he is," the older man told the group of gentlemen as they walked away.

"A visionary," she repeated, as Ash led her onto the floor just as a waltz began to play.

His eyes narrowed on her with a teasing glint that made her all the more aware of how close one had to stand to waltz. "It's much nicer than the description you would use, I take it?"

"No, only different," she said as she laid one hand on his shoulder and placed the other within his grasp.

"Now I have to ask what word you would use to describe me," he said, pulling her a fraction closer as he guided her in the first few steps of the waltz, just as he had in her father's library that day. "Wait. I don't think I want to know your answer. Not in such a public place anyway."

Did he think her so scandalous that anything she had to say would be shocking? *He* was scandalous, not her.

Though now that she was considering it, this entire dance was scandalous. Or perhaps it was simply her dance partner who made it seem so. She'd never thought the waltz shameful like some of the older matrons of the *ton* believed, but tonight, in his arms, she could see their point. Even in the brightly lit ballroom with plenty of watchful eyes upon them, dancing with Ash was thrilling. "Do I seem the type to have such wicked thoughts that they shouldn't be uttered in public?"

"After I caught you staring at my breeches at the last ball?" he asked. "It seems likely that your thoughts are less than appropriate, my lady." He said the last bit with a raised brow and a teasing lilt to his voice.

"I was not…" Her voice trailed off as the heat of a blush filled her cheeks. She couldn't lie to him. She blamed Isabelle entirely for this. Ranking gentlemen's bums had been her idea. Evangeline had to put order back into this exchange at once. "*Dangerous*. That's how I would describe you."

"Lord Crosby, a dangerous visionary," he mused. "Sounds rather nice, I think."

"I suppose so, if you're considering setting up a shop with a shingle in the front window."

"No," he blurted out, a shadow of worry crossing his face for a moment. "No shops and no windows. *They're* a bit too dangerous."

"Too sedentary for a gentleman on the move?"

"Perhaps," he answered. A bar of music played before he spoke again, the trouble seemingly set aside for now. "You look delicious this evening, by the way."

"Do I?" What an odd compliment. She didn't think a gentleman had ever called her *delicious* that she could recall.

"Mmm, droplets of maple covering vanilla." He flicked his gaze down to the embroidery on the cap sleeve of her gown. "Have you not noticed?"

"It's the warm shade of silk that was selected to complement my hair."

"And that it does. It also makes you look like a dish of maple ice." He leaned close to whisper, "You'll pardon me if I have a lick, won't you? I haven't eaten a bite since this morning and I'm starved."

Her eyes grew wide with shock. "I'm quite sure Lady Dansbury wouldn't approve of any licking at one of her events."

"Did you think I meant you?" he asked as he guided her around a corner of the ballroom. "Licking you is clearly out of the question at such a lofty ball as this one. No, your gown is giving me cravings for maple-flavored ice. Of course, I'm sure gnawed holes in your skirts would give the wrong impression as well."

A loud laugh burst from her as if begging for freedom. She pressed her lips together in an effort to suppress any further outbursts.

His amusement deepened at her terribly public show. "The solution is obvious. You should remove your gown for my dining enjoyment and thereby avoid all social embarrassment. It works for everyone, really."

Evangeline released an unladylike cackle as he twirled her around the floor.

"Meet me tomorrow for ices," he said once she'd stopped laughing. "I find I have a craving that can't be satisfied here on a ballroom floor."

She'd never heard anyone talk of ices as a craving to be satisfied. "You make ice from Gunter's sound rather scandalous."

"I am dangerous, as you say." He grinned. "Bring a chaperone, if you must."

"I suppose ice in the park is a better option than stripping me of my gown to dine on fabric."

"If you knew how famished I am, you wouldn't think so."

"You should have a bit of something before these events. One never knows the state of the refreshments being served." Of course, she was never allowed a morsel at a ball. Mother didn't think the sight of a lady eating was appealing to gentlemen, not to mention the time it took away from the ballroom.

"I hadn't time tonight. There was a bit of an…issue

at my residence." The shadow of worry returned to his eyes for a moment.

"Oh?"

"Nothing of concern," he muttered, but there was something about the tightness of his jaw that negated his words.

The dance ended too soon, without a count of smiles or lingering touches to calculate its length. She needed to let him go. If they remained staring at each other on the floor much longer, there would be talk. She tried to lower her hand from his but met a moment's resistance before her hand fell to her side, gloveless.

She looked down in surprise at her bare hand before hiding it in the folds of her gown that fell over her hip. "How did you do that?"

"Tricks of the trade, I'm afraid. It's the risk one takes when dancing with a dangerous gentleman— losing one's glove."

"Ash, give it back," she whispered, looking back up at him only to see an amused gleam in his eye.

"Lady Rightworth," he said, turning to greet her mother only a few paces away.

"Evangeline," her mother commanded. "Lord Winfield is waiting to lead you onto the floor." Her eyes darted to Ash before landing back on Evangeline with poorly concealed anger. "Priorities, darling."

"I must go. Thank you for the dance, Lord Crosby," Evangeline said with a raised brow—leaving the *Give back my glove* unspoken between them.

"The pleasure was mine." He nodded to her and her mother, the dratted picture of gentlemanly behavior, if not for the lady's glove he held in his hand.

"I'm going to walk away now to join my next dance partner," Evangeline stated, flaring her eyes in his direction but saying nothing of her stolen garment in front of her mother.

"Of course you are," her mother responded. "Lord Crosby knows the way of things. Don't you, my lord?"

"I do," he said with a wide grin.

"Do you indeed?" Evangeline asked, eyeing the glove he still held captive in his grasp.

"Evangeline, are you questioning a titled gentleman?" her mother accused with a false, simpering laugh. "I'm sure he's well-schooled in social protocol, *as are you.*"

"I only wonder at his knowledge of specific items that concern ladies more than gentlemen. Fashion, for instance."

"I have a good *grasp* on such things, my lady. Although, I do wonder at the use of a fan. Tell me, Lady Rightworth, is it truly for the use of cooling one's person, or is it simply something to keep close by with which to injure gentlemen's arms?"

"Your arms look no worse for wear to me, my lord," her mother stated. "Lord Winfield's, on the other hand, are quite empty." She looked around to find the other lord, turning her back on them for a moment.

"Yes, your arms look quite fine, my lord," Evangeline said as she lunged for her glove.

Ash pulled it from her grasp, a look of mock shock on his face. "I'm glad you noticed."

She shoved him in the chest and reached for the dratted glove, only to have him wave it in her face. She grasped at the length of fabric but Ash was faster than she was, leaving her flapping her arms about behind her mother's back in a crazed attempt at retrieving her stolen property. As their silent battle continued, Evangeline could only hope no one was looking in her direction to witness it.

In the next second, Ash dropped his arm to his side and pasted a pleasant look on his face. Dropping her arms with a huff, Evangeline looked around just as her mother turned back to them.

"Come along, Evangeline. I believe I spy Lord Winfield across the room. We must hurry—that Roselyn Grey is near him." Her disdain was evident in the manner in which she spoke Evangeline's friend's name. "It wouldn't do for him to lose interest in you in favor of such a...lady. Good day, Lord Crosby."

The second her mother's back was turned once more, Evangeline dove at Ash's hand. Her fingers tangled with his long enough for her to look up and meet his laughing gaze. With a squeeze of her fingers, he handed the glove back to her.

"Tomorrow. Scandalous ices in the sunshine," he confirmed.

"I have no doubt of the scandalous part," she muttered, stuffing her fingers back into her glove.

"You called me dangerous," he explained. "I have a reputation to keep up now."

She pulled her glove on properly and raised her chin in defiance. "I should have left you thinking yourself the visionary."

"I prefer your definition," he said as she turned to walk away.

Five smiles and a lingering arm touch later, she

was back at the side of the ballroom. Everything about Lord Winfield was respectable and true. He was everything she could hope for in a husband, even if he did drown himself in cologne before every ball. He was not a bad man, nor—as Isabelle had pointed out—was he an unattractive one. He would provide a comfortable life for her away from her mother. He seemed quite pleased with her—well, pleased with her looks, at any rate. He seemed to be seeking something to show about town on his arm, much like one would a new bracelet. She would be his shining jewel. As long as she continued to glitter, it would be a fine life. It was all she should hope for.

Why then did her attention wander back to Ash when she danced with Lord Winfield? The steps had been similar in nature, the placement of his hand against hers quite comparable, yet her dance with Winfield hadn't seemed scandalous in the least. And Lord Winfield didn't find it amusing to steal her clothing. She smiled. Unfortunately she'd found it just as amusing as Ash had, blast her wicked heart.

She watched Roselyn as she waltzed about the room with a most unlikely dance partner. Since Ash had disappeared with the group of gentlemen he'd been speaking with earlier, Evangeline was left to her own thoughts until the next dance. This was the point in the evening at which Victoria would usually say something inappropriate, but Evangeline was left to ponder Roselyn's waltz alone.

Her friend was dancing with the new Lord Ayton, younger brother to her former fiancé. General concern for her well-being could be what kept his gaze on her friend, but Evangeline didn't think that was the case. Perhaps she had been wrong to worry over the destruction of Roselyn's first season. Her friend seemed to have a better handle on things than Evangeline did at the moment. Glancing around once more for Isabelle and Victoria—even though it was now too late in the evening for them to arrive—she wondered what had happened to keep them away. Someone must have grown ill late in the day. She would send a note in the morning before she met Ash for ices.

"The flames nearly took them both," a lady said to her mother loud enough to gain Evangeline's attention.

Flames? Had someone had a house fire? Fires in the kitchen were terrible things, especially in a place like London where the homes were so close together. The poor family they must be discussing would have lost everything. Evangeline turned around, listening to the talk she usually ignored.

"I heard he carried the girl out of the shop only minutes before she would have expired from the smoke. Quite heroic," the woman finished, fanning herself.

"Really?" another lady leaned in to say. "Lady Smeltings said she was pressed to his body in a most scandalous manner."

"My, my. I do wonder if the truth will ever be known," another lady commented.

"I knew those girls to be trouble when they first claimed to be relations," her mother announced. "Second cousins, you know…quite distant."

Fear coiled deep in Evangeline's stomach at her mother's words. It couldn't be. But Victoria and

Isabelle weren't here tonight as they had planned to be, that much was true. "Mother, has something happened to Victoria and Isabelle?" Evangeline asked. "Is that why they aren't here tonight?"

"Haven't you heard?" one of the other ladies asked, clearly excited to be part of the talk of the evening. "There was a fire on Bond Street. Your cousin Victoria was in the blaze. And she was rescued by Mr. Brice."

Her mother shifted at her side at the mention of their family relationship, but Evangeline ignored her.

"Mr. Brice? What was Victoria doing with Mr. Brice?" Isabelle was the one who spoke of no one else. She'd been in love with the man as long as Evangeline had known her. It made no sense.

"That is what everyone is wondering. What *was* she doing alone with Mr. Brice?" one of the ladies asked, causing a round of tittering to vibrate through the group.

Evangeline shook her head, not understanding. "But he rescued her. She's safe."

"She's quite cozy, I hear," one of the ladies said, her eyebrows raised in accusation.

"She was in a fire," Evangeline retorted.

"Who cares about the girl? Have you heard if Mr. Brice is expected to make an appearance tonight?" she heard someone ask.

Another woman remarked, "Lady Dansbury would be pleased, I'm sure. I suspect, however, that he's resting from such a feat of heroism."

Evangeline took a step away to regain her composure. It wouldn't do to engage in fisticuffs with a pack of ladies at a ball. Forcing herself to unclench her fists, she took a breath and looked out across the sea of twirling dresses before her. Did no one care for the facts of the situation or for Victoria's well-being?

She turned to see Roselyn moving toward her, the gentleman she'd been dancing with following behind. Roselyn had intended to go shopping with Victoria this afternoon. She'd had a narrow scrape with death, and Victoria even closer. Bond Street had always seemed such a safe place, but a fire… Well, fires could happen anywhere. And what of Isabelle in all of this? To have everyone putting her sister's name together with the man she loved must be troublesome to say the least.

It was as if last season was repeating itself. That time, Evangeline had smiled at the man Sue loved. They'd walked in the garden together at her mother's insistence. But this season was different. This season she had Ash at her side. The chatter around her turned to heated voices, pulling Evangeline from her thoughts.

"I don't want your opinion," Roselyn blurted out.

"Well, I never," her mother replied, taken aback.

Evangeline stepped between them before the situation could worsen. "I'll take it from here if you please, Mother. Roselyn, did you hear about Victoria?"

Evangeline told her friend all she knew of the horrible fire that afternoon, but she needed to know more. It was too late tonight to call on her cousins. However, tomorrow morning at first light she would be at their door. Her mother could deny their closeness as a family all she liked, but Evangeline knew the truth. She wasn't going to abandon them, just as she wouldn't leave Roselyn to stand alone during an entire ball. These ladies were more family to her than her family had ever been.

Perhaps this season she could be counted upon to make the correct choices. Some of her decisions may still be questionable or she wouldn't have agreed to ice with Ash Claughbane tomorrow afternoon, but she could be a friend to her cousins. She would make wise decisions about other things in her life at some later date—after she'd spent a bit more time with Ash.

◦◦◦

Ash lounged back against a tree near the entrance to the Berkeley Square gardens, crossing his arms over his chest. It was a nice enough afternoon. If Evie was here she would comment on the sun, the green grass, and the fullness of the tree he was standing beneath. But Evie was not here—she was twenty minutes late. She could be with the clearly more desirable Lord Winfield. The memory of her on Winfield's arm last night still stung.

"Get hold of yourself, man," he muttered. He'd never been one to fall prey to fits of jealousy. Evie should be with a respectable, *true* lord like Winfield. He should wish that for her since he was only…

What was he doing, anyway?

He'd never before arranged to meet a lady for ices in the afternoon. Until he arrived in London, his life had been a series of meetings in parlors for the sake of the sale. When he did venture away from those parlors, it had always been to some shadowed place to sway some lady to his way of seeing things and better his odds in his schemes. He'd barely noticed the weather outside before he came here. Birds chirping, the spring of wet grass beneath his feet—this was all Evie's fault.

He grinned, seeing her carriage arrive outside Gunter's, and pushed off the tree to greet her. The sweet shop was located across from the park, where people regularly gathered on benches and at small tables to enjoy a treat on warm afternoons.

Lady Rightworth was the first to set foot on the ground, looking just as unhappy as she had the evening of the poetry reading. But a moment later when he caught sight of Evie, he forgot all about Lady Rightworth.

Evie descended from the carriage and looked around for a second before she spotted him in the park and began to move in his direction. She was wearing blue today, but he would still describe her as delicious. Perhaps not today, not in front of her mother, but delicious nonetheless. Evie's dress billowed out behind her like sails on a ship as she glided across the open area of the park. Meanwhile, her mother picked her way across the grass in an attempt to touch as little of nature as possible. He fought down the chuckle that tried to escape his throat, hiding it beneath a cough.

"My lord," Evie said in a small voice as she curtsied before him.

One day he would discover the full extent of why she only spoke normally when they were alone. Even though he knew her trepidation had something to do with her mother, he wanted to understand it all. A desire to know more about anyone was a frightening thought. No—he was investigating. He'd done research for his work in the past, and this was no different. Or was it?

"Lady Evangeline," he offered with a nod, quite possibly sounding as fearful as she did but for an entirely different reason.

"This outing cannot take all afternoon, because Evangeline has preparations to make for tonight's ball," Lady Rightworth proclaimed as she reached them. "Lord Winfield is very much looking forward to seeing her there."

"Mother, Lord Crosby has invited us here," Evangeline admonished, her eyes cast down at the ground.

"After you spent most of the morning looking in on those cousins of yours?" Her mother heaved an exaggerated sigh, ensuring everyone present was aware of her exhaustion. "Very well. I suppose we've taken the time to travel the distance."

Ash couldn't tell if she was referring to the ten minutes in her carriage or the trek across the rough terrain of trimmed lawn, but clearly she wasn't pleased about either. He wasn't particularly happy about her presence here, in all honesty, because it placed strain in Evie's eyes and forced her into that blasted whispery voice when she spoke. But he wasn't complaining.

"At least they have staff here." Lady Rightworth raised a hand and signaled the man crossing the grass toward them to quicken his pace. "Partaking in sweets while outdoors is barbaric enough without assistance."

Evie shot him an apologetic look while her mother was distracted, but Ash found himself more amused by her ladyship than offended.

"How may I serve you?" the man asked, reaching

them just as they were sitting down at one of the tables set up in the grass.

"I'll have a chocolate," Ash said with a twinkle in his eye. It had been years since he'd taken the time to enjoy a dish of ice. There was always a new town to visit, a new item to sell, but there was never time for things like ice in the park. Despite his travels and fast-paced life, he should take more time for the occasional simple pleasure.

"My daughter and I will have the rose-shaped vanilla," Lady Rightworth announced without so much as a glance in Evie's direction.

"Is that what you want, my lady?" Ash asked, noticing the slight sag to Evie's shoulders. It was faint, almost hidden, but it was there—disappointment.

"Of course vanilla is what she wants." Her mother turned accusatory eyes in his direction, as if he'd suggested Evangeline dine on a vat of whiskey. "Isn't it, darling?"

"I-I'm sure it will be fine."

"Oh look, there's Lady Smeltings," her mother simpered as she touched her hair to ensure it was in place. "Do excuse me. I must speak with her. Lady Smeltings!" She rose from her seat and called across the expanse of green grass. "Lady Smeltings!"

Ash really should try to win the woman over to his side. That's what he would do under normal circumstances, but he couldn't bring himself to appease her. Not only was she loud and, on the whole, offensive to all the senses, but she inspired unease in Evie—and that was a fact he couldn't overlook. He held up a hand in silent request for a moment to discuss their order before asking Evie, "Have you ever tried the bergamot?"

"No, but it does sound…" Evangeline glanced around in search of her mother's whereabouts, watching her as she moved steadily away from them. "The vanilla will be fine. It's been pleasant in the past."

"My lady, you do know the flavor of ice you prefer, don't you?"

She pressed her lips together and glanced down at the table, the light pink of a blush creeping onto her cheeks. Everyone had a favorite flavor of ice, did they not? Yet Evie said nothing.

At her silence, Ash told the man, "We'll have one of every type you offer."

"Ash…I mean…my lord, that is too much. My mother won't allow it."

"She isn't here."

Evie glanced around to see her mother now sitting with two other ladies some distance away. "She won't approve, and I'm not to have more than three bites of any sweet."

"Evangeline, you are going to try every flavor of ice Gunter's has to offer until you are able to select your favorite."

"I don't have the pin money to…"

"I can more than afford a few ices. It would be my pleasure to assist you in what is clearly an arduous decision." He nodded to the man by the table, who set off across the grass toward Gunter's establishment.

"I must apologize for my mother," Evie said after the man was out of earshot, her voice finally the smooth, relaxed one she used when they were alone.

"There is more than enough time this afternoon to have an ice or, in this case, quite a few."

"Truly, it's all part of my masterful plan to make you too ill to attend that ball tonight."

"Is it? And I have fallen into your trap just like that," she said with a small shake of her head. "Mother will be disappointed when I stay home and force Lord Winfield to find another dance partner."

"Would *you* be disappointed if you were unable to attend?" Ash asked, unable to resist. He shouldn't care if she was interested in Lord Winfield. But he also shouldn't be here with her, and shouldn't be looking forward to an entire table filled with sweets.

"I do find I grow weary of dressing for town," she admitted.

"I fully support your lack of dress. I would prefer it, however, if you attempted it at an event where I could enjoy the view."

Her eyes grew round as she looked at him. "That is not what I meant by that comment."

"I stand by my thoughts on your lack of a dress nonetheless," he teased, wishing he could unwrap her from the confines of her pristine gowns for just one night and experience everything she held back from the world.

"Do you speak with all the ladies this way?"

"No. Only you. Others would slap me."

"As did I."

He laughed at the memory as two large trays of ices were placed between them. Every type of ice offered lay scattered across the table, and they were each given a spoon. "I deserved that slap you gave me," he said when the man had left them once more. "Now, tell me of your dislike of getting dressed."

She blinked at the bounty of ice in front of her, then took the smallest bite he'd ever witnessed of the chocolate that sat at her elbow. She made a small sigh, then began. "It's an awful process, you know. Hours of having my hair pulled this way and that, being bound tighter than you can imagine into a gown, and then adorned with ten different options of jewels. I suppose I don't have the interest in fashion most ladies do." She delved her spoon into another bowl, this time taking a mouthful. He watched as her lips curved around the sweet bite of honey-covered elderflower.

"Hmmm. All of this"—he waved his spoon at her before sinking it into one of the flavors—"only serves to hide who you truly are. Are you not in town to find a husband?"

"I am." She scanned the table before settling on a bowl toward the end of it.

"It would seem that revealing your true identity would be wise before marriage." Why was he advising her in the way of *marriage*? He shook his head and scooped up some of the chocolate ice that sat in front of Evie.

"The thought that it's a bit misleading has crossed my mind."

"Yet you still come to the park with pearls and hair that's curled to perfection."

"You don't approve," she said, lowering the spoon.

"I didn't say that." He couldn't keep his clear interest in her from his voice as he spoke. She was beautiful. There was no arguing that fact. "I'm merely noting how you're leading the poor gentlemen of the *ton* astray in their search for wives this season."

"Ash Claughbane, are you claiming *I* am the one being false?"

"In a sense." He smiled at her look of dismay. "But then it only serves to make me the fortunate one."

"How so?"

"I know you would prefer a simple day dress to a gown. I alone can imagine you with your hair down, flowing around your face. At the next ball, I will smile, knowing you don't enjoy being the prim miss across the room with jewels draped around her neck. In my mind, you will be free and smiling back at me."

Their gazes locked for a moment. He'd revealed too much. He blamed the excess of sugar before him. What had begun as simple and innocent pleasure was spinning at a rapid pace toward wild and guilty desire. He shouldn't be here with any lady, but certainly not with Evangeline Green, daughter of Lord Rightworth. Yet he could more easily eat a vat of ice than walk away from her now.

She worked to swallow, drawing his gaze to her throat for a second. "I may be prim and draped in jewels, but I will still be the lady smiling back at you."

"And what of Lord Winfield?" The question was out of his mouth before he could stop it. Damn. Years of training in such things, and within an hour of her company, he was voicing every thought in his head.

"I've only ever given him his allotment of smiles."

"Ah, the numbered smiles. How many smiles do you allot him?"

"Five."

"I wonder how many smiles you have served me today," he mused. "I can't say that I've been counting this afternoon."

"Neither have I." She smiled at him brightly enough to light her eyes and remove the memory of her earlier strain. This smile was pure, unnumbered, and his.

The joy in her clear blue eyes pierced his heart. Everything with Evie was fresh and new. Even eating ices was an experience like no other—simply because she was here. And because he was with Evie, he was living this moment as if he'd never tasted chocolate ice before. What other experiences would she make new? Perhaps in all of his travels he had been missing the truly extraordinary moments that often went unnoticed.

"Evangeline?" A female voice carved through their sugar-induced euphoria. Evie's mother loomed over them, staring in outrage at the table covered with bowls of ice. "What *are* you doing?"

"Lord Crosby insisted that I try—"

"Saffron? Ambergris? Laaaavender?" her mother exclaimed, looking down at the table between them, one hand clutching her heart. "And I thought you above the antics of your foolish sister!"

"I was hungry," Ash attempted, but her mother was too busy lecturing Evie to hear him.

"Thank you for a lovely afternoon," Evie said as she stood from the table.

He rose to watch her leave. "The pleasure was mine, believe me."

Evangeline turned to walk away, rounding their

table to follow after her mother. But only a step away from him, she paused and turned back. Leaning toward him, she whispered, "The maple is my favorite. Thank you."

He could hear her mother's words as they crossed the grass. "Did you take more than three bites? You know you are not allowed such an excess of sweets. And when I already had the waists of your gowns taken in! The maid will no doubt need more time adjusting your stays. We have tonight's ball to think of."

Tonight's ball—one Ash hadn't planned on attending. He would be meeting with a few gentlemen over a hand of cards. Meanwhile, Lord Winfield would be wooing Evangeline. Even though she would be bound into a dress that hid her true beauty from the world, there was something unsettling about the thought of her dancing with another man. Was he jealous?

Damn, he was.

In an instant, his earlier suspicions were confirmed. He was jealous of the honest lord who never traveled and who would have the good luck of dancing with Lady Evangeline Green. Ash shook his head and sank back into his seat, surrounded by melting ice. He'd definitely consumed too much sugar.

Eleven

OLIVER DEAN HAD NEVER GIVEN UP ON A PROJECT. On the other hand, he considered all of his projects works in progress and thus never quite complete. He settled back on his heels, listening to the ticking of twenty different clocks—none of which offered the proper time. He'd looked at the portable steam contraption from every angle imaginable. It simply wouldn't function.

St. James, who'd commissioned the work, didn't care either way. The head of his club in London, the Spare Heirs, had only asked for a prototype that appeared to function, but Ollie needed it to work. For once in his life, he knew he was close to creating something world-changing. He was so terribly close, if only the blasted thing would function. He hit it with the wrench in his hand, frowning when it didn't sputter to life.

"I've brought you something to eat," a voice called from the door, making him smile. "Your grand-mother is concerned you might waste away in here if not fed regularly."

"I have tea," Ollie said, rising to his feet and moving toward his desk near the door where his new wife stood. "Surely that will keep me alive until this evening."

Mable set a tray on top of a pile of diagrams and touched the teacup with one elegant finger. "Ollie, this tea is stone cold and untouched. I don't believe the thought of tea is enough to keep your grand-mother's concerns at bay."

"Really?" He grinned, watching her pick up one of his drawings and study it, her face screwed up in concentration. Even if every one of his inventions failed, he would continue to try, just so Mable would make that adorable face while she attempted to work out what he was building. He prowled closer to her. "I find thoughts of you rather filling."

"Flattering, but not helpful at the moment." She tossed the plans aside and shoved a biscuit at him when he neared.

"A biscuit? How am I to eat when you have me so distracted?" he asked, wrapping his hands around her and pulling her close.

"You need some distraction. You've been in here for weeks."

"Ten days," he corrected. "If I could only deter-mine the proper alignment of the gears in this assem-bly... Let me show you." He tugged her hand and pulled her across the room, weaving between stacks of abandoned instrumentation and broken bits of clockwork of various sizes. Finally, he stopped before the blasted steam contraption he couldn't get to work.

"What does it do?" she asked, reaching out to poke at it with a finger.

He scrubbed a hand across the back of his neck as he considered the function of the machine again. "At the moment? It spews water across the floor in a most wondrous display."

Mable reached out and turned one of the gears with a finger. "It seems complicated."

"I had to cross belts and gears in more directions than you can imagine to get it to this point."

She giggled. "It reminds me of my attempts at knitting, yarn darting in every direction. My sister used to say I could make a larger mess of a ball of yarn than anyone she knew. It would take hours weaving the yarn back and forth between our hands to make sense of it. I'm sure you'll get it sorted."

He pulled her to him and buried his face in her hair, still studying the pile of metal in his workroom. "I hope so. This could change everything. It would be revolutionary if I could only work out how to make it function."

"You don't need to change the world for me to love you, Ollie. The amount of pressure you're placing on yourself is hardly good for you."

"Pressure...pressure! That's it! Pressure!" He pulled his gaze from the machine to look at his beautiful wife. "You're brilliant!"

"I am?"

"You are!" He lifted her from the ground and spun her in the air before setting her back down in front of him. "I've gone about this all wrong. I can see it now."

Mable smiled up at him. "That is because you, sir, are so very intelligent."

"The smartest thing I ever did was marry you. What

did I do before you dropped into my life, a charming English girl claiming to be a French heiress?"

"You certainly didn't eat, I'm certain of that much," she said, prodding him in the stomach.

"For you, I'll stop work to eat a feast. In fact, let's go now."

"Ollie, we don't eat for another three hours. Cook will have fits."

"Three hours before we can dine together." He curled his hand around the back of her neck and drew her into his kiss. "How will we pass the time?"

"I have a few notions, but since you're the expert on clockwork, I'll let you decide." She turned and sauntered from his office, tossing a wink over her shoulder that promised three hours wouldn't be enough time together.

Most wouldn't view steam, pressure, or the closeness of grinding gears as aphrodisiacs, but with Mable around, they were. Abandoning his work until tomorrow, Ollie followed her from his workshop.

Twelve

EVANGELINE NODDED GOOD NIGHT TO HER MAID—who gave her a sympathetic smile in return—and waited for the door to close, then removed the binding ribbon and ran her fingers through the tight braid in her hair. Shaking loose the plaited strands, she pulled her fingers through them a few more times before climbing onto her bed. Who could sleep with their hair bound up in such a manner? She'd been forced to do so until now, just as Jane had been forced to braid it as instructed, but Evangeline refused to endure it any longer. Every night Jane pulled Evangeline's hair into the braid that almost kept her eyes from closing. Every night she suffered for the sake of her hair.

But not tonight.

It was a small rebellion. Only Jane would know. If Evangeline laid the ribbon on her pillow, even if her mother woke her in the morning, she would think it had come loose in the night. Yesterday Evangeline had tasted a table full of ices, and tonight she would sleep with unbound hair. Truly, she was a hoyden. She chuckled as she carefully placed the ribbon Jane had used on the edge of her pillow.

She was fortunate that tightly bound hair was her current problem, really. When she'd been to visit her cousins, she'd had to work to keep the shock from her face at Victoria's new short length hair. Apparently the ends of her hair had been singed in the flames. She was still beautiful, and the style seemed to suit her temperament, but Evangeline quite preferred the longer length of her own hair.

The repercussions of that blasted fire on her cousins' lives were unending. Shorter hair was the least of their worries now with the news of their father promising Victoria to Mr. Brice for his bravery. Or should he be called Lord Hardaway now? How quickly things had changed for everyone involved. Brice had tried to refuse the courtesy title, according to Evangeline's mother, until his own father forced his hand.

Evangeline shook her head and drew her fingers over her sore scalp. There was nothing to be done for any of it. She'd attempted to speak with Isabelle on the subject, although that had done little good. Isabelle wasn't speaking to her sister, and Evangeline couldn't blame either of them. Sisterly love was a delicate thing. She would know.

Just then, a scraping sound on the other side of the room drew her attention. Her window slid open. An intruder! Her heart pounded in her chest. She'd heard stories of the dangers of London, but she'd always thought their home was safe. What should she do? She had to do something.

Evangeline picked up the nearest weapon she could

find to defend herself against the threat climbing into her bedchamber—her silver-backed hairbrush. She shifted to her knees on the edge of the bed, holding the hairbrush up in preparation to beat the thief senseless. The only sound was her heart pounding in her ears. Time seemed to slow as she watched one Hessian boot drop over the windowsill, followed by the large form of a man. Rather nice boots for a common thief, weren't they?

"Your home is surprisingly easy to break into," he said. "You should have that seen to."

She froze, the brush still held high in her hand, blinking into the shadowed side of the room. It lay too far beyond the reach of her candle for her to see the intruder properly.

"A hairbrush?" he asked. "This is how you defend yourself? Really, Evie."

"It was all I could find." She tried to shake some sense into her addled mind. Ash was standing in her bedchamber. "What are you doing here?"

"There wasn't any entertainment tonight," he replied as he shook his coat back into place on his shoulders.

"If you came here to be entertained, I may yet have to beat you with this hairbrush."

He chuckled and dropped into a chair. "No need to brush me to death. I was passing by, and I wanted to inform you of my plans."

"Your plans," she repeated. "You scaled the side of my home to inform me of plans?"

"I was passing by."

"You mentioned that part." She was staring at him with the faint notion that everything about this would make sense if she only looked a bit closer. It didn't work.

"Haven't you ever had a thought to go somewhere you shouldn't?"

"I suppose."

"I wanted to come here—to see you." He lounged back in the chair as if it was made for him and surveyed his surroundings. "You have an interesting decorating style, Evie. One would think you were quite concerned with fashion by the fashion plates and...do you have *three* wardrobes?"

"Everything was delivered here for my use." She shifted from her knees and moved off the bed to stand. "You wanted to see me?"

"I did break into your home," Ash conceded with a small nod.

"So you did," she prompted, and said no more in hope that he would explain what he was about.

"You look better than I'd imagined," he said after a moment's silence.

"You imagined me?"

He grinned as he watched her. "Not exactly like this, but..."

She looked down, realizing only then that she was dressed for bed in just her night rail, not even a robe. Of course, she hadn't been expecting a man to crawl through her window. She crossed her arms over her breasts in an attempt at decency. "If I had known you would visit me, I would have remained dressed."

"If you find this discomforting, I'm glad you don't know how I imagined you," he mused.

Heat rushed through her body as her heart began to

race. She took a step away from him, but bumped into the edge of her bed.

"Evie," he said, standing from the chair. "I didn't climb in your window to take advantage of you. There's no need to be fearful." Closing the gap between them in only a few paces, he placed his hands on her shoulders and slowly moved them down her arms. "You don't have to hide from me."

"I'm not afraid of you. I'm afraid of me." She was known in her family for making terrible decisions. She couldn't be trusted, especially when he was looking at her like that and making her limbs turn to noodles.

"You have my word that I won't touch you," he reassured her as he looked down into her upturned face.

"Ash?"

"Hmm?"

"You're touching me now."

"That would appear to be true," he said as if noticing his own grasp on her shoulders for the first time. "Well, I am a swindler by trade, but I'm also a gentleman."

"That's unfortunate." Her hand flew to cover her mouth as her eyes went wide with horror. She never spoke the thoughts that ran through her mind. What would he think of her?

He chuckled and pulled her hand from her lips, wrapping her fingers within his. She couldn't look away. There was no judgment in his gaze, only something dark and hungry that matched the emotions swirling through her body. He bent his head and placed a kiss on her hand.

"See? Quite the gentleman."

"Quite," she whispered. He was standing close enough to unbalance her if he hadn't been holding her hand within his. The heat of his body warmed the air around her as she looked up into his eyes. "I could be wrong, because I don't have vast amounts of experience on the subject, but I don't think an *honorable* gentleman would be standing in my bedchamber in the middle of the night."

"Do you want me to leave?" he asked with a raised brow as he lowered her hand to her side with a gentle touch.

A moment passed before she spoke. No, she didn't want him to leave. She didn't ever want him to leave. "You said you wished to tell me of your plans."

"I did. Of course when I had that thought in my carriage, I didn't know how difficult it would be to talk of plans and other mundane minutiae with you standing here looking as you do." He lifted a hand to her hair and let it fall through his fingers.

Her eyes drifted closed. After a lifetime of elaborate styles tugging at her scalp, his gentle touch had her leaning in to him for more.

"And this certainly isn't helping my concentration."

She opened her eyes to look at him. "Do you want me to stand across the room?"

"No." He continued to trail his hand through her hair.

"I could move away if it would help…"

"Could you?" he asked.

"No. I should. But somehow…"

"I like you like this, with your hair hanging in every direction and no adornment. Do you like it?"

"Mmm-hmm," she murmured in reply as he continued to slide his fingers through her hair.

"That lady you portray in every ballroom isn't you. This is you. This is the true Evangeline—thoughtful, delicate, and quietly bold."

She'd never considered herself to be bold. "Do you think so?"

"I think you want much more than you allow of yourself or will even admit," he said, watching her.

"You tempt me to want more," she admitted. He'd already made her realize there was happiness to be found in knowing the flavor of ice she truly enjoyed, and how lovely it was to laugh aloud. "Do I tempt you to do the same?"

"You have no idea." His voice was deep, gravelly, and more than a little suggestive.

She flicked her hand out and hit him on the chest. "That wasn't how I meant that at all."

He caught her hand and held it close. "And yet it is no less true. You tempt me beyond reason. You tempt me to want something more."

His heart beat beneath her hand.

"Ash, this is dangerous—whatever is happening here…"

"I know." He grinned the wicked grin of a swindler about to steal the prize. "Say that you enjoy it as much as I do, Evie. Admit that you like breaking your rules with me."

"They aren't my rules," she said, suddenly fearful.

"Then why follow them?"

She swallowed and looked up at him. "I make poor decisions on my own."

"I disagree," he said, still holding her close. He toyed with the hair that fell over her shoulder. "You made the perfect choice yesterday."

"I ate six bowls of syrupy sweetness to discover one small detail."

"Did you enjoy them?" he asked.

She grimaced, hating to admit the truth. It was unladylike. "Unfortunately, I did."

"Then you made the best decision available to you at the time." His deep voice rumbled through her as he spoke, calming her and setting her nerves on edge at the same time.

"I haven't thrown you from my bedchamber. I'm quite certain that is a poor decision."

"That's a matter of opinion," he said with a grin. "What is your opinion? What do you want, Evie?"

You, her heart screamed, but her mouth refused to form the word. Her gaze dropped from the depths of his eyes to his lips. He was so close, and yet he only touched her hair and held her hand to his chest. It would be so easy to rise to her toes and show him what she wanted. And yet it wasn't easy at all.

"Meet me tomorrow night at Vauxhall Gardens," he said without preamble.

"What?" she asked, trying to follow the quick change of subject. "I couldn't possibly."

"Your aunt and uncle are attending. I'll be among their party. Meet me there."

"It would be scandalous. Surely Victoria isn't planning to be there. The fire. Perhaps Isabelle…" Her voice trailed off as she tried to put the pieces of the invitation together in her mind.

"Do you want to go, Evie?"

"It would be improper," she responded, but even she could hear that her heart wasn't in it. "My mother would never approve," she tried again and failed once more.

"Do you want to go?"

"I have heard it's lovely," she mused.

"Do you want to see it for yourself? Experience it for yourself?"

Evangeline licked her lips and gave him a small nod.

His eyes lit up at her agreement. "Then I will see you at Vauxhall tomorrow night."

"I shouldn't," she said with a shake of her head.

"Yes, you should." He tilted her chin up to meet her gaze. "Evie, you want to attend. You want to taste life. You want to see the fireworks. You don't have to hide—not from me."

She nodded. Was that what she'd been doing—hiding?

"Perhaps I'll even kiss you again if I can make you ask for it. You think I haven't noticed that you've been staring at my mouth for the past ten minutes?"

"I have not…" She began to disagree, but it would have been a lie and he knew it.

"Say that you want me to kiss you, Evie."

"I would never…" she began, but fell silent.

"Tell me you want me. Say the words and I'll kiss you."

"I…"

"Say it," he implored.

Evangeline's lips parted, but she said nothing.

"Say, 'I want your lips on mine, Ash.' That's all you

have to do. I could show you so many things, Evie. Do you want me to? Say the words."

Her breathing came out harsh as her heart pounded in her chest. How was he making her so unsettled simply with words, and why couldn't she utter anything in return?

"I could bring you so much pleasure, Evie. Do you want me to touch you? To truly touch you? If you asked me, I would fit your breasts into the palms of my hands just like this." His hand hung in the air over her breast, close enough that she could feel the heat of his skin through her night rail. "Then I would lower my mouth to take your nipple between my teeth, tugging at your polished exterior until the real Evie pulled me closer. I would take your breast into my mouth and with my tongue…" He sighed, dropping his hand away from her. "But you have to tell me you want it."

"Ash," she whispered, already missing the heat of him close to her skin.

"There's a world out there that you could experience. All you have to do is stop hiding and tell me what you want."

It wasn't that simple, was it? She opened her mouth, unsure how to speak of her own desires. She never talked that way, not like Ash was able to do. But the truth was, she did want him to kiss her. She wanted everything about this man. That was also the trouble. She couldn't be trusted to speak—not just now. "I…"

He grinned and brushed a strand of hair from her face, placing a kiss on the top of her head as he did. "You're almost there. Just a few more words. Perhaps you need more encouragement."

"No." She took two steps backward until her heels bumped the wall. "I–I'm quite…"

"Evie, has anyone ever spoken to you this way?" He took slow steps to close the gap between them.

"No," she breathed.

"Do you like it when I do?" He grinned down at her as if he could hear all the thoughts she was too afraid to voice aloud. "I think you do. Do you want me to continue?"

"Do I have to say that as well?" she asked.

"No. I've learned in my line of work that it's sometimes necessary to give someone a taste of what they want before they'll pay the price."

"Is that what you're doing to me? Is this a taste of what's to come?" Heaven help her, she hoped it was.

"Only if you want it. That's my price." He shifted her hair from her shoulder as he spoke, letting it fall down her back.

"That seems…" Whispers of his touch brushed down the side of her neck as he moved her hair. She worked not to lean into his palm and feel the full force of his hand on her skin. "…reasonable."

"I thought so as well." He shifted even closer to her, leaning his arm on the wall above her head and surrounding her without the benefit of his embrace to steady her. "If you tell me you want me to kiss you, I'll kiss you here." He spoke the words against the sensitive skin beneath her ear before moving down her neck, not touching her, but close enough that she could feel the warmth of his lips.

She splayed her hands on the wall behind her to

keep from tipping sideways. He wasn't even touching her, and still she struggled to breathe.

"I would kiss my way down your neck to just here where I can see your pulse beating rather fast. Is it beating fast because you want me to kiss you, Evie?" he asked against her skin. "You know my terms. Say the words. This is only the beginning. I could show you a lifetime of pleasure if you want me to."

"A—a lifetime?" Her voice came out thick, the words heavy on her tongue.

He lifted his head from her neck and looked at her. He seemed as surprised by his words as she had been. He hadn't meant anything by it. She knew that. He had always been about to walk out her door. And she didn't want one misplaced word to stop what he was doing right now.

"You don't have to explain," she almost begged. "I understand."

"So, you are able to speak. This would lead one to believe you were simply enjoying the thought of what I might do to you too much to stop me."

"I was not," she lied.

"Then you don't want me to kiss you." He pushed from the wall and turned away from her.

"Ash!" she exclaimed a bit too loudly, grabbing a fistful of his coat and pulling him back toward her. She rose to her toes, prepared to kiss him and be done with his games, when she saw the gloating grin on his face. The man knew precisely what he was doing to her. He'd done just as he'd said—given her a taste of what she could have, and now she did want it. The devilish salesman.

But before she could make any further move toward him, a knock sounded at her door. Evangeline jumped, and Ash was already moving toward the open window.

"Just a minute," she called.

Looking to the window, she met Ash's gaze for just a second, but in that second was the promise of what would happen tomorrow night.

"Vauxhall Gardens," he whispered and she nodded.

"Evangeline, did I hear you yelling something about ashes?" her mother called from the hall.

"Yes. The wind outside, you know. Ashes blew from the fireplace."

"I'll send for a maid."

"No need, I've just swept every ash from the room." She grimaced at the truth of her statement as she watched him disappear into the night. "All is fine. Good night."

"Very well, but do try not to bellow in such a manner. It's quite unseemly."

Evangeline raced to the window when she heard her mother's retreating footsteps, looking out into the black of night. He was gone. Sinking into the chair Ash had lounged in only a few minutes ago, she touched the pulse at her neck where he'd spoken his last words. Unseemly. Unladylike. She'd spent years in training to *not* be something. All Ash asked was for her to be. He'd accused her of hiding, and perhaps he was right.

Tomorrow night she would go to Vauxhall Gardens with her aunt and uncle, because she wanted to do so. She would enjoy her evening because she wanted to, and then she would tell Ash everything she wanted him to hear—beginning with asking for his kiss.

≈

He spent a great deal of his time waiting beneath trees for Evie to arrive places. It wasn't that Ash minded, because a tree always provided one a convenient place to lean, but he would rather spend that time with Evie than the tree. The rough bark of the trunk pulled at the coat he'd worn to guard against the night chill. What was he doing? He should be wooing Lord Knottsby's guests into investing at least a small amount in steam— that was why he was here. He didn't need much from any one gentleman present, but he couldn't only target Rightworth or it would look suspicious.

St. James had somehow managed an invitation for the two of them to join the Knottsbys' party at Vauxhall Gardens. He'd also asked that Ash not involve Knottsby himself. Of course there had been no explanation—there never was with St. James. But there were other gentlemen for Ash to focus his efforts upon. And the small gathering would make that task much easier. Evie being here, on the other hand, would only make his true task more difficult. He knew that fact, and yet…

"If you continue to skulk about out here in the dark, the other guests will become suspicious," St. James said in a low voice as he stepped out of the thatched roof pavilion.

"She isn't here," Ash grumbled. He shot one more glance up the path before joining St. James.

"Nor should she be," his friend hissed. In his dark

gray attire, it sounded as if the night itself had spoken. "Have you considered how this will end?"

Ash sighed and ran a hand over his weary eyes. "Not well."

"She should either be used as a pawn in your scheme, or she shouldn't be involved at all. There was never a chance of it ending well between you."

"I'm aware." He knew he and Evie were not destined for a happy ending. That knowledge, along with the threat she posed to his plans, should be enough to keep him away from her, but it wasn't. He'd known what an idiot he was when he scaled the side of her home last night, and he knew it now. But that knowledge didn't keep him from looking up the path toward the iron bridge one last time before following St. James toward the open structure where their party was gathered.

"Lord Crosby, do have some champagne," Lady Knottsby offered when they came into view. "We're celebrating our daughter's upcoming nuptials, you know."

Ash accepted a glass of champagne and stepped into the pale light of the pavilion. Thousands of colored glass lanterns hung around the garden, making the trees look alive with fairies. Warm light of every color spilled onto the stone floor where they gathered, aided by several lanterns that had been placed on the table at the rear of the structure. Refreshments were set out there as well, giving the gathering an intimate overtone. It would have been a lovely party, if Evie had found the courage to come. As it was, he was left to focus on his work and chat with the hostess. He hid his sigh behind his glass as he took a drink.

St. James waved away the offer of drink as he always did, instead lacing his fingers behind his back. "I hope your family is well after the fire last week."

"Oh, quite," Lady Knottsby replied as she took a fresh glass from the footman who circled the gazebo, offering champagne and arrack punch. The remnants of beautiful youth clung to Lady Knottsby's cheekbones, and she tossed Ash and St. James a smile before lifting the glass to her lips.

"One never expects such tragedy to strike." Something dark and unspoken passed over St. James's usually stoic face. The man had never intended a fire to break out when he sent Brice to the jewelry store on Bond Street. Ash knew that without a doubt. But one couldn't offer sympathies too heavy-handedly in such a situation.

"Terrible circumstances—that fire," Lady Knottsby said with a shake of her blond head. A pout lingered about her lips for a second before her face lit up with glee. "But those flames led to quite the happy event for our family. The soon-to-be bride will be here shortly. She wanted to look her best to see her fiancé, you know. We came along without her. Isabelle was quite ready to be off." Lady Knottsby indicated her other daughter with a wave of her hand, sloshing champagne to the floor in the process.

At the mention of her name, Isabelle turned around. She barely spared a glance for Ash or her own mother. Instead, her gaze locked on St. James. Her eyes held a desperation that most wouldn't notice, but Ash had carved a living from looks like that. The desperate would pay any price for a bit of hope, and he was a purveyor of dreams.

"Would you excuse me a moment?" his friend asked, moving across the pavilion.

Interesting. It seemed St. James was indeed playing the part of hope this evening. Ash watched him join Isabelle. St. James was as secretive and difficult to read as ever, but Isabelle wasn't. Her eyes lit up as he moved across the room in her direction, as though she'd just spotted her oldest childhood acquaintance. Even now she was laughing at something he'd said. St. James knew how to jest? Who could have guessed it?

"Lord Crosby, are you enjoying all that London has to offer?" her ladyship asked, pulling his attention away from the urgent whispers and laughter from the other side of the gazebo.

"I believe I am," Ash said in a rare moment of complete honesty. "This is the longest stay I've ever had in the city."

"I do hope you aren't planning to leave too soon. It would be a shame for society to lose such a fine gentleman as yourself." She tipped forward a bit when she moved to tap his arm with her fan, spilling more champagne on the floor.

"I have no plans to leave just yet," he said, eyeing the woman's husband across the gazebo. The man was so consumed in his own conversation that he hadn't noticed his wife had become quite foxed.

"Do you have an interest in any of the ladies this season?" She took a small step closer to him and lowered her voice to say, "You're quite handsome to be unattached, you know."

"Unfortunately it is business that brings me to town, my lady." He walked a fine line. In his experience, ladies beyond their limits for alcohol could be easily offended by a lack of interest. One second she could be doing nothing but batting lashes, and the next she would be raising the alarm to her husband. He shot a glance toward the man once more, but he didn't seem in the habit of looking in his wife's direction.

"Mmmm, then perhaps someone with a bit more experience in life is more to your taste?" She grabbed another glass of champagne and lifted it to her lips. "Everyone should have companionship, Lord Crosby."

She was almost correct. Someone like her who needed such things should have companionship—her husband's companionship. Ash didn't live such a life. *Never stay. Never become attached.* He took a sip of his champagne, searching for the right way to proceed.

On occasion he had used women like her to aid him in whatever he was selling at the time—within reason, of course. He didn't have to agree to all a woman desired to gain her assistance. A few well-placed words of encouragement and she would help with his scheme. After all, ladies had a great deal of influence over how their husbands' funds were spent—even ladies desperate for those same men's attention. But when he looked at Lady Knottsby, all he could see was Evie's aunt. St. James was right—he'd well and truly mucked up this job. "I believe I'm otherwise spoken for."

"Oh? Lucky lady."

"As are you." With a slight tip of his glass, he indicated Lord Knottsby across the pavilion. "Your husband boasts of your beauty to all who will listen."

"He does?" Her eyes went round as she searched for the man in question.

There it was—hope. There were many less desirable aspects of Ash's work, but he'd always enjoyed the look in someone's eyes as they wondered if their lot in life might finally change. "How could he not? Your beauty lights the gardens more than lanterns ever could."

She batted her lashes at him and listed sideways a step. "Lord Crosby, you flirt."

"Then I'm in good company." The woman was indeed a flirt, but he could see why. It came from the same desperation that he'd seen in her daughter's eyes only a minute ago. Lady Knottsby didn't truly want him. She wanted what she clearly didn't possess—the admiration of her own husband.

She lifted the glass to her lips and took a drink, her eyes dancing over to where her husband stood. When the man became aware of her gaze and looked in their direction, Lady Knottsby smiled. Hope was a beautiful thing. She turned back to Ash and opened her mouth to continue their conversation. But when a twig crunched and movement caught his eye, his attention snapped to the path outside.

Moonlight shone off pale skin and the lanterns lit tiny pins in her hair, making Evie look like she was made of the night sky. He couldn't turn away. She was chatting with another lady as she moved down the path. Ash didn't notice the other woman, beyond noting it was the woman from the fire. His eyes were trained only on Evie and how she was gliding in his direction.

"Lord Crosby?" Lady Knottsby leaned to the side to gain his attention, almost tipping over the pavilion railing with the movement.

Ash blinked at her, disoriented as if just waking from a dream.

"I daresay you weren't listening to a word I said," she remarked, pouting. "What has captured your attention?"

He watched as Evie rounded the tree he'd leaned against only a few minutes ago, her fingers trailing the leaves of a low-hanging branch. A shy smile appeared on her face and grew wide with wonder, no doubt over the decorations and the beauty of the night. He imagined that caged birds would have the same look when allowed to take flight. He pulled his gaze back to the lady's aunt, realizing too late that the look on Evie's face was reflected on his own. "I've only just seen…"

She turned. "Otherwise spoken for, are you?"

"So it would seem," he grumbled, knowing the truth of his thoughts about her niece had already been revealed.

Lady Knottsby cackled with champagne-infused laughter. "The business you're in town for is becoming quite interesting, Lord Crosby."

"You have no idea, my lady. No idea at all."

Thirteen

SOME NIGHTS WERE SIMPLY MADE OF MAGIC. Anything was possible, if one only dared to climb out the window and shimmy down the rose-covered trellis in her best gown to get there. Tonight, Evangeline had dared.

Colored-glass lanterns lit the leaves of the trees around her, giving the woods the appearance of an enchanted forest. Even Victoria's sour mood hadn't dimmed the moon that glowed just for Evangeline tonight. The stars twinkled promises from above, held fast by the cool night air that met her cheeks. It was lovely, and she was in it.

Nothing could dampen her spirits this evening, not the wide-eyed look of her aunt upon spying her, the tense moment between her once-close cousins, or the mysterious gentleman lurking at Isabelle's side. All she saw was Ash.

"I didn't think you would come tonight," he murmured once they were able to speak in private. They strolled at the rear of the group who'd chosen to wander along the Grand Walk instead of dining on thin-sliced ham and tarts.

"You made quite the argument in its favor."

"Did I?" He grinned, slowing their pace to allow a larger gap between them and their party. "It was the mention of fireworks, wasn't it?"

She slipped her hand farther around his arm as she glanced up at him. "You know it wasn't the fireworks."

"Hmm, really?" He frowned, a playful gleam still dancing in his eyes. "Everyone likes fireworks."

"Really."

"I wonder what it was, if not the lure of fireworks. I have it on good authority that I need to work on my salesmanship. I wouldn't want to miss the opportunity for some constructive thought on my ability to provide persuasive argument. I wouldn't want my skills to suffer." His suggestive tone left no room for interpretation of which skills he was truly referring to.

Evangeline sighed. "You are the single most irritating man of my acquaintance."

"Good. I attempt to excel at everything I do."

She attempted to excel at everything she did as well, although she suspected their motivations were quite different. Still, it was nice to have good intentions as common ground. She intended to enjoy every night breeze, firework, and perhaps most of all, every kiss this night had to offer. Tomorrow and the day after that would sort themselves to rights. As long as Ash was at her side, she could be brave and crawl out her window to face the world. When she glanced up at him, a smile covered her face.

Were his intentions good? When tomorrow and the day after came, he might choose to walk away as he had before. Then she would be left to face life alone. "I hope it is true—your desire to excel," she finally replied.

"In respect to what in particular?"

Your staying by my side and making a life here. She swallowed that truth and looked up at him. "In…life. I wish the best for you."

"There's no need to choose your words so carefully, Evie." He placed his hand over hers and met her gaze. "You can say anything you wish to me. I won't hurt you. I wish you'd believe me."

They slowed their steps until everyone in their party had rounded a bend in the path ahead. No one seemed to notice their absence, which was just as well since she had no desire to be among their number. Everything she wanted was here—she only wished to keep it a bit longer. How long would they have together tonight? A few stolen minutes, perhaps an hour if they were fortunate? If tonight was all they could possess, she wanted to live every second of it.

"The things you said last night in my bedchamber, about the manner in which you would kiss me." Her words were rushed. "Did you mean that? Or were you simply spinning a yarn to make me meet you here?" She'd taken a great leap by coming here this evening, and now she was caught in the air, unsure where she would land but hoping it would be in Ash's arms.

"I meant everything I said." All humor disappeared from his face as he spoke. It was a rare occurrence, the lack of a mischievous smile and twinkle in his eyes. The intensity that replaced it made her short of breath. "I want all of that and more with you. The question is, what do you want?"

Life was just in front of her. All she had to do was reach out and grab it before it passed her by. "I want your lips on mine, Ash Claughbane."

"Come with me," he murmured as he pulled her from the path.

She didn't know where he was leading, but she knew she wanted to go with him. Stumbling over tree roots, branches snagging the hem of her gown, leaves stuck in her hair, she wanted it all. The warmth of his hand enveloped hers even through her glove as he pulled her deeper into the cover of the woods. His stride was long, forcing her to scurry behind him to keep pace. Laughing up at the canopy of the trees, she lost herself in the wild moment. She'd never run through a forest before, ignoring the branches that pulled at her gown. How was she to explain... Never mind; she cared not a whit!

Before she could blink, she was in his arms, her breasts pressed to his chest as he backed her toward the trunk of a large elm. The laughter that had bubbled through her only a moment ago simmered into anticipation.

He paused, his hand trailing over her cheek as he watched her. The moonlight dripped down between the leaves, landing on his skin in sultry, glowing dollops of light. Was he waiting for her to speak?

"Ash," she began, but fell silent as he shifted closer to her. His fingers dipped into the hair at the nape of her neck with intoxicating tenderness. Caught between the desire to savor each second as if it were a delicious spoonful of ice and the desire to rush forward into the night, she tipped her chin up, offering herself to him. She waited with parted lips and lowered lashes, wanting this, wanting him.

She rose to her tiptoes, her heartbeat filling the night air as his lips finally descended onto hers. Commanding a response with his gentle caress, he pulled her into the kiss. Slowly drawing her into some place dark and needy, he pushed past her guarded exterior.

Perhaps *guarded* was going a bit far. There was no barrier between them, no guard, only his mouth on hers. She opened to him before he could ask, tangling her tongue with his, tasting him as he did her. Melting into him even as new tension buzzed within her, she reached for more.

He must have felt the same, because he slipped one hand around her waist while his other hand delved deeper into her hair. Everything about him was warm, inviting her into the dangers his kiss promised. Needing something to root her to this place, she laid her hands on his shoulders. The solid strength of his body surrounded her and pulsed beneath her light touch. His grasp was more reckless than hers, his hands roaming over her back, her neck, holding her steady and making her weak.

He broke their kiss, but only long enough to give her bottom lip a playful bite. The kiss that followed muffled his amused laugh until she darted her tongue out, wanting to taste that mischievous smile that always lingered on his face. His amusement died away as he groaned and pulled her closer.

She pulled back on a ragged breath a moment later, smiling as he pressed his forehead to hers.

"Kiss my neck as you said you would," she whispered.

"Demanding," he murmured against her skin, already kissing his way down the line of her jaw. "That's my Evie. Tell me what you want."

His lips slid down the column of her neck, giving her more than she had asked for. She'd asked for a kiss, but the desire that seeped through her limbs hadn't been expressed in words. Anything she said, he would give her. This was her chance to live, to dive into this experience and not come up for air. She was bold. She could make demands of him—this man who had haunted her dreams was here to fulfill them.

"Touch me…as you described it to me." She could be open with him. Ash wouldn't judge her like others. "I want to feel…"

"What do you want to feel?" he asked as he trapped the pulse in her neck beneath his lips, teasing her skin with his tongue.

She whimpered and tightened her grip on his shoulders. "I don't know… I've never felt this way before. Or at least, only the times when I've been with you."

"Put your hands on me," Ash told her.

"My hands are on you." The only knowledge she possessed came from him. Other than the way he touched her, she'd only seen couples embrace on the dance floor. Some ladies thought even that was scandalous. Apparently there was a great deal more scandalous behavior to be experienced, and she had Ash to show her all of it. "Is this not how I should touch you? When couples waltz…"

"They are in the middle of a ballroom," he explained. "We're alone in the woods. Give me your hands."

"Wait." She ripped off her gloves and threw them to the ground at their feet.

"Excellent idea," he murmured against her lips as he kissed her again. He lifted her hands in his, guiding them until the flats of her hands were pressed to his back beneath his coat. Every breath he took, the carefully reined in tension he held in his muscles, every sensation of his body coursed through her hands.

"Ash?"

"Mmm," he answered against her lips.

He was right. She didn't need to hide anything from him. "I want you. All of you."

There was a moment's pause in which he stared into her eyes before he curved his hand over her hip, lifting her from the ground. Fireworks cracked through the night sky somewhere above them with great booms of explosive light. His lips slashed over hers in a desperate plea. She wasn't sure whose plea it was at first, but it was matched in equal parts. He pressed her back into the smooth trunk of the tree, letting her feel how much he wanted her as well. Her breath caught in her throat at the pressure against her hips. She tightened her grip on his back, wanting more.

Somewhere in the outside world that had all but vanished around them, a familiar, terrible sound invaded her ears. She didn't want to hear it. She wanted to discover more about Ash. Squeezing her eyes shut, she wished for this night to never end. But then she heard it once more.

"What was that?" she asked, hoping it was only her imagination.

"I can show you, but not in public gardens beneath a tree."

"No, I heard something."

"Oh." He paused. Was he listening too?

Then the sound cracked through the air again, like a whip snapping at the warmth of her skin—her mother's shrill, false laugh. It was the laugh she used when making a show of finding someone amusing.

She focused on Ash. There was no time to explain. She had no time for good-byes. Her only hope was that he understood what she was doing by some shared knowledge visible in her wide eyes.

If Mother was here, and that laugh meant what Evangeline knew it to mean, then Mother knew Evangeline was down this path. Shoving Ash hard in the chest, she pushed him back, catching him off his guard as he staggered backward a step. Ash watched her with a confused look on his face, but didn't move back toward her.

Tugging frantically at her skirts, she looked down to ensure she was put together. It would have to do. There was no time. With quick motions she forced the loose pins back firmly into her hair. She touched her lips, wishing she could trap this night and his kisses there. But she couldn't linger about wishing and dreaming—she needed to leave. Turning, she ran back toward the path from the shadows.

Branches pulled at her skirts and tree roots threatened to trip her, but she pushed past, finally stumbling onto the path. She straightened and began walking toward the bend where she could hear her mother's voice.

As she came into view, her mother's eyes narrowed on her as she made some excuse to the lady at her side. The seconds stretched out as she watched reality crash in on her with every swish of her mother's gown. Like the waves of an unforgiving sea, her mother moved toward her, pulling Evangeline under. How had she dared to imagine she could navigate these waters without Mother's consent?

"Mother," Evangeline said in greeting once they were alone.

Her mother liked to think her daughter ignored every piece of instruction she'd received in life. In that moment, however, Evangeline stood with perfect posture and completed the most difficult feat of all— she acted as if Ash didn't exist.

෪

Ash leaned out from the trunk of the tree where he could just see Evie. He'd followed her only a few steps before he heard people approaching. Clinging to the shadows of the woods, he now looked through the low-hanging branches, his eyes on the path just ahead. He rested his hand against the tree, watching as Lady Rightworth reached where Evie now stood. She was standing as close to Evie as he'd been only seconds ago. Seconds, and yet he could feel everything changing as if what they'd shared had just disappeared down the winding path.

"Alooone? Out after the sun has set, on a garden path, with your maid at home? And where are your gloves? It is a good thing I found you when I did, Evangeline Green. I owe my thanks to your aunt for sending a footman for me and alerting me to your arrival."

"Damn," Ash whispered to himself. He'd brought this upon Evie. Leering at her in front of her aunt as he had, what had he expected? Even if Lady Knottsby had been foxed, she hadn't been beyond all thought of protecting her niece from him. *Idiot!* He should have known better. He did know better.

"I thought we were beyond such behavior," Evie's mother hissed over the rustle of the leaves as a breeze blew through the trees. "I should have known someone like you could never change."

"I have changed, Mother. I do all that you ask of me."

"I was under the impression that the additional lessons had eliminated the threat of such foolishness. Apparently I was mistaken."

"I'll try harder, Mother. I shall rededicate myself to the task of—"

"I should think so! I suspected during your summer of madness that you were the same waste of flesh as your sister, but I'd convinced myself otherwise."

Ash drew back. Waste of flesh? Who spoke to their daughter in such a way?

"This isn't the same," Evie pleaded. "I've changed. I would never..."

"You were to be special—the shining gem of society. My darling daughter." Evie's mother grasped her chin between her long fingers, and lifted Evie's face toward the moonlight filtering through the trees. "This strumpet who struts about in the dark is no daughter of mine."

"Mother, I'll do anything you ask." Evie staggered back a step as her mother released her. "Please, don't send me away—not until season's end. I'll be the lady you wish me to be."

"Your lessons will begin at daybreak tomorrow, and there will be no tea and biscuits, no rest from our task. Clearly I've been too lenient with you." She sneered down her nose at Evie, seeming to relish the way she was treating her daughter. "If you prove your worth, perhaps I'll allow you dinner tomorrow."

"Thank you, Mother." Evie dipped her head to the woman. "I won't disappoint you."

"That, Evangeline, is doubtful."

Ash couldn't listen to any more. He pushed from the trunk and began to prowl through the trees, not knowing what he may do once he reached Evie's mother and not caring one bit. He was only a few paces from the path where they stood when a hand wrapped around his arm and dragged him back into the shadows.

"What the…" Ash turned to face his attacker, only to find Kelton Brice staring at him.

"You can't help her," Brice said in a whisper.

"The hell I can't." Ash pushed against his friend's hold only to receive a shove back toward the conceal-ment of the woods.

"If you wish to marry her by special license in the morning, be my guest." He released Ash's arm and waved for him to lead the way.

Ash didn't move. His body still reeled from his time with Evie. He longed to surge forward, but his mind refused to budge. He didn't get involved—it was his own rule. "I…"

"That's what I thought. No man wants to gain a wife in that manner. I would know." Brice sneered at the thought, clearly thinking of his own situation.

"I can't hide here and allow her to take the blame for my ideas. The things her mother said..." Ash's voice trailed away with a shake of his head.

"There is no assistance a gentleman can provide a lady on a moonlit path in Vauxhall Gardens without it involving a leg shackle."

"Are you suggesting I allow her mother to berate her and browbeat her into submission while I watch?"

"Yes." Brice eased his grip on Ash's arm but he didn't release him. "You must. Save her tomorrow, but not tonight, not like this. Or you seal your own fate."

"Why are you even here?" Ash finally asked, shaking free of his friend's restraint and pulling his coat back into place.

"Meeting with my future father-in-law," Brice bit out. "People speak of wives as if it's a prize to be burdened with a woman for the rest of one's life." He turned and started walking through the woods toward a different section of the path. "This lady in particular... I don't mind telling you, she's a right nasty piece of work."

Ash fell into pace with his friend, glancing back one last time to where Evie and her mother had been. They were moving down the path toward the garden's entrance now. He knew his friend was right, but his thoughts were still fixated on her. *There is nothing you can do for her tonight*, he reminded himself fiercely. Forcing his attention back to his friend, Ash said, "You have my condolences. St. James mentioned you got a title for heroism as well. It's Hardaway now, isn't it?"

"I was doing Spares business. Do you think I want

a title and a wife to draw attention to my work with the Spare Heirs?"

The new Lord Hardaway didn't pause for Ash to answer, only plowing forward with, "Now, everywhere I go I'm getting congratulations and thanks. *Oh, how heroic you are, Lord Hardaway. Tell us how you saved your future wife from the fire,*" he mimicked. "I'll thank them to keep their bloody traps shut about that fire. If anyone guesses why I was there when it happened…"

"Why were you there?" Ash stepped over a log and kicked aside a fallen branch in their way. "St. James didn't reveal much after it happened. It had nothing to do with my business dealings—that much I know."

"Do you think yours is the only work the Spares are involved with?" Hardaway shook his head with a frown. "St. James has his hands in more pies than we could eat in a year, and I enjoy pie. Cook makes one with a sauce so rich—"

"Then it *was* a different Spare Heirs job," Ash cut in. "I can see why you don't want the title linking you to the fire."

"Who gives two damns about the title? I don't want a blasted wife."

Ash couldn't blame the man. As much as he wanted to help Evie this evening, he didn't want to trade his freedom for a life he hadn't chosen. "Did the lady's father see reason tonight?"

"I never got around to speaking with him on the subject," Hardaway ground out, his blond hair catching the lantern light as he looked up and sighed. "My *betrothed* stormed off when I arrived, and had her mother chasing after her. I thought I had my chance when she fled. But the lady's twin sister kept shooting me these looks across the gazebo. Like a wounded puppy, that one. At any rate, I couldn't very well discuss the matter while someone who looks just like the lady herself stared me down with sorrow-filled eyes."

"Bad luck, that," Ash offered as he pushed a branch away.

"It's not my favorite encounter with twin ladies, to be sure. There was this time in the country…"

Ash stopped listening. Hardaway didn't seem to require someone to listen when he told one of his stories, and Ash's mind still lingered on the other side of the patch of woods and Evie's encounter with her mother.

He'd often wondered what scared Evie so terribly that she couldn't speak her own thoughts. Now he knew. A few pieces slipped into place even though he had no details of her story. Summer of madness. What the devil had that meant? Whatever she'd done, it couldn't justify the way her mother was treating her. Nothing justified such treatment.

It was no wonder she'd hidden herself from him. From the world, really. She was scared of revealing everything her mother hated, everything that woman had stripped from her one hurtful word at a time. Sometimes words were more powerful than the strongest fists. And yet, she'd told Ash that she wanted him. She'd laughed and smiled up at him, kissing him with the command of a woman who knew her own mind. He knew the real Evangeline Green—she'd shown him.

The knowledge of what she had risked to meet him, to open up and let him into her world, made tonight that much more precious. He would treasure every second. No regrets. Even if it had ended badly, the taste of Evie was still on his lips. She'd told him she wanted him, and he'd held her in his arms. He wanted her too. The memory of her body pressed close to his seeped through every crevice of his mind, filling him with longing even while a slow grin began to cover his face.

Was Evie smiling over their time together as well? Or had fear taken the place of such memories? Her mother's arrival had certainly stomped on any embers that had burned bright between them tonight. Would that fear keep her beyond his reach from this day forward?

He didn't know where things were headed with her, but as long as he stayed, he needed her to stay with him. He couldn't lose her, not yet.

Fourteen

ASH MOVED THROUGH THE PEPRIDGES' GARDEN PARTY like a dog on the scent of a fox. Hang his objective, his commitment to his parents, or his responsibility to the Spare Heirs. He needed to see Evie.

"You're certain this was where she was to be today?" Ash asked Ethan, Lord Ayton, as they moved through the crowd gathered in the shade of the trees near the Pepridge home.

"I've told you yes twice already, Crosby," Ayton ground out.

"And?" Ash glanced back at his friend, who was now a step behind him as they squeezed between two groups of chatting ladies.

Ayton caught up to him in one long stride, muttering in a low voice only Ash could hear, "St. James arranged your invitation today for Spares business."

"I'm not sure of your point," Ash lied, tossing out a smile for the ladies they passed.

"This lady of yours seems to be falling into the category of your business, not Spares business," Ayton said with a lopsided, sympathetic smile.

Ash surveyed the side of the garden where they now stood. There—Evie was talking with a friend on the outskirts of the party. "It's rather complicated, to be honest," he said as he watched her for a second.

"Nothing involving a lady is simple," Ayton grumbled in return as he stared in the same direction. It only took one glance to see who held his friend's attention, as his gaze locked on the lady speaking with Evie.

Ash shot his friend a smile, already moving in Evie's direction. "I've always enjoyed a challenge."

"Does my hat match this dress?" he heard the lady beside Evie turn to ask as he moved within earshot.

"Your hat always matches your dress. As does mine." Evie was staring off into the distance. She hadn't seen him yet.

He slowed his pace, taking in how together she appeared today. How odd. Ash felt bruised from her encounter with her mother last night, and yet she showed no evidence that anything had occurred.

"Roselyn," Evie asked, "do you ever want to *not* wear a matching hat? Perhaps arrive at a garden party with no hat at all, lift your face to the sun, and encourage freckles?"

"One of my dear friends has freckles, and I find them charming on her," Roselyn returned. "I don't know that I could pull off the look myself."

Ash glanced back over his shoulder in search of Ayton. He'd clearly had his eyes on Roselyn a few minutes ago, and Ash hadn't intended to abandon him to society so quickly. Perhaps Ayton had been wise, unlike Ash, and had decided against tempting fate by going near the woman. But then Ash spied him caught in conversation with a gentleman Ash didn't recognize. So much for abandoning him to society. "Sorry, mate," Ash whispered to himself as he turned back to Evie and her friend.

"I find I no longer care how it will look," Evie was saying, her face lifted to the sun. "I want to feel the sun on my skin and the breeze in my hair."

Ash paused at her words. That was his Evie, the true Evie. Perhaps her mother hadn't stomped out every burning ember of rebellion she possessed after all. Hope surged through him, making him realize why people were willing to pay such a high price for a vial of it.

"Who are you, and what have you done with Evangeline?" her friend asked.

"I know. It's shameful, isn't it?" Evie chuckled. "Mother would scrub me down and cover me in perfumed powders at the mention of such a thing."

"I won't tell anyone," her friend told her as Ash moved with silent steps through the thick grass.

"I may not be as trustworthy," Ash said from just behind them, making both ladies jump.

Evie turned, her expression somewhere between surprise and relief. His mind was a bit muddled at the moment as well. His need to see her again had led him here. Now that he stood in front of her, what the devil was he to do? Silence stretched out between them, laden with the heat and turmoil following last night.

"Lady Roselyn Grey," Evie blurted out as she blinked up at him. "This is Lord Crosby. Crosby, Lady Roselyn is—"

"Far too busy to talk to the likes of you," Ayton finished with a grin as he joined them.

"Never," Roselyn said. "I hope you will pardon my friend Lord Ayton, who has *no* control over *my* schedule."

"I believe I approve of this friendship, Ayton." Ash gave the lady a nod, then turned to his giant of a friend. "Anyone who can put you in your place deserves a medal of some sort."

"I fear she would be so weighed down with awards, she would cease to move," Ayton said as he stared at the lady.

"Then she won't mind when I steal her friend away for a turn in the garden?" Ash asked.

"Of course not," Roselyn replied, glancing back and forth between the two of them with a curious look in her eyes.

Evie gave him a small nod. "Roselyn, if my mother comes looking for me, tell her I've gone inside to avoid the sun. *That* activity I'm sure she would condone."

His heart clenched in some way he should most likely avoid as she slipped her hand around his offered arm. Where should he begin, when he wasn't even sure what needed to be said? He only knew that what he'd seen last night overshadowed any thought of what they had shared beneath that tree, and that was a difficult task. "I need to speak with you." *Good start, Ash. Statement of fact. Facts are helpful.*

"Is it about last night?" Her smile was false. One of the numbered ones, no doubt.

Any hope he'd possessed when he first saw her

today was snuffed out at the sight of that smile. But he had to try. He needed to see her true smile again as much as he needed air, water, and a stiff drink about now. He sighed. "Yes, it's about last night."

"Then, no, you may not." She nodded to another lady as they strolled around the end of the hedgerow.

"Why not? Evie, what I witnessed wasn't right. You can't tell me that you…"

Evangeline laughed to cover his words with a glance over her shoulder to where a group of older society matrons had gathered to gossip. "Oh, Lord Crosby, you do jest. I too have had a fine morning."

What? He blinked for a second, before following her gaze and catching on. She couldn't risk being heard. Searching the surrounding garden, he spied a gate in a tall wall of greenery and adjusted their direction. "My morning was less than grand due to my concern over rain clouds."

She glanced up at him as they moved step-by-step closer to the gate and the ability to speak without blasted weather metaphors. "It rains here every day, my lord. Every day."

"Then you understand my concern." He couldn't bear the look of complete sorrow in her eyes that one glance held. He longed to knock her mother to the ground in a most ungentlemanly fashion.

"I've become quite resistant to a few puddles."

"You shouldn't have to be." His voice sounded harsh, even to his ears. He swung the gate open a bit harder than he'd intended because it slammed into the wall of shrubbery and became stuck in the dirt.

Was her father aware of her treatment? Surely he

was. How could he not be? They lived in the same home. Ash tensed at the thought of Evie trapped there, a prisoner in her own family.

Anger surged anew within his veins. The revenge he would enact on Rightworth would be sweeter because of what her father had allowed to happen to Evie. What kind of man said nothing while his daughter was held captive in a life not of her choosing? But Ash knew the sort of man Rightworth was—he'd known that unfortunate truth for some time. Rightworth was the sort of man who destroyed families, and after what Ash had witnessed last night, apparently the man's own family was included in the number. He would pay not only for what he had done to Ash's family but what he was still doing to Evie. She had no one—no one but Ash. He had to protect her.

"Not all of us are free to appreciate the sunshine, my lord." She stepped through the gate, taking in the maze they'd entered. She turned back to him with a thin smile. "But enough about the weather."

"This has nothing to do with the weather." His words were harsher than he'd intended as he worked to tamp down the rage that filled him. Glancing in both directions, Ash turned left, since either direction led into a vast green unknown.

"I know." She gave him a shy smile. "Any chance of us discussing something happy? The gardens last night were beautiful. I enjoyed...my time with you." She blushed and looked down at her feet as they walked into the vibrant green maze. "I didn't want it to end."

"Neither did I." He squeezed the fingers that wound

around his arm, holding on to her as if she might dart away like a wounded animal. He sent a questioning glance in her direction, but otherwise remained silent. In the absence of words, they moved farther into the maze, turning one corner, then another. The only sound was that of crunching gravel beneath their feet as they twisted on a directionless path.

"Mother has always had great plans for me. I'm sorry you had to see that."

"I'm not," Ash said in complete honesty.

"Yet I find myself embarrassed by it today."

"You shouldn't be. Now you're not alone in your dealings with her."

She nodded as they rounded another corner of the maze. "I try to act as if all is well."

"You don't have to act with me, Evie."

"I know."

"What great plans does your mother have for you that I threatened to spoil last night?"

"Marriage," she stated.

"Is that all?" he asked as he studied her. Surely there was more to it than that. Marriage was accomplished rather easily, wasn't it? He'd escaped it with Hardaway's assistance only last night.

"Marriage to a gentleman who meets her needs—someone with wealth and a title greater than Father's," Evangeline clarified. "She sees me as her second chance at success."

"Did she do so poorly in her own attempt?" She was Lady Rightworth with an estate, a house in London, his family's money... What more did she want?

"I believe she wishes to look down in disdain on

all those around her who have the misfortune of not being her."

"A noble goal," he teased. "What's success in life without being able to throw stones at those who are less fortunate?"

"Indeed." She laughed and her hand relaxed a bit on his arm.

"Evie…" He shouldn't ask, but his curiosity needed to be sated. "What was the summer of madness your mother mentioned?"

"Oh that." Evie took a breath, her blush deepening to a dark pink on her cheeks. "She finds a way to remind me of that failing every day. I suppose she doesn't want me to mistakenly forget the largest regret of my childhood. It isn't likely that I would dismiss it, even without her reminders. Mistakes large enough to shape the remainder of our lives aren't often forgotten. I was twelve when it happened. Old enough to know how a lady should act, but sometimes people can be pushed…" Evie pressed her lips together and stared down the winding path ahead for a moment before continuing.

"My great-aunt—and benefactress to our family at the time—was visiting us for the summer. My sister and I disliked her. She was and is a hateful woman. The season never seemed to end that year. Such cruelty. Sue and I would sit together at night and dream up ways to be rid of her for good. We kept a list. False letters calling her home, painting her skin a hideous color while she slept—that one was Sue's idea. It was innocent.

"But then Great-Aunt Mildred taunted Sue one

day, told her she would never find a husband. She said that she would take away all funding for Sue's paints and canvases. You would have to know my sister to know how hurtful that was. Anyway, I couldn't stand by and watch for another day. Sue was devastated, and I was angry. So we took the most horrible items from our list. That night while she was in the drawing room with our mother, my sister and I stole into my great-aunt's bedchamber. We replaced her face powders with flour, poured oil on the floor beside her bed, and wrote awful insults on every piece of paper on her desk." Evie squeezed her eyes shut for a second as if blocking out the memory. "Then we went to the kitchen and put…ipecac in her evening tea. Or so I thought. It was childish."

"Actually, I find I wish I knew you when you were twelve. You sound quite amusing."

"Great-Aunt Mildred didn't find it so amusing. You see, it wasn't ipecac that we put in her tea. It was strychnine. It was a mistake. I don't know why they were kept together in that old mess of a cupboard, but they were. The bottles were similar. It's no excuse, but that is what happened. She was so vile. But I didn't mean… The doctor arrived in time to save her, but not the situation. When she was well enough to return to Scotland, she did so, and she took her funds with her. My family was left destitute. And it was my fault."

Silence fell between them for a moment as numbers crashed through Ash's mind. Nineteen, twelve, seven…seven years… Her family was left with no funds because Evie had accidentally poisoned a cruel relative seven years ago. Rightworth had taken everything his family possessed around the same time. That was more than coincidence.

Her actions when she was only a child had destroyed his family but had ultimately led him here to walk arm in arm with her. The knowledge should make him despise her, and yet all he could feel was grateful that he was here walking on this path with Evie at his side. He must be losing his mind. It was poor timing indeed, since he'd just realized the mess he'd mired himself in. If he completed his task in town and had his revenge on her father, Evie would watch as her family lost everything once again—just as had happened when she was twelve. But the man deserved Evie's wrath as well, didn't he? Somehow Ash didn't think Evie would see things in those terms.

With her hand wrapped around his arm, they walked in synchronized steps. When Ash took all the man had, would Evie take the blame again, even though she had no knowledge of his plans? Ash had never considered Lord Rightworth's family when he'd dreamed of taking his revenge. He'd known the man had daughters, but they hadn't been real people to him then. And he certainly hadn't imagined he would meet Evie and feel... He didn't know what he felt for her, but he knew whatever it was, it was going to complicate everything. Ash blinked the passing shrubbery back into focus.

"I never admitted my sister's involvement in my great-aunt's poisoning," Evie continued. "There was no sense in harming her with the truth. Therefore it was my summer of madness and my burden to bear alone."

"It was a mistake," he said in defense of the person

who had inadvertently caused so much harm in his life. "That's hardly cause to drag it back out and discuss it day after day."

"I know, but that's what my mother does. *Without that reminder, how will I learn*," she mimicked. "The truly sad part of it all is that I believe it to be my far lesser crime. What I did last year to Sue…" She trailed off with a shake of her head.

What could she possibly have done? This was prim and proper Evie, after all. "Did it involve sneaking out at night to go to Vauxhall Gardens?"

"A masquerade ball on the neighboring estate," she replied.

"I'm impressed by your daring, Lady Evangeline Green."

"You shouldn't be. What began the night of the masquerade ball will forever be my own quiet summer of madness. No one aside from my sister and my cousins know of it, but I'll always know."

"I have nowhere to go. And I'm not certain I could leave if I wished to do so. Did we take a right and then two lefts, or a left and two rights to get here? I'm not sure. I think, however, our best bet at ever seeing the outside of this maze is to continue forward."

They walked for a moment in silence. The green walls of the path grew narrow, brushing against their shoulders. He wasn't sure if Evie would continue to speak. He had asked a great many questions of her. But just when he'd given up and opened his mouth to make some amusing commentary on mazes, she began.

"I couldn't fail again, not after what I'd done as a

child. I couldn't even make a misstep again. I wouldn't survive it." Evangeline's eyes were haunted. "If my mother had known I was with Sue that night—that it had in part been my doing…"

She fell silent for a moment in which he didn't dare speak. "I decided to let her take the blame. I allowed my own sister to be threatened. I was cruel in order to appear good in my mother's eyes… I let her suffer as I had when I was a child. Alone."

By the look in her eyes, Ash knew there was more. But he couldn't stand the pain he saw there anymore. "I'm sure you wanted to assist her. If you could have helped her situation, you'd have done so."

"You don't understand. If you knew, you wouldn't…"

"I wouldn't what? Think you worthy of this stroll through a garden maze? Believe you're a beautiful person? …I wouldn't stay?"

She bit her lip, tears pooling in her eyes that she quickly blinked away. He stopped, turning to face her there between the walls of green. Placing his hands on her shoulders, he turned her until she was looking up at him.

"Evie, do you know nothing of me? Sometimes, we do what we must for survival. I do understand. I understand that you love your sister. You did what you knew how to do. You did the proper thing."

She nodded as she looked up at him. "The proper thing." She turned away and took a step down the path, making him hurry to catch up to her.

"Mother has always had ideas," she bit out. "Her version of the reality of our lives. I knew when I was a child who I would become. She made me, crafted me from pieces of silk pressed together over years of expectation.

"Most ladies have some fond memories of times when their governess's back was turned. Some afternoon where she slipped down to the pond or…I don't know what. I can't imagine what one would do with such freedom. I was always working. Lessons to make me into this." She held up her arms before dropping them back to her sides.

"I made one mistake when I was twelve, and I'm still reminded of it—as you saw last night. My summer of madness." She shook her head.

He wished he could take her pain away, but the only thing to be done was listen.

"After the night of the masquerade ball last year, Mother truly wanted Sue's blood. She'd never been kind to her, but it became worse." She took a small breath. "When Mother forces me upon a gentleman for a dance or for a walk in the garden, I accept it. I always do what I'm told, don't I? I can't afford the luxury of rebellion. But last year, Mother forced me upon a gentleman who clearly had eyes for my sister. And I let her. I should have stopped it. But instead I was thrown between Sue and the man she loved. I wasn't strong enough. I had to do as Mother instructed me. I knew if I didn't…" She shook her head and looked away. "They're married now. Lord and Lady Steelings. And I lost my sister and closest friend in the process."

Ash stroked the back of her hand as they walked, wishing he could strip away her pain. "Evie, have you explained this to your sister?"

"I've never spoken these words aloud before. Only now. Only to you."

"I think it's time you told your sister this. Where does she live now?"

"She's on an extended wedding trip to France. I'm unsure where. She doesn't write letters, only sends small sketches of places she's been, people she's seen. She's an artist," she explained.

"She would want to hear from you. I'm sure of it."

Evie stopped, turning to look at him. "How do you know?"

"I haven't seen my brothers in years, but I still care for my family…very much so."

"But what I did was too awful. I—"

"Listened to your mother," he cut in as he reached for her, cupping her cheek in his hand. "You did exactly what you were taught to do. The question is, what do you want to do now?"

"Not being strong enough is no excuse for my behavior."

"You're strong enough to repair it. You're allowed mistakes." He pushed a tiny piece of hair behind her ear as he spoke.

"No, I'm not allowed flaws."

"I allow you mistakes then," he said with a smile. "Until the day you allow them of yourself. I can't very well have you perfect around me. What would I appear to be by comparison?"

"Perfect. In my eyes, at any rate."

His heart sped. He held her gaze for a moment before she blushed and glanced away. He trailed his hand down her arm until his fingers tangled with hers.

"I shouldn't have told you any of this," she muttered, still looking down the maze path.

"Why not?"

"Admitting my mistakes to others only stands to hurt me."

He wasn't *others*, he was Ash. How could she think otherwise? "Evie, I would never do what your mother did last night. I would never hurt you in such a manner." He swallowed his anger and tried for a bit of levity. "Anyway, I'm a safe one to talk to since I have no one to tell. I've only kept one person in my life for any length of time, and he's in my employ."

"And you'll be gone soon." Her grasp on his hand tightened. "You didn't say that part, but it's true, isn't it?"

"Unfortunately, that is true. I would like to enjoy our time together while I'm here, at least."

"Was that what you were doing last night? Enjoying your time?"

"It was enjoyable, but not in the way you mean it," he said, a bit offended by her low opinion of him.

"But you *are* leaving. That hasn't changed, even though we…"

"I will have to leave town, Evie. That hasn't changed. I wish I could explain…"

"And this is simply a stroll in the garden to pass the time."

"Nothing about this is simple." He didn't know what this was, but he knew damn well it was no simple stroll in the garden. He also knew he could make her no promises. He was leaving town when his work here had ended, no matter how sweet

Evie's kisses were, no matter how he enjoyed her company or the fit of her body in his arms. He would have to sort out how to protect her from her family in the process, but he knew he would have to leave her.

"Some things are that simple, Ash."

He didn't know the proper response. He always knew what to say to turn the conversation around in his favor. It was his damn life's work to know how to turn this around. But Evie, who didn't believe herself strong enough, had struck him into silence with her words. *Pull yourself together, man.*

She looked away, down the path where a sundial was perched at the center of the maze. "It's certainly a lovely day," she said to fill the silence that had come between them.

"The weather, Evie? Has it come to such dire circumstances?" He reached for her, but she'd already stepped too far away from him.

"It would seem it has indeed come down to the weather. Will you excuse me? I find I'm growing overwarm in the sun, and we have reached the end of our path."

"Evie," he called after her, but she didn't turn around, instead disappearing into the hedgerow on the opposite side of the sundial.

"It's for the best," he murmured to himself. He hadn't known what he was going to say if she'd stopped to listen to him. All he knew was a small voice echoing in his memory. *You may call me the lady who left you standing alone in the library.*

He squinted up into the sun. It was a maze, not

a cold library, but the day chilled him to the bone nonetheless. He couldn't let her leave him. Cursing under his breath, he turned back to retrace his steps through the maze. Perhaps then he would discover where he went wrong.

⁂

Evangeline descended the steps to the main floor of her home with practiced grace, all evidence of a fitful night's sleep tucked safely away from view. Her past might have been horribly exposed to Ash in that dratted garden maze yesterday afternoon, but there was nothing to be done about it this morning.

Jane had informed her only minutes ago that her mother had summoned her to the drawing room. As much as Evangeline longed to spend the morning sorting out her thoughts where Ash was concerned, she knew she couldn't leave her mother waiting too long. Evangeline took a small breath at the bottom of the stairs and released her grasp of the rail, determined to face this day and her mother as she always did.

"Lord Winfield," Evangeline said a moment later from the drawing room door, stopping short of entering the room. She darted her eyes to her mother and back again. The smug look on her mother's face explained everything. She'd somehow managed to detain the lord she'd chosen for Evangeline, and she wasn't going to release him anytime soon. Taking a step into the room, Evangeline resigned herself to spending the following few hours on display like a hat in a shop window.

"Lady Evangeline, your mother has been

entertaining me in your absence with tales of your embroidery talents."

"Has she?" Evangeline shot her mother a quick glance as she moved farther into the room. "I wasn't aware that my skill was of particular note."

"Evangeline, darling. You know you are quite skilled at all the domestic arts." Her voice was light to disguise the warning that resided beneath. "There is no need for modesty."

"It's quite all right, Lady Rightworth," Winfield chimed in, unaware of the unspoken battle between the two ladies in the room with him. "Your daughter's beauty far exceeds any need to prove herself worthy as a lady."

Evangeline looked at him for a moment. He must have meant the comment as a compliment, but something about his words grated at her nerves. "And if I was less fortunate in my appearance, I would need to work to better myself?" she finally asked.

"Evangeline!"

Lord Winfield shifted in his seat to face her. "We all have attributes to contribute to the world, my lady."

"You mean to my future husband's home. I can't imagine I would contribute anything beyond the country estate where I'll reside." She shouldn't challenge his thoughts. She should accept his opinion that she only had beauty to offer the world. A week ago she would have, but not anymore.

"Isn't that quite enough for a lady to manage?" he asked with a smile meant to charm. "Home, family, appearances at the right events on a gentleman's arm?"

"I suppose it is." And it was what she'd claimed she wanted—marriage to a gentleman, a fresh start in life.

Escape from her mother was within her grasp. Winfield could offer her a life outside these walls with just a bit of encouragement. Only, he thought her finest accomplishment in life was her looks. She was more than an assortment of fine cheekbones and batting eyelashes...wasn't she? Ash had thought so. Today, the future Winfield represented—the one she'd wanted for so long—appeared terribly hollow in her mind's eye. She would be trading one prison for another of a different sort. In no way did marriage to one of any array of gentlemen set before her lead to her freedom.

"The season's entertainments alone would fill your days, I'm sure. It's a great responsibility to help a man appear successful in the eyes of his fellows. But it would be a simple task for a lady of your distinction," his lordship said with a kind smile.

She should give him smile number two in return— she should. But something about his expectations for her was bothersome. She wasn't certain where her talents lay, but she knew she was more than the image her mother had created all those years ago. Ash had seen more in her, and even without him at her side, she saw it now too. She deserved more.

She reached for a teacup from the service on the table. "A lady's looks and their ability to reflect her husband's worth *are* all that matter."

"Indeed." Lord Winfield laughed at what he took to be a jest, which stopped the set-down that hung on her mother's lips.

"Perhaps I shouldn't eat too many of these biscuits then." She dipped her gaze to the platter that lay between them. "My mother is always saying so."

"My daughter enjoys teasing those she holds in esteem, my lord," her mother said with a wild look of panic in her eyes.

And my mother enjoys bettering herself in society, Evangeline thought. "Mother is correct, of course," she said a moment later. "Though I should in truth refrain from eating all the tea biscuits. I wouldn't want to deny his lordship his share. Anyway, I find I prefer ices. Tell me, my lord, do you have a favorite flavor of ice?" she asked, thinking of Ash and their shared table of sweets.

"Evangeline," her mother warned. "I'm sure Lord Winfield is too busy to spend afternoons eating ice."

"Then I consider myself fortunate that he found time to call on us today."

"It's my pleasure to be here. Though it is true it's been too many years since I had ice to recall my preferred flavor."

"Just as I thought," her mother snapped with her eyes on Evangeline. "Gentlemen with titles as grand as Winfield's don't indulge in such frivolities."

"That is unfortunate. I hope you find more time for leisure pursuits in the future, my lord. It's quite lovely to enjoy a dish of ice in the park."

"I'll keep that in mind," Winfield returned.

"Evangeline, it looks to be a fine day outside. Don't you enjoy days like this?" her mother asked, clearly steering the conversation.

Evangeline parted her lips to reply with a rehearsed line, but then she looked at her mother as she glared back over the rim of her tea cup. The woman was forcing this courtship forward regardless of Evangeline's clear misgivings on the subject. It was to be expected, but one thin thread in the knotted embroidery of her life demanded rebellion.

Her mother had starved Evangeline, controlled her words, forced her to train daily to be someone she was not, and threatened to send her away to Scotland to live with the aunt she'd almost killed. But above all else, her mother had ended the one night she'd had with Ash. Evangeline would never forgive her mother for ending what had only just begun. He would leave London, and she would never know what might have happened under that elm tree in the park. And for that, she refused to claim that the trees provided nice shade in the park. Silence—it was the only rebellion she dared, but she exercised it now in full force.

"My lady," Winfield said to gain Evangeline's attention a long moment later. "If days seen out in the park please you, I would be honored if you would join me one afternoon soon for a ride—at the proper hour, of course."

"She would like that very much," her mother answered for her.

"Until then, I will keep every image of you with me as I leave here today." He offered her a kind smile. "Every smile and turn about the ballroom floor is locked away in my mind for safekeeping."

"How kind of you, Lord Winfield," her mother crooned.

It was kind. And yet...those smiles hadn't been true smiles. Her only true happiness had been with Ash, and she'd left him standing alone in the center of a garden maze. She'd left him there before he could leave her. He'd become too close. He knew too much. Surely it would fall apart now. And so she'd walked away. She'd acted out of fear of losing him, but she'd spent too much of her life being afraid and refusing to live. She wanted to experience all that life had to offer. She wanted a table of ices to choose from and the freedom to eat from every dish. Perhaps Ash was already on the road out of town after their cross words yesterday, but his strength remained with her.

She smiled and stood from her chair. "If that is settled, will you excuse me? I am sorry to cut our tea short, but I must leave now."

"Now?" Her mother drew back in shock. "His lordship came here to call on you."

"It's quite all right," Winfield said, rising. "I have business in town I must see to as well. I trust that I will see you at tonight's ball, my lady?"

"Of course." She would be at every ball. She didn't want to miss a chance to see Ash again if he was still about, and if Lord Winfield was there as well, so be it.

She watched Winfield leave the room before setting her teacup on the table with a clatter of china. "I'm off as well, Mother. I'm going to visit my friend Roselyn Grey." Evangeline didn't spare her mother a glance as she shook out the folds of her day dress. She didn't know how to find Ash to make amends, but she could begin taking the correct steps in her life by supporting her friend when her help was needed.

"She's steeped in scandal," her mother hissed. "I forbid you to go to that home of madness. The things that must happen under that roof are unimaginable."

Evangeline turned, facing down her jailer. "My friend needs me, and I will not disappoint her as I did my own sister."

"Do *not* speak to me of your sister!" Her mother rose to her feet, looming over Evangeline like the monster she was.

"Very well," she murmured. She wouldn't speak of her sister, but she also wouldn't turn her back on her friend when support was needed. She turned and walked away from her mother. If only doing so permanently was as easily accomplished as finding the perfect flavor of ice.

Fifteen

"Have you lost your capacity for clear thought?" St. James asked.

"Most assuredly, yes." Ash sank back onto the carriage seat opposite his friend, who didn't seem to feel very friendly at the moment.

"You're aware of the familial relationship between your lady and Lord Rightworth, and yet you seek her out after she's left you alone in a garden only yesterday? Even if you were using her as part of—"

"She isn't my lady," Ash grated out. The thought angered him, even though it should simplify his life. He should be glad she had walked away from him, yet he wasn't.

"Interesting."

Ash glared at St. James as he folded his arms across his chest. "No, it isn't interesting in the least."

"I fail to see how *this*"—St. James paused to indicate their chase across town—"will benefit your plans, *Lord Crosby.*"

"Neither do I," Ash muttered to himself as he watched building after building slide past the window.

"Then why take such a risk?" St. James asked. His sharp eyes took in every detail of the situation. "Damn."

"What? I can fix this, quite easily in fact. I'll sort things out with Evie. And her father has already agreed to invest heavily in Crosby Steam Works…"

"You love her. You went and fell for your enemy's daughter like the plot of some novel. You know they're called tragedies for a reason, don't you?"

Love? Ash uncrossed his legs and leaned forward, staring down his friend. "Slow your pace there, St. James. I do not *love* her. I don't go about handing my heart out while working." Did he? No, what he felt for Evie was concern mixed with lust, nothing more. "Evangeline and I met a year ago, and she discovered my identity when I first arrived in town. I had to further a relationship with her to keep her quiet."

"Did you?" St. James raised one dark brow. "How much further did you further?"

"Rather personal, don't you think, mate?"

"I do." The carriage grew dark as they rounded a corner onto an unlit side street. St. James's voice had a rather ominous quality that Ash attributed to the night, but it went deeper than that. The man's specialty was secrets, after all.

St. James continued, "I also think the Spare Heirs are wrapped up in this business of yours. If she turns cold on you—which she appears to have already done—we're all in deep trouble."

"I…" Ash began. "There have been a few instances of… We…"

"When a salesman can no longer speak in whole sentences, it points to a larger problem."

"I'm aware," Ash grumbled, sinking back into the seat once more.

"I should begin taking measures now to protect the Spares. It seems the society requires a great deal of protection these days."

"No," Ash snapped. "Don't get involved. Not yet."

"Very well. You have two days to clean up this mess, or I will see it done without you." He rapped on the roof of the carriage for Stapleton to stop. A moment later, St. James had vanished into the night.

"Love," Ash muttered once he was alone. St. James's usually sharp mind had led him astray. Ash didn't love Evie—he couldn't. Love meant attachment; attachment meant staying; and staying wasn't possible. Especially not considering her surname.

But in spite of all of those sound reasons… Bollocks. He loved Evie.

He'd kept her close in the beginning out of necessity. But the need to keep seeing her had turned in quite a different direction some time ago. St. James was right—she now threatened everything Ash had put together over the last seven years. And yet, he risked it for her. He spent his days seeking out her company and his nights dreaming of her. Even now, he was rushing across the city in hope of finding her.

Blasted love. How had he allowed this travesty to happen?

He was Ash Claughbane, a gentleman meant for the road. The carriage rolled to a stop outside the ball, mocking his need to keep moving. He almost laughed, but as he reached for the door, he saw her. Gliding out into the quiet night alone, Evie had emerged from the ball before he'd even arrived. Her usually ornate hair was different tonight, as was her jeweled neck—or lack thereof. She wasn't wearing any jewelry aside from the small pearls in her ears. She looked…pleased, happy. This was the true Evie, the one that he loved. His hand tightened on the carriage door.

Would she be so pleased if she knew he was sitting in his carriage watching her? Grinning from ear to ear at the mere sight of her? She'd made it rather clear that if he was planning to leave, he should get on with it. It was selfish of him, but he wanted more time with her. He couldn't stay. One more night, however…

"Evie," he called out before he could think better of it.

She turned and blinked into the darkness before a smile lit her face and she moved toward him. "I was hoping I might see you tonight."

"I only just arrived." He opened the carriage door and crouched in the doorway, waiting to move once he knew her direction. "Are you leaving?"

"I complained of a headache." She grinned up at him in such a mischievous manner that he had no need to ask after her health.

"I may turn you into a swindler yet. May I offer you a ride home?"

She cast a glance to each side, clearly checking to make certain they were the only ones present. Taking a small step toward him that made his entire body go on alert, she looked up at him and lowered her voice, "What if I don't want to return straight home?"

"Then you should without a doubt come with me. I know of just the place." He held his breath, not knowing if she would come with him. It wasn't proper; he knew that much to be true. But she was already outside the ball with an excuse in play. Yet she hesitated, looking to her maid several paces away. But when she looked back at him, a ray of hope shined in her eyes—one of pure rebellion. In the next second she smiled and gathered her skirts.

Turning back to her maid who stood a few paces away, Evangeline murmured a few quick directions. Ash watched as the woman disappeared around the corner of the building, clearly on her way to ensure Evie's headache was a believable excuse.

After he'd assisted Evie into the carriage while ensuring no one near the entrance to the ball was looking, he leaned out and called up directions to Stapleton. Dropping back into his seat, he noticed Evie had seated herself across from him. She'd agreed to come with him and yet she kept her distance.

"Do you know you have a pair of odd-looking dogs in the seal upon your door, Lord Crosby?"

"They're symbolic."

"Of what, exactly?"

"The hurry I was in a while on the road to London."

"They suit you."

"Two ugly dogs suit me? I believe *you* are the one who needs to practice key skills if you believe that to be flattering."

"Dogs tend to run free, turning wild and taking scraps from the neighbors if allowed to do so."

"They also bite," he countered.

"Bite? No. Your painted-on dogs look quite docile."

"Do they?" He reached for her without warning,

lifting her from the opposite seat and depositing her in his lap.

"Perhaps *docile* was the wrong word."

"Why were you escaping the ball tonight?"

"You weren't in attendance," she admitted.

"You went there to find me? When you left the garden yesterday, you were quite clear that you didn't want to see me."

"Yet you called my name when you next saw me."

"You know my opinion on following rules."

"Then what is my excuse?" she asked.

"Poor judgment?"

A small sigh escaped her lips as she gazed into his eyes. "That goes without saying."

"Then let's not say it." He stretched his fingers into her hair, silky strands tickling the backs of his fingers. He wanted to touch every part of her, to study each in wonder as she lay before him. Pulling her close until their lips met in the flickering light of street lamps, he tried to tell her in that kiss everything he couldn't say aloud. He wanted to protect that fragile moment, even as his body hummed with tension and the slight weight of her across his thighs had him wanting to drive into her and make her his right there on the velvet-covered seat of his carriage. She must know how much he wanted her, since at the same moment her eyes met his with a combination of curiosity and need. He would not lose control of the situation. He would take things slow with her. Tonight he wanted to show her...

But in that instant, as if making a snap decision, Evie lifted the hands she'd kept folded in her lap and delved them into his hair. With her sweet lips pressed against his, he threw off any idea of what he might have shown her on the slow tour of what could be and deepened their kiss. Holding her exactly where he wanted her to be, he angled his lips over hers, tasting her. Her lips were soft and willing beneath his, and soon that languid desire spread into her limbs. He needed her, more of her.

He moved his hand up her waist to the outside of her breast, his thumb teasing her nipple into awareness through the layers of her clothing. She gasped against his lips, breaking their kiss to stare into his eyes. She barely breathed, and even her fingers ceased their desperate tugging in his hair. Was she struggling to keep her composure? She should know she didn't need to worry about such things with him. He looked deep into her eyes and palmed her breast, challenging her to let go. Her breaths grew shallow, but otherwise she didn't move.

As much as he didn't want to say the words that were a growing warning in his mind, he did. "Do you want me to stop?"

"No. I'm worried you will stop. I don't want it to end." Her voice cracked as she spoke.

He let out a harsh laugh of relief and pulled her close, wrapping his arms around her. "Trust me when I say I will only stop when you tell me I must."

"Truly?" she asked into his shoulder.

He shifted her in his lap so he could see her face. "Evie..." He almost said the words then. *I love you.* But the truth was a rather resistant thing at times, and now was one of them. Instead he kissed her with all the frustrated, desperate longing he possessed, his need for her growing instead of diminishing.

She grasped the hair on the back of his neck, dipping her fingers beneath his cravat to drag against his skin. He ripped the damn length of fabric from his neck and threw it aside in a heartbeat before returning his hands to her body. She trailed her perfect fingers down his neck, making him turn his head into her touch. But when she leaned forward to press her lips to his skin, as he'd done to her only a few days ago, it was the undoing of any control he still possessed.

He ran his hands up her sides, needing to feel more of her. He'd never hated clothing more than he did at this moment. Tugging at the fabric of her already low-cut gown, along with her stays and shift, he pulled her breasts free of the fabric. Beautiful. Even in the dark, her skin glowed in the glimpses of moonlight that moved across her body as the carriage rolled gently down the street. Her pert nipples were poised above the wrinkled mess of her gown, begging for his touch. Looking into her eyes, he touched her soft skin, roaming his hands over her. He kissed her again as he took her nipple between his knuckles and grazed the surface until her hands grabbed fistfuls of his shirt.

He tipped her back a fraction over his arm and lowered his lips to her collarbone. She became restless in his arms, squirming and torturing him in the process as she ground into him. Refusing to cut short his exploration of her body, he moved to her breasts on a trail of kisses. He loved the way her skin felt against his lips. He could kiss her forever. When he reached the already sensitive peaks of her breasts, she arched into him with a small moan. He dragged his teeth across her with playful bites before soothing those peaks with his tongue.

Evie sat up straight at this, the look in her eyes one of pure wanton danger. She splayed her hands on his chest, pushing his coat back from his shoulders as she moved. He wrestled out of the sleeves and let the coat fall around them on the bench seat.

He slid his hands up her spine, drawing her back into his embrace before trailing his hands down over her hips. Supporting her with one arm wrapped securely around her, he ran a hand down her leg. Tracing a line up the back of her knee and dragging her gown with him as he moved, he pulled her legs up onto the seat beside them, one hand on the bare flesh of her inner thigh.

"I don't know what to do," she admitted.

Ash froze. When he looked up, he met her shy yet intent gaze. He was rushing into this just as he'd said he wouldn't do. "You don't have to do anything," he assured her before forcing himself to ask, "Should I stop?"

"No," she almost pleaded as she ran her fingers over his shoulders.

"You can do anything you want, Evie. I'll give you anything." He meant his words beyond this night of pleasure. He would give her anything in this world if it made her smile.

"Then I want to do this," she said, shifting to a new angle and flicking her tongue out to taste him, kissing him with an inexperienced fervor that drove him wild. She was pressed close to his body, her breasts dragging against the linen of his shirt while she breathed in small gasps. Clearly she enjoyed the sensation because she moved against him again. She was intoxicating, and he was drowning in her warmth. He had no need of air, only her.

He slid his hand up the inside of her thigh a little faster than he'd intended. Needing more of her, he took control of the kiss as he reached the apex of her legs. Grazing his knuckles over the soft core of her body, he explored her reactions to his touch. He wanted to run his hands over her entire body, memorizing her, learning her, claiming her.

He palmed her, not insisting on more just yet, only to feel her body's response to the intrusion of his fingers. Her breath caught even as she melted farther into his arms. She blinked her eyes open and met his gaze. There was something unreadable in her eyes, but he was certain desire mingled there with other unspoken emotions. A moment passed in which he didn't move, only existing on the slight shivers that ran through her body. When she finally relaxed into his touch, he released the breath he hadn't realized he was holding.

"Evie," he whispered, a plea for more. Tugging at her bottom lip with his teeth, he pulled her back to him with playful kisses. He couldn't take her here on a moving carriage seat, but he couldn't let her go yet either.

A second later, she encircled his neck with her arms, dipping her hand into his shirt to grasp his bare shoulder. His lips slashed over hers, making the demands that coursed through his blood reality. He heard the fabric of his shirt rip but didn't care. Let her tear it from his body. He needed her touch, needed to feel her against him.

He pressed the heel of his hand against the springy hair beneath his palm. Any thought of moving too fast vanished as she whimpered and arched into his touch.

He gave her what she wanted. She might not know what to do, but her body certainly did.

Deepening their kiss, he rejoiced when she opened to him, allowing him better access to her body. He stroked her with teasing touches, pulling at the fragile walls she'd placed around her heart. Every pass of his thumb over the small bud of her sex, every circle he made there, tumbled another piece of her guarded exterior to the floor. She was trembling in his arms, exposed to him, flushed and perfect.

She gave a small squeak of alarm as he slipped a finger into her wet heat, but he captured the sound with his mouth. As he brought her to the tipping point, the pleasure unrelenting, she arched into him. Her body was pliant in his hands. He ached to be inside her, but right now she was his—offered up like a gift he could never repay. With every movement, he attempted to return the happiness she gave him.

She clung to him, fingernails digging into his shoulders, and he wasn't much closer to stable than she was. Breathing his name at his lips, she pushed against him, begging for more.

"Come apart for me, Evie. You don't have to hide. Not with me," he coaxed her.

She stretched for the freedom he promised as he pressed his thumb to her core and drove into her, beckoning her over the steep edge into bliss.

"You don't have to be afraid anymore," he murmured against her skin. Her body tightened around him, and her grasp pulled her closer to his chest. He pushed into her with one final movement as she pressed her face into his shoulder, burying her scream there. He worked to keep from shaking from the impact of her climax.

It was a beautiful sight. Her dark hair fell around her shoulders, and her dress was a crumpled mess gathered at her waist as she lay over him like a blanket. She pulsed with the warm remnants of desire as she grew languid in his arms. He continued to touch her, drawing lazy circles over her exposed hip.

He was still unbelievably hard, and every bump of the carriage while she sat in his lap made that painfully clear. But she was happy and lounging in his arms, and for tonight that would have to be enough.

Seeming to have the same thought, although a much more innocent version of his own, Evie asked, "Should I? I don't know how to do what you just did, but I could try to—"

"No." It was too tempting an offer—one that would lead to her naked and straddling him as they rolled through the streets. "Let me hold you. That will be enough for tonight."

"And tomorrow night?" she asked, a note of hope threaded through her voice.

"We'll see," he murmured. Another night of this was dangerous—he knew that for certain.

He held her as the carriage continued down the street. He peppered her bare shoulder with kisses as she rested her cheek on his shoulder, then smiled and pulled her closer.

He could stay here forever, circling London with a sated Evie in his arms.

Forever. He'd never thought of forever before. It was a foreign word he associated with death and desolate lands. But when he thought of Evie beside him, that desolate land became lush and hopeful. Love, hope, and forever. He was in trouble. Perhaps one of his love tonics actually worked, and he'd mistaken it for the decanter of whiskey he kept in his bedchamber. He smiled against Evie's skin at the thought.

"Ash?" she finally asked, the warmth of his name blowing across the side of his neck.

"Hmmm?" He didn't trust himself to talk just now. He was likely to blurt out that he loved her, and now was not the time, after what she'd just shared with him.

"Where are we going?"

"We're already there." He slid his hands over the bare skin of her back, keeping her warm in the night air as he held her to his chest. Her heart beat through his body in time with his own. He wasn't ready to let her go. "I told my driver to keep moving in circles if he must, but not to stop."

Her soft chuckle reverberated through his body. "I suppose he's accustomed to such directions with your line of work."

"He is, but not for as good a reason as I had tonight." He brushed the hair that had fallen down her back to the side. He couldn't stop touching her. Although his body still ached for release, he only wanted to hold her a bit longer. Blasted love.

She straightened enough to meet his gaze in the dim light. "You haven't…offered other ladies…assistance home, have you? You do have quite a nice conveyance. Almost as if it was made for this sort of activity."

"No, actually. But I'll try that in the next town over, if you think it would be successful." His voice still held the deep rasp of desire as he spoke. "Imagine the number of ladies I could fit in here," he said, looking around in consideration.

She shoved him in the shoulder. "I shouldn't have asked."

"Five? Six if they're on the small side," he added, still looking around his opulent carriage.

"Ash," she reprimanded even while she laughed.

"One, only one," he said a moment later, pressing his forehead to hers. Their gazes locked in the constantly changing light from the windows. Before either could read too much promise into those words, he quipped, "I only got this carriage two months ago."

"You're impossible," she said.

And then he was kissing her again. He would have to return her to her home soon, or her parents would know she hadn't gone straight there from the ball. Yet he didn't want this night to end. Returning her home meant giving her back to his lifelong enemy.

"Meet me tomorrow night," he murmured against her lips, knowing that was the quickest he could see her again once he released his hold on her tonight.

"For another ride in your carriage?"

"No. Tomorrow there will be a destination."

She made a small sound of complaint and squirmed closer on his lap, making him groan with unfulfilled longing.

"Trust me."

"I do," she said in a soft voice.

Perhaps Evie's poor judgment did need to be mentioned after all. But instead, he signaled Stapleton with a quick bang on the roof and drew her into another kiss.

Sixteen

IAN CLENCHED THE FIST THAT REMAINED HIDDEN beneath the rough surface of the inn table. They needed to be on the road chasing after this Crosby fellow, but instead they were here—debating if they should be here at all. Far too much time had been spent already gathering the men who sat around him, then nearly a week had been wasted on the road toward Oxford. But they were near London now. With each day he came closer to the man who'd swindled his grandmother, but he also came closer to killing the other gentlemen traveling with him. *Gather the neighboring gentlemen*, Rockwale had insisted.

Blasted Rockwale. What did he know? This was the last time Ian would take advice from a foxed butler. Now he was trapped with these men, swilling ale instead of completing his task.

"Perhaps it's time we turned back, Lord Braxton. We have homes and lives waiting for us, after all," Lord Feathsly said to the murmured agreement of the other gentlemen around the table.

Ian shifted to keep from tapping his foot in his

impatience. "If you wish to return to your families without accomplishing the task we set out to do, by all means return. Lord Feathsly, I believe you invested rather heavily with our quarry. If you want to return home to your wife and inform her of your failure, then go ahead. I hold no ill will toward you."

"Now see here, Braxton—"

"I'm planning to travel the few remaining miles into London, where I will make further inquiries." Ian indicated the road outside the Cross Keys Inn where they'd stopped hours ago to water the horses and *rest for a bit*. Rest, ha! Who needed rest? Not Ian. "I will find this Lord Crosby, as he is now known. If you want no involvement in the last of our journey, so be it." He took a long drink from the tankard in his hand, allowing the underlying taunt to find its mark.

"I suppose we've come this far," Feathsly muttered.

"Right you are, Feathsly," another gentleman in their group encouraged. "We know the man's alias now, as well as his direction."

The youngest of their group—though still older than Ian by at least ten years—chimed in, eager to be on the winning side of the argument. "Think of how celebrated we'll be as the heroes who brought the villainous Crosby to justice right in the heart of London society."

"I suspect there will be celebrations in our honor," the gentleman at Ian's side mused.

"No doubt," Ian agreed with a raised tankard of ale. In truth, he had his doubts about how celebrated they would be for bringing to light the fact that half the ton had bought into the man's schemes. In Ian's experience, gentlemen didn't enjoy admitting their flawed thinking. But he wasn't about to argue when the idea was helping his cause. The other gentlemen at the table raised their glasses and drank.

They would be in London by tomorrow, but then began the trouble of finding the elusive *Lord Crosby*. He had seemed to be everywhere at once in Bath, but that was the nature of Bath, wasn't it? This was London.

A different gentleman in his group had wanted to return home every day of their journey thus far. What would a city the size of London bring? How many calculated statements of persuasion would Ian have to make to these men before he was able to find Crosby? He took another drink and ran his hand over the pocket where he kept that page of the *Times*. The ink had faded and blurred from him unfolding it and reading it again and again.

That blasted man would pay, not only for what he'd done to Ian's grandmother but for Ian's present inconvenience. He'd been under the impression that managing his sisters was difficult. He'd been wrong. Managing six gentlemen in search of justice and their investment funds was far more difficult. Crosby had no idea the storm that was brewing for him.

Ian smiled and stood from the table, unable to sit in these stagnant waters any longer. He needed to move, needed to act. "Let us return to the road. If we leave now, we can reach London by nightfall."

"Quite the quick pace you've set for us, Braxton."

Quick? They thought this quick? "I only want to see this matter settled in a timely manner. You can rest once we're in London."

"We'll have to rest after traveling at such speeds."

"And I would like to visit my tailor while in town."

"Capitol idea, Feathsly. I wouldn't be opposed to stopping at my club. It's been some time since I've been to town."

Ian stopped listening and strode out the door. The other gentlemen in his party could do what they pleased. He was going to town for only one reason—to find Crosby and bring him to justice. Ian would not be *resting* until he accomplished his task.

The afternoon sun filtered down on him through gray clouds. Not too far away, under these same clouds, Crosby was no doubt busy hoodwinking some poor member of good society. Ian wouldn't stop until he found the man.

Seventeen

EVANGELINE CRUMPLED THE SHORT NOTE IN THE PALM of her hand and tossed it into the parlor fireplace before her mother could ask what it was about. She'd already memorized the words anyway. Like a promise whispered in her ear, it made her smile.

Garden gate at eight o'clock tonight.

Yours,
Ash

She blushed at his salutation. *Yours.* Was he hers? After chasing after him for a year, and then having him chase after her, was this it? It certainly had felt like something real in his carriage last night. He'd told her he couldn't stay after his work was done. She knew the truth of their situation, but she also knew the truth of her own heart for the first time. Her decisions weren't steering her astray as her family thought—they were steering her in the unlikely direction she was meant to go.

Tonight, that direction was wherever Ash was going.

After a terribly long afternoon filled with lectures from her mother, quiet plans with her maid, and anticipation for tonight, she was at the garden gate with ten minutes to spare. She'd been taught not to pace; however, she'd also been taught not to climb from her window to meet a gentleman at the garden gate. She turned and had begun walking back to where she'd come from when she heard his voice over her shoulder.

"Leaving so soon?"

"Ash," she exclaimed as she turned back toward him. He stood on the opposite side of the fence. The street behind him was empty, making him look as though he'd simply appeared at the garden gates without the need of movement. "Where is your carriage?"

"You sound disappointed. Are you using me for my fine conveyance?" A look of mock shock drew his brows together.

"Of course I'm using you," she teased as she neared him at the fence. "I have a weakness for pairs of strange-looking dogs."

"Doesn't everyone?" He held the gate open for her.

Glancing over her shoulder, she saw no sign of watchful eyes in the windows of her home as she slipped out onto the dark street.

Ash took her hand in his and led her around the corner to where his carriage was waiting. "Did you complain of a headache again?"

Her plan this evening had been carefully thought through. Jane would make certain she was seen going into Evangeline's bedchamber in another hour. A scripted, one-sided conversation would take place, and at the end of it, Jane would leave, locking Evangeline's door, yet leaving her window open for Evangeline's return. It was a brilliant plan. "Tonight I'm reading in bed," she said with a satisfied smile.

"Would you like to return to it?" He glanced at her, a grin tugging at his cheeks. "I would happily join you in your bed. Although your book may go unfinished."

"Where are you taking me?" she asked to cover the deep blush that heated her skin.

"It's a surprise." He handed her up into the carriage before joining her.

Tonight he didn't pull her into his arms, leaving her somewhat disappointed. Instead, he sat across from her, his long legs stretched across the floor of the carriage, trapping her feet between his ankles. From this position, she was forced to sit straight with nowhere to look but into his blue eyes. Perhaps *forced* was a strong word, as she had only a moment ago considered climbing onto the man's lap for the ride. But there was something quite intimate about sitting in a darkened carriage and staring into a man's eyes. He nudged the sides of her feet with his boots and smiled at her as they began to roll away from her home.

For the duration of the short ride, she guessed their destination while Ash made wild claims of where he *should* take her—to the park to swim in the Serpentine, to the harbor to smell the dead fish, to a brothel to have her cheeks rouged. By the time they arrived in an alley between two tall buildings, she was out of guesses. Where were they? But just as she leaned near the window to investigate, Ash produced the cravat she'd pulled from his throat the previous night.

"Have you decided to move into your carriage now?" she asked as he stretched the length of fabric out between his hands. "If you brought in a few options of coat, you would never need to leave."

"This is to be a surprise." He held up the cravat and nodded for her to comply with whatever he had planned for her.

Her heart sped as she looked at him. "You want to blindfold me."

"Have you never been surprised before?"

"Not with anything pleasant," she admitted.

"Then I'm glad you're with me tonight." His smile was warm, easing her fears.

She leaned forward on the seat until she was poised in front of him. He lifted the cravat to her face. His fingers grazed her cheeks in a light touch as he carefully wrapped the fabric over her eyes and tied it at the back of her head.

"It smells like you," she murmured.

"Hopefully that isn't a bad beginning," he said with a laugh as he secured the knot behind her.

"No, it's…" Her voice trailed off as she inhaled the scent of his skin. Memories of last night overwhelmed her as she sat in the dark surrounded by the entirely male smell of shaving soap mixed with something that belonged only to Ash.

Without warning, he pressed his lips to hers in a quick but heart-stopping kiss. He gathered her hands in his own as he said, "I'm right here. There's no need to become intoxicated on the scent of my cravat."

"I wasn't," she began but stopped, knowing it was a lie.

"Come with me." There was a smile in his voice as he lifted her from the carriage and placed her in front of him on the ground. "Wait. I almost forgot..." She heard him step away for a second before returning to pull her bonnet from her head and replace it with a different one.

She reached up to touch it, but he grabbed her raised hand and placed a stick of some sort in her grasp. "And hold this just so. Very well, you're ready."

She couldn't keep the giggle from her voice. She felt completely ridiculous holding some unknown object in her hand while blindfolded and wearing an unknown hat. "Ready to go where?"

"With me." He wrapped her arm around his and began leading her away into the unknown.

"Where are you taking me?" she asked again as the smell changed from London alley to something lightly floral.

"Do you trust me?" he asked against her ear.

"Yes. But I would still like to know if I'm in the park or the center of a ballroom."

"You're in neither place."

"Ash, that isn't helpful in the least."

"Watch your step."

She stopped walking and looked toward where she imagined his face to be. "How am I to watch anything at all?"

"That's true," he mused, his voice coming from a completely different location from where she'd focused her glare.

While she turned, attempting to find him, he slipped his hands around her waist, lifting her from the ground. A second later she was in his arms and he was moving. She buried her face in his neck, hoping they were not in the middle of a ballroom after all. When he was through with this charade, she was going to kill him. He jostled her close to his chest. Was he climbing stairs? Stairs… Where were there stairs? But she gave up a minute later, realizing she'd never been anywhere with this many stairs.

His heart pounded through her body. She enjoyed the feel of it through her hands, but he must be exhausted from carrying her up so many steps. If he'd only remove the cover from her eyes, she could walk. "If you allow me to see, you won't have to carry me," she muttered against the soft hair that curved behind his ear.

"That's a fine offer, since we've reached the top now." He released her legs and allowed her to slide down his body until her toes touched the floor.

"The top of what?"

"You aren't going to stop asking questions and simply experience the moment, are you?"

"No," she replied with a smile, the cravat stretching across her cheeks as she did so.

"Very well. Have it your way." He pulled the cloth from her eyes.

She blinked as her eyes adjusted from dark to the dim lighting of… "We're…in a hall of some sort."

"Right you are." He laced his fingers with hers and tugged her toward the far end of the hall.

Glancing down, she now saw that she held a large masquerade mask on a stick that would make her look as if she were an insect of some sort. "Is this a masquerade ball? Because those don't usually end well for me."

"No." He chuckled and took the mask from her. "That was simply for my amusement. You looked like you might sting me the whole way up here—quite frightening."

Sighing with exasperation, she looked behind them to see a service door that must lead to the steps. Sparse candles held in shining metal sconces cast angled shadows over the floor as they progressed down the hall. It was quite dark, yet it was a fine building, with dark wood moldings surrounding the occasional painting, and a thick rug beneath their feet. It reminded her of the elegance of the British Museum, where Isabelle could often be found, but there weren't enough paintings or sconces for this to be some lesser-used upper room.

How would anyone see the art, even during the day? What type of building was elegant yet shadowed? Voices rumbled somewhere in the distance, but all was empty and silent where they were. She glanced to Ash for answers but he only smiled. As they progressed, she noticed the series of doors they passed were only on one side of the hall. Evangeline squinted at one of the small plaques outside the last door as they slowed. *The Duke of Kilburn* was embossed into the ornate piece of metal that hung there.

"Ash, where are we? And who is the Duke of Kilburn?"

One of her two questions was answered as he opened the door for her, leaving her breathless. Chandeliers piled high with candles hung from an ornately painted ceiling in the center of the large room. Where they stood, in a shadowed box above the gathered crowd, they were almost level with the ceiling. She stepped forward, counting four levels beneath them all filled with people. Gasping, she stepped back again. Someone could see her.

"No one will know you're here," Ash said, reading her thoughts.

"The theater? I've always wanted to attend. Mother calls it vulgar. How did you manage it? What if the Duke of Kilburn finds us here?" She knew she was blabbering, but she couldn't stop herself.

"I knew this box to be free."

She narrowed her eyes on him. She was now an accomplice in his crimes. Breaking into a duke's private box at the theater must have some penalty. "Someone could see us," she said without any heat to her voice. She didn't want to leave. "We shouldn't be here."

"That is why I brought this." He tapped her hat.

She shrank to the corner and removed the hat he'd placed on her in the alley to investigate it. It was by far the largest, ugliest hat she'd ever laid eyes upon, adorned with giant faux flowers and bunches of ribbon in a green that reminded her of a muddy bog. "It's hideous," she said with a laugh.

"I know. No one would believe you would wear something so unfashionable." He tucked a stray bit of hair behind her ear as he spoke. "Your secret visit to the vulgar side of London is safe."

"This may become my new favorite fashion." Replacing it on her head, she murmured a quiet thank-you.

"Thank *you*," he countered. "I believe we have some time before the production begins. Would you care to sit?" He indicated the row of chairs in the center of the box, but she didn't move from the shadowed back corner.

"What are you doing to me, Ash Claughbane? Breaking into a ducal box at the theater… What's next?"

"That, Evie, is entirely up to you." He ran his hands down her arms.

Her heart pounded at the look in his eyes, as if she were the only person in the world, only her. "Anything I want?" Her gaze dropped to his mouth. She was staring. She knew it and yet she couldn't stop herself.

"Whatever you want," he murmured. His voice was soft, rolling over her in waves of warmth with every word. "All you have to do is say it."

"Kiss me."

The corner of his mouth quirked up for a split second before he stepped too close for casual conversation. "Here before the prying eyes of society?" he teased, but his hands were already on her, pulling her to his body as he trapped her against the back wall of the box.

The giant hat pushed to the back of her head as her shoulders found the cool plaster wall. He closed the gap between them, kissing her with much more intensity than he had in the alley. This was a kiss of declaration, of direction, and she wanted to follow with all of her heart. She didn't know where this path led, but she knew it would bring Ash closer to her. She reached out, tasting him and seeking more…and he matched her. For every move she made, he upped the stakes as if it was a game—a game he played quite well.

His hands moved over her body in knowing strokes, up her sides, down over her hips to the curve of her bottom, pulling her into a frenzied pool of wanting. Their bodies pressed together, both seeking more.

She delved her hands into his coat, tugging at the back of his shirt until she'd ripped it loose from his clothing. Running her hands up his back, she reveled in the heat of his skin against her wrists, the movement of his muscles beneath her fingers, his body so close to hers.

Just when she thought she was as close as she could be to this man she'd dreamed of for the past year, he nudged her feet apart with the toe of his boot and stepped closer. He lifted her until they were on eye level. He broke their kiss but only long enough to meet her gaze for a second before his lips were on hers again.

There was some emotion in that short lock of their eyes that she couldn't quite define. All she knew was no one had ever looked at her that way, and no one else ever would. She splayed her hands across his back, needing more of him as she deepened their kiss. He matched her desperation and rocked his hips into hers with a small groan—his or hers, she wasn't certain.

His hands slid over her hips in a gentle caress that was in direct opposition to the harsh kiss they shared and the grind of his hips into hers. She grasped at his body, her fingernails dragging across his back in a fashion that would surely leave marks. She would apologize for that later, but just now she'd lost all control. Years of training had not prepared her for the reality of what courtship led to. There were no controlled smiles or touches, only raw emotion and need. The hard force of his body dragging against hers was overwhelming.

"Ash," she choked out a moment later against the rough evening stubble of his jaw. She didn't know what she was going to ask, only that his name hung on her lips as if he was the answer.

He lifted his head to look into her eyes and she saw something wild there, matched by the rampant beat of her heart. Releasing his hold on her until her feet were on the floor, he threw the hat she'd forgotten across the box and plunged his hands into her hair, sending pins clattering to the floor around them. She pulled his coat off his shoulders in the next second and let it drop to the floor before stretching up to run her hands over his broad shoulders.

He peered down, eyeing his coat with a dubious expression, before kicking it out to lie like a blanket at their feet. "Perhaps I should have joined you in your bed after all," he mused.

On a slow, seeking kiss, he gathered her in his arms and knelt on the inside of his coat, holding her in front of him. The soft lining met her knees as her gown billowed around her on the floor.

"I like this better."

Here he was hers without risk of intrusion from her family. It was odd to feel so secluded and alone with him when half the town was below them waiting for the opera to begin, but at their elevation, only the birds in the rafters above the ornate ceiling could see them. Only with Ash could the floor of a stolen box at the theater become a romantic escape into bliss. He made her dare to live life. His acceptance gave her strength, and yet in his arms she yielded to his touch and allowed herself to be weak. What sort of man caused such a reaction? Only Ash.

She loved this man. Perhaps she'd always known this in some locked-away portion of her heart, but Ash had thrown those doors open. There were no locked doors with him. When had she started to love him? She couldn't find a time or day in her memory when love began, only that it had grown within her wild and free.

"What are you thinking?"

That I love you, she almost said, but even bravery had its bounds. "Locks and doors," she muttered.

His hands glided over her body in a heated embrace as he looked into her eyes. "You're safe here with me," he said, misunderstanding her disjointed thoughts.

"I know." And with that she began to shimmy her arms out of her gown.

Moments later, her gown had been tossed aside, and Ash had unlaced her stays and stripped off her shift, leaving her kneeling before him in only her stockings. Before she could reach for it, Ash had tossed his shirt aside and returned to her, his hands covering every inch of her exposed skin in turn. She slid her hands over the muscular planes of his chest. A dusting of hair covered his powerful body, tapering down to his hips. Her gaze dropped to watch his hands roam over her bare skin. His thick forearms flexed with almost reverent restraint as he touched her breasts, her waist, her hips.

"Evie," he whispered as he laid her down on his

coat and braced himself over her. "You're perfect like this, tousled hair and no adornment. You don't need jewels to make this neck beautiful." He trailed his fingers down her breastbone, making her shiver.

His lips followed the same path. He traced a line with his fingers down her stomach with the promise of his lips following in their wake. But when he touched her as he had last night in his carriage, she flinched. Would his mouth follow his fingers even there? Her breaths grew ragged with anticipation of what might be as he nudged her body open for his exploration. She lifted her head, watching the look of wonder and appreciation on Ash's face as he gazed down at her.

It was wrong—the excitement that buzzed through her body at being displayed before him in such a manner—but she wanted to share this with him. She was breaking a long list of rules as she opened to his touch...but someone wise once told her rules were malleable things and would snap back when one was done with them.

Hang the rules, anyway.

He placed a hand on the inside of her thigh and guided her leg to the side, exposing every part of her body for him to see. After a lifetime of being wrapped in pristine gowns, she was fully revealed to him with no adornment. She was free to be anything she wanted, and tonight she wanted to be his. In the next instant his lips were on her as she'd wondered, even hoped, they would be. His mouth did things to her body she didn't think possible, as he first ran his tongue over her in delicious strokes, then drew her close with his lips, and finally invaded her. Plundering and taking everything she offered, he pulled at the last strands of her rational mind. All thought was on what he was doing to her and how she wanted more.

She sank her fingers into his hair, needing to touch him. She pressed into him even while it overwhelmed her, catching her in a torrent of confusing desire with Ash the only source of relief. She shifted and arched beneath him in fretful movements, but he held her still with one hand on her hip. With the other, he... She didn't know what he was doing with his wicked taunts against the most intimate part of her, but she dug her fingers deeper into his hair in a silent plea for more. Then she was shaking beneath him as he coaxed her over the edge into pleasure as he had last night with his words—only now he spoke silently with his lips, his hands, his tongue flicking against her until she couldn't hold on any longer.

A moment later he was still caressing her with the backs of his fingers as she lay before him both satisfied and yet starved for more. Would she ever have enough of this man to be sated?

He ran his lips down the inside of her thigh to her knee, the slight stubble on his face scraping against her sensitive skin and sending shivers up her spine. He took a playful bite at the inside of her knee and began to move back up her leg with slow scratches of his chin and soothing kisses leading the way.

He slid back up her entire body that way, hard planes against soft, rough skin against smooth. The dark, intent look in his eyes would have frightened her even a week ago, but now she wanted the same thing he did. This was the man that she loved, and there was nothing to fear with him. The delicious friction of the hair on his chest against her breasts made her curl into his body. Her knee came up to cradle his hip, dragging against the fabric of his breeches. She wanted to touch him as he had her, to feel the heat of his skin against her entire body. She wasn't certain what to do, but it began with the removal of his clothing.

Reaching between them, she trailed her fingers down the ridges of his stomach, then grabbed the waist of his breeches. Her fingers dipped into the top edge of the already taut fabric, making Ash flinch above her, his arms tensing on either side of her head.

Even though she was enjoying the tickle of his hair against her knuckles, perhaps she wasn't doing this properly. She'd never removed a gentleman's clothing before, after all. She required assistance to dress— perhaps he was the same. She slid her other hand over the bulging fabric, searching for the buttons that must hold his clothing on somehow. Ash pushed into her grasp, and the entire bulge pulsed beneath her hand. She froze, her eyes flashing to Ash's in alarm. But he only raised a brow at her as if she should have expected such a thing to happen.

She hadn't expected such a thing to happen. She hadn't expected any of this, but now that she was here, she wanted more.

Returning to her work, she discovered the secret to removing a gentleman's breeches was, in fact, all in the wrist. Ash grew more and more still by slow degrees the longer she worked on the fall of his breeches. He twitched beneath her knuckles when she grazed his skin, but remained otherwise frozen. Watching her with a dark, almost pained expression, he waited for her to finish. When the fabric of his breeches lost the battle to her persistent fingers, she blinked at the length of him that she'd released.

She looked up and met Ash's gaze.

"If you want to touch me, you can," he rasped.

With a tiny nod she placed her fingers against the length of him and skated her hand down over the surface. Lifting a curious gaze to Ash's face again, she watched his expression as she curled her fingers around him. His breaths were harsh and he looked at her as if he might perish at any moment, but he didn't move away. She tested her boundaries with him and moved her hand over him as he'd touched her in the carriage.

Ash groaned and bent his head to her bare shoulder, but did nothing to stop her exploration. She slid her hand over him again, this time dragging her thumb over the tip of him. He groaned louder at that and bit at the fleshy part of her shoulder. His lips trailed up the side of her neck now, as if poised to inflict punishment if she dared to continue.

She dared, and he sucked at the base of her neck until she squirmed beneath him in response. Releasing him, she trailed her hands over his hips and up his back. He was hers to enjoy tonight. She'd wished for this for so long without knowing what exactly she was wishing for.

She moved her hands down his back, beneath his now-loose breeches, and grabbed entire handfuls of his quality bum. She'd have to tell Isabelle about it later. Or perhaps not, since this was rather incriminating.

She wanted more of him. The way he covered her

body yet still held himself braced on his arms above her was infuriating. She spread her fingers over his skin and grabbed him again, this time pulling herself up to meet his chest. The length of him pressed heavily against the core of her body. The sensation was thrilling. She couldn't look away from the heavy-lidded desire in his eyes.

"Evie," he warned. He pulled his hips away from her, and she dropped back to the floor. That was when she noticed his arms were shaking. "I hadn't intended on things going this far. I didn't bring you here to…"

"I know you didn't." She released her hold on his backside to trace the lines of muscles that began at his hips and stretched up his sides.

He took a ragged breath and looked in her eyes. "I've stolen a great many things, swindled wealth away from unsuspecting gentlemen." His voice rasped as if his words came at a great cost. "I've done large amounts of wrong in my life, but I won't steal this from you." He lowered a hand to cover the core of her body where it still hummed from his efforts. "I won't take you unless you want it."

Was he asking if she wanted this to end? She didn't ever want this to end.

She wanted to wake at his side every day and find herself in this exact place by nightfall, but perhaps on a bed instead of the floor of a London theater. She rocked into the palm of his hand. "I want it," she assured him, wishing she could explain how much, but knowing this wasn't the time for such talk. "I want you, Ash Claughbane. Steal me away. Swindle me. I'm yours."

He exhaled with what she thought might be gratitude and moved his hand to her hip. Her grip on him tightened, willing him to stay with her and lead her into the unknown. His gaze met hers and held her there as he rocked her hips up and entered her in one quick motion. She couldn't move—the contact she'd craved now had her pinned beneath him. Had he pierced through to her heart? It was possible. His body was pressed against hers as he filled her, covered her, surrounded her. She'd tensed and bit her lip as her body stretched in ways she'd never imagined. The pain that was rumored among ladies was overshadowed by the excitement of finally possessing every bit of the man she loved. She wanted to share this with him.

As if he could read her thoughts—and with the way he was watching her, perhaps he could—he moved his hand over her hip, encouraging her to relax and trust him. "I won't hurt you again, Evie."

"You aren't going to stop, are you?"

He only chuckled in response as he withdrew and drove into her again. This time there was no pain. Somehow knowing she'd recovered from the initial shock of his intrusion, he changed his rhythm against her. Her body became more and more pliable in his hands as she now arched to meet him. The sheer power of his body mixed with something lighter—fun and rebellious—into a potent concoction of need, driving her steadily forward into pleasure-filled darkness.

She clung to him as she moved into a world she didn't know or understand, trusting he would show her everything there was to see. Everything around her crackled with the fire that burned brightly between them as she reached for some unnamed peak. She would surely perish if she didn't reach the point he was steering her toward. But then she was pulling him closer as she fell into a boneless heap beneath him. The bond that seemed to tie them together in that moment made her eyes prickle with the heat of tears. She loved him, and right now he was hers. He stilled in her, watching her spiral down from the heights he had pushed her to.

Eyes sparkling with mischief, he lifted her from the floor and pulled her with him as he leaned against the wall. She blinked at the sudden change, realizing she now straddled him, her hands landing on his shoulders and her knees on either side of his hips.

"It's not over?" she whispered.

"Hardly. You're mine, remember?" He sucked at her neck as his hands held her hips steady on him. "I'm not done swindling pleasure from you."

He flexed his hips off the coat-covered floor in a quick motion that drove him deeper into her body, daring her to play his game. Her breath caught at the new sensation of their position and she clutched his shoulders in response.

A pleased grin tugged at the corners of his mouth as he guided her hips over him for a minute. The pace was too restrained and she couldn't handle it, surging forward. He was watching her move on him, a look of awe on his face. He mouthed something without sound that might have been either *love you* or *look at you*, she wasn't certain, but she didn't spare it any thought as she stole her pleasure from his body.

The power of her position over him, the ability

to make him look at her that way, make him mutter soundless words to himself, was intoxicating. She could move how she wanted, take what she wanted, and he allowed her that—without judgment.

There in his eyes she could see how his confidence in what he was doing warred with his control slipping away. Sly smiles were replaced with a look of wild desperation that was building again in her as well. He moved one hand to reach between them and toy with the same sensitive place that had made her wild earlier as he pulled her down onto his body with more force than she alone possessed. She bent to his clear skill and allowed him to do what he wished with her. Arching into his thrusts, she almost cried out when he pulled her down to him in one last forceful action. He reached for her mouth, covering it with his as he pulsed inside her.

A minute later, they still clung to one another in a heap of sweat-slick and still-shaking body parts. Somewhere beyond their private world an orchestra began to tune their instruments. The intensity and power of what they'd just shared was too fragile for words. All she knew was she had to find a way to keep Ash Claughbane in her life.

They sat there until the opera began, the music filling the air around them, but neither moved to claim their seats. He'd only left her once and that was to retrieve a cloth dipped in the cool water of the bucket where a bottle of champagne sat in the corner. Returning to her, he'd pressed the fabric between her legs with a gentle touch. She would no doubt be sore tomorrow, but the gesture made her heart clench.

After throwing the handkerchief back in the direction of the champagne pail, he propped himself against the wall and pulled her toward him until she was resting between his thighs, curled on top of his coat with his capable arms wrapped around her.

Turning her head to the side, she reached up to press her lips to the edge of his jaw. "The theater should always be viewed in this manner." Her voice was a raspy whisper beneath the high notes of the soprano.

"Naked and not watching at all?" he murmured into her hair with a chuckle, the sound vibrating down her back.

"It's beautiful."

"You're beautiful," Ash whispered as he continued to roam his hands over her body, over her hip, down her thigh, then back up across her stomach to her breast. He traced a random pattern of warmth and awareness over her body, lulling her into equal parts comfort and anticipation of where he might touch next.

She squirmed farther into his embrace, resting her hands on his thighs. "Have you ever wanted to hold on to a moment and keep it forever? I would keep this one."

His hands tightened around her as some emotion passed across his face, but when he looked down at her a second later the emotion was gone. "It's difficult to hold on to anything for very long in my life—such that it is."

"It doesn't have to be." She turned her cheek into his chest. "I could hold on with you."

"Things like moments don't like to be captured that way." He sounded almost sad. If he wanted something, all he needed to do was say it. Wasn't that what he was always telling her?

She took a breath and voiced the questions that consumed her mind. "What about things like being together and happiness? Could we hold on to that?"

"I'm not letting go—not tonight." He tightened his grip on her in a fierce and possessive manner that soothed her even if he hadn't answered her questions.

She could focus on where that would leave them when the sun rose tomorrow. Just now, she didn't want to think of any time beyond right now on the floor of a stolen box at the theater.

"Good," she said, twisting in his arms. "If you aren't letting go, that leaves my hands free to roam—for tonight, at any rate."

"The rules of your games aren't fair. You know that, don't you?" he chided jokingly, his hands sliding around her waist as she moved.

"Neither are yours," she countered with a grin. "I learned from the best."

Eighteen

He slid his hands through Evie's hair in an attempt to gather it at the back of her head and grabbed one of the pins that still littered the floor around them. Ash preferred her hair cascading down onto his shoulders as she rode him, but he would have to leave here with her at some point this evening.

"I like you better than my maid," she almost purred as he combed his fingers gently through the waves of mahogany.

"Considering what we just shared, I'm glad of it." He laughed as she elbowed him in the ribs.

"I meant that Jane has been instructed to pull my hair impossibly tight. You're gentle." She tossed a smile over her shoulder at him before returning to her stance before him. "It's lovely, actually."

"I would recommend you look in a mirror before you say that." He pulled a concerned face as he twisted her hair up onto her head and stuck a few pins in it to hold it there. It wasn't to Evie's usual standards, but neither was the rumpled dress she now wore nor the crushed coat that he'd slung over one of the chairs.

What she was wearing would, however, be enough clothing to slip out the service door to his carriage without notice.

Turning, she looked up at him. "We should leave soon, shouldn't we?" There was a resigned sadness to her voice that he didn't like. "I've heard that many lords don't arrive until after intermission, and that's already begun. We could be discovered here. The Duke of Kilburn could find us."

Ash ran his hands down the short sleeves that covered her shoulders, partly to smooth the wrinkles in the fabric, but mostly because he couldn't stop himself from touching her. "He isn't even aware he possesses this box, not to mention the great distance he lives from here," Ash said truthfully.

"How do you know that?" Her eyes narrowed on him, but he kept his expression blank as he looked down at her. "I'm not certain I've heard of the Duke of Kilburn. It's surprising that my mother would overlook educating me about a dukedom. She would be fortunate to tie herself to a duke by throwing me at him. The duke must be quite happily wed or a doddering old man with no use for ladies. Either way…"

Ash laughed. "Doddering, yes. That is precisely how I would describe the duke."

"Would you? You know him, then—the owner of this box?" She sighed as she watched him. "You didn't swindle his investments away from him, did you?"

"No." Perhaps it was time to tell her the truth anyway. He wasn't certain if this was the proper time to discuss it, but the subject was here, surrounding him as they stood by the Duke of Kilburn's box seats. Ash took a breath. It was time. "Actually, I'm attempting to return his fortune to his family."

Evie's delicate brows drew together in confusion as she studied him. She opened her mouth, no doubt to ask some difficult-to-answer question that would have to lead to truth between them.

He couldn't hide his true identity and the ramifications of that truth from her any longer, even if it led to the end of their time together. His mind raced with where to begin. The supposed friendship between their fathers? Or perhaps how that friendship had fallen apart when her father had destroyed his? She already knew what had become of him after that. "There are things about my past, Evie. Things you don't know."

And that was when the Duke of blasted Kilburn decided to walk through the door.

Ash ground his teeth together as he eyed the man. Evie jumped away from Ash and folded her hands at her waist in an attempt at innocence, but he pulled her back to his side with a hand on her lower back.

"Brother," Brennen said with his eyes on Ash. "So this is where I find you." He shut the door and turned to take in the scene before him, exhaling through flared nostrils in the same manner Ash had seen his father do when Ash had done some wrong as a child. But this man was *not* his father. Ash had a father, and that father was gone.

"Good of you to come," Ash lied with an attempt at a pleasant smile, though he was fairly certain it fell short of genuine. "The performance is quite entertaining tonight. Don't you agree, my lady?"

Evie almost choked on a gasp at his side. "Quite

nice," she finally managed in the small, whispery voice she used when she was afraid.

Ash draped his arm farther around her waist to comfort her. Damn his brother for frightening her so. He could kill Brennen for coming here and intruding on their evening together.

"What the devil are you doing here?" Brennen asked with a defeated shake of his head. Years they'd been apart and this was how he was greeted?

"Welcome to town to you as well." Ash turned to Evie to say, "Forgive my eldest brother. His manners have always been somewhat lacking."

His brother's gaze swept from Evie to Ash as if trying to solve some riddle. "You shouldn't be here."

"And yet I am." This moment was just a further example of why they'd never seen eye to eye. Everything with his brother was about expectation and rules, and Ash had never measured up to Brennen's standards. Of course he'd made it a point to try not to, but that hardly mattered.

Brennen had the good grace to look uncomfortable. It was likely due to physical confines, considering his brother's height and size in general, and not the intimacy Brennan had interrupted, but it did assuage Ash's anger a bit to see his brother feeling awkward.

"I can see I have poor timing," Brennan said, his gaze on Ash's arm around Evie's waist. "Or perhaps my timing is better than I could have imagined." He shot Ash a disgusted glare before offering Evie a small bow. "My lady."

She pulled herself straighter, seeming to find her strength. "If you are brothers, then I believe I wrote to you earlier in the season. I never received word back from you."

"Ah, you are the lady who wrote to me. Your words about my dear brother were so poignant that I thought I would come see him in person."

Ash shot Evie a look that could freeze bathwater, but said nothing.

She struck the pose she maintained at every ball as if it were armor, shielding herself from his blasted family. "May I ask how you tracked us here tonight? This is all rather sudden. I find I'm a bit taken unaware by it all."

"You don't know? Ashley, did you not tell her anything of our family? My lady, I'm the Duke of Kilburn and you are in my opera box."

"You're a duke," she stated, turning toward Ash with accusation in her eyes. "Your brother is a duke. That means you're the son of a duke."

"No, the title skipped my father. He passed seven years ago. The illustrious duke here is still growing accustomed to his fancy new title. Aren't you, Brennen? It's shocking his giant head was able to fit through the doorway."

"Ashley," Evie muttered, cutting off any retort his brother might have made. "Your given name is Ashley and you come from a titled family. How could you keep such secrets from me?"

"I haven't been called Ashley since—"

"Ashley Lashley—that's what our brothers always called him when he was young," Brennen filled in for her. "On account of the eyelashes." He shrugged. Did Brennen believe it was his place to dole out the family history for Evie's benefit? He wasn't a blasted volume in a library to recite such facts. How he shared a bloodline with this man was beyond Ash's comprehension.

Ash's hand fell away from Evie as he took a step toward his brother. "Go ahead and say it in its entirety," he spat out. "It always did have such a nice ring to it. You've come here tonight, so you might as well truly have a time of it."

"Ashley Lashley, do you have a sashley?"

"And you wondered why I never returned home. My name is Ash. Do you know what rhymes with that? Bash, smash, crash—do I need to continue, Brother?"

He took another step toward Brennen, but stopped at Evie's hand on his chest. "Ash, I know who you are. You have nothing to prove tonight."

It was remarkable the calming effect of one gentle touch. He relaxed and looked down at her, a stirring concoction of fragile and strong as she stood between him and his brother. Against all odds, he smiled. "I told you he was old and doddering."

"Although not as far away as you presumed," she murmured.

Ash took a breath and did what he should have done from the first moment he saw his brother tonight. He took Evie's hand in his as he spoke. "My apologies for not introducing you sooner. This is Brennen Claughbane, Duke of Kilburn, and my eldest brother. Everything else I told you was the truth. I am the fourth son in my family. And my eldest brother is, in fact, a horse's arse."

"Pardon?" Brennen straightened his coat on his shoulders as if he could physically shake off the insult.

"You are," Ash assured him.

Brennen shook his head. "I'm a benevolent leader. It isn't easy, you know."

Ash ignored his brother, looking only at Evie. "I've been honest with you about everything for at least eight days."

"That's quite possibly a new record for him," his brother added with a great deal of disapproval. But he wasn't wrong.

"It's true," Ash conceded.

He held his breath, but then Evie smiled and her smile quickly turned into laughter. "Trustworthiness for eight entire days. I'll count myself among the fortunate."

"No, *that* honor is mine." When he looked into her eyes, the future seemed to unfurl before him. For the first time, he didn't want to pull away from it.

"And what of eight *more* days of trustworthiness?" she pressed.

She still didn't know of the connection between their families, but he would deal with that later. There was time. "I might be able to manage that," he said with a wince of pain over the unfortunate turn of events tonight. "Make me one promise, though. Don't call me Ashley."

"You have my word."

Ash turned to his brother a moment later. "Might we continue this delightful reunion after I've returned the lady to her home lest she be missed?"

"Certainly." Brennen gave her a nod of farewell. "I don't believe I caught your name, my lady."

"Lady Evangeline Green, Your Grace." The words were out of Evie's mouth before Ash could redirect the conversation.

"Green," Brennen repeated, his voice hollow as he looked first at her, then at his brother. "Hurry and return her to her home. Then, we have much to discuss, *Ash*. You'll find me at the Humpleby Hotel."

Perhaps they did have matters to discuss, but Ash didn't plan to seek out that conversation tonight. Not after the evening he'd spent with Evie. Some dreams one simply didn't want to wake from.

❧

"Evangeline, darling, you have a gentleman caller," her mother said from the door of her bedchamber. Her already pinched mouth was drawn in more than usual as her assessing gaze raked over Evangeline's ensemble. Evangeline wasn't sure whether her own simple day dress and loosely knotted hair or the gentleman waiting in the parlor had her mother in such distress, and she didn't particularly care. She gave her hair an approving pat and rose from her dressing table.

All of her thoughts were focused on Ash this morning. Her body ached in the most delicious fashion, reminding her of their night together with every movement. She hadn't wanted the carriage ride home to end. She didn't want anything with Ash to end, and for the first time, she believed he felt the same. He'd made her no promises, but there had been something in his eyes, something that looked like hope. She suppressed the smile that remained in her heart and met her mother's unceasing gaze of disapproval.

"Is it Lord Winfield?" she asked in a chipper tone that made her mother's eyes narrow. Let her glare. Nothing could shake Evangeline's bright mood today.

"I know Lord Crosby had a prior engagement this morning. He told me… Well, never mind that. I'll be right down."

"It is not Lord Winfield. It's a Lord Braxton." Her mother twitched the calling card between her fingers with a wary eye to check the quality of the paper on which it was printed.

"I…can't remember meeting a Lord Braxton."

Her mother's eyes flashed. "He asked for you. Clearly you have met. Chatting and dancing with Lord Crosby when you should be furthering your acquaintance with Lord Winfield, and now there's a Lord Braxton in the picture whom you can't recall? What shall Lord Winfield think of you?"

"That he isn't the only gentleman in London? Mother, I have no memory of this Lord Braxton."

"A crime unto itself. Gentlemen should be studied, their qualities memorized."

"I quite agree," she said, thinking of Isabelle's rating of bums and Ash's body last night. Clearing her throat, she took the calling card from her mother. "Perhaps if I see him…"

"This is the height of unladylike behavior," her mother stated with a shake of her head, reminding Evangeline of an irate chicken with twitching feathers. "Seeing a gentleman of whom you have no memory in the parlor, all the while keeping Lord Winfield on a string."

"I haven't kept anyone on a string, Mother. If Lord Winfield is hanging about on a string, then it is because you placed him there. My interests lie elsewhere." She moved past the woman into the hall, beyond the fear that had surrounded her most of her life.

"Of all the common…"

Evangeline sighed and turned back to her mother, giving her the same look of disapproval she'd learned so well. "Save your outrage. I know you long to give it full range, but I seem to have a caller waiting for me."

"Is this the influence of your cousins?" her mother hissed as she moved forward toward Evangeline in a continuous snake-like motion, threatening a strike at any time. "I will not have you speak to me in such a manner. After all I have done for you."

"Actually, Mother, this isn't their influence at all. This is the true Evangeline, and I like her. Now, if you'll excuse me, I have a caller." She turned and left her mother gaping after her as she descended the stairs to the parlor.

"Lord Braxton?" she asked, stepping in the door of the small receiving parlor.

"Yes. Thank you for seeing me." The gentleman paused in the middle of what might have been pacing and turned to look at her. His hands were on his hips, displaying his broad shoulders and trim waist to perfection. Evangeline had no interest in the sandy-haired gentleman, but she had a feeling she would be the only lady in town to dismiss his intense stare and chiseled jaw. "I'm aware this is highly irregular since we haven't been introduced."

She glanced behind her to ensure the door she'd just entered was open and felt a wave of relief at seeing Jane in the hall. Taking a breath, she moved farther into the room. "I'm quite relieved. I was concerned that I'd forgotten our dance entirely."

"No. I only arrived in London yesterday." He

shifted to the side and back again as if requiring the movement to continue. "I'm afraid this is somewhat of a delicate matter."

"That sounds rather foreboding," she mused, her smile still firmly in place. Even the discussion of a *delicate matter* couldn't dim her spirits today. "Please sit. Delicate matters shouldn't be discussed while standing."

He nodded and sat, even though he looked as if he disagreed with her reasoning. "Lady Evangeline, it is said that your name is linked with that of Lord Crosby."

"Is it?" Something in Evangeline tightened. "I suppose people do talk in this town. It's nothing untoward, of course," she lied, everything beneath her skin going on alert.

"I'm glad to hear it. My lady, I don't know quite how to phrase this, but Lord Crosby is a confidence man, a swindler."

"*Swindler* is such a nasty word," she said, repeating what Ash had once said to her. "Surely Lord Crosby hasn't done anything so vile as to deserve that."

"He's done plenty."

"I suppose you have proof of such an accusation." She raised her brows questioningly. If this man had evidence that would harm Ash, she needed to understand what it was. She had to save him.

"Lord Crosby doesn't exist," he replied, a grim expression on his face.

"Well then. That does put him in a poor light." Was that all this Lord Braxton knew? She wasn't certain how she would contain such information, but for Ash, she would try.

"I'm terribly sorry to bring you such news, but

this man has walked away with a portion of my grandmother's fortune, as well as that of several other families in Bath. He claims to be gathering investors for the development of a new type of steam engine—a small one. He sells it quite well, but it's complete rubbish. And now, he has come to London."

"I see. Tell me, Lord Braxton, have you come here entirely in the generous spirit of warning me of danger?"

"That…and I'd hoped to enlist your aid." His words were as careful as his watchful gaze.

"You believe I might have information on this Crosby fellow," she supplied, wanting this interview to end.

Braxton nodded. "I was hoping he'd mentioned where he was living while in town."

"He didn't even tell me his true name, Lord Braxton." She gave him a mournful look, thankful for once for the lessons that her mother had forced on her. She had learned well how to speak without revealing anything.

"I understand how difficult this must be for you. It seems he has a routine of befriending a lady in every town as a means of easing his entrance into that area's society. I'm sorry he selected you while in London."

"What do you mean by that, my lord?" she snapped. She wasn't like any other lady in any other town, was she? And she wasn't sorry she'd known Ash.

"I only… I apologize if I offended you…"

"You believe I am his entrance into good society?" She was many things to Ash Claughbane—as he was to her—but his entrance to society she was not. Had she introduced him to anyone while he was here? She couldn't recall anyone except for her friend Roselyn, and he hadn't been the least bit interested in talking to her. This man had things all wrong—he had to.

"I suppose I misunderstood your friendship with the man. I thought he'd acted in the same manner here as he had all the times before. My apologies."

The word *all* stuck in her mind. *All the times before.* "Lord Crosby and I have scarcely shared a dance." Evangeline brushed nonexistent lint from her skirts before glancing back up at Braxton. "I'm afraid your sources are incorrect."

"That's pleasant news, then. I have sisters, but a man can never become impervious to tears." His smile would have been charming if they weren't discussing such a painful matter.

She banished the image of a long line of ladies standing on the side of the road to London, all having experienced what she had last night. "Allow me to put your mind at ease, my lord. Lord Crosby means nothing to me." She was only able to make this statement with such authority because it wasn't his true name. Taking a breath, she pressed forward. "Out of curiosity, however, how many ladies has he left behind in such a fashion?"

"The number is quite unseemly, my lady," he leaned in to say in a low voice. "I really shouldn't discuss such things."

"It is a sizable amount, though?" Her voice came out in a squeak and she swallowed.

"It would appear so."

"Thank you for the warning. I'm sorry I don't have any information for you as to Lord Crosby's whereabouts." She worked to keep the discussion conversational, though she wanted to simultaneously throw this man from her home, interrogate him for information, and wallow in the truth of Ash's past. "What will you do when you find him?"

"I will have him punished to the full extent of English law."

"I see," Evangeline murmured. She needed him to leave. She needed time to think. "Well, you have quite a pile of work ahead of you. I won't keep you."

Ian nodded his thanks and stood. "If you see him, do me a kindness, if you don't mind, and don't mention our discussion here today."

"Of course. I'm quite good at keeping secrets, Lord Braxton."

He left the room, but Evangeline couldn't move. *The number is quite unseemly, my lady.* How many women had Ash used and then abandoned in his schemes? He'd used her that way last year. But this time was different—wasn't it?

Of course this season was different. She knew him now. None of those other ladies knew about his family or his childhood. None of them had ridden in his carriage or gone to the London theater with him. She blushed, knowing those ladies she'd pictured standing alongside the road into town were part of his past, not his future. None of them loved him like she did, and none of them ever would.

She was already moving toward the door. She had to find Ash and warn him before it was too late.

Nineteen

ASH CLAUGHBANE PROVED DIFFICULT TO FIND.
Truly, she shouldn't be surprised. When one came
and left town as quickly as he was known to do, a
solid home overlooking a park wasn't likely. And
in his line of work, he most likely didn't wish to
announce his whereabouts while in town. It was
odd, though. In all of their time together, he'd never
discussed his accommodations.

Did some part of her believe he was made of smoke
and vanished into the night when he wasn't with her?
Evangeline shook off the thought as she looked out the
carriage window. Ash was talented, but not to that extent.

Her carriage rolled to a stop outside the hotel where
the Duke of Kilburn had said he was residing, and
she blinked up at the large structure. The Humpleby
Hotel took up the entire block. She'd never entered a
hotel before today, and she'd rushed out without her
maid like a complete ninny. "Mother would fall over
in a dead faint if she knew I was at a hotel to find a
duke—alone," Evangeline muttered to herself as she
stepped down from the carriage.

The Humpleby looked cheerful enough with greenery outside the front doors and a helpful-looking footman. Perhaps this wouldn't be the clandestine meeting she'd imagined after all. The Duke of Kilburn had been decidedly easier to find than his youngest sibling. She only hoped the man would help her find Ash, especially considering the two brothers' less-than-ideal reunion last night.

Would he even know Ash's whereabouts?

It was a chance she must take. She pushed forward into the hotel with only a quick nod to both her driver and the footman who held the large door open for her to enter the building. She scanned the open room, moving past a large flower arrangement set beneath a shimmering chandelier. Hotels were hardly the frightening places her mother had led her to believe. There was something enchanting about the bright, open space where a few well-dressed ladies and gentlemen were gathered.

Spying a dark wood counter across the room, she moved toward it, her shoes making a pleasing clicking sound against the marble floor with every step. "Please inform the Duke of Kilburn that he has a caller," she stated before the man behind the desk could say a word.

"Of course, my lady. May I tell him who is calling?"

She opened her mouth to answer but someone behind her said, "No, you may not."

Evangeline spun on her heel, knowing that voice quite well.

"I hate to make anything too easy for him," Ash explained with a grin.

"Ash!" She half exclaimed and half breathed his name in relief, the resulting sound coming out breathy and wanton. "Thank heavens you're here."

"I'm pleased to see you again as well," he hedged, clearly trying to discern why they were meeting at the desk in the Humpleby Hotel.

"I came here to find you. You've never told me where you reside," she explained.

Ash glanced over her shoulder to the man behind the desk, waving a hand to indicate their business was settled before guiding her away a few paces. "It's somewhat of a secret."

She smiled up at him as they strolled across the open room. "Isn't everything a secret with you?"

"Yes. This secret, however, isn't mine to share."

"I would pry to satisfy my curiosity, but I have more important things to discuss with you."

His expression grew concerned to match her own as he watched her. "I believe there are some tables set up for tea near the back of the hotel. I passed them on my way in."

He must have entered the building from some service door again today. "Do you always leave your carriage in a back alley?"

"Except when I mean to be seen, yes. It's a habit that has served me well, especially when sneaking into your bedchamber at night," he said with a smile.

"Shhh!" She looked around to see if anyone had heard him, but only a few others were in this area of the hotel, all involved in their own conversations.

Ash and Evangeline entered an adjoining room filled with small tables and flooded with sunlight from the tall windows that overlooked a courtyard filled with exotic-looking plants. He led her across the floor, clearly waiting to begin their conversation in earnest until they reached the far side of the room.

"A Lord Braxton from Bath came to my home this morning," she said as she took a seat close to the corner where they could speak without being overheard.

"Lord Braxton called on you," Ash confirmed with polite interest as he joined her at the table.

"Yes. He's here in London, Ash. He's looking for you."

"Are you frightened for me?" His brows drew together into a rarely seen frown as he leaned forward, grasping her hand beneath the table in his secure grip. "Evie, I've escaped men like Braxton before, and I will do so again. You have no cause for concern."

"He knew information about your past—your patterns." She blushed even as she made the vague reference to women in his past.

"What patterns? I'm careful about such things."

"Patterns," she repeated, willing him to understand without her having to voice the words. "He said…"

"Evie, whatever it is he said to you, please understand that Braxton doesn't know *me*. He knows whatever evidence he believes he has gathered against me, but he doesn't know me. Not like you do."

She exhaled on a small sigh as she looked into his eyes. "Which is exactly what I thought. I knew even if you did leave ladies scattered in your path—"

"Is that what he claimed?" Ash laughed and shook his head, clearly relieved at the awful news, which only made her glare at him. How could he be pleased about such a statement about his person?

"You didn't remember my name when we met this year," she reminded him.

The amusement in his eyes was instantly replaced with something warmer, softer, something she couldn't quite define. "Everything is different now. You know that. I could never forget you, not now. Not after our time together."

"You aren't using me for an entrance into society?" Even as she said it, she gripped his hand tighter under the table, refusing to let go.

"Lord Braxton will pay for putting such a thought in your head," Ash muttered. "Evie, what could I possibly gain by eating every flavor of ice in existence with you? Did it benefit me to take you to the theater last night? The truth is that I enjoy our time together."

"I do too." Her voice sounded shaken and tight even to her. "I thought when Lord Braxton said this was your pattern, that you use ladies in your plots... I thought for a moment—"

"I'm not using you," he cut in.

She wasn't certain how long they sat there staring into each other's eyes before she whispered, "I believe you." But she knew she was nothing like those other ladies in other towns along Ash's path. When he looked at her, she knew the truth—she was the only lady who mattered.

"All is well then?"

"Ash, Braxton wants to see you suffer for what you've done. He mentioned the authorities." A still silence fell between them, both knowing what her next words would be, but neither wanting to hear them. "You have to leave town. Run. Flee."

"I...can't."

"You must." She leaned closer over the table to

beg him. "I couldn't live with the knowledge that you were imprisoned when I could have saved you."

"You have saved me." His smile was warmer than the sun that flooded the room around them as he looked at her. "But I won't leave."

"I don't understand," she said with a small shake of her head. "Whatever funds you're making in town matter little if you lose your life to gain them."

"For the first time, this isn't about the money," he said before his gaze lifted to a point over her shoulder.

"No, it's about revenge," someone said behind her. "Isn't it, Ashley?"

Evangeline spun in her seat, taken aback by the intrusion in their conversation. The duke stood over their small table. Why must the man interrupt every discussion of consequence they had? Did he possess some sort of brotherly instinct that drew him near at such times? It was unnerving.

"This doesn't involve you, Brennen," Ash warned, his hand tightening around hers.

"I disagree," the duke countered as he pulled up a chair and wedged himself into the larger of the two spaces between them. "We're of the same family, last I checked."

"And that gives you the right to barge into *my* conversations with *my* lady?"

His lady. Some small part of her rejoiced at the words even with their harsh delivery. Evangeline tried to keep the smile from her lips. She was his and he was hers. Perhaps he would have to flee town, but they would sort that out later. As long as his hand was wrapped around hers, all would be well.

"Considering who you're calling *your* lady? The family to which she belongs?" the duke countered. "Yes! I have every right, and she has a right to know the truth, Brother."

All Evangeline could do was look back and forth between the two warring brothers and wait for someone to explain what they were going on about. What truth should she know? And had he mentioned something about revenge?

"You have nothing to do with this, Brennen." Ash sat forward in his chair with an elbow braced on the table as if he was struggling not to lunge across the white cloth-covered surface at his brother. "This matter is between Evie and me."

"We're brothers, Ashley. Whatever you do in town affects me as a result. Our family has no need of your assistance, no matter what promises you made to Mother. This mad chase for revenge has to end."

"Quite demanding now that you have a dukedom to cling to, aren't you?" Ash mocked, the usual good-natured smile on his face replaced with a sneer. "It isn't as simple as you think it is, I'll have you know. *Everything* here has become complicated."

"Clearly." The duke's gaze slid over Evangeline before returning to his brother.

A maid moved closer in the ensuing silence. Her eyes were wide on the unfolding scene, as if she'd been watching the entire affair from nearby. She likely had. Ash and his brother were doing nothing to keep their voices at a reasonable level.

"Tea? Yer Grace? M'lord? M'lady?" Her voice held traces of a cockney accent.

Evangeline blushed. If her mother would faint at knowing her daughter was at a hotel, she would surely be sent to an early grave if she knew Evangeline was in the middle of a brawl in a hotel. She was about to wave the maid away when the duke spoke.

"Tea with some of those biscuits I was served earlier would be perfect. I'm starved."

The maid bowed out of the room, and Ash glared at his brother. "Tea and biscuits? By all means, have refreshment while you set out to destroy my life."

"I didn't come here to destroy your life. I came here to stop you."

"I need nothing from you. I never have, Bren."

"Have you not noticed the clear mess you made of your plans here in town? Give it up, Ashley."

"I told you not to call me that!"

"Perhaps all of this is clear to you, but I have no idea what the two of you are discussing. Could someone please explain what this conversation is regarding?" She looked to Ash but his brother replied.

"Revenge." He stated the bold, undeniable word.

She blinked. "Revenge against whom?" He'd mentioned that before. Evangeline looked to Ash for answers. "Ash, what is he talking about?"

"Tea, m'lady?" the maid asked as she placed a tower of biscuits in the center of their table and began filling cups.

"No. No, thank you." Evangeline leaned around the tower of food to maintain eye contact. "Ash?"

"None for me, either," he said with a wave of his hand.

"I meant for you to explain—"

"I know." He shot a cold look at his brother before returning his gaze to hers. "When I first came here,

I didn't know you. It wasn't until later that I learned which family was yours…"

"What does my family have to do with anything?"

"Everything," the duke pronounced from the opposite side of the biscuits.

"She didn't ask you."

"Then tell her already," the duke complained. "Or I will."

Ash exhaled and looked at her. Resigned defeat had removed the sparkle from his eyes, and he suddenly looked quite weary. "When I was eighteen, my family lost everything. Even our furnishings were hauled out of our home to be sold." He entwined his fingers with hers and held her hand tight. "The look of frantic rage on my father's face as his house was emptied is one of the last memories I have of him."

"That's terrible," she muttered.

"He ended his life—gambling debts to another lord satisfied, but nothing left behind for his family. Mother's health began to fail after that. She couldn't accept the hand fate had dealt her."

"Oh, Ash." Evangeline longed to pull him close and offer him the comfort he hadn't known when he was younger.

"Tell her who is to blame, Ashley," his brother interjected.

She was starting to see why Ash didn't care for the man. She'd never met anyone so heavy-handed in her life. "Who is to blame?" she asked, even though she hated dancing to the man's tune.

Ash didn't answer for a moment. The only sound was the crunching of biscuits on the opposite side of the tall service. "I promised my mother I would fix things for our family. I promised I would get our funds back… and make the lord who destroyed our family pay."

Her stomach clenched as the details of their earlier conversation fell into place. Revenge. What family she belonged to. What she had a right to know. "My father?" she whispered. She needed Ash to say the words. Surly this wasn't happening. That day in the park, he'd claimed her father wasn't involved. Had he lied?

He nodded, but she needed to know more. She had to somehow understand.

"You targeted my father in your plots?"

"I-I made a promise to my mother that your father would pay for what he did to my family," Ash said in a low voice.

She studied him. "You told me you weren't going to swindle my father. You told me and I explained away your actions. If you were to take from my family, you were only after a small amount. You claimed that's all you ever did."

A sound of dismay come from Ash's brother, but she ignored it.

"Taking advantage of your father is what I set out to do, what I've been committed to doing, but then I began spending more and more time with you," he tried to explain, but her ears were already ringing with his lies.

"All the while lying to me." Evangeline tried to dislodge her hand from his, finally shaking her fingers free after three tries. How could he have deceived her so after all they'd shared? All of their time spent together, the conversations… He'd convinced her to sneak out to Vauxhall to meet him. He'd happened to arrive just in time to give her a ride home in his carriage. Last night…

She stared at him, seeing him for the first time for the true swindler that he was. He'd sought her out at every turn, even going so far as to climb in her window at night. Why would he go to such lengths unless that was all part of his plan as well? All of his actions pointed in one clear direction, one she'd been blind to until this moment. Ash had seduced her in order to ruin her. "You had it all planned out? What happened between us?"

"No. God, no! I never planned for this."

"When you took…" The words stuck in her throat. He'd taken her virginity. Certainly she'd given it over freely at the time, but he'd known exactly what he was doing. And now she was ruined. Any chance she'd had at a good match—the match her family wanted for her—was gone now. She'd given herself to him, and he'd only been with her out of revenge?

"I never meant to hurt you, Evie," he said in the most serious voice she'd ever heard him use, but it didn't matter.

"Yes, you did. You came here planning revenge on my father. And you accomplished your task on all levels. You plotted this all along, didn't you?"

"For seven years," the duke supplied.

She almost choked on her rapid breaths. She needed air. "I was to find a husband this season. Instead, I allowed you to… Oh, what have I done?" Her hands flew to her lips to stop the tumble of words. No one needed to know what she'd given to him last night, but she knew. She would always know. Ash Claughbane had seduced her and ruined her to further hurt her father. And she'd enjoyed it. What kind of wanton had he turned her into that she'd relished every moment of her demise? She was Evangeline. She didn't do that sort of thing—she couldn't. She gripped the edges of her chair, holding on as the world spun around her.

Ash reached for her across the table, but she leaned away from him. "I never meant for this to happen, but I don't regret it. You've changed everything."

How could he be so callous? Her jaw dropped open. She'd thought she knew him. "You don't regret what you've done?"

"It brought you into my life." His voice was rough.

"What a boon that must have been for you," she said in mock politeness.

"It was, but not how you're perceiving it, Evie."

"Don't call me that," she demanded. "You lied to me. You used me in your games and I thought..." She'd thought he cared about her, that she'd been special. She'd told herself that perhaps one day he could have grown to love her as she did him. But that day would never come now. He'd only wanted revenge on her father, and she was the fool who'd fallen for his tricks.

"Are you certain you wouldn't like some tea?" the maid asked, returning.

"I don't want your blasted tea!" She pushed her chair back with a loud screeching sound. She couldn't fall apart here. She'd worked for too many years to descend into public hysterics now. She was Evangeline

Green, and she would walk from this room with some dignity left intact. "I'm leaving."

"Don't go." Ash was on his feet, the look in his eyes one of wild determination. "Please, don't go."

"Ha! I've spent so long begging that same thing of you. I shouldn't have come here. I shouldn't have done a great many things. That changes now. I have to fix my mistakes before my poor decisions destroy my family once again. I trusted you, which proves what a fool I am."

"No, you aren't." He reached for her arm but apparently thought better of it as his hand dropped back to his side. "None of this is your fault. You at least have to believe that. I'm to blame in this, Evie, not you."

She studied him for a moment. Why was he so insistent that she wasn't to be blamed? There was some detail that he was avoiding in all of this. She could see it in his eyes. And then she realized the truth. The facts settled into place in her mind even though he'd worked not to say the words. "Seven years. That's what you said, wasn't it? This began seven years ago? My father gained back what I lost our family, and he did that at *your* father's expense." She stared for a second at the truth of her words reflected in Ash's eyes. "This all happened because of me. It *is* my fault."

"It's not your fault. Don't you dare say that," Ash said, taking a step toward her.

"You knew." She took a step backward, away from him and his lies. "You knew that day in the garden maze." She pressed her lips together as tears stung the backs of her eyes. "You knew before your carriage. You knew before the theater. Yet you didn't tell me?" She would not cry—not here and not for him. "I'm sure that made this portion of your revenge that much sweeter."

"No!" He had the good grace to look appalled at the suggestion. "Evie…"

"Don't," she warned with a finger pointed at his chest. "You don't get to tell me lies anymore."

"We are making a scene," the duke said.

"I don't *care*." And for one blinding moment, she didn't. She turned, wild emotion rampaging through her heart, and grabbed a biscuit from the tower. Raising her arm, she flung it at the duke who'd been sitting watching them as if at the theater. She grabbed another fistful and slung them at Ash. It didn't assuage her anger and it was worse than crying in public, but she didn't care just now. Her heart and her virtue lay in crumbs at Ash's feet—why shouldn't the blasted tea biscuits as well? She would walk away from this afternoon and never look back.

"Evie," Ash called after her, but she was running. The clicking of her shoes on the marble floor sounded in her ears with a sickening hollowness. The flowers she'd thought were enchanting only an hour ago now assaulted her nose with noxious perfumes. She had to escape this place. The dark, dank interior of her family's carriage called to her.

The first tear slipped from her cheek as soon as the carriage door was closed. She'd left him. After all this time trying to hold on to him…he'd never cared for her. Revenge—that was all he had wanted.

"Father's fortune. My future. It's my fault. All of this is my fault." Regardless of the prying eyes of passing traffic outside the carriage window, she fell to the side, pressing her face against the serviceable fabric of the seat. This summer had been nothing but madness, but she couldn't allow her family to pay for her foolish behavior this time. Not again. She pulled her arms around her body to keep from shaking as she bumped down the road.

Ash was just a memory. Perhaps one day she would look back on this afternoon as a casual observer, with no longing or anguish. Perhaps one day she would even be glad she'd left him standing in that hotel calling after her, and her life would be better for it. But somewhere deep inside, where she knew the flavor of ice she preferred and how she wanted to be touched by a man, she knew those were lies.

Against all reason, she wanted to throw open the carriage door and run back to the man who'd set out to destroy her family, the man to whom she'd given her heart and her body so willingly. He'd looked at her as if she was his future, and she'd wanted him to be hers. "Ash…" She cried his name into the empty carriage. A loud sob caught in her throat, and she wrapped her arms tighter around her body.

Her mother had been right all along. She couldn't be trusted to make decisions regarding her life. And she would never stray from her family's wishes again.

✧

He should leave. He had no right to be here in Evie's home after what happened yesterday afternoon. Of course he never did have a true right to be here. Ash's mind was caught in a loop, and no matter what he did, it brought him back here to Evie's door. He hadn't slept. He hadn't eaten. He didn't think he could ever ingest a tea biscuit again. The sensible thing to do was to leave town, and that was the one thing he couldn't do.

He'd been shown into the front receiving parlor—Evie's room. The gray skies outside left the empty room cold and devoid of life. When the butler had returned and said Lord Rightworth wasn't available, Ash hadn't been surprised. He likely knew Crosby Steam Works was an empty shell of a company.

With a nod Ash moved back toward the door. There was no use lingering. Evie didn't wish to see him. He didn't blame her. He was, after all, an untitled gentleman and a swindler by trade. But then he heard it.

Humming. Happy, no, *delighted* humming.

He couldn't help himself. He moved toward the sound, ignoring the butler's murmurs at his back. Rounding the corner of the doorway into a large drawing room, he saw Evie standing on a platform. A mirror stood before her as the same young maid he'd seen many times before knelt at her feet with a needle and thread, and her mother circled her, humming.

Evie was wrapped in the finest silk. Tiny flowers trailed from her narrow waist to the floor. Everything about her was elegant perfection, and it couldn't be more wrong. He wanted to scoop her up and carry her from this place to somewhere she'd be safe from her family. But she wanted nothing to do with him. She'd left him. His mouth went dry, and all he could do was stare. *I should leave. I have no right to be here. I never did have a true right to be here.*

Evie's gaze shifted from the far window to the mirror and she saw him. He knew because he saw her small intake of breath. Otherwise she didn't move. Tiny smudges marred her skin beneath her eyes. She hadn't slept last night either, it seemed. He wished he could explain away his actions, but he couldn't. He hadn't been honest with her from the start. This was his fault. It was all his fault.

He should turn and walk away, out of her home, out of her life. But he was rooted to the floor, looking in on a scene he had no part of. He was meant to travel on alone; that had always been his destiny. He would pack this image away and take it with him—not the ornate gown or the shining locks of hair pinned with precision, but the look on her face. If he tried, he could imagine longing in her eyes as she watched him in the mirror. But no matter what she wanted to say to him or throw at him today, he knew she wouldn't move. It was time to leave.

"Lord Crosby," her mother exclaimed, for once pleased to see him. "We weren't expecting you today. Were we, Evangeline?"

"No," Evie whispered, still watching him in the mirror.

Ash cleared his throat so that he could speak. "I came to see Lord Rightworth."

"He's with his man of business, changing some investments about and seeing to a few things for Evangeline," Lady Rightworth said, waving away the cryptic yet telling news like it was a troublesome bug. "You're fortunate enough to catch a glimpse of Evangeline's gown, though. It's beautiful, isn't it? I had it made for her and set aside for the occasion. She'll make a fine bride. Don't you agree?"

"Bride." The single word fell from his lips as he looked at Evie in the mirror. Bride?

"Oh yes. She accepted Lord Winfield's suit just this morning." The woman beamed as she adjusted Evie's sleeve. "He's been quite patient waiting for our Evangeline."

Evie shifted and looked down at her toes, no longer meeting his gaze in the mirror.

"Do be still, darling, and stand up straight. It's as if you haven't been taught proper posture." Her mother clucked her tongue in disapproval. "I've done my best with you, but Lord Winfield will have his hands full to be sure."

Evie straightened, her face devoid of emotion as she whispered, "Yes, Mother. I'll try to please him when the time comes."

The unspoken boundary that kept Ash at the door crashed to the floor at Evie's words. He moved into the room until he was standing beside the mirror she faced in that blasted ornate gown. Evie shouldn't try to please anyone but herself. She deserved more than this paltry offering of a half-life.

"Do you wish to offer your felicitations, Lord Crosby?" Lady Rightworth asked as she circled to Evie's other side. Her hands were clasped at her waist as she looked down her nose at him.

Ash ignored the woman looming over them and looked up to where Evie stood above him on the platform. "Is this what you want?"

"It's for the best, my lord," Evie whispered, her chin quivering slightly even as she kept it raised. She was staring straight ahead into the mirror as if he didn't exist. Perhaps, to her, he no longer did. "Mother believes—"

"I don't give a damn what your mother believes," he roared, stepping in front of the mirror until he was facing her. His stomach was in knots. He would be thrown from the house any minute, but he had to try. "Is marrying Lord Winfield what you want, Evie?"

Her mother drew back in shock at his harsh words. "I have never heard such talk—"

"Yes, you have, Mother," Evie snapped at the woman, seeming to draw strength from his exclamation. Perhaps Evie wasn't completely lost after all. "You heard such talk last year from my sister and her husband. Don't pretend otherwise."

The maid stilled at their feet and watched as Lady Rightworth's eyes widened. "I never!" Evie's mother placed a hand over her heart and excused herself from the room, claiming she needed to sit for a moment.

Ash thought it more likely that she was gathering her forces to strike again, but he was glad he had a moment to speak with Evie alone. "Is this what you want?" he asked again with a nod of his head to indicate the gown she was wearing and everything that came with it.

"This is the match my family has arranged for me," she said carefully in a small voice that was no longer a whisper but not her usual voice either.

He took a step forward. "You didn't answer my question."

"I require a husband. This is for the best."

"Is this what's best for you, or what's best for your mother?" Ash asked, trying to shake her from the trance she was in.

"What would you have me do?" She stepped down

from the platform, thread trailing from a half-sewn hem, but the maid said nothing of it.

"Don't marry him," he said with a shake of his head as he searched her face for answers.

Evangeline swallowed and pressed her lips together for a moment before speaking. "Why not?" she finally asked, breaking the silence. "Why shouldn't I marry him?"

Ash's voice faltered. She shouldn't wed Winfield because he couldn't make her happy. Winfield didn't know the real Evie. He didn't know to protect her from her mother. He didn't know what she liked, or how to make her truly smile. Ash did, and he'd gone and mucked everything up with his lies.

"You used me," she said, her voice thick with emotion that barely showed in her eyes. "You lied to me. And we both know you won't stay."

"I made a terrible mistake—it's true. You don't have to forgive me for that. I don't deserve your forgiveness. But you don't have to marry Winfield either." How could he make her see? If he couldn't have her, he wanted to think of her smiling and laughing somewhere—not with a lord who didn't even know her.

"It's best if I don't make my own decisions just now," she stated as if she'd repeated the words to herself many times over to memorize them.

"Just now is when you do need to know your own mind, Evie." He muttered a curse and ran a hand through his hair. "You're to wed Winfield? Only two nights ago—"

"Don't you dare," she warned, finally finding her voice. "We both know what that was about, and I'm fortunate to have this opportunity." Evie turned to the maid and dismissed her with a nod of her head before turning back to him.

"Actually, I don't know what that was about the other night," he said, cutting off anything she'd been about to say. "I don't know what any of this between us has been about." He motioned between them with his hand. "But I do know I don't want you to marry blasted Winfield!"

"Revenge—that's what this is about," she retorted, mimicking his hand motion between them.

"No," he said, even as his heart began to crush in upon itself. "I wasn't honest with you about why I was here, but it was *never* about revenge where you were concerned. Never."

"Then what do you want with me?" Tears pooled in her eyes, but she blinked them away and pulled her spine straight with some sort of mental warning he couldn't hear. "Why are you doing this?"

"I want you to be happy." He sounded like he was begging, and in many ways, he was. He needed her to go on to live a happy life without him if he had to lose her. He couldn't bear the thought of her married to Winfield. The man was too polished and pompous. That couldn't make Evie happy...could it?

"Do I look happy? Do I look pleased with this conversation?"

"No. You look like your mother's creation, and I know you're more than a bit of silk and lace." He sighed, fisting his hands at his sides to keep from reaching for her. "Evie, don't marry him."

"Everyone tells me what to do." She raised her hands to twist around a bit of loose ribbon at her waist before dropping the ribbon and clasping them together in a white-knuckled grip. "Who to be," she continued. "They tell me what I like, what to wear…" She swallowed and looked him in the eye. "You don't get an opinion, Ash Claughbane."

The sharp sting of her words hit him harder than if she'd slapped him. "Your opinion is the only one I'm fighting for, Evie."

"I make poor decisions. Therefore, my family was kind enough—"

"To marry you off for their gain in society?" He reached for her, unable to resist any longer. He wrapped his hands around her arms as he looked into her eyes, begging her to understand. "They're using you."

"As opposed to what you did to me," she countered as she fought back tears.

"I love you."

She took a breath and closed her eyes. "You need to leave."

"I suppose those are cheap words from a swindler like me, but they're true nonetheless."

She opened her eyes, but stared straight ahead at his cravat instead of meeting his gaze. "Go." Her body shook beneath his hands as much as her voice did when she said that one word.

"Evie," he tried, but fell silent.

"Please go," she whispered.

"I wish you all the happiness in the world, Evie." He lifted her hand to his lips and kissed her knuckles. He couldn't bring himself to say good-bye, but only to nod farewell.

Then he did what he should have done over a month ago and walked out the door.

Twenty

A SELECTION OF DRESSES HAD BEEN SLIPPED OVER HER head, examined, pinned, and discussed while she stood in the modiste's shop on Bond, yet Evangeline hadn't really seen any of them. The sun dipped lower in the sky, streaming light into the front window of the shop. The tea that had been offered when she'd arrived with her mother had grown cold on the table in the corner. And Evangeline's mind could not be further from the small shop where she was destined to spend the remainder of the day draped in various silks. Today didn't matter.

Yesterday he'd said he loved her. Ash's face swam before her as it had for the past day, but as she did every other time, Evangeline blinked it away.

She would find a way to continue breathing without him. She would move her feet forward in the hope that they would meet solid ground. And one day, long from now, it would no longer feel as if her heart had been ripped from her chest. That day would come, wouldn't it? As she stared unseeing into the shop mirror a full day after he'd claimed he loved her and she'd told him to leave, she doubted it.

Her body ached for just a glimpse of him, just one more moment in Ash's presence. Had she been wrong to send him away?

He'd lied about her father's involvement in his past. He'd lied about his plot of revenge against her family. He'd stolen her virginity. Only...that last bit didn't feel precisely true. She frowned at herself in the tall mirror that stood before her as the dressmaker shook out the skirts of her gown. That night at the theater with Ash had been one of mutual desire. She'd wanted that night every bit as much as he had. And he hadn't intended things to go that far; he'd told her that and she'd understood. She'd felt the same as he did. He hadn't taken anything from her—she'd handed him her heart on a platter.

The next day while angry and confused, she'd accused him of compromising her as a means of revenge against her father, but today she couldn't quite make the claim ring true in her heart. The way he'd looked at her yesterday as if she were the only lady in the world...

Then he'd said he loved her. Was it true? Could she trust him? He'd told her about his family—about being the youngest of four brothers. That had been proven true. He'd even admitted he was a swindler, and that—now that she was aware of the details—had been quite a dangerous move. But beyond specific examples of truth versus lies, when he looked at her there was an honesty in his eyes that even now she trusted. But could she trust herself? Theirs was never meant to be the happily-ever-after sort of romance. He was always going to leave her. *But I made him leave when he wanted to stay*. She pressed her lips together and forced herself to take one breath, and then another. Everything about her life was wrong.

"No, no, no. That gown is all wrong," her mother complained at her side. "Would you have my daughter's betrothal to Lord Winfield be announced while she walks about in raaaags?"

She blinked into the mirror, noticing the gown she was wearing for the first time. It was actually…pleasant looking with simple lines and a lack of ornamentation. "It isn't rags, Mother." Evangeline smoothed her hands over the pleats at her waist. "It only needs to be hemmed and taken in a bit here and there."

"It's all wrong for you, Evangeline. My special daughter needs a suitable gown for her special evening." Her mother sang the last bit in a voice that made Evangeline feel nauseated.

The gown had an understated grace that she appreciated, all soft creams and pale-green trim. "The color is—"

"Awful, I know." Her mother shuddered. "Do you have anything in a nice blue?"

"I like this color," Evie said in a small voice, but no one was listening to her while her mother was bellowing orders.

"A *nice* blue! Not that." Her mother drew back from the woman holding the rich blue gown draped over her arm. "We aren't in the tropics. Indigo, really." Her mother sighed and touched a hand to her head to secure an already firmly attached lock of hair. "Perhaps we should visit the shop down the street— this one seems to be on the decline." Although the comment was directed at Evangeline, it was intended for the two women who bustled around the shop in an attempt at making her mother happy.

Evangeline shot the woman holding the blue gown a sympathetic look in the mirror, hoping her wordless apology was understood.

"I can see now that we shall go elsewhere for your trousseau." Mother sank down to perch on the edge of the nearest chair with a shake of her head.

Evangeline turned to face her mother, dislodging pins as she moved. "I would like this gown to be included in my trousseau if I'm not to wear it tomorrow night."

"That?" Her mother's eyes raked up and down the cream-colored gown with clear dislike. "Evangeline, I thought you had a discerning eye for such things."

She straightened her spine. Ash wasn't here to hold her hand, and he never would be. She could do this alone. She could face her mother and survive. She'd done it before. "Nevertheless, I like this gown."

"Absolutely not." Her mother dismissed Evangeline without a moment's thought and stood and turned to look at a table piled high with bolts of fabric. "You will wear clothing that suits your new station and will make you appealing to your new husband."

"I should be appealing to my new husband with or without this gown," she countered.

"Evangeline, don't be vulgar," her mother hissed, turning to hold a scrap of fabric up to the light from the front window. "Your husband will require heirs of you, but that deed will be done quickly enough. What will *appeal* to him is your ability to carry out your responsibilities as his wife in a proper style."

Evangeline hadn't intended to be vulgar. She simply wanted to wear a different gown. *Is this what you want?* Ash's voice echoed in her memory. "I'm to wear what you select for me, marry who you select for me, be the lady you trained me to be…"

Her mother turned in a flash, appearing dark and ominous with the light of the window at her back. "I'm here to help you, my darling." The angry clip of her voice negated the term of endearment and drew the watchful gaze of the shopkeepers. "Without my guidance, you wouldn't know how to handle such situations. You know you can't be trusted to make important decisions." She lifted the sleeve from Evangeline's shoulder before dropping it back again and rubbing invisible dust from her fingertips. "I suppose you would survive, but not well. We both know that. That is why I will always be here to oversee things for you."

Evangeline looked at her mother, studying her in a way she never had before. She wasn't the all-powerful creature of doom Evangeline had always envisioned, but a grasping lady out for her own gain. Her mother was never going to relinquish control over her. Marriage had seemed an escape, but it wasn't. The only escape she'd ever experienced had been when she'd followed her own heart. She'd accused Ash of using her, but her own family had used her to a far greater degree than he was capable of doing.

"I will wear this gown," Evangeline said with a raised chin, relying upon every fiber of defiance she possessed. "Its lines possess a simple beauty."

"Beauty is never simple, darling."

"Yes, it is."

"Pardon me?" Her mother took a step closer as if preparing for battle.

Evangeline swallowed a lifetime of fear and continued, "Daisies have a simple beauty. Swans on a lake. Changing leaves…"

"Swans are filthy, and daisies are horribly out of fashion. Freesia—that's what everyone is using now in their arrangements. You would do well to remember that once you're wed. Lord Winfield wouldn't care for daisies, I'm certain. I'll advise you in such things, of course. We can't have you requesting the wrong flowers in his lordship's home."

"I don't care for freesia," Evangeline announced as she turned back toward the mirror, signaling the woman with the pins to take in the waist of the cream gown she still wore.

It was as if floodgates of bold behavior had been thrown open with her mother's announcement that marriage wouldn't end Evangeline's entanglement with her. She was as strong as she'd been with Ash at her side. He believed in her. He had loved her, and that knowledge, even though he was gone now, was enough to steel her against her mother's wrath. She was worthy of being loved, and she would settle for nothing less. "Freesia smells like a brothel, and I will not have it in my home."

The gasp from behind her made Evangeline fight back a smile of satisfaction. "I've dedicated my life to bettering you in preparation for marriage, and this is how you repay me on the eve of your engagement announcement?"

"No. You're correct, Mother. You deserve much more than this." She offered her a polite smile in the mirror. She would indeed get much more than what Evangeline was dishing out today. She would get everything she had coming to her from years of mistreatment. Ash had been right—this was the exact time when she should know her own mind.

❧

Ash moved down the dark street, his boots falling hard on the wet stones. In the past four and twenty hours, he'd told a lady wearing a wedding gown he loved her, and then he had unpacked his trunks for the first time in seven years. Of course, in line with his standard crooked way of life, the lady in the wedding gown was to wed another, and he'd unpacked his trunks into rented rooms in his gentlemen's club. He mumbled a curse. Even when he broke his only two rules in life, he cheated when he did so.

The unpacked trunks—or more accurately what he'd found while unpacking his trunks—had led him toward Rightworth's house tonight—not the lady who was no longer his. It was rumored that Evie's engagement was to be announced at tonight's ball. Everyone would be there, including the reason he was striding in that direction—Lord Dillsworth. He'd taken a page from the man's ledger book, and he should return it. The fact that Evie would be there—smiling a false smile while wearing some ornate gown that didn't suit her personality and being congratulated on her upcoming nuptials— hardly mattered.

"Doesn't matter at all," he whispered into the damp night as he increased his pace down the street.

He'd told her he loved her, and she'd told him to leave. It was fine. He was fine. He'd survived so far alone, and he would continue to do so.

"Do you mind?" St. James asked as he stepped up beside him. "You're stomping and soaking my breeches in the process."

Couldn't the man see he wanted to walk alone in the dark tonight? "I'm not stomping," Ash growled.

"No, of course not," St. James replied in his usual smooth voice, as if he were making idle chat over tea instead of chasing Ash through the London streets. "You also aren't brooding at all. The fists at your sides and the angry gleam in your eyes are merely signs of your overall indifference."

"You *aren't* annoying, and *shouldn't* return to headquarters," Ash countered without slowing down. Didn't St. James have something more important to do than to follow him around town? Everyone at headquarters was talking about the former Spare Heir who'd returned to town to take the secret society down. Shouldn't St. James be in pursuit of that villainous chap rather than Ash this evening? But the man at his side didn't seem concerned with such things at the moment.

"I assume we're attending the Rightworths' ball," St. James mused, clearly not accepting Ash's dismissal.

"How did you find me, anyway?"

"Your man, Stapleton, told me you set off on foot with the Dillsworth ledger page in your pocket."

"Stapleton." Ash exhaled a harsh breath. "He has

the unfortunate habit of speaking when he should remain quiet."

Ash didn't shift his gaze from the street ahead. Homes lined the streets in this part of the city. Rightworth's house was now a block away. When he'd set out tonight, he'd thought the walk would do him good. He didn't feel good. He felt angry and lost. His only option was to keep moving forward, and tonight that would lead him into further heartache. He deserved it. He deserved Evie's wrath and everyone else's for keeping the truth from her. "I suppose you're going to attempt to keep me from attending tonight."

"No."

"Good," Ash replied, taken aback by his friend's response, but not questioning it.

"What we need is time," St. James mused.

"Her engagement is going to be announced tonight," Ash bit out through a clenched jaw. "What time do I have?"

"I was speaking of Crosby Steam Works, but it's good to know you aren't attending a ball simply to fall upon your sword with that stolen ledger page."

Ash looked at his friend for the first time since the man had found Ash on the street. "But that is what I'm doing. I'm making amends for all of my wrongs, St. James. Turning over a new leaf." He tried to smile, but was certain it looked more deranged than optimistic when he saw the look of concern in his friend's eyes.

Ash didn't care. He was deranged, lost, heartbroken, and angry—which all seemed much the same in the dim moonlight. But if he couldn't set things right with Evie, he could at least set everything else in life back as it should be. "I made light of those hideous cherubs painted on the ceiling of headquarters. Apologies, mate."

St. James didn't respond.

"And I told Hardaway and Ayton about my scheme and my false name after you said to keep it quiet. Apologies for that as well. Then there was that time not a week ago when we were helping Ayton save his lady and I went to the mews to head off any chances that lord had of escape. I took that hit after I hustled one of the grooms in cards, not because we had a brawl when I acted valiantly on the Spares' behalf. And yesterday when I said—"

St. James held up a hand to stop him. "I don't know that total honesty is wise in these situations, Claughbane."

He didn't understand. Ash couldn't sit about while Evie married another gentleman because of him. He'd done nothing but make mistakes in his life, and he needed to fix something or he would go mad. "I hurt her, St. James. I hurt her and now she's going to marry Winfield."

"I know," St. James said in as close as he could come to a comforting tone. "Do you have some sort of grand plan for tonight to win her back? The Spares could help you somehow."

"No." They'd done enough to help him with his failed scheme. He didn't want their assistance now. This was his burden to bear. Not to mention, at this point, there was no winning her back. He'd tried. He'd failed.

I love you.

You need to leave. The exchange played out again in his memory as he supposed it would for the remainder of his life.

"You're part of this society, you know," St. James offered, not mentioning how Ash had failed that society already. "You don't have to do this alone."

"No." Ash glanced at the man at his side. "I mean that I'm not going to stop her. I have no grand plan. I'm going to set my wrongs to rights and drink heavily in the corner while Evie dances with another man."

"That's a terrible plan," St. James mused.

"Plans are more your territory, aren't they? I simply have a document to return."

"And she wonders why I'm always working," his friend muttered.

"What?"

"Nothing," he replied as they neared the front of Evie's home. "Ah, quite the crush tonight. This should be interesting."

Ash didn't want to discuss his plans for tonight. He only wanted to unmake his mistakes, and right now that started with Dillsworth. He moved away from St. James, his eyes scanning the crowd for the older man. A moment later he became aware that he was searching for a young lady with dark hair, not a man old enough to be his father—treacherous eyes. The truth was plain—he did want to catch just one glimpse of Evie tonight. He needed to see her. Perhaps he could live the rest of his life this way, lurking in the shadows, waiting to see her for just one moment before returning to his life of misery and regret. It sounded…promising.

"To clarify," Brice—no, it was Hardaway now—said a few minutes later as he joined Ash in the main hall, "you're attending this ball, the engagement celebration for the lady you lost to another lord, for the purpose of returning documents that I offered to return for you...all while there's some lord asking after you all over town."

"St. James told you already?" Ash looked around for the leader of their club, but he'd already slipped away, no doubt to see to business of some sort while here.

"He said you deserved to listen to me because of the cherubs. I don't know what he meant by that. He could have taken up drinking, though that doesn't seem likely after all these years."

"So much for making amends on that score," Ash muttered, his eyes still sweeping the room as he pushed his way through the crowd with Hardaway at his side.

"You know you're seeking out my father, a man I see every morning while I try to down enough coffee to erase the previous evening?" Hardaway confirmed.

"You rise early enough to see the morning?" Ash asked, deflecting his friend's concerns.

"It's morning to me, and that wasn't the point. I could return that paper to my father's desk, and he would never know it had been missing."

"You think I'm taking an unnecessary risk," Ash said, filling in the gaps of the discussion his friends must have had behind his back a moment ago.

"I think you've lost your bloody mind," Hardaway countered. "It happens to the best of us. My uncle Herbert lost his mind over a woman. Of course in his case she was the parish vicar's wife. Needless to say, he was banned from services, and there was some bit about not being allowed to show himself in town. Come to think of it, I think that was meant in the literal sense of showing his bits to the ladies, which is simply good standards for anyone. You can't go about naked in town, no matter who you believe yourself to be in love with."

"Since I'm not naked but wearing proper evening attire…"

"To attend this ball." Hardaway spread his arms to indicate Rightworth House, almost hitting a lady in the process, but he didn't seem to notice. "This ball. The one where announcements will be made about your former lady and Lord Winfield."

"I'm here for a valid purpose." Ash patted the pocket of his coat where the ledger sheet was folded. He was repairing a wrong. That was all. "I need to return this document."

"Just make sure you don't find yourself naked in town with the vicar's wife, if you know what I mean."

"Oddly enough I know exactly what you mean." But it was too late for him. Ash's crimes were already exposed, and he had been left raw by the experience. No clothes could cover that sort of wound.

"No one wants to see your bits and pieces, Crosby."

"Noted." Ash walked into the large drawing room, now emptied of furniture to allow for dancing. Evie stood with her friend Victoria along the far wall beneath the windows. He stopped. "I see your betrothed is here tonight."

"Bollocks. I'm going to slip down the hall to the

terrace before her father spots me. Have fun destroying what's left of your life so your wallow in misery can be complete."

"Much appreciated," Ash muttered, not shifting from where he stood with its perfect view of Evie.

She wore a blue gown covered with so much adornment and jewelry that it almost blinded one to look at her. She was beautiful beneath the frills and shine, but it was the false Evangeline she had out for display this evening. His heart clenched further. Then, she smiled at something her friend said—a real smile. Under the show of ladylike excess, was she happy about this fiasco? She appeared to be pleased until she turned and her gaze met his across the room. The smile slipped from her face.

Ash couldn't move. There was no forward. There was no plan for his future or even making amends for his past. There was only now and the clearly unrequited love he was drowning in. She'd asked him to leave her. He should leave now.

He should, but he didn't.

Twenty-one

INVENTOR OLLIE DEAN COULD WALK FASTER THAN THIS carriage was moving. He'd been on the road to London on Spare Heirs business for an eternity.

In truth he'd left his home two days ago, but an eternity seemed more fitting since his travels had taken him away from Mable's side. And this blasted trip to see St. James didn't appear to have an end in sight with the other carriages blocking the road. He leaned toward the window to determine the reason for their slow pace. "Precisely why I never come to town."

His quiet home life called to him like a siren on a damn ocean cliff, but he had business to see to with the Spare Heirs Society. He'd worked secretly for the group of gentlemen for years now, consulting on technical matters for various endeavors. He'd often wondered why he'd been recruited to join the group. St. James had been sure of his decision, though. Secretly Ollie had always thought that as an inventor specializing in clockwork, he wouldn't ever have a large role to play in the sort of work that was popular within the society. Until now. This... He glanced to the newly drawn plans that lay on the seat at his side. This might be something.

Sighing, he settled back in his seat and forced himself to relax. He would enjoy this as best he could even while rolling down the road toward London at a snail's pace. Crosby Steam Works. He'd thought it a mad idea to attempt to produce steam from such a small apparatus. They'd *all* considered it mad. He almost smiled, and he would have if so much were not at stake.

He tugged at the dark-brown waistcoat his grandmother and his wife had insisted he wear. "No one will notice if it matches my eyes," he'd complained. But grandmothers were an unstoppable force when teamed with any other female.

The thought of his family had his toe tapping on the floor. He glanced to the diagrams of the steam machine once more. St. James and Lord Crosby would be quite surprised indeed to see him in town.

That was, if he could ever manage to arrive in London.

❧

Afternoon had turned into evening. A footman had stoked the fire; empty glasses had been taken away and replaced with clean ones; and the draperies had been closed on all the windows except the one Ian kept returning to with every pace of the room. The accommodations for his party were at least pleasant, even if the company he kept was not. Ian exhaled in an attempt to remain patient and turned on his heel, walking back across the private parlor they'd been offered use of at the hotel.

"I found him!" Feathsly announced as he stepped into the room…alone. He closed the door behind him.

"Crosby? You have him?" one of the gentlemen asked.

"I saw him not twenty minutes ago." Feathsly rocked up on his toes, his chest puffed out with obvious pride.

"Yet he isn't here," Ian muttered, trying to understand the situation.

"No. But I saw him. Laid eyes right upon the scoundrel," Feathsly returned.

Ian stepped toward the man. "You saw him walking down the street, and you didn't think to stop him? We've been chasing Lord Crosby for weeks."

"I know we have. I couldn't take the man alone and exclude all of you fine gentlemen. Now that we've bonded on the road and such, I thought we should confront him together. I didn't think it was right to take the credit for finding him after all we've been through."

"Quite honorable of you, Feathsly," one of the other gentlemen offered. "We should all have a piece of the celebration that's to come."

"The celebration," Ian repeated as he ran a hand over his weary eyes and turned away from the men to keep from throwing a punch. He simply wanted to find Crosby so that he could return to life as usual in Bath. Was that asking overmuch? With these men involved, it indeed did appear to be. "There will be no celebration since the quite honorable Feathsly let the man go."

"Now see here, Braxton…" one of the gentlemen began, but Ian wasn't listening.

"We've been in London for days now, and this is the first news we've had," Ian informed Feathsly, turning to face him once more. "We've scoured the city's inns and rented rooms. If Crosby sleeps at night, we have yet to find evidence. Not a soul will speak against the man. Yet you spy him and let him go?"

"I came straight back to tell you about it," Feathsly defended.

"Do you even know the man's direction this evening? Where did you see him?"

"He was with another gentleman and dressed for the evening."

"Where?" Ian practically yelled before he reined in his temper.

"On the other side of the park, in the fashionable area."

Ian turned and began pacing the room again. "What entertainments are being held this evening? I haven't a care if we must attend three balls in one night; this chase ends today."

"I was invited to a dinner at the Appleby residence," one of the men said.

"The Rightworths' ball is to be the big one tonight," another lord chimed in.

Ian turned back to look at the men in the room. "We'll start with the Rightworth event. Whatever we must do, this so-called Crosby will be found by night's end."

Twenty-two

ARRIVING AT A BETROTHAL BALL AT WHICH ONE HAD no intention of becoming betrothed was much like attending one's own funeral. People had gathered together; the excess of flowers was profuse enough to cover any stench; and soon everyone would learn the truth—she wasn't deceased. Or in this case, she wasn't planning to marry. The lack of expectation on her part left her free to enjoy the festivities—as much as she could, anyway, when there was blasted freesia as far as the eye could see and she was trapped in a gown she disliked.

Evangeline glanced down at the ornate gown she wore, topped with such a show of jewels that her arms grew weary of lifting the weight of them. She touched the large necklace at her throat and looked down the wall to where her mother stood talking with a group of ladies.

This would be the last night she would be forced to wear such an ensemble, and since it was, she was almost relishing the pull of her hair into the elaborate style and the heavy jewels that tugged at her earlobes. It was like the last required smile of a dance with an undesirable partner, and much in the same way she savored the discomfort.

"Would you like some whiskey to numb the pain?" Victoria asked. "I always carry a flask in my reticule." She raised a salute with a glass of lemonade that didn't look like lemonade at all.

"Thank you for the offer, but I find I'm quite looking forward to the announcement." Evangeline nodded in greeting to two ladies who moved past their corner of the large drawing room.

"I thought the gentleman in question swam in cologne and wanted to use you as a trophy to trot out at parties."

"Oh, that's all true," Evangeline replied brightly.

Victoria eyed her over the rim of her lemonade-disguised whiskey. "I'm certain there's an explanation here somewhere."

Oh, there was quite the explanation. Evangeline adjusted one of the bracelets at her wrist and watched her mother holding court with some other ladies halfway down the wall from where she stood. "You'll quite enjoy it, I'm sure."

"Now I am curious."

"I only wish everyone was here tonight," Evangeline mused as her gaze swept over the sizable crowd.

"It's quite the crush, Evie," Victoria countered. "No need to get down on things now."

"I mean Isabelle and Roselyn," Evangeline turned to say, eyeing her cousin's glass.

"I don't think Roselyn is sparing us a thought." Victoria returned as she handed her glass to Evangeline with a roll of her eyes.

Evangeline took a sip and immediately regretted the action, handing back the glass while choking out, "True." Roselyn had left town in rather a rush last week. With her elopement and a wedding trip, she would be gone some time, and Evangeline missed her already. But her friend had finally found happiness, and Evangeline was glad of it.

"What of Isabelle?" Evangeline asked once she'd recovered.

"I couldn't say." A tightness entered Victoria's usually smooth voice that Evangeline had never heard before. Victoria downed the last of her whiskey in one swallow and handed the empty glass to a passing footman before she continued. "She doesn't speak to me these days. We've become strangers. She spends most of her days at the museum. I believe she may have a new love interest." She shrugged, not meeting Evangeline's gaze. "I don't see her, not that she minds the space away from me."

"But you mind being away from her," Evangeline filled in.

"I do, but don't ever tell her I said as much," Victoria warned.

"Your secrets are safe here."

"Speaking of secrets, I sense that you're planning something devious for this evening, and you know I enjoy being involved in devious plots."

"You're a walking devious plot."

"Then you see why you require my assistance tonight. It's simply what I do."

Evangeline smiled at her cousin. For all the flaws of her family, she was grateful to be related to Victoria.

Life would never be dull with her around. Evangeline only hoped Lord Hardaway knew what lay ahead of him with her as his wife. As if she'd conjured up the man, she saw him just inside the far door to the room—speaking with Ash.

What was Ash doing here? He'd come back?

Her smile slipped from her face as she calmed her overwhelming desire to run to him. She'd destroyed things there quite well when she'd commanded him to leave her be. But if she ran to him anyway, heedless of shoulds and oughts, then what would she do? Aside from any wrongdoing he'd committed against her family, this void between them was entirely her fault. He was no longer hers. Would she walk up and chat about the weather as if nothing had happened? There were no words for what was in her heart, save three.

She heaved a sigh. It was too late for such confessions, and tonight she must remain focused on the task at hand.

Ripping her gaze from his, she found her mother in front of the bank of windows that lined one wall of the room. "On with the show," Evangeline muttered to herself. She left Victoria's side to move toward them.

"Evangeline, my darling daughter," her mother said for the benefit of the ladies who surrounded her. The bracelets on her wrists caught the candlelight as she beckoned Evangeline forward.

"Mother," Evangeline said with a gracious smile for the group.

"We hear you might have exciting news for us this evening," Lady Smeltings said, clasping her hands together. "We couldn't imagine a more perfectly suited couple, could we, ladies?"

"Truly? May I ask why you think so?" Evangeline asked.

"Evangeliiiiiiine," her mother warned through a thin smile. "Of course everyone can see what an ideal match you and Lord Winfield will make."

"Is that because of our well-matched social standing or how fine I will look in his family's jewels? As long as he has a title worthy of marrying your daughter to and a home ideal for hosting the *ton*'s elite, what more could you ask for? We know what's really important, don't we, ladies?" Evangeline gave the group a much-rehearsed wink. A few titters of amusement rolled around the gathered group, along with more than one wide-eyed look of shock. These people didn't know the real Evangeline, but they were about to meet her.

"*Evangeline.*"

"You see, my mother has spent a great deal of time turning me into the type of lady a lord of Winfield's level would find appealing. And tonight is the culmination of her hard work. I believe she's earned a round of applause for her efforts, especially after I nearly wrecked our family when I was twelve years of age—"

"There's no need to discuss this, Evangeline," her mother sang through teeth clenched into a smile.

"Do you not think so?" Evangeline turned to ask her mother. "That's odd, since you don't miss an opportunity to remind me of my faults behind closed doors." Shifting her gaze to the circle of ladies who were all staring and hanging on her every word now, she confided, "She even denied me food for several days this season. The effort she's put forth for this day is…astounding."

Fans fluttered around them, stirring the

freesia-scented air as the ladies looked around the group. No one knew how to respond, since no governess or finishing school had ever covered how to react to the sort of show Evangeline had planned. She looked at her mother, daring the woman to contradict her words.

"All of this is for you, darling. Now, I believe we should make the announcement," her mother said in a clear effort to change the direction of the conversation.

"Yes. Yes, we should," Evangeline agreed. "Let's announce it."

"Lord Winfield," her mother called to him. She sounded nervous. She should be.

"Ah, is it time for our happy news?" Winfield asked as he left his conversation to join them.

"I believe that would be wise," her mother said, eyeing Evangeline.

Evangeline stepped forward and laid a hand on Winfield's arm to gain his attention. "Do you mind if I say a few words before you make the announcement?"

"Already taking the lead at society events." He gave her mother a nod of appreciation. "You were correct. She'll make a fine wife."

Her mother only tittered uncomfortably and shot Evangeline a look of such warning that it required no words.

"Everyone, might I have your attention?" Evangeline announced and waited for the room to quiet. Heads turned and conversations paused until everyone looked in her direction.

There was no turning back. She'd worked her entire life to be the proper lady she was expected to be, and now, with all of society's eyes upon her, she was about to toss aside every bit of that work. She swept her eyes across the room before her gaze landed on Ash. He still stood just inside the far door of the room, watching her. *Everyone* was watching her, but somehow his gaze went deeper, touching her soul without words. Ash wasn't at her side, but somehow his presence steeled her for what she was about to do.

Swallowing the last shred of fear she possessed, she began. "A few moments ago, I was sharing with these lovely ladies a bit about my mother and our gracious host's kindness. Mother, step forward if you please."

"Oh, I wasn't expecting this." Her mother clutched a hand over her heart and glanced around uncomfortably at the crowd. "What are you doing?"

Evangeline didn't answer her. "When my mother, Lady Rightworth, was making arrangements for this event, we...had a quarrel." She held up a hand to stay any comment. She'd spent years memorizing her half of every conversation, and it was finally her own turn to write the words she would speak.

"I'm aware that it does happen between mothers and daughters. You see, I stated that I preferred to wear a cream-colored gown with no adornment or jewels, and that I was fond of the simplicity of daisies." She turned to her mother with a polite smile to ask, "You remember, don't you, Mother? It was just after you made that dressmaker cry with your insults. At any rate, my *dear* mother, being the wise society matron that she is, instructed me on the *correct* flowers and gown that you see before you tonight.

"What do I know of my own likes and dislikes, after

all? Therefore, tonight I would like to recognize my mother, whose insistent influence can be seen in every single bloom this evening, every bit of abundance used for the sole purpose of impressing everyone here, and every piece of my own ensemble."

Evangeline raised a glass of champagne intended for the toast to the newly betrothed couple as she continued, "As you can see, there is freesia in every available vase present this evening, and I am dressed in the gown in which she saw fit to display me."

"Evangeline, you do jest." Her mother batted her arm playfully, yet hard enough that a bruise would form by tomorrow. "I hope you have a liking for humor, Lord Winfield."

"I hope so too, Mother." Evangeline glanced at Winfield, who had a confused look on his face but was otherwise remaining silent. "Of course, you will always be around to make such decisions as flowers and gowns for me so Lord Winfield won't truly know his wife at all." She released a false laugh just as her mother had taught her to do and forced her to practice until her voice was hoarse. "He'll have no idea that I think freesia smells like a brothel at sunset before all the men arrive for the night."

She took a bloom out of the nearest vase and flung it at her mother. This hadn't been part of her plan, but blast it all, it felt wonderful. How much pain, fear, and sorrow had she experienced at this woman's hand? The very woman who should have cared for her had used her position to hurt her. And now that she'd begun she couldn't stop.

"Lord Winfield won't know that I find an

abundance of freesia blooms perhaps more overbearing than my mother, which is a rather difficult feat to achieve." She flung two more flowers at her mother, watching as they fell to the floor between them.

"He won't know that I'm capable of discussing more than just the weather." She pulled out more flowers and threw them, smiling when they hit their target. There were gasps, but she didn't care. She wasn't listening to the gasps. She didn't look around to confirm the looks of dismay on every face present. She'd wasted far too much of her life trying to be the perfect lady. Everything with her mother was a show.

She wanted a show? This would be one to remember.

Evangeline was going to shed the false identity she'd been forced to wear for so long. She was Evie Green, precision in smiles and gowns be damned.

"Of course, none of my preferences matter since I'll have no say in my own home, just as I have no say in my life." She ripped a bracelet from her wrist and hurled it at her mother.

"You'll tell me what to wear as you always do." She pulled an earring from her ear and tossed it.

"You'll tell me what I'm allowed to eat—or not eat, as the case may be." She removed the other earring and smirked as her mother held her hands up to block her face from harm before Evie hit her arm with the shot.

"You'll tell me what I must say and force me to rehearse conversations." She removed the other bracelet and sent it sailing in her mother's direction. Then she ripped the necklace from her throat and threw it at the woman now surrounded by flowers and jewels, just as she'd forced Evie to be covered in adornment.

"You'll tell me who I am and what I want for the rest of my life. How do I know this? Because you always have!" Evie exclaimed as she threw the last bracelet at her mother. "And for what? To marry me to a gentleman for your own social gain? How high must you climb in society to be happy, Mother?

"It ends today. I will not allow you to manage my life any longer." She turned and grabbed the half-empty vase of freesia in her fist. But as Evie looked away, her mother grabbed her arm, attempting to drag her away from the watchful eyes of the crowd. Her grip was tight, but Evie was used to such a stranglehold on her person. Wrenching free of the woman, she turned back to face her.

"What a shameful disappointment you are," her mother hissed at her, but in the silent room her voice carried. "Do you even realize the hardship I've suffered? Day after day. It isn't an easy task putting a shine to something this dull. But I accepted that you were what I had to work with. And I fought every day, dedicated my life to the effort of turning this… *you*…into something a gentleman might desire. And this is how you show your gratitude? Daft girl. You're rubbish, just like your plain-faced sister."

"Don't speak of Sue in that manner. She deserves both of our apologies after what you forced me to do to her," Evie warned in a low voice. The vase in her hand grew heavy with the weight of her mother's words. "For years I've been bruised from your effort and hardship. But you won't force me to do anything ever again," Evie murmured before upending the vase over her mother's head.

Evie heard the gasps around her, even a quickly hushed burst of applause, but she didn't allow it to distract her from the woman before her. Instead Evie stared her down like an opponent in battle. Her mother stood shaking with rage. Evie would have been fearful of the look in her eyes only a few days ago, but not now.

The room was still. She had the attention of everyone present tonight, and for the first time, she was proud of the image they saw before them. She was no longer a fabrication held together by jewels—she was real. She was Evie. "Who I am is enough," Evie said only loud enough for her mother to hear. "Sue was right about you. This is where we part ways."

Evie turned. Looking through the crowd of stunned, silent guests, she signaled a footman by the door. A second later a procession of servants entered carrying platters piled high with white daisies. It was every servant that Mother had let go over the past two seasons in London. They'd been more than willing to assist Evie when she'd contacted them this morning. Even on such short notice, there was an army. They moved through the crowd, passing out daisies to everyone in attendance.

A few ladies drew back in horror and refused the simple blossoms, but Evie had wasted enough of her efforts on ladies of their ilk. That ilk could rot. They didn't understand the beauty of a daisy and they never would. Lady Smeltings shook with what Evie could only assume was indignation over the entire scene while another lady attempted to calm her.

Evie scanned the crowd with an odd sense of

detachment. For so many years, she'd lived in fear of just this occurrence, and now that she'd caused such mayhem at a ball, the only thought that washed over her was that she was finally free. She was free of her mother's reign of terror, but she was also free of society's expectations for her. And freedom was a grand possession indeed.

"Throwing the family jewels…" she heard a lady say, but they could keep their family jewels. Evie had no need of them anymore.

She moved into the crowd, hearing a gentleman say, "If my daughter ever…" But she stopped listening. If his daughter ever, Evie would be the first to congratulate the poor dear.

As for Evie, there was nothing further her parents could do to harm her. That gentleman's daughter may never dare to speak her own mind, but Evie had dared. She had dared and now she would dare to live every day in the same manner as she had tonight.

"I never suspected such…" she finally heard on the lips of an older lady, but the woman's gaze wasn't focused on Evie, but on the freesia-covered lady that Evie had left behind. No one had suspected how horrible her mother had been to her, but now they knew the truth.

"No more lies," Evie whispered to herself.

She moved with slow steps through the room, watching as the simple flowers replaced the freesia arrangements, covering every surface with their beauty. Servants were still filing through the doors with tray after tray as the orchestra began playing once more.

She moved toward the door of the drawing room

where she'd last seen Ash. Was he still about? Had he seen her spectacle?

"Lady Evangeline," Lord Winfield said, stepping into her path and stopping her progress.

Drat. She'd been so caught up in seizing her life back from her mother's grasp that she'd forgotten about their engagement. He was searching her face as if seeing her for the first time, but Evie had no desire to stand about while he struggled to understand what had just happened.

"I won't be able to marry you, my lord. Apologies for any inconvenience this may cause you." She gave his arm a pat and veered around him, continuing on her way.

She heard him stammer something behind her, but she didn't stop. She needed to find Ash.

"That was quite the announcement," a gentleman said as she passed.

His voice. Where had she heard that voice before? Her stomach clenched before she'd even turned to see who was speaking to her.

"Lord Braxton," she choked out. "What are you doing here?"

"This was reported to be the event of the evening. It seems the gossips were right on that score."

Evie stared up at the man, her mind racing. What of Ash? Was he still here? He wouldn't be safe with these… She raked her gaze across the group of men. Oh dear, they looked like the makings of an angry mob. "Well then." She swallowed. "I hope you continue to have a lovely evening. If you'll excuse me…"

"I would appreciate it if you didn't warn Lord Crosby of our whereabouts," Braxton said as if he could read her thoughts.

"Certainly." She took a step away from the man before turning back to him. "In fact, I'll assist you. He asked me to meet him on the terrace in but a few minutes' time. I'll show you the way."

"Magnificent news," Braxton exclaimed as he fell in step beside her. "I had my fill of London days ago. My home won't survive my absence much longer. The sooner I find this man, the sooner I can be gone from this place."

"He's terribly difficult to find, isn't he? You have my sympathies, my lord." She laughed, thinking of the last year when she'd searched for him as well, although for entirely different reasons.

He grumbled in response as she led the way out the door to the terrace.

"My thanks for your assistance," he offered as the group of irritable-looking men stepped out with him.

"I'm always happy to assist you in such a manner," Evangeline said with her most charming smile.

A moment later, the last of the men was through the door and she made her move, slipping back inside and turning the key in the lock. Her heart was pounding as she looked through the sea of people before her in the hall. The buzzing of the crowd had increased with the scene she'd caused. Somewhere in this madness of her own creation, Ash stood unaware of the danger he was in. She only hoped it wasn't too late.

❧

Ash didn't wait for the flowers to be doled out to everyone—he knew a finale when he witnessed one. Instead, he moved through the crowd until he reached the front receiving parlor where Evie spent her days and slipped through the door. He braced a hand on the wall and tried to settle his racing heart, while an odd mix of pride and sorrow threatened to drown him.

She'd done it. She'd stared down her opponent and thrown flowers in the face of danger. She *was* still his Evie, the real Evie. Only…she wasn't his anymore. He shook his head and pushed off the wall.

Moving to the opposite end of the room, he stood staring at the settee where he'd once had tea with Evie. It seemed a lifetime ago that she'd chatted about the weather nonstop. If he'd told her then about her father's connection to his past, would things be different between them now? Would he be the one in the next room being congratulated, or would she have thrown him from the house months ago like an unwanted freesia blossom?

Behind him, the door slammed shut and he spun on his heel. "Evie," he murmured.

"I locked the lot of them on the terrace," she said, eyes wide and face flushed. "I can't believe I did that. Of course, I can't believe I did a great many things tonight."

He moved toward her, unable to resist the pull she had on him. "If you ever desired work at a traveling festival, I think you'd lead a fine show." He lifted a hand toward the wall that separated the parlor from the drawing room. "That was…"

"Long overdue," she finished, straightening from the door.

"I was going to say brilliant, but yours is true as well."

She twitched the ribbon trim of her gown with her

fingers as she looked at him. "I couldn't have done this without your encouragement."

He nodded, unsure how to respond without further pouring out his heart for her to refuse. "Congratulations on your engagement," he finally blurted out.

"Is that why you're here?"

"No." The paper that had brought him here was still in his pocket and quite forgotten until this moment.

She took a breath and looked at the floor between them. "You have to leave."

He released a harsh breath that almost sounded like a bark of laughter, but there was nothing amusing about the way his heart was aching for her. "I suppose I should have known that was coming. After all, it isn't the first time you've asked me to leave."

"This isn't about that," she corrected, taking a step in his direction. "Lord Braxton is here, and he has a band of men with him."

"Braxton," he repeated. "And you've come to warn me away."

"Yes." She looked at him with pleading eyes. "He wishes you harm. I...feel otherwise."

"*Otherwise*, and yet we're at your betrothal ball." He gave her a wry smile before looking away.

"It was never about that for me. You must go. Now."

His entire life had led him to this moment. His promise to his mother. His scheme to exact his revenge on Rightworth. The years of practice to be ready for the task. Evie. It was the last in the list that stayed his movements. He couldn't leave her, not now, not even for the evening. He would spend the remainder of his life undoing the wrongs he'd done. It wouldn't undo where their relationship had gone sour, but it was a start.

"I'm not going to leave," he said in a low voice.

"What of your rules? You never stay," she pleaded, but he didn't move. "Why now when you have so much to lose?"

"Turns out even malleable things like rules can break if you truly want them to be broken."

"They'll send for the authorities. It would mean prison, Ash. You have to leave. Run!"

He turned back to her, resigned determination meeting the worried look in her eyes. "I've already unpacked my trunks."

She shook her head, clearly not understanding the significance of his statement. "Pack them again."

"No. I won't run from this. A very brave person I know threw flowers in the face of her enemy tonight, and I won't turn tail and run from mine."

"It's not the same, Ash." She took a step closer to him, looking up at him as she spoke. "If you stay, you'll leave here in chains."

"And you with a leg shackle." He laid a hand on her shoulder, the most he dared to touch her. "I have to do this, Evie. I've always slipped out the side door when things got difficult. I have a pile of wrongdoings in my past and I don't want to live in that manner any longer. I never thought I could have more in life until I met you." He dropped his hand away from her, drawing his fingers into a fist at his side. "I…" *love you*, he finished to himself.

He wouldn't leave her, he couldn't. Not now, not

ever. He would never abandon Evie, no matter what that meant for him. But he did need to allow her to walk away for her own good. "I'm glad for your newfound happiness in your situation. Now, I have to sort out my own situation."

"It will lead you to a prison cell." Her voice was raspy as she spoke. "This path, it will only lead you to harm."

"So be it," Ash murmured as he walked out the parlor door.

~⚬~

She had to do something. He was here because of her, Evie knew it. He'd come to support her tonight even though she'd forced him from her life, even though his presence here would end in his imprisonment. He was walking toward his own demise and under the impression it was for her. He was righting wrongs? What did she care about that nonsense? She'd loved him, even knowing he was a swindler. She couldn't allow him to make a sacrifice like this on her account. She had to stop him.

Evie made it as far as the parlor door before realizing she didn't know what to do. There was no stopping Ash from destroying his own life. She'd tried. Lord Braxton would be angrier than her wet mother with flowers on her head by now. Had anyone found a key and allowed him back into the ball? Perhaps she had time to repair this situation.

She spun around the hall in search of someone or something that could help. She wasn't certain what she required, but she knew she couldn't allow Braxton to hurt Ash. She needed something, someone…anything really! She just needed assistance. Grabbing a walking stick her father sometimes used when he took walks in the park from the corner behind the front door, she turned, brandishing it as one might a sword. Only, she'd never used a sword before. Blast her useless training in embroidery!

She turned and gave the walking stick a testing jab, only to hit their butler in the back. Wincing as he cried out in pain, she rushed to his aid. "Terribly sorry. You were not my intended target."

"My back begs to differ, my lady," the old man grumbled.

She needed to escape this little mishap and find Ash. Would he be in the drawing room by now? Where was Lord Braxton? As well-planned as the earlier portion of her evening was, this was not going well at all. "Would you like to sit?" she offered, looking around the hall for a chair.

"During a night of entertainment? Certainly not." He seemed more affronted by her offer of assistance than the jab to his ribs. "This evening has been quite eventful. I can't imagine the chaos if I chose to abandon my post."

"Yes, quite eventful," she agreed.

"In addition to your…display," he finished, clearly struggling to find a polite word for what she'd done, "there have been quite a few uninvited gentlemen attempting to enter through this very door. The last of which I refused. His attire—"

"*Refused*. You turned someone away?" she asked.

"He awaits entrance still. On the steps outside."

"You left a guest waiting on the steps on a damp night such as this?" She reached for the doorknob, but the butler wouldn't budge. "Perhaps you *should* abandon your post."

"My lady!" he exclaimed and steadied his mulish stance in front of the door, blocking her from opening it beyond a small crack.

She glared up at the man standing between her and the door. "If Lord Braxton is allowed entrance—and he has a band of men in his company, all of whom mean one of our guests harm—then I see no trouble in admitting the poor gentleman you left to stand outside in the dark. What is his name?"

"It's a Mr. Dean." He drew back a fraction in disgust, reminding her of her mother. "He doesn't even possess a title, my lady."

"Neither do you," she retorted. "Stand aside so I may open the door, or you may do the job you were hired to do and open it yourself."

He drew himself up to his full height. "I have worked in this home for ten years."

"And you have clearly spent far too much time in my mother's company. Open the door," she commanded.

Then a new voice sounded over her shoulder, making her turn. "My lady, at the risk of having you turn your weapon upon me, I believe I can help in this matter."

Evie looked up to see the man she'd seen Ash with on several occasions. Perhaps she could send him in search of Ash while she quarreled with her butler. Would he listen to a friend over her? She tried to remember his name from the gardens that night he'd chatted with Isabelle. They'd been introduced, but Ash had been there that night and he'd been quite distracting. "St. James, isn't it?" she asked, hoping she was correct. "I've seen you with Lord Crosby."

"You have."

This was it, the assistance she needed. "Perhaps you can speak with him. There's a lord here who's set on hurting your friend."

"Lord Braxton," St. James replied. "I'm aware."

"He has a band of men at his back. And Lord Crosby insists—"

"Lord Crosby has a band of men at his back as well. Now, if I could allow Mr. Dean entrance?"

"A band of men?" Evie muttered. Ash worked alone and only kept one man in his employ. Or had that been a lie as well?

But before she could inquire over his meaning, Lord Hardaway joined them in front of the door, with her butler still standing sentry. "St. James, I think you need to come into the next room. It's worse than we imagined."

"I knew it would be," St. James stated.

"My lady, perhaps you should excuse yourself from the festivities," Hardaway began.

"What?" She raised the walking stick in her hand, preparing to use it if necessary. "Not likely."

"Very well," he said, easing away from her. "I know Crosby is sweet on you, and I thought it would be best if you didn't see…"

"See what?" She didn't wait for an answer. She was running toward the drawing room door.

When she rounded the doorway, she heard

Braxton's clipped tones over the rustling of the crowd. Everyone was looking toward the middle of the floor. Shoving people aside, she made her way to the front of the audience and gasped.

Ash was there, a line of angry-looking gentlemen blocking his escape. He wore chains at his wrists and was shackled to the chair he sat upon. *No.* She tried to scream the word, but no sound came out. She was too late to save him.

"This man has stolen funds from many of you," Braxton announced. "He claims to be gaining investors for his steam works, but it's a lie. This man is a fraud. His name isn't even Lord Crosby. I have it on good authority that he's without a title and from the Isle of Man."

"Where he is the younger brother of a duke," Evie cried out. "Mind your wording, sir."

Murmurs carried across the crowd, but Ash didn't look up from the point he stared at on the rug before his feet.

"I heard the steam works was true. Release him," a gentleman yelled from the back of the room.

"Yes, release him," another man joined in to rumblings of assent.

St. James's claim of a band of men at Ash's back flashed in her mind. Was it true?

"You heard lies," Braxton countered, turning back to Ash. "Your *Lord Crosby* doesn't even defend himself."

"Nor should he have to," Evie said, stepping forward into the open section of floor around Ash and his enemies. "He's an honorable man, Lord Braxton. Otherwise, he wouldn't be present tonight."

"Honorable?" Braxton asked. "He swindled funds from every one of these gentlemen you see before you. He's a common thief."

"No, he was gaining investors," she tried.

"Investors in Crosby Steam Works? Crosby Steam Works didn't even exist until he arrived in London. In Bath his name wasn't even Crosby. Oh, but he claims to be on the edge of a breakthrough. He claims steam will be a part of everyone's lives and not simply for factories. They are lies, my lady."

"You don't know that," she bluffed. She wasn't sure what she was doing, but she couldn't allow Ash to remain there shackled to a chair.

"If what he claims is true, where is the proof? Where is the steam?"

She had no answer. The crowd around her rumbled. There was no proof to be given, and even with a few men in the crowd supporting Ash's claims, the weight of fact was on Braxton's side. She looked down to where Ash sat, beaten by his own life choices and with heavy iron holding him to this place. It was too much. Lord Hardaway had been right—she couldn't watch this. It was too painful. Soon the authorities would arrive and he would be led away from here, away from her. Trapped forever.

"Where is *Lord Crosby's* much-promised steam?" Braxton pressed further.

"Here," someone behind her called out.

At the same time, a loud grinding noise had everyone turning and placing their hands over their ears. A moment of confusion passed before a stream of white vapor began to rise to the ceiling of the drawing room.

"Steam," Evie murmured.

She turned to look at Ash, who wore the same look of shock as everyone else in the room. Turning back, she saw St. James, Lord Hardaway, and a man she'd never met before pushing a contraption farther into the room. *A band of men at his back.* But what was his connection to these gentlemen?

"Make a path, if you please," she called out, shooting a smile over her shoulder at Ash.

The sputtering machine was pushed to the center of the room over fallen daisies, and everyone began to applaud. The unknown dark-haired man in the brown waistcoat nodded his appreciation as St. James and Lord Hardaway clapped him on the back. Even Ash, still chained to a chair, was grinning in amazement.

"Lord Crosby may not be this gentleman's true name; however, Crosby Steam Works is quite real, as you can see," St. James stated.

Evie marched forward until she was in front of Lord Braxton. "Remove Mr. Claughbane's restraints immediately."

Behind him, the other gentlemen were suddenly gleeful and congratulating one another for having the foresight in their investments. Lord Braxton, however, was studying the contraption. Probably searching for weaknesses.

"Lord Braxton," Evie said again to gain his attention. "Release Mr. Claughbane. He has just earned you a great deal of money, and I believe is owed your thanks."

"Perhaps," Braxton muttered with his gaze still locked on the swirls of steam. "But if he ever comes near my family again, I'll see that he goes straight to prison."

"I believe you're safe there, my lord. I've heard that Mr. Claughbane is attempting to leave the swindling business, intent on righting wrongs."

Braxton shifted to look at her, an understanding of some sort dawning over his face. "See that he does so." With a final nod, he turned, gave the command to have Ash released, and left the room.

A moment later, Ash was free and swept up in the congratulations surrounding him.

"To Mr. Claughbane and Mr. Dean, founders of Crosby Steam Works," Hardaway called out and glasses were raised beneath the gathering cloud of steam.

Through the group all vying for his attention, Ash's gaze met hers for but a moment. In that look there was hope. Then he was pulled away, and she took a step backward. She didn't belong at his side, no matter how she longed to be there. He had a new business venture to sort out, and she…well, she wasn't certain where she would go from here. Taking another step back from the group, she became aware of Victoria at her side.

"We look like drowned rats covered in daisies, and I couldn't be more pleased," Victoria said with a playful nudge of her cousin's arm. "I have my work ahead of me, though."

"How so?"

"If I'm to keep the moniker of the wild one of our group, I'm going to need to improve my play. Well done, Evie."

In spite of the steam now falling like rain on their heads in the middle of the drawing room, and the desire to rush across the room to an Ash who was no longer hers, she laughed. Her mother's precious furnishings were destroyed along with everyone's gowns and formal clothing, yet no one appeared to mind. Merry chatter continued around the room as everyone enjoyed the novelty of it raining indoors. Perhaps in some situations, the weather could be an interesting topic of conversation.

Evie linked arms with her cousin to take a stroll around the room, which currently resembled a sodden garden.

"What will you do now that you've banished your mother from your life and ended your engagement?" Victoria asked.

"I'm not sure," Evangeline said, but as she spoke her gaze found Ash's once more. "Your sister advised me to listen to my heart."

"Your heart is leading you toward steamy rooms and rain showers?"

"It is," she admitted. "Even though I believe my time in this steamy room in particular is at an end."

"Last week I was down all of my pin money playing cards when I finally was dealt a winning hand. I won every bit back, plus some. Don't give up hope."

Evie ignored her cousin's admission that she'd gambled again and focused on her words. "Hope," she repeated as she looked across the room to Ash once more. He'd told her he loved her once. Did she dare hope he loved her still?

Twenty-three

ASH STOOD IN THE CENTER OF THE SWIRL OF excitement that had migrated from the drawing room to the terrace by the early hours of the morning. Glasses clinked together repeatedly, and steam mixed with the smoke from cheroots as the gentlemen celebrated success.

"I, for one, am glad you didn't take another day to polish the damn contraption before arriving in town, because I'd be across town in prison if you had," Ash said with a thankful nod for Oliver Dean.

"St. James didn't mention a deadline," Dean countered.

"I can't be expected to know when one of our own will decide to throw himself on his enemy's sword," St. James said, stepping into the conversation.

"Really?" Hardaway drew back in surprise. "You know everything else."

"Except for Claughbane's idiocy, it would seem," St. James retorted.

"This was all part of my plan," Ash said with a smile.

"You're a terrible liar." Hardaway laughed. "How did you make a single coin selling potions and tonics?"

"Desperation, mate. Neediness makes my lies more palatable." Ash took a sip of his drink. "An honest company should be interesting, though."

"That'll be something new for all of us," St. James mused in a low voice only the other Spare Heirs could hear.

"Mr. Claughbane, I believe," Lord Rightworth said as he joined their conversation. "You're quite the hero of the evening, much to the dismay of Lord Winfield and Lord Braxton alike."

Ash turned and took a step away from the other Spares to respect the group's secrecy. He looked at the older man. So much of his life had been spent in anticipation of destroying this man. Yet Ash hadn't accomplished that task at all. If anything, he'd further lined his pockets.

Evie would be pleased at this outcome at least. Ash wasn't certain of his own feelings on the matter—only that he now saw this man as Evie's father and not a faceless man who'd destroyed his family. His long-ago promise to his mother would have to go unfulfilled, but somehow Ash thought she would understand. The plot against Rightworth was at an end, and if that didn't please his mother, it certainly would please his living family members. And someday long from now, he would get an eternity to explain to his mother how everything had changed once he arrived in London and set eyes on Evie.

Either way, it was done.

But what did any of this mean for Ash?

"My apologies for interrupting your celebration," he told Rightworth, with his mind still on Evie despite every other distraction the night had produced. "It wasn't my intention."

"Not your intention to find yourself in chains in the middle of my drawing room? I'm certain it wasn't. I came as soon as I heard the commotion, but you seemed to have things well in hand by then." The older man gave him a nod of approval.

"I had help." Ash resisted the urge to look at the Spare Heirs, who were still gathered around Dean's steam machine only a few paces away.

For the first time in his life, he was part of something greater than himself, and that alliance had proven its worth this evening. They'd created the first portable steam engine. Crosby Steam Works was real. He hadn't sold a lie—he'd gathered investors in his steam works. He still hadn't worked out what this meant for him, but he imagined it entailed being honest and staying in one city. Was he wealthy from legitimate funds now? He supposed so. Who would have guessed this outcome? Not Ash.

Lord Rightworth looked down at his feet for a moment before he spoke again. "I knew a Claughbane from the Isle of Man."

"My father," Ash stated. He'd waited for this conversation for seven years, and just like his expectations for the rest of this evening, this wasn't the conversation he'd envisioned.

"Yes, I suspected as much," Rightworth said, running a hand through his hair. "I didn't think your appearance here was one of coincidence. I…regret what happened all those years ago. I was desperate and…"

"I already know," Ash said, thinking of Evie.

He knew why this man had taken what he had. Ash's father had lost everything on a poor hand of cards—a hand of cards he never should have played. Rightworth hadn't stolen from them, no matter what Ash had convinced himself to believe to fuel his rage in his youth. He was willing to admit the truth now. Every circumstance in life was much more complicated than he'd once thought.

"Nonetheless, I'm sorry," Rightworth said. "Regret is a terrible thing."

"Yes, it is." Ash took a breath. "I've enjoyed spending time with your daughter this season. I wished her well in her betrothal when I saw her earlier tonight. I hope she'll be very happy as Lady Winfield."

Rightworth paused, studying him. "You don't know?"

Ash's heart was somewhere between beating a wild rhythm and stopping altogether. Had something happened to Evie he wasn't aware of? "Know what?"

"She refused Winfield." There was a knowing gleam in her father's eye that made Ash uneasy as Rightworth continued. "I believe her heart lies elsewhere."

"She…" Ash's words faded away as he tried to piece together their conversation in the parlor, but came up empty-handed. "She refused Winfield? She isn't…"

"No," Rightworth confirmed. "And Winfield was pleased enough to back away, after the spectacle of the evening. I don't think he wanted a wife who knew her own mind, and I have no intention to force the issue. Evangeline deserves to be happy after what she's endured at her mother's hand. I should have intervened years ago." He gave a humorless bark of laughter. "Yet another regret."

Ash only nodded in response. Evie wasn't going to marry another gentleman. The gray night tipped sideways as everything else he thought he knew came into question.

"I married that woman to align our families, out of duty to my title," Rightworth continued. "I would call it a mistake if not for my daughters. One shouldn't marry for such reasons." The older man stared off across the dark gardens, lost in thought for a moment. Ash didn't move, sensing their conversation wasn't at an end. "I was never in favor of Winfield," Rightworth finally said. "What does social position matter when you must spend your life in the company of someone whom you can barely tolerate? That's no life, believe me."

"Then, you're advocating a love match for your daughter? Rather unconventional, don't you agree?"

"You seem the sort to appreciate a lack of convention, Claughbane, much as I've seen you appreciate my daughter."

"I…" Ash didn't know how to respond. Of course he appreciated Evie. More than that, he loved her. Evie had made her views clear on the subject though, hadn't she? She'd wanted him gone. And then she'd attempted to save his life…

"If you wish to call, we plan to be at home tomorrow. Excuse me, I have many things to see to now that the festivities are ending."

Ash watched Evie's father walk away. After years of planning the perfect revenge for the demise of his family, the moment had come and he was the one left reeling.

The excitement and surprise of the previous evening boiled over into a sludge of exhausted confusion the next morning. While her father had taken the news of Evangeline's failed betrothal rather well—a fact she contributed to his anticipated wealth in steam—her mother had yet to emerge from her bedchamber.

Evangeline had seen her father for only a few minutes this morning before he disappeared into the library for the day. He'd looked uncomfortable for a moment before informing her that her mother would be taking some time away from city life to visit Great Aunt Mildred in Scotland. Evangeline would remain with her father while her mother was away—a fact he seemed quite pleased about.

"How long will she be in Scotland?" she'd asked.

"Indefinitely," he'd replied, and they'd said nothing more on the subject.

Her mother's reign over their family was at an end.

Evangeline had spent the remainder of the morning making a list. She wasn't sure what her future held now, but she was determined it would contain at least some activities that interested her. She had to focus on herself now. Life must somehow go on. She curled further into the corner of the settee in the sunny front parlor, pulling the lap desk into the crook of her arm.

Learn to make an arrangement of daisies.

It was true, her heart was broken and would likely never mend, but she had helped set things right for Ash. She'd done the right thing for him. He was free to live his life as he chose now. And he'd chosen to walk away, just as she'd known he would since the beginning.

Watch birds in the park.

Her short-lived engagement had been shredded, the plan she'd maintained all season to find a husband falling to the floor with it. After last night, there would be no finding a husband, after all. She would need some means of…well…means, now. She could stay with her father for a time, but even that should come to an end. But she wasn't afraid. Life wasn't a thing to be feared; it was to be lived.

Learn to gamble on horses and cards.

Her mother had been mortified at the scene she'd caused, but Evangeline held no regrets for her actions. For the first time since that day when she was twelve, she wasn't afraid of her mother. There was no pain or torment that woman could inflict on Evangeline that she couldn't withstand—not anymore. And now they would likely never see one another again. Her father hadn't said many words on the subject, but she now wondered if he'd spent many of his days being beat upon by that woman as well. Somehow with Evangeline's show of force last night, her father had found his strength to stand up to his wife as well.

Visit the museum.

Evangeline was free. Alone, but free. Ash had seen to both outcomes in the end. She swallowed and closed her weary eyes for a moment. It was true that she'd become strong enough to overcome her fears at his side, because of him. But she would have to find a way to continue on by herself.

Eat more flavored ice.

Send weekly notes of apology to Sue.

Go back to the theater.

Purchase gloves that fit.

She squeezed her eyes shut again. She could spend the rest of her days eating ice and attending the theater, but neither would ever be the same as it had been with Ash. She no longer needed his strength to survive her life; however, she would want his company forever.

It wasn't to be. Would he have left town by now?

She wasn't sure how long she sat there envisioning him arriving in a new town, picturing the style of house he would make his home, his sly smile as he made plans for his future. He would be the centerpiece of her daydreams until she was old and wrinkled. For a time he'd been hers. He'd loved her, and she would carry that small serving of happiness with her forever.

A floorboard creaked by the parlor door and she opened her eyes. To her astonishment, Ash was standing in the doorway—but it wasn't the sly smile she'd envisioned that covered his face. It was confusion.

"Ash," she whispered as she stood.

"I was passing by… Damn." He stopped, raking a hand through his hair. "That's not true. I was on the other side of the city this morning."

"My father is in the library if that was what you—"

"No, that's not why I came."

Her heart was in her throat. "What are you doing here?"

"Blundering my way through this conversation it would seem," he admitted as he moved across the room toward her.

"Would you like…"

"Some tea? I don't believe I could properly discuss the weather just now."

"I was going to ask if you wanted to take a turn

around the garden. I've yet to be outdoors today." She glanced down at her day dress. It was pale pink with no adornment, but she liked how soft it was beneath her bare fingers.

He stopped. "Of course," he murmured and lifted his arm to offer her escort.

As she wrapped her hand over his arm, for a moment it was as if nothing had changed between them. Yet everything had. They walked in silence until they reached the outdoors, only communicating in small, curious glances.

They were down the steps and moving into the grass when Ash finally broke the silence. "I wanted to thank you for what you did last night."

Was that the only reason he was here? To express his thanks? "You already thanked me," she countered.

"So I did."

"I find I rather enjoy causing a scene in the middle of a ballroom—much to my mother's dismay," she mused in an effort to lighten the strain of their conversation.

"I'm pleased I could be of service, then." He took a breath and turned to look at her, stopping their movement through the garden. "Evie, I find I'm troubled by one small detail of last night."

"Oh?"

He nodded. "When you came to my defense and tried to explain away my actions before Mr. Dean with the steam machine, did you do so because it was the proper thing to do? Was it in the name of honor that you did it? Or was it...was *I* the reason you took such a risk?"

And there it was. The question she'd been steadily

avoiding since yesterday. He was waiting for an answer, of course. He'd made no commitment to her. He was likely only curious, one last question before he left town. She wanted to be honest with him anyway. She had to, if only for her sake.

"I wanted to help you. When I saw the opportunity to mend things for you, I did what I must."

"Then it was out of a sense of right and wrong." He released a breath and cast his eyes down, his hands resting on his waist. "I thought there was a chance... but I suppose I should have known."

"A chance? A chance of what?"

"You ended your betrothal to Winfield and assisted me in the same evening. I was hoping..." He muttered a curse and turned away from her. "This is clearly why I was able to sell bottles of love potion for such a high price."

Was he mumbling about...love? She wasn't certain if he loved her still, but she placed her hand on his shoulder anyway. "You have no need for bottles of love potion, Ash."

"They're raspberry liqueur," he admitted, turning back to her.

"I'm not surprised."

"Of course you aren't." An overwhelming sadness filled his eyes as he looked at her. "You're fully acquainted with my worst qualities."

"I'm well acquainted with all of your qualities," she replied. It was time to know her own mind. It was time to dare to live, to seize an opportunity for happiness and hold on tight. "I loved you last year when you left me in that hall wondering when I would see you again."

"Oh, well, about that—" he began to argue, but stopped when he truly heard her words.

"I loved you when you kissed me to make your escape at the first ball this season."

"Evie…" He murmured her name as he studied her face in awe.

"I loved you when you had my father invest in a scheme you thought to be false."

"When you list it out in such a manner…" he began, but stopped when she grabbed his hand and wrapped her fingers through his.

She stepped closer until she was looking up to meet his gaze. "I loved you when you took me to the theater."

"Clearly that didn't go exactly as I'd—"

"And I love you now," she declared as she pulled his arm around her waist with their entwined hands.

"You do." It wasn't a question so much as a confirmation of fact.

"I do. Even if I must borrow Lord Braxton's manacles and chains to keep you with me, I want to be with you, Ashley Claughbane."

"You can keep me without chains, Evie. You've already done so for some time. I couldn't run last night, not even to save my own skin. I couldn't leave you."

"And now? What if you leave *with* me?"

"Stapleton has my carriage out front, but I won't steal you, Evie. I want you to be my wife. I want a home with you, a future that stretches out forever."

"I want you, Ash. I want you to kiss me, steal me away in your carriage, and make me your wife."

"You only need ask," he said against her lips as he kissed her.

As Ash swept her up in his arms and carried her away, she saw her father watching from the library window. A strand of her hair caught on the breeze and whipped across her face, reminding her that she wore no hat, no gloves, and not a single bit of jewelry adorned her neck. Yet, none of it mattered. Ash loved who she truly was beneath her veneer of lies, and she loved him—this untitled swindler who'd stolen her heart. She grinned and wrapped her arms farther around Ash's shoulders, and her father nodded in return.

Her summer of madness, this season of rebellion, and following her heart had led her to Ash. And she would spend the remainder of her life happily telling the man she loved that she wanted him to kiss her again and again and again.

Epilogue

"You're more beautiful than the bride," Ash leaned close to whisper in Evie's ear.

"You've yet to see the bride," she whispered back in the quiet of the church.

"That hardly matters." He traced the backs of his fingers over the curve of her elbow as he spoke. "I know the truth."

They'd only arrived back in town yesterday from their brief trip to Scotland's border. It was fortunate they'd returned when they did, because Evie's cousin, Victoria, was to wed Kelton Brice, Lord Hardaway, today. Of course, if they didn't start the wedding soon, it would be tomorrow before it began. Weren't these ceremonies supposed to take place in the morning? It was nearly noon and the bride had yet to arrive.

"Do these wedding proceedings seem a bit lifeless to you?" Evie asked, her eye on the somber groom and the stifled yawn from the man of the cloth.

"I couldn't say. This is the first wedding I've ever attended, aside from ours." He entwined his fingers with hers. He was married to Evie. They would begin searching for a home this week. A wife, a home—he glanced at her sitting at his side and smiled.

"Our wedding lacked this level of formality," she murmured, nodding through the gathered crowd toward the front of the church laden with flowers.

"Do you think so? I thought the foxed blacksmith really added something."

Evie laughed, the sound carrying in the quiet church. She touched her lips with her fingers, her eyes still dancing in amusement. "I thought the rings we'd stopped to purchase in York were going to be tossed in the fire in his haste to be rid of us."

"Who knew Gretna Green would be such a treacherous place? I'd rather pictured the entire town covered in floral patterns the way it's spoken about," he mused in a low voice.

"I thought it was perfect," she whispered with a sigh, looking up into his face.

"Keep that sense of delusion about old buildings and cranky townsfolk when I take you to visit the Isle of Man."

She grinned. "I can't wait. I want to meet the other members of your family and see your home…"

"My home is with you, hopefully within a day's journey of London. We'll find an estate where we can share our lives. I might take up farming."

Evie giggled at his side. "Your future in farming is about as promising as my future in embroidery."

"Then we shall endeavor to find a new pastime together. I have a few ideas on that subject." He slid his gaze to hers to give her a mischievous smile.

"Bird-watching?"

"If that's what you wish to call it," he teased.

Evie squeezed his arm and smiled up at him. "I received a missive from Sue this morning. She and her husband are set to return next summer, and she would like to visit us then."

"We should be settled well before that. I never thought I would have a wife and a home, much less that I would make plans nearly a year in advance to entertain a lord and lady."

"I never thought that I would wed the founder of Crosby Steam Works and the man responsible for an invention that will change the world. I've always had my heart set on an unsuitable swindler and a generally disreputable rebel of a gentleman."

"I always knew the steam works was true and not a ruse to steal money," he replied.

"You're a terrible liar. Truly, you need to work on your skills, sir."

He leaned close to whisper in her ear. "I vow to practice my skills the moment we leave here in the carriage."

"May this wedding be as fast as our own," she muttered, making him laugh.

Just then, music from an unseen orchestra began to play and everyone began shifting in their seats with restless anticipation. "At last. It appears to be beginning."

"Your friend Lord Hardaway looks to be quite angry," Evie whispered.

"He doesn't seem pleased, does he? At least he made a timely appearance. More than I can say for your quite late cousin."

"Victoria? Do you see her?" She craned her neck to see over the sea of hats blocking her vision. "I've never seen such a crowd at a wedding."

"No, I was referring to her sister, Lady Isabelle."

"It is troubling that Isabelle isn't present today." Evie shook her head as she looked around for any sight of her cousins. "Poor dear. Should we go look for her after the ceremony? She threatened to wear black, you know. Perhaps she thought in the end not being present for one's sister's nuptials was better than appearing in bombazine. But there's certain to be talk of her absence tomorrow."

"She's the one who has eyes for Hardaway?" Ash asked, looking at the man standing at the front of the church. "Why anyone would want that man is beyond my understanding."

"Isabelle claims she has moved on and is interested in some other blond and broad smiling fellow. But never mind that. I thought you and Hardaway were friends."

"We are." He nodded, not understanding her comment.

Evie mumbled something that sounded like, "Men, *humph*."

"Do you see the bride anywhere?" he asked a moment later when the orchestra moved on to their second selection of songs. "I'm looking forward to this ending; the ride away from here sounded so appealing."

"I already told you I can't see a thing."

Another melody passed with Hardaway shifting on his feet before the watchful eyes of the *ton*. Then Ash saw Evie's cousin Victoria come into view, her gaze focused on a point at the front of the room, beyond where he sat with Evie. Her eyes were wide and her face rather redder than he remembered it being. She was panicked. He'd seen the look before on the desperate faces of people buying love potions and healing waters.

Ash shifted his gaze to see what had given her the

wild look in her eye and saw only Hardaway. Ash had only shifted his gaze for a second, but when he looked back, Victoria was turning, her gown in hand as she hitched it up to indecent heights and set off at a run. Gasps carried over the crowd like crashing waves on a beach as Hardaway stood watching her leave. His friend blinked, clearly trying to make sense of the situation before a harsh look crossed his face and he took off running after his wayward almost-wife, calling after her.

"Did Victoria…" Evie looked up at him with wide eyes. "Did she leave Lord Hardaway at the altar?" She looked around as if her cousin might be hiding somewhere in the shocked crowd. "Where has she gone? Should we do something?"

"Yes, we should do something—let her flee."

Evie only stared at him as if he'd lost his mind. In the past few months, he quite believed he had.

"You should know, Evie. You can't stop someone from leaving until they're ready to stay."

Her look of shock turned to one of resigned acceptance. "And then *this someone* will stay forever?"

He smiled down into the face of the woman he loved and wrapped both of her hands within his. "Staying forever sounds like an exciting adventure."

"I suppose you're right—Victoria will figure it out, the way we did. In the meantime…I'll race you to the carriage."

With that, Evie pulled away from him and scurried down the church pew toward the door. When she shot a playful glance back over her shoulder, he knew—he would only run when it was in the pursuit of Evangeline Claughbane, his wife, his love.

Acknowledgments

When Lady Evangeline Green first appeared on the page, it was in her sister's book, *Desperately Seeking Suzanna*. Evie was only supposed to be the beautiful and overly perfect sister in the background of that book, but there was something about her strained efforts at perfection that spoke to me. I knew then that I had to write her story.

Have you ever attempted to be perfect to make someone happy?

I tried for more years than I care to admit to be perfect enough to please a few people in my life, but it was never enough. No matter what I did, I could not live down the mistakes I'd made years before. Then one day, after I'd allowed things to progress in this manner far too long, always listening to the reminders of my wrongs, always trying to be a bit more or a bit less to achieve some ideal version of myself to please them, I walked away. Although there were no vases of flowers upended at a ball, in the end I found the same strength that Evie did and faced down those who thought so little of me. It wasn't until I was halfway through writing this book that I realized just how close to home this story was for me. So it's only fitting that the acknowledgments should speak from my heart as well.

I write romance novels because I want to make readers smile. If you've ever met me in person, you know I'm a fan of smiling. Through these stories, I want to share love and happiness with the world, and like Ash, I want to be a purveyor of hope. If anyone has ever held it against you that you once had a summer of madness, a semester of insanity, or a year of complete lunacy, know that you are perfect just as you are. You, dear reader, are beautiful. Keep smiling, and thank you for reading.

Special thanks to: Mary Altman, Michelle Grajkowski, Mr. Alpha Male, my sweet little monkey, the Bad Girlz of badgirlzwrite.com, and the entire Sourcebooks team. Hugs to all!

E. Michels

About the Author

Elizabeth Michels is the award-winning author of the Tricks of the Ton series and the new Spare Heirs series. She grew up on a small Christmas tree farm in South Carolina. After tiptoeing her way through school with her focus on ballet steps and her nose in a book, she met a boy and followed him a thousand miles away from home to Kansas City, Missouri. They spent their summers visiting his family in Middlesbrough, England, soaking up culture, history, and a few pints along the way. Elizabeth attended Park University, where she graduated magna cum laude with a BA in interior design.

Elizabeth now spends her days creating plots and concocting characters at her home in a small lakeside town in North Carolina. When she is not typing as fast as human movement will allow, she is caring for her husband and little boy. Elizabeth Michels is a lover of happily-ever-afters; whether in her writing life or in her home life, she spends her days with one word on her lips—*love*. She invites you to read her stories, get lost, and enjoy. Elizabeth loves to hear from her readers. Please visit www.elizabethmichels.com for more information.